The Cook-General

A JOAN KAHN BOOK

BOOKS BY JOHN CASHMAN

THE COOK-GENERAL

THE GENTLEMAN FROM CHICAGO

The Cook-General

*An Account of the Barnes
Mystery of 1879*

by

JOHN CASHMAN

Harper & Row, Publishers

New York, Evanston, San Francisco, London

A HARPER NOVEL OF TERROR

THE COOK-GENERAL. Copyright © 1974 by T. F. T. Davis. All rights reserved. Printed in the United States of America. No part of this book may be used or reproduced in any manner whatsoever without written permission except in the case of brief quotations embodied in critical articles and reviews. For information address Harper & Row, Publishers, Inc., 10 East 53rd Street, New York, N.Y. 10022.

FIRST EDITION

Designed by Janice Stern

Library of Congress Cataloging in Publication Data

Cashman, John.
  The cook-general.
  1 Webster, Katherine, 1849–1879—Fiction. I. Title.
PZ4.C3412C03   [PR6053.A822]   813'.5'4   74–1879
ISBN 0–06–010658–1

For Mikum

FOREWORD

This tale is a work of fiction based on fact. Kate Webster (alias Lawler) was in the employ of Julia Martha Thomas from about January 27, 1879, until she murdered her mistress on March 2 of that year. She was arrested at Killane, County Wexford, on March 28, and returned to England. Her trial commenced at the Central Criminal Court, Old Bailey, on July 2 and concluded on July 8, when she was sentenced to death. Kate Webster was executed at Wandsworth Prison on Tuesday, July 29. A full report of her trial can be found in *The Trial of Kate Webster* of the Notable British Trials series, edited by Elliott O'Donnell in 1925.

Real characters and events have been used, but various activities and incidents have been invented. No fact positively proved has been altered.

Following her arrest, Kate Webster made a series of long-winded statements to the police accusing others, quite falsely, of the crime she had committed. These, together with her final "confession" made on the eve of her execution, are included at the end of the book for the sake of interest. But Kate Webster was an ingenious and inveterate liar, and the contents of all these statements, including her confession, cannot safely be regarded as the truth.

A glossary of thieves' "lingo" of the period is also included, together with an explanation of other contemporary terms and some observations on the case in general. Some may not be strictly accurate, but Kate—whose language was famous— would have liked them.

J. C.

PART

1

A LITTLE INDEPENDENCE OF
HER OWN

I

The house he was watching was the center of a group of three
and set back so as to be flanked by its neighbors. The front
garden was therefore larger than those on either side. It was a
well-planted garden—with stubby firs and low thickets of ma-
honia aquifolium—and, on this moon- and starless night, the
approach to the house lay in shadow. And Strong noted with
satisfaction that not even the hissing flame of the solitary gaslight in the street could pierce that shadow.

Strong looked up and down the street and across to the three
houses for perhaps the thirtieth time. Everywhere windows
were curtained and blank, or darkly obscure. Not that he expected to find things any different; at three o'clock in the morning good people lay in their beds and slept. And Strong had
been told that he would encounter no dogs.

Strong left his vigil in the bushes and walked slowly and
quietly off to a clump of withered planes. These trees cast their
own gloom, but Strong could see his woman—lurking and
frightened—where he'd ordered her to stay, and he cursed her
under his breath. Did she not realize, idiot child, how every

movement could attract attention? Mary Durden, he decided, was no good for his purposes, and the sooner he returned her to her hattery the less damage she might do them both.

He came up behind her, his boots silent on the pavement, and tweaked her bottom.

"Hush!" he hissed when she squealed. He moved her farther under the shelter of the trees and put his mouth close to her ear —a nice ear, but pressed flush with her head by the bonnet she wore. Had she designed such a bonnet for herself? "I'm about to go in," said Strong. "You stop 'ere, and don't you move—not a muscle, mind? You stop 'ere and watch up and down like I told you. If you see anyone—anything—you just start to do like I told you." And he'd told her this and that all morning. Would she remember his instructions, follow them to the letter, when an emergency arose? Strong doubted it now and wondered why he had placed any confidence in the girl by day. "Nowse I'm orrf," he said and squeezed her arm above the elbow, a hard squeeze caused by the anger he felt toward himself. "Just don't you move, hear?" And she nodded, one eye still on the hand that gripped her upper arm.

Strong retraced his steps to where he had hidden before, wishing that he were somewhere else or that he were accompanied by someone else, even wishing that he were all alone, for he was sure he could take the Mitchell house with ease.

He crossed the street in two bounds and slid into the laurel hedges over the low brick wall. Once within the leafage, he paused, lying on his back and holding his breath, although he knew he had not been seen. Dogs—it was his fear of dogs that trespassed so upon his courage.

Strong left the hedgerow and slipped from shrub to tree to bush as he approached the front of the Mitchell house. He kept his eyes very much to the ground, to grass now beginning to whiten with frost; but his ears listened with uncanny hearing, for such was his gift and a tool of his trade. At French windows to the side of the front-door portico Strong stopped and flattened himself against the wall on bended knee. His breath formed small puffs in the cold; but still he made not a sound, and his motionless form merged into the butts and outline of the house façade. His hands went into both his jacket pockets and reappeared with a curious assortment of iron implements—a pair of fine pliers for grasping the end of any key positioned in a lock, and a thin hacksaw. Thus armed, Strong crept up to the French windows and inspected the catch. Yes. As he had supposed, the key had been left in the solitary lock, and this he turned with comparative ease, using his pliers.

Once inside the house, in a room Strong rightly determined to be the drawing room or parlor, he paused to listen before lighting a tiny wax candle. Then he set about his business quickly and quietly. The drawers and various compartments of a tallboy, a mahogany chest and a sewing box were opened and searched, Strong being able to assess possible value by touch as well as by inspection. But there was nothing of value in this room—just as he'd been told all those weeks ago—and Strong moved on, shuffling into the hall and entering the dining room. Silver—plate if not sterling—was his aim, but the dresser and cutlery canister in this room contained only chinaware and bone-handled items. Not a single article of worth, and again Strong was reminded of what he had been told: "They're poor folk, Mr. Strong. You'd be a-wasting yer time."

Out in the hallway again, Strong stopped and looked up the stairs. Perhaps the treasures of the house were kept in the bedrooms? But in the bedrooms slept the Mitchell family, and

5

Strong dared not venture farther. If he had his pistol, matters might be different. But he didn't have his gun, for he had forgotten to make up ammunition. All he had was the memory of those words, "They're poor folk, Mr. Strong," and an incompetent girl bunting for him outside. No, the risk was too great. His greed dampened, Strong left the way he came—through the French windows of the drawing room, which he did not trouble to relock. In the front garden he turned and looked up at the house for a last time. No doubt his informant had been correct —these *were* poor people. But, to adopt a favorite expression of his informant, "Bad cess" to them all.

The Durden girl he found where he'd left her, but she was examining a tear in her sleeve rather than minding the street, and Strong gave her a light cuff about the ears as he came up.

"What's that for!" yelped the girl, but Strong said nothing, taking her by the arm and hurrying them down Stanley Road and away from the scene of his frustrations.

"I done no wrong, honest," pleaded the girl when she judged it safe to talk again. Strong mouthed an obscenity.

"How's that?" asked Mary Durden.

"I said, 'Shut your teeth or I'll do 'em dentistry.' "

They were approaching the village of Teddington now, a built-up area, and Strong did not wish to attract the attention of some nosy peeler on his beat—should any policeman be foolish enough to be out at this hour of the morning. In a few minutes they would reach his donkey and cart, left in a secluded copse and stacked with oil jars to avoid suspicion, and then they would be safe.

"Please be nice to me," said the girl, still wheedling. "I told you I was no good for this sort of thing, I did."

"No good for nothing," Strong mumbled and quickened their pace.

"I suppose you wish *she* was here!" said the girl.

Strong laughed shortly and increased the pressure on her arm.

"I suppose you'll be off back to her!" Jealousy could make Mary Durden brave. Strong eased the grip on her arm a fraction. Would that he *could* go back to her. How long had it been since the two of them had house-robbed together? He looked down at the Durden girl. And now he was saddled with *this*. No good at work, no good at play.

"No good for nothing," Strong repeated.

What was it Katty had said when he'd taken up with Mary Durden? "Sflesh!" or something equally strange—an Irishism of some kind. But then Katty always had said peculiar things, most of which Strong was unable to comprehend. And now Katty was behaving in a peculiar manner—abandoning her natural talents, shunning Strong, giving up her meal tickets . . .

"I suppose you'll now be leaving me," said the girl at his side, and she began to weep.

"Shut your face," Strong said quietly. They had reached the copse, and he could see his donkey munching by some bushes. He'd take Mary back to her shop in Kingston, but he'd not stop there himself. He'd away to Wandsworth for a few hours' sleep, then he'd put his ear to the ground and track down the elusive Katty Webster.

II

As Mrs. Thomas passed the Hole in the Wall she averted her eyes. The public house was little more than a converted corner house, a stone façade with a side door leading to a small bar, and it had more the appearance of a shop than of a tavern. But it was, nevertheless, an establishment wherein strong ale was sold and, as such, an embarrassment to Mrs. Thomas. Outside the tavern was an old man in shabby clothes, the gas-lighter, holding a long pole, and she saw him reach up to spark off a lamp screwed into the wall. A miraculous lamp in many respects, fed mysteriously through a copper pipe that disappeared into the paving stones. Mrs. Thomas had never ceased to wonder at the inventive use of so foul a substance as gas. In many ways she suspected gas for its noxious self, but it pleased her that the Richmond borough could boast a series of well-lit streets; people tended to rush home less fast and furious when darkness began to fall.

The Hole in the Wall stood at the top of Park Road, a narrow street falling away sharply to a busy avenue. Part paved, part cobbled, the road was strictly residential, and there were villas of various descriptions and sizes, each with a small front garden on either side of it. Mrs. Thomas approved of the unchanging atmosphere and quiet of the street, although its steepness sometimes troubled her rheumatic legs. But at the moment, having been to the shops on Richmond Hill, she was walking downhill, and her pace was brisk. In the gathering gloom of late afternoon she was happy that her shopping was done and that in a moment or so she would be in her own house enjoying a cup of tea.

Halfway down the street she stopped, looked carefully from left to right as if afraid some racing coach might materialize out of thin air, and then crossed over.

Outside her house, a semi-detached of Mayfield Cottages, Mrs. Thomas stopped again. Her villa was Number Two, and she looked over the garden gate to Number One. Both houses were the property of Miss Ives, who lived in Number One with her aged mother, and Mrs. Thomas wondered if the former might be about her garden. But she was not—not on a day as chill as this—and Mrs. Thomas passed through her own gate and up the garden path to the front door of Number Two. If she'd seen Miss Ives, Mrs. Thomas had it in mind to complain to her, to express her concern as to the amount of horse droppings dirtying Park Road. It was too bad that tradespeople used the street as a short cut between the hill and Queen's Road, permitting their nags to soil both road and pavement. Mrs. Thomas was anxious to discuss the matter with Miss Ives so that Miss Ives might raise it with Logan, the roadsweep, whose responsibility it was to brush away such mess.

After letting herself into the house with a latchkey—one of many keys on a bunch—Mrs. Thomas waited a moment for her eyes to become accustomed to the dark. The hallway was dark as a dungeon. There was no fanlight over the front door, the walls were papered brown, and the bare floorboards painted pitch. There was also a perpetual musky smell, something Mrs. Thomas never seemed to notice.

Mrs. Thomas took off her coat and bonnet and sat down on a small hall chair. She was wearing her cayman shoes, and she proceeded to change them for a pair of patent slippers. She regretted having worn her best shoes on this shopping expedition, as they were now muddy and scuffed. She put them by the umbrella stand and decided to clean them later, after tea.

Mrs. Thomas stirred her tea and then abruptly left the armchair for the window, one of two tall bay windows, heavily draped in brocade. She pulled back a curtain to look out into the back garden. Shadows crossed the lawn outside. It was a small garden, dominated by a bushy fir, and it was upon this fir that Mrs. Thomas now concentrated her attention. She was looking for a squirrel she had noticed that seemed to make it a custom to explore the lower branches in the late afternoon, its furry red body darting about the trunk with frenzied movements. She had told Miss Ives about it, but the latter had been skeptical, for she was convinced that the red variety had been made obsolete by the onslaught of the gray. And Miss Ives had given her a strange look. Not that Mrs. Thomas was unused to such looks. On the contrary, people in Richmond tended to stare at her, even to whisper among themselves, when she ventured out to take her constitutional. Mrs. Thomas appreciated that she was considered eccentric, and that knowledge troubled her not at all. She was sure that people did not intend their gossip to be spiteful.

Eccentric or not, she *had* seen the squirrel, and she moved closer to the pane, one jeweled hand holding back the curtain. Soon nightfall would deprive her sight of the squirrel if the little fellow appeared. She pressed her face to the glass. Standing there surrounded by the massive fall of material, Mrs. Thomas looked old and fragile, tiny-boned in her bustle dress. She was also away from the warmth of the fire and conscious of the cold. And staring out upon a drear January afternoon made her even colder. But she would not forsake her vigil, and she adjusted the tippet about her shoulders.

A short movement and quiver among the branches of the fir caught her attention. Mrs. Thomas jumped with excitement. But her rheumy eyes, the gloom, and the grimy panes were all against her. The movement ceased and within seconds it was too dark to see anything at all.

"Nitwits!" said Mrs. Thomas and allowed the drape to fall. The word was her closest approach to an oath and was uttered only in private. Once her late husband had overheard the expression, and she had been scolded. Mr. Thomas, a devout Presbyter, had eschewed swearing of any kind.

She returned to her chair by the davenport desk. It was high-backed, deep-buttoned, and very comfortable. Laying her head against the fabric, she stretched her legs out toward the coal fire. But she was still cold. The fire was inadequate for so large a room, and she had not laid it well. It was the same in every room; the whole house was drafty, and her fires never burned to satisfaction. Mrs. Thomas often wondered why she had rented the old villa from Miss Ives in the first place; Mayfield Cottages were far too large for one person, let alone an old lady. How could she be expected to keep it clean? How could she be expected to make and light the fires, to adjust the gas, to dust and swab and launder all by herself? Mr. Thomas, were he alive, would be very cross to observe the state of things at the moment. And her explanations he would have dismissed with a wave of the hand. Mr. Thomas had been a stickler for order and cleanliness. But Mr. Thomas had been dead these five years now.

Mrs. Thomas picked up her cup and peered at her tea. It was

cold and unpalatable. Dearly would she have liked another cup, a small luxury to make up for missing her squirrel. But to obtain hot tea she would have to leave the drawing room, cross the wide hall in darkness, and descend the stone steps to the basement area. There she would be obliged to light the grate and wait about that bitter place for the kettle to come to a boil again. All of this for a cup of tea. How she wished that Edith were still in her employ—for all of Edith's faults.

Mrs. Thomas sometimes admitted to herself that she had "difficulty" with servants. But she refused to believe that this problem was something of her own making. Having a little independence of her own, she was able and willing to pay her servants a respectable wage. Nevertheless, Edith had groused to Miss Ives about her pay and conditions, chatter that had cost young Edith her situation. Mrs. Thomas humped her shoulders as she thought upon the treachery of her maidservant, and she felt pleased that Miss Ives had reported the complaint to her immediately.

"She says you are too finicky and do not give her sufficient to eat," Miss Ives had told her. "She says that she is forced to live on bread and vegetables, never seeing a morsel of meat from one week to the next."

And young Edith had wept when given notice. Well might she weep! Had not Mrs. Thomas salvaged her from a workhouse, clothed her, protected her, and given her decent opportunity? And Edith had repaid such kindliness with deceit. Mrs. Thomas might pray for her, of course, but now the girl could face the world alone.

Since the death of Mr. Thomas his widow had lived in a series of rented accommodations in the southwest London area, and it had become her practice—her good deed—to lend a helping hand to the poor hopeless daughters of the lower orders. Staring into the dying embers of the fire, Mrs. Thomas reflected that she had provided many with honest work and spiritual guidance. The Reverend Doctor Cummings had recently complimented her on her efforts, and she knew that Mr. Thomas—and indeed her first husband—must both look down upon her from the Above with satisfaction.

Mrs. Thomas relaxed in her chair at the thought of their benign and silent approbation. But it was the very least she could do. Her last husband had been a thrifty man in his lifetime and left her moderately well provided. And Mrs. Thomas secretly enjoyed the sacrifices she made to repay society for the good life she had led, not only with Mr. Thomas but also with her first husband, Mr. Murray from Troon. Yes, she had been wife to two good men, and although she had borne no children, her joy had been complete. So now, in the evening of her own life, she would pay them homage by the doing of good works. She held that the upper classes sadly neglected the care of those less fortunate—paying them lavish wages, yet totally unconcerned as to how their charges spent their money. Mrs. Thomas was of the opinion that the soul was as much in need of nourishment as the body; it followed, therefore, that an employer was responsible for the incorporeal needs of a servant. Mrs. Thomas was firm in this respect. Not only were her maidservants forbidden to visit public houses and the music halls, but she also kept a close eye upon other aspects of their behavior. Evening prayers were the order of the day, and her servants were encouraged to openly confess any unseemly thought or deed that might have occurred over the past twelve hours. Discipline and method were essential.

Mrs. Thomas left her chair and prodded the dying fire with

a brass-handled poker. The bar was heavy in her hands, and her efforts useless, so she went back to the button-back in despair, allowing her thoughts to return to the question of servants.

Had she not probably saved the souls of at least three young things by her careful guidance? Would they not have led a life of prostitution or died in the gutter but for her active encouragement? So her conscience told her. Why then did the girls choose to leave her employ so quickly? This was something she would never understand; she could only surmise that girls of the poorer classes were lacking in both sense and gratitude. A small frown came to her face as she recalled one particularly distasteful episode. Molly Jones had been her name, and she had come to Mrs. Thomas direct from the Clerkenwell House of Correction—an utter degenerate. Molly Jones, at seventeen a woman of the streets and a "garrotter." Mrs. Thomas had then been living in Kingston upon Thames, and the vicar had advised her against taking the girl at all, pointing out that she had been sentenced for violent robbery.

"She'll do you nothing but harm, and her soul is lost," had been his words. But Molly Jones could boast a childhood spent among the hills and valleys of Wales—the country of dear Mr. Thomas—and until her family had moved to the slums of north London she had been free from sin. As a gesture to Mr. Thomas, his widow had taken the girl in, risking all to employ her as her cook. And, as if a miracle were being performed by St. Jude, a transformation occurred. Molly Jones became quiet and obedient, busying herself about the house by day, kneeling in prayer with Mrs. Thomas by night. As a result, greater privileges were extended to this girl. She was permitted to dust and clean; she was allowed access to her mistress's bedroom. Oh, what folly! The girl's servility was little more than a wicked ruse, and that very bedroom the final target. The girl began to prey upon Mrs. Thomas's jewel case and its precious contents collected and cherished over the years. And, like a magpie, the awful girl had hoarded the stolen pieces in her bedroom. Then one afternoon Mrs. Thomas returned home unexpectedly, to be greeted by strange noises from her servant's room. Investigating, she discovered the malicious child in the arms of the coalman, while scattered about the bedclothes were her rings and brooches. Molly Jones begged forgiveness, as might be expected, but such misdoings could scarce be overlooked. So she was returned to the House of Correction, and the coalman was sentenced to hard labor as the girl's receiver. "In God's name, have a care whom you take in in future!" rebuked the vicar.

So she had taken greater care, and on her removal to Richmond she had used the services of local village girls. But Mrs. Thomas was not fainthearted; a Molly Jones was not to put her off. And accordingly she had engaged young Edith, and again her trust had been betrayed. A girl capable of airing her grievances in the manner adopted by Edith must be capable of anything. But once again young Edith should not be allowed to deflect Mrs. Thomas from her mission with young girls of doubtful character.

Slowly she left the comfort of the chair. She must stoke the fire again before this cold caused her to perish.

"I'll find a general this time," she said aloud as she moved. The coarse chunks of coal refused to burn, and she pushed the snout of a pair of bellows into the fire basket. "I'll see to it tomorrow," she added as she pumped the air. She would speak to Miss Ives or to Mr. Deane, her coal merchant. Or she might do best to consult her friend Miss Loder. Yes, Miss Loder would know of somebody available. Miss Loder was the daughter of a person of position within the community. *She* would know the domestic situation in the neighborhood. Perhaps Mrs. Thomas might do better to select a more mature person this time. Mrs. Thomas doubted she could bear the ingratitude of the young again. A lady more mature this time. She hoped that Mr. Thomas—Mr. Murray too—would not scorn her for this sudden lack of "grit," but Mrs. Thomas was beginning to feel her sixty years of age.

OUT OF SERVICE

I

"*Red* squirrels are virtually extinct," said Miss Ives.

Mrs. Thomas saw that she would never be believed, but she objected to this high-handed rejection of her story.

"I tell you I saw him," she repeated.

"But you didn't see it last night, did you, Julia?"

"No, it was too dark. But I'm sure he was there, bless his little heart!"

Miss Ives shrugged. Why not let the old lady have her fancies? She had very little else—no family, few friends, just a life of aimless drifting. Miss Ives studied her latest tenant for a moment; strange how she always regarded Julia Thomas as "the old lady," though she was little older than herself. Sixty-five or so? But Julia Thomas was small and bent and fussy.

"How have you been managing without Edith?" Miss Ives asked her.

"It's very difficult." Mrs. Thomas looked about Miss Ives's parlor and noted the high polish on all the furniture. "Very difficult indeed." Just as she'd thought, Miss Ives decided. The old lady was unable to cope. The villa had been built to house

17

a young family, not a diminutive lonely widow. Miss Ives had originally considered advising Mrs. Thomas against taking the property, but Miss Ives was only a leaseholder herself, and one rent was needed to pay the other.

"Are you proposing to remain in Richmond for long?" she asked.

"Where else can I go?"

"You have your brother in Brighton. Why not go down there? I hear that the air is very healthy. We are too near the river in Richmond."

Mrs. Thomas sighed. Would that she *could* live with or near brother Charles. But she knew that Charles would not take kindly to such an idea. Charles regarded her as "bossy" and called her "The Schoolmarm" and implied that she was prone to interfere.

"My brother has his family and is much too busy," she said. "He's a doctor, you know."

Miss Ives nodded, slightly impatient. How many times had she been informed of the fact that brother Charles was a medical man. Mrs. Thomas was forever making reference to him, as if she held a professional relative essential to establish her gentility.

"Well, if you stay at Mayfield you must have some help," Miss Ives said.

"Ah! And that's just why I called upon you, Elizabeth!" And to have done so had taken courage, for Mrs. Thomas found Miss Ives an awesome lady—haughty and sharp, although kindly toward herself. "Now! I made a little note of it in my Memorandum. I always make little notes of things in my Memorandum in case I forget things. And I *do* tend to forget things, Elizabeth.

And I *do* so need some help, my dear, and I *do* so hope that you will be able to advise me!" Mrs. Thomas produced her Memorandum for Miss Ives to see.

Miss Ives declined to look at the book. "What kind of help do you want? A char or a general?"

"Oh, a general! It's such a great big house."

"Generals are expensive these days, you know."

"I know. They have become thoroughly spoiled of late. But I don't mind. I can pay." Mrs. Thomas's tone became confidential. "I *have* means, you know!"

Well did Miss Ives, and many others, know of Mrs. Thomas's private income. Indeed, as in the case of her doctor brother, Mrs. Thomas spoke of little else. She was clearly desirous of impressing upon all the extent of her riches. Miss Ives felt that Mrs. Thomas was not really possessed of great wealth; she suspected that if the truth was known, her income would turn out to be meager. Mrs. Thomas had a full wardrobe, certainly; but most of her clothes were old and worn, and the style and fashion of some were positively antique. Nor was Miss Ives much impressed by her tenant's jewelry.

"The person to see is your friend Miss Loder," she said. "She will be of far greater assistance to you than myself."

"Quite so, my dear." Mrs. Thomas held up her Memorandum. "And I had noted down her name alongside your own, to remind myself not to forget to see her this very morning. And now you have also jogged my memory into consulting my little book, to find that I must pay call on Miss Loder as well as upon your own dear self. Now I'm simply bound not to forget!"

"You think and talk in riddles, Julia. No wonder you get so confused." Miss Ives stood up and brushed down her skirts.

Mrs. Thomas allowed herself to be escorted to the front door. Miss Ives took her along by the arm, as if aiding someone very infirm, or a simpleton.

When she was gone, Miss Ives turned her attention to a Christmas tree in the hallway. The tree was brown with death, and needles lay everywhere. As she worked, Miss Ives thought upon Mrs. Thomas. Rumor had it that she was a "tartar" toward servants and tradesmen. Strange, for Mrs. Thomas was timid when in the company of friends and acquaintances of her own station. She had been a teacher until the death of her last husband. Could it be that she regarded and treated her inferiors as children? Miss Ives had her own views as to the treatment of staff. Treat the uncouth as mere children, then they tended to behave as such—to lie, to steal, and become indolent. Far better that they be regarded as household pets—fed, nurtured, and punished if they misbehaved—and Miss Ives loved cats and dogs.

II

But Miss Loder did not share Miss Ives's misgivings, and she was happy and smiling to see her friend Julia Thomas. They sat in Miss Loder's upstairs parlor—a jungle of heavy furniture and potted palms—and Miss Loder listened patiently to the other's involved explanations as to why she now required the services of a cook-general.

"Her duties would be simple," Mrs. Thomas concluded, looking at the organized clutter of the room. Miss Loder lived in a Regency house, one of several in the Crescent, and the four stories necessitated a bevy of staff. Mrs. Thomas had encountered no less than three girls and a tweeny, and she suspected more were tucked away, as it were, in the lower regions. Not that she resented the good fortune of her friend for one moment; Miss Loder was a wealthy spinster, her father a respected builder and a Mason, and it was fit and proper that she lived in so august a style. Mrs. Thomas valued her friendship for some of those very reasons.

"What you really need is a good cook *and* a housekeeper," her friend said at last.

Mrs. Thomas flung up her hands. "No, no! That would be *far* too extravagant for my simple needs, m'dear!" She did not choose to add that a good cook's salary—say forty-five pounds per annum?—was way beyond her income.

"Well, if that is your decision, I think I can help you without further ado," Miss Loder said, twiddling a ring on her finger. "I have a Mrs. Crease, from Mitchell's Row, charring for me sometimes on a Saturday. Poor woman, her husband is a shoe-black and not well these days, for he was sadly injured at the Alma and has never been the same since that dreadful war. But I'm wandering off. Anyway, sometimes Mrs. Crease is forced to attend upon her husband, and she sends along a friend to help my girls. I only know this friend as 'Kate,' but she strikes one as both willing and cheerful, and I am aware that she is seeking a permanent situation."

"As a general?"

"As a general."

"Then perhaps you will speak to your Mrs. Crease on my behalf."

"I shall. I shall send for her when she comes this Saturday."

Mrs. Thomas made a noise of satisfaction, but she thought it right to ask more of this "Kate" so that she might gauge a possible salary. Twenty pounds?

"Tell me about 'Kate'," she said.

"There is very little I can say. I have barely spoken to her. I can only repeat what cook has told me."

"Well, do you know how old she is and where she comes from?"

"It's difficult to say just how old she is," Miss Loder said slowly. "She might be thirty or as much as forty. And I know nothing of her immediate past, although her origins obviously lie in Ireland."

Mrs. Thomas pulled a face. "In Ireland?"

"Yes. She has this lilt to her voice—what they call a 'brogue.' "

"Ireland," Mrs. Thomas repeated. Her distaste was evident.

"That disturbs you, Julia?"

Mrs. Thomas did not reply at once. She must overcome her prejudices; she was not in a position to be choosy at the moment. "I have found the Irish rather slapdash," she said. "But you tell me she is cheerful and willing, and it is not for me to prejudge her. Pray tell your Mrs. Crease to send her friend so I may interview her, but I shall want to see her Character."

And then the two ladies spoke of other things—of the possible hole in the roof at Mayfield Cottages, of their health, and of their neighbors. Mrs. Thomas limited her calls to the customary fifteen minutes, and after that time she took her leave, being escorted from the house by some nameless member of Miss Loder's superabundant staff.

For the remainder of the morning Mrs. Thomas did her shopping, which included a visit to Mr. Thorpe, hardware merchant, for the purpose of starch and black for the grates. Mounds of washing had accumulated at Mayfield Cottages, and the grates were in a forlorn condition. A little task for this "Kate" perhaps, and the sooner "Kate" made herself available for service the better.

III

It was arranged that "Kate" present herself for Mrs. Thomas's inspection on the morning of Thursday, the 23rd. The interview was to commence at eleven and terminate at twenty-five past, so that Mrs. Thomas might put on her coat and bonnet and start her morning calls at half past the hour precisely.

One minute before the appointed hour Mrs. Thomas went into her dining room and positioned herself at the head of the long mahogany table, facing the door and the hall beyond. The front door she had left ajar. Mrs. Thomas decided it preferable to endure a few moments of icy draft than to answer the knock of a potential servant herself. And from where she sat by the window she would be able to observe the progress of her caller up the front path. Before her on the dining table lay her Memorandum, and she waited with a pencil poised in her left hand.

But time passed, and her irritation grew. Mrs. Thomas consulted Mr. Thomas's half hunter—a watch she now always wore close to her heart—and saw to her surprise that it was ten minutes past eleven. Where *was* the stupid woman? Did she not appreciate the importance of punctuality?

The minutes ticked on, and Mrs. Thomas began to tap the table with her pencil. Seventeen minutes past and no "Kate"; Mrs. Thomas started to turn the pages of her little notebook, tut-tutting whenever an entry reminded her of something she had forgotten to do. At one page her scribbling was too small

23

to be decipherable, and she held the book up close to her nose. She was thus preoccupied when a strange feeling caused Mrs. Thomas to look up quickly. There, framed in the doorway, stood the tall figure of a woman.

She was dressed entirely in working-class black, and dark hair was tucked back severely under a black straw hat. Sun streaming in through the window blinded Mrs. Thomas, and she was unable to see this woman's features clearly.

"Kate?" she asked after a while, forced to speak first.

The woman nodded, but made no other move.

"I have been waiting for you," Mrs. Thomas said. Why had not the woman announced her arrival instead of just wandering into the house like this?

"And here I be," came the reply. The voice was very soft and without a hint of apology. Mrs. Thomas was puzzled.

"You *are* Kate—Mrs. Crease's friend?"

"Kate Webster, missus." The woman took two steps forward, and Mrs. Thomas could then see her face. An unusual face.

"I was expecting you at eleven o'clock," Mrs. Thomas said. She still expected an apology or some excuse, but none came. "Well, better late than never, Miss Webster!"

"Mrs. Webster, missus."

"Mrs. Webster? I'm so sorry . . . Mrs. Webster." No one had told her the woman was married. Mrs. Thomas felt embarrassed, and vexed that here was she making apology.

"Miss Loder of the Crescent informs me that you are anxious for employment as a general," she added with a sniff, endeavoring to recover her composure.

"That's the manner of things, missus." The woman had moved again, and Mrs. Thomas found herself examining that unusual face once more. It was a hard forbidding face, although

24

the features were not coarse. The brow was high and wide, and the nose short and well modeled. But the eyes and mouth she found unsettling—the former oblique and dark as a beetle's wing, the latter broad and pale and turned down sharply. The face bore an air of haughty indifference. Then Mrs. Thomas's eyes met those of Mrs. Webster for a second time, and Mrs. Thomas looked away.

"What experience have you had?" she asked.

"I've done before. Mrs. Crease will speak for me, I daresay."

Mrs. Thomas marked what her friend Miss Loder had termed a "brogue," but she did not find the sound displeasing.

"Oh, she has! Or so I am led to believe. She spoke of you to Miss Loder."

"That'll be a lady I've done for then."

Did Mrs. Thomas detect a note of impatience in the woman's voice?

"And where do you hail from, Mrs. Webster?" she said.

The other appeared to weigh the question for a moment. "From County Wexford, missus. A long time back, that is."

"Oh yes? And since coming to England?"

"Liverpool, London, these parts. I've been travelin', missus."

"With your husband?" Mrs. Thomas prepared to enter details in her book.

"Captain Webster's been dead these past ten years."

"Captain Webster—army?" Mrs. Thomas was surprised to find her the widow of an officer.

But the Irishwoman laughed, a melodious laugh. "Not he, missus! He skippered his own craft and commissioned himself, up in Liverpool."

"And so you came down to London with your grief, poor woman."

25

Another laugh, and Mrs. Thomas saw white and even teeth. "Not so much of the grievin', missus. The cap'n was a wrong 'un, and I'm pleased the Locker took him. Drowned by the weight of his sins he was."

Mrs. Thomas was shocked by such lack of respect for the dead. "And now you are on your own, Mrs. Webster?"

"Not entirely. There's me boy." And Kate Webster's face softened visibly.

"You have a child! Bless me, I didn't realize! A boy—how old is he?"

"Coming up six."

Mrs. Thomas did some arithmetic. "But I understood you to say that you have been widowed ten years?"

"And so I have. And I'm not ashamed to admit me boy's a spot of Irish toothache."

"I beg your pardon?"

"An accident, missus. A little bastard, if you like."

Mrs. Thomas grew flustered again. Her face reddened and she took short gulps of air. First the husband, now this. How could a mother treat the stain of illegitimacy in this offhand way?

"Where is he now?" she managed eventually.

"With Sarah Crease. She cares for him when I can't. And I pays her for the pleasure. Up to four shillen a week, I does." And this was said with pride. Well at least the woman faced up to her responsibilities, Mrs. Thomas conceded. And perhaps the existence of a child made her reliable.

"Would Mrs. Crease continue to do so were you to enter my service?" she asked.

"That she would."

Mrs. Thomas nodded. It was well that she would not be forced to have the boy about the house. Not that Mrs. Thomas disliked children; much of her life had been spent educating them. But they tended to get in the way and make noise. Moreover, there was something rather grotesque about the children of the very poor.

"When would you be ready to start, Mrs. Webster?"

"Whenever you be giving me the nod, missus."

"Capital!" Mrs. Thomas would take the woman. "Now, if I could just take a peep at your Character?"

It was Kate Webster's turn to look surprised. "She didn't tell you, missus?"

"Tell me? No, I fear not. Who was supposed to tell me what?"

"Sarah Crease was to be telling Miss Loder so you'd know. I haven't got no Character, missus."

"None at all!"

" 'Tis some time since I been working for a lady. Oh, I had me a pack of references, but I've lost the entirety of them. I daresay Mrs. Mitchell of Stanley Road in Teddington will spake up on my behalf." Kate Webster's eyes were downcast, as if she knew the job was lost, and Mrs. Thomas decided to take pity.

"Never mind," she said. "You have charred satisfactorily for Miss Loder, and that speaks for itself." But she considered it untidy for a girl to lose her Characters. She got to her feet and crossed the floor to the other—to stop short suddenly. Mrs. Thomas was amazed to find how tall the woman was—at least five feet, six inches against her five. And broadly built as well, with strongly corded hands, red bony hands with long straight fingers. So much the better, she thought, for such hands would be capable of much work.

"I shall show you the house," she said, and Kate Webster stepped aside to let her pass, then followed after, dwarfing her new-found mistress.

"I shall show you the kitchen area first," Mrs. Thomas said in the hall, and they began to descend the narrow stone steps. At the bottom Mrs. Thomas turned to Kate. "I'm afraid it is a basement. Very dark and dingy. But I expect you will be able to brighten it up."

Kate entered the kitchen and looked around. It was as Mrs. Thomas had said—and very cold. A roughly hewn wooden table and a dresser dominated the first part, and along the wall lay an old-fashioned range. Quarry tiles on the floor, dirty and moist.

"As you can see, we still have to burn wood," Mrs. Thomas said of the range.

Kate touched the black surface. "The fire's out, missus."

"Again? Dear me, I never seem able to keep it going. No doubt you will be more successful, Mrs. Webster." Mrs. Thomas opened the drawers of the large pine dresser.

"Cups and saucers and so on," she said. "Cutlery in the middle drawer."

But Kate was paying her no heed, her eyes peering into the second part of the basement—an annex, darker still and vaulted like a cellar.

"The copper," Mrs. Thomas explained.

" 'Tis a funny place for the washing."

"It's connected with the copper next door. Miss Ives's house, you see."

"Still a funny place for the doing of the washing." Kate returned to the foot of the steps. Her inspection was complete, and it was time to move on. The basement had an atmosphere she did not like.

Mrs. Thomas led the way up to the hall again.

"My sitting room," she said, opening a door. She did not invite Kate to enter, nor did Kate appear anxious to do so. But she had noticed that Mrs. Thomas was left-handed.

"I shall show you upstairs." Mrs. Thomas closed the door quietly and began to ascend the broad staircase. The stairs were steep, and Mrs. Thomas was obliged to pull herself up by the banister. While she climbed and panted, Kate followed a step behind. She observed that Mrs. Thomas's back was curved into the beginnings of a hump, and she felt compassion for her frailty.

The villa had only two floors, and the landing ran the length of the building. Three bedrooms and part of a converted attic led off, the doors painted a somber shade of brown, like the hall below.

"My room," said Mrs. Thomas, indicating a room to the front of the house. "I keep it locked."

"I'll be needing a key," Kate said.

Mrs. Thomas looked up sharply, with thoughts of Molly Jones. "Absolutely no need whatsoever," she said. "I can cope there on my own. Besides, you are lucky. My room is the largest in the house."

Kate shrugged. So be it. If the lady wished a pigsty upon herself, she was surely welcome.

"This will be *your* room." Mrs. Thomas announced, flinging open the askew door of the converted attic.

Kate went in. Fourteen by six or seven, with a sloping ceiling and a mass of lead tubing in a corner. Someone, somehow, had managed to slide in a narrow bed.

"I'll have to be losing a bit o' weight," Kate said. She came out and looked up and down the landing. "What's in there then?" she asked, indicating a promising door.

"The spare room. I use it for trunks and boxes."

Kate grunted. She was unhappy with her room; it recalled to her the measurements of a cell.

"Perhaps yer'd be telling me where I'd obtain the benefit of soap and water, missus?" she asked. She had heard that some houses had a tap above stairs.

"In the kitchen area. But I am sure you will find it most secluded."

Kate smiled. Years fell away from her face, and the brown eyes twinkled. "I'm not scary, missus," she said. Both sexes had seen her in less than pantaloons in her time. "I'll do me lavitations in the place provided."

Mrs. Thomas was impressed. Here was a plucky woman who showed much promise.

"Come downstairs, Mrs. Webster, and we will settle matters."

Kate stayed close behind on the stairs, frightened that the older woman might slip and tumble.

"I am minded to pay you nine shillings a week," Mrs. Thomas said in the hall, and Kate's concern for her faded.

"Ten shillen, and all found, missus."

"I see. Very well then. Nine and thruppence—and a week's notice if required."

Kate shook her head. "I got me boy t'be thinking of."

Mrs. Thomas was inclined to reject this outrageous demand, but the other's eyes bored into her. "So be it. Ten shillings," she said with heat. This Mrs. Webster plainly had a will of her own.

Kate acknowledged the change in her value with a bow, then

yawned without covering her mouth. "I'll be off and away," she said. "I'll be round with me baggage this evening, missus." She walked toward the front door, and Mrs. Thomas took note of her clumsy stride—a sloppy swaying motion, as if her upper body were disjointed from the lower part.

At the door, which was still open and shaking with the freezing wind, Kate turned. "Till this evenin' then." And she held out her hand. Mrs. Thomas was unused to shaking the paw of a servant, but she took it, her own hand being enveloped in a gentle squeeze. Kate bent down slightly. "That'll be a dandy watch you're wearing," she remarked of Mr. Thomas's half hunter. "And I do believe that chain's of solid gold."

To flatter Mrs. Thomas's jewelry was to compliment Mrs. Thomas, and the lady beamed, forgetting their differences over the subject of salary. If this Mrs. Webster was a trifle brusque and outspoken, these were minor faults capable of correction in due course. No doubt Mrs. Webster was of earthy stock, a large and familiar farm girl from the wild marshes of her native land. No doubt she was very ignorant, but her mind would therefore be open to instruction. She would be both willing and grateful to be taught the proper way of things; from rough materials could be fashioned the brilliance of a gemstone.

"I'm sure everything will be most satisfactory," Mrs. Thomas said happily.

THE CRACKSMAN AND HIS BUNTER

I

Kate sat herself in the corner alcove of the public bar with her back to the wall. In this way she could survey the whole room and take note as to whoever came through the swing doors. At present the bar was empty, and Mrs. Hayhoe—proprietress of the Hole in the Wall—nowhere to be seen. So much the better, thought Kate, for Mrs. Hayhoe tended to buttonhole customers with her chatter, and Kate wished to speak with the man called Strong in private.

She took out her pipe, a tiny clay with a broken stem, and inspected the contents of her tobacco pouch. No more than three strands of shag and some dust. She dearly wanted a smoke, and her face creased into a frown as she delved into the side pocket of her cape. But there was no tobacco to be found there either, just the butt end of a penny-starver.

She was muttering invective and squashing the cigar into the bowl of her clay when a man suddenly sat down beside her. Kate jumped, for she had not seen him enter and approach. But Strong always moved this way, and invariably took her by surprise.

"Ye sent for me, O prince of the jemmy," Kate said in a loud voice, and Strong looked about him in alarm.

"Hush your tongue, woman. D'you want for to spoil our nice relations."

Kate held out her pipe. "What I want is a spot of beef."

Strong leaned over and peered into the clay. "Horse shit!" he said and gave her his pouch. "Beats me why you don't give up that thing and take to Woodies like a respectable lady."

"Like a Haymarket doxy." Kate scratched a match on the marble tabletop. "Now get me a glass of red heart if you're a man worth knowing at all."

Strong smiled and took out his change. Two pennies and a silver threepenny bit. It was not his custom to treat ladies, but Kate Webster made an exception to that rule. Slow with masculine pride, he ambled over to the bar and smacked the brass bell. Mrs. Hayhoe came through from the taproom and took his order, and Kate turned her face to the wall until she had gone again. Sometimes it was better not to be seen in company with the likes of Strong.

"Yer rum," Strong said, returning with their drinks. He sat down again, and sawdust flew up and about his legs. "And how's Mrs. Webster then?" he asked, brushing down his trousers.

"Poor as a Connaught man, Mr. Strong."

This mock courtesy had long been a private joke.

"I've no money for you," said Strong.

"It's only the child I'm thinking of, Mr. Strong."

"He's not my child!" Or was he? Strong would never know.

"Perhaps. But he's mine, and I care for him. Five shillen would tide me over." Kate hated to beg, and her manner was graceless.

"I thought you was in work?"

"Me money's spent. But I starts a fresh situation tonight. A proper situation, Mr. Strong, so I'll be paying you back this time."

But Strong shook his head. "You owe me nigh on ten bob as it is. You'll get no more till that's paid, unless . . ."

"Unless what?" Kate's eyes were sharp over the top of her glass.

"Unless you want to *earn* a bit."

Kate had expected the conversation to turn this way; it always did. And why else had she been summoned to this meeting?

"You let me down bad over the Mitchells," Strong whispered. "I took the trouble to put you in and prepare the way, and then you rats on me." This was true. Strong had found her the job as maidservant, and at the last minute she had refused to allow him to carry out his plan to burgle.

"The Mitchells were poor folk," Kate replied. "And Mrs. Mitchell was sick. It was no time for robbery, Mr. Strong." Moreover, she had been happy with that family, remaining with them in Stanley Road for more than a year. She would still be there perhaps, had it not been for Strong.

Strong fell silent. What Kate Webster had said about the Mitchells had now been verified. But he did not feel inclined to confess his blundering expedition in company with Mary Durden.

"What's this new job you got?" he asked casually.

Kate jerked a thumb. "Just down the road here for a Mrs. Thomas, as a general."

Strong laughed. "Trust Katty to find a nest near a boozer!"

"Mrs. Webster to you, Mr. Strong."

"Yes. This Mrs. Thomas—she rich?"

Kate considered the question. "Aye, that she is. As rich as

34

crazes." She was thinking of the gold half hunter and the rings on Mrs. Thomas's fingers. "And a silly old biddy t'boot," she added.

"Hows about it then!" said Strong, quick as a flash. "Settle in nice and cozy, find out where things are kept, give me the nod, and I'll nail her drum simple!"

Kate finished her rum and set down the glass. She looked at Strong with a look both sad and baleful. "And land me twelve months' hard like last time?" she said. "Get me another tot, Mr. Strong." And she pushed her glass toward him.

"Last time was unlucky," Strong said when he came back.

"Unlucky, you calls it! Yer use me as your bunter, yer gets all the pickings, I gets a year at the Slaughter—and you calls it unlucky. Bad cess to you, Mr. Strong!" And Kate downed her drink in one.

"I made sure your kid was cared for," muttered Strong.

Kate shook her head. " 'Tain't right for a boy to be without his mother. No, Mr. Strong, I'll thieve no more on your behalf. Use that whey-faced slut of a hat girl if you will."

Strong began to fill his own pipe with unnatural preoccupation, and Kate guessed that all was not well with regard to Mary Durden. "You two fallen out?" she inquired with a sly smile.

"Pah!" Strong lit his pipe and puffed furiously. How Kate had laughed when he and Mary had started living as man and wife.

"I said you would," Kate went on smugly. She had been secretly jealous of the other girl's good looks. This turn of events was most satisfying. She was about to pursue Strong with her teasing when others began to come into the bar, and a blind man felt his way around the tables selling tin whistles. It was time for Kate and Strong to leave, and they got up simultaneously.

"How about half an hour of it back at my place," Strong suggested outside in the street. "For old times' sake. I haven't had a bit of jam in weeks."

"No, Mr. Strong."

"I'll pay you—"

Kate's ferocious look cut him short.

"Sorry, Mrs. Webster. Can we meet again?"

Kate shrugged.

"Here? Next Thursday dinnertime?"

"At noon then, Mr. Strong," Kate replied. "Good day to you, sir." And she swept past him and up toward Richmond town.

II

Kate's boy was small and dark, with the black curly hair and pale blue eyes of his father. Now, as he played, Kate watched him. Her son would be called Master Webster, but Captain Webster had been no more the father of the child than he had been husband to the mother. "Captain" Webster had managed a doss house on the Liverpool waterfront—the scene of every crime listed in the Calendar—and Kate had been his woman until sent to prison by the city quarter sessions.

No, her boy's father might have been someone different. Perhaps a porter at a Hyde Park hotel with whom she'd dallied for a while, perhaps a Bayswater tinmaker man—her son had his eyes, and Kate had loved the fellow furiously for a month and more. But perhaps it had been Strong after all.

"You're a little basket, but I loves you," she said aloud and laid aside her broom.

It was customary for Kate to sweep out Mrs. Crease's kitchen when she called, to clear up some of the mess left by the boy. And now she would give him his tea. "Bread and drippin'?"

She cut a slice from the loaf on the kitchen table and spread the dripping thick. Mrs. Crease wouldn't mind; she was very fond of the boy. Mrs. Crease was a good woman, and someday Kate would reward her for her kindness.

"Now you come here and ate up all your tay," she ordered her son and hoisted him up onto a chair. "Ate it all up, and you'll be as big and strong as your ma!"

She paused on her words. The boy needed a father, without a doubt, and for a time Kate had searched for someone suitable. But to what avail? No decent man, drunk or sober, would hitch his prospects to one so ugly. And others? Well, they might use her company and her body for the passage of a night, and give her short shrift and half a sovereign in the morning—if she was lucky.

Strong? She could always marry Strong—and what a fearsome thought was that! A safe companion in crime for life, without the risk of her turning Queen's evidence against him in a court of law. How happy she could make him.

There had been George, of course, but her association with Mrs. Crease's son—ten years her junior—had been ill-fated from the outset. There were those who considered that she'd led the lad astray. Not his mother, glory be; Mrs. Crease fortunately had known nothing of the relationship from start to finish. But the police in Teddington had their records, and they'd turned informer on her. They had told George's employers at the King's Hotel, and he'd lost his job as potman.

"Nosy mutton-shunters!" Kate said to herself.

Never once had she tried to seduce the lad; her intentions had been quite honorable. But she'd taken him out drinking in the town, that constable had seen them, and a report had been made. George was scared away, and it certainly was well that Mrs. Crease remained outside the secret.

"Have you eaten it all up then?" Kate addressed her son. "Then come to yer ma, and I'll clean you up neat as a pin!"

The small boy eased himself off the chair and ran to her. She took him by the elbows and swung him around, at the same time singing and dancing a little jig.

The kitchen door opened and Mrs. Crease came in. "My, what a party you're having!" she said, removing her head shawl. A short dumpy woman, Mrs. Crease reminded Kate of a hedge-hog.

"How's himself?" Kate asked, lowering her child.

"Mr. Crease? Just going up to see. Better, I think, bless you. I've brought him muffins for his tea. You know how he loves his muffins." Mrs. Crease produced a paper bag from her shopping basket.

"I'll toast 'em for you," Kate offered.

"No, no thank you, Kate. I'll do them. I know just how brown he likes them, and he's ever so particular about his muffins!"

She did not add that Kate had a tendency to burn things.

Kate watched the older woman impale a muffin on a toasting fork and solemnly hold it close to the kitchen fire.

" 'Tis a bitter shame such a man as himself lies in his bed," she said suddenly. Ill health frightened Kate.

"As you know, it's been this way ever since the winter of 'fifty-five," Mrs. Crease said. "It's the cold, you know. Gets at the very marrow in his bones!"

Kate nodded. Many was the long night she had spent sitting beside Mr. Crease in his pain.

" 'Tis a bitter shame," she repeated. "One of me own uncles

was the same. Off to the Crimay with a cockade in his hat; back
a year later with an elegant leg made o' wood. I was a girl at the
time, but I have the memory of it well."

Mrs. Crease turned the muffin. Kate spoke rarely of her past
or family.

"Were many of your family soldiers, Kate?"

Kate laughed. "Too many. I come from a line of warriors. If
they weren't a-fighting against the Yeos, they were fighting for
the British in some ferrin clime. Croppies or the Dublin Fusi-
liers, it made no difference."

"And now?"

"Ah, that's a tale I cannot tell, not having set foot o'er the
water these past twelve years. But I'll imagine they're all Feni-
ans now, snicking the tails off cattle—if they're not all railroad-
ing in Americay."

Mrs. Crease started on a second muffin, while Kate's boy lay
on his back before the fire, thumb in mouth. How very little she
knew of Kate Webster. Some had cautioned her in vague terms
about the woman, but she had experienced nothing but good
humor and devotion. And Kate's nursing of Mr. Crease this
December had been wondrous kind.

"We will both miss you when you are gone," she said.

"Fiddlesticks! I'll be callin' for to see me boy each week."

"Mr. Crease likes to have you about, you know."

Kate's hand touched her shoulder. "If he gets poorly again,
you just have to holler and I'll be back to stay—and there's me
word on it!"

Mrs. Crease sought and found Kate's hand with her own.
"The doctor is most anxious for him," she said, and her voice
broke.

It was Kate's turn to pat Mrs. Crease. "Pay no attention to the physics, mother." She laughed. "A man who's spent his days married to Brown Bess is hard to kill! You take me word on it. He's as tough as a tacker!" Then she put out her foot—huge and booted—and turned over her son in his resting place. "Up now, you! Time fer bed! Come an' give your poor ignorant ugly old mother a kiss!"

III

Saying goodbye to the boy had been a dismal business, and Kate had cried into his neck as he clung to her. Finally she had pushed him hard into the grasp of Mrs. Crease, seized her bags, and left without a backward glance. She had not been separated from the child since her last period of imprisonment, and for such injustice she now mentally cursed her world, the cases in her hands swinging angrily as she strode down Park Road to Mayfield Cottages.

She passed the Hole in the Wall and saw the lights and heard the laughter. A light drizzle had begun to fall, and she felt the urge to call in at the public house for gin. But she suppressed this desire and walked on. In her present state alcohol might influence her tongue, and she had yet to get the measure of Mrs. Thomas. Anyway, she had a bottle in her bags, and she promised herself a nip before she retired to bed.

Number Two Mayfield Cottages was in darkness when she arrived, and Kate walked up the garden path with care lest she stumble on the verges. There was no porch at the door, and she stood in the rain waiting for an answer to her knocking. She tried the handle, but the door was locked. The weather became worse, and Kate feared for her bonnet; the straw of a two-shilling hat could be quickly spoiled in a heavy downpour, and Kate owned only one.

At last, the unfastening of bolts, and the front door opened a fraction to show the features of Mrs. Thomas—pinched and pale in the light of a single candle.

"Another minute and I'd be surely drownded!" Kate said, and Mrs. Thomas moved aside to let her pass into the house. Kate tripped on the step, and her bags banged against the wall.

"Take care, the paper!" said her new mistress.

Kate put down her bags and took off her cape, shaking the garment furiously.

"In the kitchen!" said Mrs. Thomas. "Hang it in the kitchen. I don't want water in the hall!"

It was difficult to see by the candle, and if Kate gave her a certain look, the latter missed it.

"Can I borrow your candle, missus?" Kate asked. She did not want to negotiate the basement steps in the dark.

"I'll show you down," came the answer, and Mrs. Thomas led her down.

The kitchen was as damp and cold as Kate remembered, and she watched Mrs. Thomas fumble with matches to light a lamp.

"You've no gas, missus?"

Mrs. Thomas adjusted the wick. "You will find oil lamps under the dresser," she said. "I seldom use gas. I find it very wasteful." And very costly too.

Kate sniffed the moist atmosphere, and her action was taken for something different.

"You have a more, er, *extravagant* nature, Mrs. Webster?"

"How's that? No, not at all. In fact, I like the dark. It conjures up the path of ghosts." She laid her cape across two chairs to let it dry.

41

"We have no ghosts in this house, I assure you!"

Kate chuckled. "More's the pity of it then!" She ran her hand along the edge of the dresser, and soot came away on her fingertips. "Scross, but you've a lot of dirt down here!"

Mrs. Thomas nodded. "The copper. It's from the copper."

Kate looked over to the cramped cellar part of the kitchen, but now it lay pitch black beyond the range of the lamp.

"You burn coal for the copper?" she asked.

"Cheaper than firewood, Mrs. Webster. But I expect you will be able to deal with the smudges."

"Surely, missus. But you'll not be minding if I use wood for the copper in future?" Why was her mistress so niggardly about light and fire?

"I should prefer that we continue to burn coal," she was told. "Its disadvantages are far outweighed by the question of cost."

Kate shrugged. She could see that argument was wasted breath and decided Mrs. Thomas was a "crab apple." Why, she had even put out her candle now the lamp was burning.

"Is there anything you'll be wanting of me before you retire, mistress?" she inquired. For herself, she'd like a cup of tea.

Mrs. Thomas consulted her half hunter under the oil lamp.

"It is now eight o'clock," she said. "A glass of water in the drawing room, if you'd be so kind. I shall then be at prayer for a while." She paused. "Perhaps you would care to join me, Mrs. Webster?"

"With your prayers, missus?"

"Yes indeed. It is fit and proper that devotion be companionable." Both Molly Jones and young Edith had been required to kneel at prayer with Mrs. Thomas. Why should Mrs. Webster, even if she was older, be made an exception to this rule?

"I shall be upstairs then," Mrs. Thomas went on. "I shall hope

42

to see you in a few minutes." And she relit her candle and left.

Alone in the basement, Kate smiled to herself. No harm in humoring the old lady, she supposed, although Kate had not said a prayer—in company or alone—for many a year. But had Mrs. Thomas forgotten she was papish?

Kate took a glass from the dresser and filled it from the pump. As she did so, a framed picture nailed to the cupboard door caught her attention. Putting down the glass, she raised the lamp. It wasn't a picture, but a notice in the nature of a sampler. "Never change your place unless The Lord clearly shows it will be for the good of your Soul," she read. Gothic script, and upon the lower part of the mount were engraved the words "A Reminder to All Good Domestics."

Kate was not surprised by the notice—she'd seen many of that kind before—but she did not wholly agree with its caution. Perhaps she might engineer its fall onto the hard quarry tiles of the floor in due course.

She took the lamp and the glass of water, mounted the steps to the hall, and went into the drawing room. Mrs. Thomas was already on her knees, hands clasped before her on the davenport desk, two candles in matching brass sticks on either side. Her eyes were shut in prayer, and Kate waited for them to open before she spoke.

"I brought you your water, missus."

"Hush!" Mrs. Thomas held up a hand. "Hush now, and kneel beside me!"

Kate crossed over from the door and did as she was bade, her body coming down heavily so that the room shook and china rattled in a cabinet.

"The Lord's Prayer," Mrs. Thomas said with a frown. "We shall recite the Lord's Prayer."

Kate strove to remember the words, and mumbled beside her mistress. But at the conclusion of the prayer, she became nonplussed.

"For Thine is the Kingdom, and the Power, and the Glory, forever and ever, Amen," her mistress was saying while Kate stayed silent.

Mrs. Thomas bowed her head and then looked at Kate.

"You did not attempt to say the latter part, Mrs. Webster," she said.

Kate stared back at her. "No, missus. I've never heard that bit before."

"Never heard it before! How can that be! Surely you know the Lord's Prayer!"

"To be sure I does, missus," Kate replied. Her voice was calm although she was slightly annoyed. "But not that bit at the end. The Fathers back home never learned us those particular words."

Mrs. Thomas was inclined to remonstrate further, but she got to her feet instead as she recalled one peculiarity about her servant.

"Of course, you are a Roman Catholic," she mumbled and took a sip of water. "I imagine that many of your prayers are different."

"And a sight older too, missus." Kate pulled herself up, to tower over Mrs. Thomas.

"Antiquity is not always a sign of the best, Mrs. Webster!"

Mrs. Thomas was sharp, and Kate anticipated a lecture. But she was tired. She wanted her gin bottle and her bed.

"Well, there you'd be speakin' of things beyond me education," she said with a yawn. Mrs. Thomas did not like this woman's habit of yawning at her. But she said nothing, settling herself down on the chair before the davenport. She opened the lid of the desk and withdrew her Memorandum and a pencil.

"Before you retire, Mrs. Webster," she began, "I would like some hot water in my room. You may place it outside the door in the blue jug you will find by the kitchen sink." She opened her notebook and found the proper page. "But before you do that, I must take some details about your good self. Now then, Mrs. Webster. You were born in Ireland. Forgive me, but what year?"

"Eighteen forty-nine."

"And your parents?"

"Both dead of the hunger."

"I'm very sorry. Any relations in England—those of your late husband, for example?"

"Not that I know. Dead and gone or moved away, I suppose." Kate's manner was more bored than wary. She stood in a slouch, hand on hip.

"And the father of your little boy?"

"If I knew that, I'd be havin' him for a shillen a week or more!"

Mrs. Thomas knew nothing of the intricacies of maintenance payments, so she pressed on. "What about your last employment? You mentioned some people in Teddington, I recall."

"Aye. Mr. and Mrs. Mitchell, Bridge Cottage, Stanley Road."

"And why did you leave that house?"

Kate could scarcely mention Strong. "Me child got took with an ailment. I had t'be on hand," she said.

"And so you went to Mrs. Crease?"

"That's the way of it, missus." It was well that Mrs. Thomas did not seek to delve more deeply into her past.

Mrs. Thomas now looked at what she had written. "You spent a year at Mrs. Mitchell's?"

"I did. And she was a lady fine and fair to me, missus."

"And before that?"

A long spell at the Wandsworth House of Correction. Kate must be careful with her answer.

"I was dairying in the country," she decided. "Way up in County Essex."

"Really? I used to live in Essex. Which part of Essex, Mrs. Webster?"

"Witham Village, missus." Just the name of a place Kate had heard she knew not when. Now she regretted her choice of county, fearful that Mrs. Thomas would probe and expose the lie.

"Ah, the south. I only know those parts north of Chelmsford, I'm afraid," said Mrs. Thomas, and Kate was greatly relieved. Mrs. Thomas closed her book and studied her new employee. An unusual person this, with her enormous stature, her clumsy ways, her variety of facial expression.

"If there's anything else for the asking, spake up and I'll supply the answer!" Kate said suddenly, unnerved by Mrs. Thomas's silent stare.

"No thank you. You may go."

Mrs. Thomas watched her servant leave and close the drawing-room door with more than necessary force. Yes, Mrs. Webster certainly *was* different. Her sudden changes of mood, the soft way in which she was able to say things that might otherwise be considered brusque or even rude . . . Mrs. Thomas decided to speak of her to her good friend Miss Loder on the morrow.

46

A RARE OLD SWINE-UP

I

Mrs. Thomas woke early and ill-humored, convinced that her mattress must be damp to give her such aches and pains. She washed in cold water, dressed quickly and hurried downstairs to make her own breakfast, grumbling at her servant all the while, although she realized that she'd given Kate no specific instructions for the day. Then she should have asked! she told herself. What was the use of a general if she was lacking in initiative? But Kate still slumbered in her attic den when Mrs. Thomas let herself out of the house in search of Miss Loder.

The morning air was cold and it was still raining. Passing carriages, driven at speed by the thoughtless, splashed muddy water over the pavements and onto her skirts, and by the time Mrs. Thomas reached the Crescent her lips were tight with irritation.

Daphne, Miss Loder's tweeny, answered the door, and Mrs. Thomas pushed by her with a terse demand to see the mistress of the house.

"Madam's yet abed, marm," she was told by the adenoidal Daphne.

Mrs. Thomas inspected the long-case in the hall. It was after eight. Surely her friend could not still be sleeping? A house should be a hive of useful activity at this hour.

"Go knock on her door and see if she is awakened, girl!"

But Daphne was reluctant.

"Step lively, girl! Inform Miss Loder that it is Mrs. Thomas who would speak to her on a matter most important!"

So Daphne left and returned shortly. Madam would see Mrs. Thomas in her boudoir.

Leaving her umbrella and coat to drip in a corner stand, Mrs. Thomas followed the tweeny upstairs to the first landing, where she was ushered into a small room papered in pink. Miss Loder sat before her dressing table brushing her hair, fat and friendly in a puff-sleeved robe.

"My, you are an early one!" she exclaimed, her smile anxious at the sight of Mrs. Thomas's bad temper.

"In the case of both my late husbands," Mrs. Thomas said, perching herself on a narrow settee, "it was our practice to begin the day while it was still fresh."

Miss Loder went back to the doing of her hair. She could see her friend in the mirror. Something had upset her.

"I'll send for tea!" she said and tugged a bellpull. "Or would you rather coffee?"

"Coffee? Certainly not. But tea would be most refreshing." Mrs. Thomas did not drink coffee. It was a beverage that smacked of Continental countries and the Church of Rome.

"It is about my Mrs. Webster I have called," she reminded herself. "I want your guidance, m'dear."

"You find her unsatisfactory?" Miss Loder began to pin her hair.

"No. She has scarce had opportunity to justify herself. But I do find her"—Mrs. Thomas picked the word with care—"somewhat *unusual.*"

Daphne came and departed with her orders.

"You were saying that you found her unusual, Julia," Miss Loder took up when the maid had closed the door. "How so?"

"Her manner is strange!"

"You mean mysterious?"

"No. Strange is the word."

"Mrs. Crease has said, I think, that life has been very unkind to Mrs. Webster," Miss Loder said.

Mrs. Thomas thought of dead parents and dead husbands and nodded. "That is what brings me here," she said. "You see, I know as good as nothing about her background. Why, she's even lost her Characters!"

Miss Loder completed the intricate styling of her hair and inserted a tortoiseshell comb. "Mrs. Crease speaks well of her. Have you heard some dreadful tale to the contrary?"

"Of course not! But I still find her strange."

Miss Loder considered the problem as she stared at herself in the mirror. Then she solved the puzzle. "That's because she's fey!" she announced with delight. "She is Irish and a Celt, my dear. As such, she is simply fey!"

"She is also a papist," said her friend gravely.

"But all the Irish are of that denomination, Julia! And we are positively invaded by the Irish these days!"

Mrs. Thomas remembered Logan, the roadsweep. "So I have observed. And I daresay the very lowliest of employment is reserved for them. I cannot say, with hand on heart, that I entirely approve of their presence in such numbers."

A knock on the door was followed by Daphne bearing a tray. When she had poured and gone again, Miss Loder spoke.

"I disagree with you about the wretched Irish. They serve a useful purpose, after all. Who else would work our factories for us?"

"Mrs. Webster comes from Liverpool." The accusation was matter-of-fact.

"Oh, dearie me! That horrid city is *teeming* with the Irish! I hear that they live in the utmost squalor, and that their children die as quickly as they are bred. Dearie me! Hence the reason for Mrs. Webster coming south! . . . Sugar?"

Mrs. Thomas took her cup of tea and searched the surface for strangers.

"Do you think it proper," she said, "for me to call upon our local constabulary and ask one of those nice young policemen whether he can tell me anything about Mrs. Webster?"

Miss Loder stirred her tea before answering. She was vexed to find a small chip in the gilt rim of her cup. Daphne—her habit of catching the lips of cups on the kitchen tap when she washed them; very well, Daphne must pay a halfpenny into the "Forfeit Box."

"If you are so very worried, yes," she told her friend.

Satisfied, Mrs. Thomas now sipped her tea in peace. She would go to the constable's office in Richmond that afternoon. But first she must visit the grave of Mr. Thomas at Kingston Cemetery. Then she would lunch at Mrs. Gordon's establishment in the High Street and further her inquiries afterward.

"I do believe it a trifle warmer today," she observed in better humor.

"But wet and clammy," came the reply. "It is not a healthy time of year."

50

II

Kate had risen at half past eight to find her mistress gone. So she went below, lit the fire under the range, and made herself some porridge. Tepid porridge and tepid tea were followed by an attempt to clean up the basement area. But the grime and mold made hot work, and she soon despaired, abandoning her mops and pails for a simple feather duster, which she took to the drawing room.

In the light of day Kate was now able to take note of the contents of this room. To her surprise, austerity reigned; the davenport desk was of poor quality, and the chairs and sofas tattered. A standard cabinet was filled with inferior glass and china, and no pictures hung on the walls. A wellington chest of drawers had handles missing and chipped veneer.

But if the furnishings and objets d'art failed to occupy Kate's professional interest, there remained one notable exception. A piano, decorous and inlaid with costly woods, stood upright against the near wall. And a canterbury, worked as if to match the piano, held sheafs of music and song. Kate selected samples at random. "Woodman Spare That Tree" and "Song of the Troubadour." Kate was bewildered. Hymns she had expected, not popular ditties. Now Kate loved music, and she became excited. She lifted the lid of the piano. The ivory keys were yellow with age and use, but they were intact. Note by note she tried them, and none fell false. A tuned piano—and Kate's ear was perfect—was rare except in the houses of the aristocratic or the talented. Captain Woolbest had owned such a piano when she'd been in his employ. But that gentleman had been an enthusiastic songster, as well as a boon in her bed. And that had been six years back, when Kate was but four and twenty.

Still daydreaming, she picked up another sheaf of music. Another song—but what was this? "A Maiden So Tricked," with quite risqué words. Kate smiled. Did her mistress really entertain her guests with such renditions? It was inconceivable! But if it was so, then her mistress played two parts.

"Why, the wicked old woman!" Kate laughed.

She closed the piano and returned the song to its stall. She must ask Mrs. Thomas to instruct her in the way of music, to show her how to pick an air on this incredible mass of wire and hammers. For that Kate would indeed be grateful.

"As I was walking through Dublin City," she began to croon as she dusted. "At the hour of twelve in the night, Who should I see but a Spanish lady, Washing her feet by candlelight."

Kate continued to sing as she worked throughout the house. Only when she attempted to gain access into Mrs. Thomas's bedroom did her lips become still. The door was locked with two brass eyes, and she recalled the bunch of keys carried by her mistress. No matter. Why should the lady trust her? Time itself would relax this situation, for Kate had no intent to thieve. Nor would she allow Strong to lever his irons in this house. She had too much to lose this time. The Beaks could order an extended sentence in her case, and force a final separation from her child. Kate's hands clenched hard around the bamboo stick of her duster at the thought.

The morning passed, and at midday Kate went down to the kitchen area. She was hungry, and she had seen some bread and cheese in the larder. She would have preferred a bit of meat, but her employer obviously ate little flesh or fowl. Kate would volunteer to shop for her that afternoon and get some chops for their supper. And if Mrs. Thomas made complaint, then Kate would eat them all.

She took the loaf from the slate shelf and searched in the dresser for a knife. The one she found was old and blunt, and she was obliged to hack the stale bread rather than cut it clean. No butter to be had, and the cheese was rancid.

"O for a glass of porter," she wished aloud.

Never mind. Her little boy would be eating his fill right now. Bacon sandwiches, and Mrs. Crease's bacon sandwiches were of the best.

Kate finished her bread and cheese and washed away the nasty tang in her mouth with tepid tea from the pot. With the housework done, she'd now be free to do her sewing. She left the basement and went upstairs to her room. Sitting on the edge of the bed, she began to sew strips of brownish fur onto the lower hem of her one and only coat. The fur was dyed to imitate beaver, but Kate knew its true origin lay with a kidnaped household cat. She sewed quickly and badly—with fingers tutored in various houses of correction—and she cursed her awkwardness from time to time. Then a heavy banging on the front door reached her ears.

Kate came down and opened the door. It was misty outside, but no colder than within the house. On the doorstep and front path stood a group of four—two men and two women. All were small and swarthy and dressed in garish clothes. Kate recognized them for gypsies.

The nearest—the man on the step—was their spokesman.

"My nabs has nante dinali," he said, and his smile was false and ingratiating. "My nabs has nanti numgare."

He had no money and no food—mummer's slang Kate had

heard before in Kingston. These Romanies must be caravanned on the common near the park.

"My nabs can sharpen churi for dinali," the man said.

Kate was about to turn them away when she remembered the carver in the kitchen.

"Wait," she said. She closed and bolted the front door and fetched the knife.

"Sharpen this," she told the man on return.

"Dinali?"

"When you've done with the sharpening."

The man took the knife, and the nearest of the two women came forward. She gave the man a stone, and he began to scrape the blade up and down, spitting on it occasionally, his eyes never leaving Kate. This was their fashion, of course—to stare you out, with the threat of the "evil eye." But Kate was not afraid. These were cheap-jack fair people, vagrants and standing patterers, and beneath even her contempt.

The man finished scratching the knife and handed his woman the stone.

"Cha borus," he said. "Dinali?"

Kate took a farthing from her apron, disguising the coin in her fingers. The man gave her the knife and took the money.

"Bawlor!" he shouted when he saw what he'd got. "Pig! Dinali —more!"

Kate shook her head, amused by his anger, for the man had begun to dance up and down.

"Dinali!" the other gypsies took up the chorus, but Kate remained impassive. Seeing that Kate could not be frightened, the man on the step spoke to his woman in their tongue. Kate did not understand what was said, but she noticed how the other gypsies came closer. Finally, the woman with the stone approached her. She was wrinkled and sinewy, aged by open living rather than by the passage of time, and her eyes were black and hard. She wore a pearly band around her forehead and a red velvet skirt with a satin stomacher. The latter she now pulled aside, to reveal a small tray of goods for sale. Thread, tapes, stay laces, and nutmeg graters. Kate wanted none of them, and again she shook her head.

"No dinali," the woman said. "Maybe fogare or beware?" She licked her lips as if to explain, but Kate understood her to be demanding tobacco or liquor by way of payment for her knick-knacks.

"I'll be wanting none of your trinkets," she said.

"Fogare, for smokey?" The woman came closer.

"No 'baccy, no beer. Now be off with you!"

Kate turned toward the door. A hand caught her by the sleeve—the woman with the tray still insisting. Taking a deep breath, Kate spun around and seized the woman by the wrist. She gave it a hard twist, and the woman yelped with pain.

"Touch me, and I'll give yer what Paddy gave the drum, yer stinkin' heathen witch!"

The gypsy woman tried to bite Kate's hand, bending over to use her teeth, and Kate's control deserted her. Letting go of the woman's hand, she took hold of the tray, tearing it from its strings and flinging the contents into the air so that they fell in a cascade over their heads. The gypsy began to howl like a North African, and her cries were joined by a yowling from her fellows. She came at Kate with her hands hooked into claws. But her fury was equaled by the big woman on the doorstep. Kate drew back her arm and punched the woman in the eye, knocking her into a bundle down the pathway. Kate then squared up to the nearer man. He cringed and turned to run, and Kate's booted right foot struck him full in the seat of his pants, driving him headlong into a clump of rose bushes. Kate came off the doorstep and challenged the entire party of gypsies.

"I'll have yer tripes and not yer ribbons!" she shouted. "I'll teach yer to play the patter at the house of a dacent woman!"

But the gypsies knew their match, and short of drawing knives they must retreat. Two were running for the gate, and the fallen man and woman slunk off to join them.

"Come back, you cowardly turds!" called Kate. Then she laughed to see the man rubbing his behind. She picked up a handful of stones from the path and hurled them after him. "Come back, and I'll boot the arse off you, man!"

At that moment Mrs. Thomas came into view by the gate.

Mrs. Thomas stopped in her tracks, and the gypsy man squeezed past her through the gate. Mrs. Thomas observed scratches on his face. He was followed by his woman, red-eyed and sobbing with rage.

"What is all of this?" Mrs. Thomas asked.

The gypsy woman paused. She stared at Mrs. Thomas and then shook her bony fist.

"Her nabs is a keteva muler!" she said, pointing at Kate. "Bad sort!" She pulled down the under lid of her left eye. "Beware!" And she ran off up Park Road to join her fellows.

Mrs. Thomas entered her front garden and walked up the path to Kate, stepping over the trinkets strewn around. She took note of the battered bush.

"Those wretches have completely ruined my roses," she said when she reached Kate.

Kate laughed. "I was obliged to help the one of 'em on his way with the toe of me boot," she said.

Mrs. Thomas had seen her throw the stones and heard her

shouts, but this was something worse.

"Come inside, Mrs. Webster," she said firmly.

In the hall Mrs. Thomas removed her hat and coat before speaking. Kate now sensed that she might be in bad odor and stood quietly to one side.

"Are you seriously telling me that you *kicked* one of those people?" Mrs. Thomas asked at last.

Kate was puzzled. "To be sure I did, missus," she said.

"Kicked him?"

"And I gave the woman the flavor of my knuckles, missus."

"You hit one of the women?" Mrs. Thomas remembered the face of the gypsy woman at the gate.

"Yes, missus." Kate thought that she'd better explain. "You see, they was tinker folk, come to swindle, putting on a poor mouth about having no money. I know the tinkers, missus. They're the bane of our lives across the water. If they don't get what they wants, they'll make a row-de-dow. But this time Kate's shown them, gave them a rare old swine-up!"

Mrs. Thomas saw the flush of excitement on the other's face. Far from the incident causing her fear or distress, the woman had plainly enjoyed herself.

"I find your behavior and your attitude extraordinary," she said to Kate.

"How's that, missus? But they was travelin' people, missus!"

"Harmless gypsies, Mrs. Webster." Kate shook her head. "Please do not contradict me! They were poor gypsies from the Ham encampment. I know, because I have had occasion to see them before. They performed *Fair Rosamund* only last September. And now you have done them a great injustice!"

Kate grew sulky, so that Mrs. Thomas felt the urge to scold her further. But Mrs. Thomas was weary. She had walked far that day, and now she wanted to rest. Perhaps when she was refreshed she would return to the matter.

"I will take tea in the drawing room, Mrs. Webster."

Kate refused to move. "I did what I did for the protecting of your home and property, missus," she said.

Mrs. Thomas sighed. "Then your motive was mistaken, and your means quite unforgivable. Now please go about your duties at once!"

The look on Kate's face changed from sullen to defiant.

"That's no way to be talking to me!" she snapped, and she regretted her words at once.

"Mrs. Webster!"

"I'm sorry, missus, I really am."

"And I should think so! My word, I'll not tolerate such impertinence! Do you hear?"

Kate nodded.

"Do you hear me?"

"Yes, missus. I'm sorry like I said, missus." And Kate hung her head while her hands clasped and unclasped behind her back.

"Good! Now fetch me my tea, and then you may stay in your room until I send for you. Pray meditate upon your appalling behavior."

And Mrs. Thomas went off into the drawing room.

Kate made her way downstairs with a heavy heart. She realized that she had come within an inch of instant dismissal, and she must not lose her service. To be without work was to fail her little boy, and to lay her open to the temptations of Strong. And all of this because of a band of tinker folk. Kate's eyes went strangely vacant, for her thoughts traveled far away to the green-brown hills of County Wexford. Itinerant tinkers and charcoal burners. Woodsmoke and the smell of cattle. Then her mind returned to the gloomy kitchen and her employer.

"Damn her for a snaggle-toothed old cow!" she said in a loud voice and felt better.

MUTTON-SHUNTER

I

Police Constable Pew aspired to make sergeant before the year was out. But his ambition had been precisely the same at the beginning of 1878, and the more sensible recesses of his mind advised that his arm would sport no stripes this year or the next. The truth was that, in order to succeed in the Constabulary, it was essential to make arrests and secure convictions. PC Pew made many arrests—he was apt to produce his handcuffs and execute a seizure in the case of the most paltry misdemeanor —but to obtain a conviction was another matter. During the year he had been severely censured both by his superiors at the station and by the local magistrates. "You must not," they would tell him, "make arrests without evidence!" And his cases had been dismissed. In order to allay such criticism, PC Pew sometimes resorted to unfairly clever means—fabricating that vital bit of proof the silly laws of the land demanded. In such cases a culprit might protest his innocence and avow that the testimony of PC Pew was false, but then the constable had only to appear hurt or surprised for his version of the matter to be accepted by the authorities—his boyish good looks being something of an asset. But the times whena PC Pew could produce incriminating evidence to "down" a rogue were limited, for PC Pew's powers of imagination were in themselves very limited. And now he had not secured a notable conviction since Christmas, and he was despondent.

Mrs. Thomas's visit to the station occupied his mind as he walked his large feet up the hill to that lady's house. Mrs. Thomas was obviously a respectable member of the community, a lady of quality. Usually Sergeant Thatcher attended upon the old ladies of the town, and so popular had he become among that sisterhood that he was called by them "Sergeant Rusty," by reason of his red hair and mustaches. This popularity had earned for him his promotion in the force, Pew suspected. But happily Sergeant Rusty had not been on duty when Mrs. Thomas had called. PC Pew had been left at the desk, and he had dealt with the old lady with as much unction as he could muster. She had been impressed—Pew could see that—and he decided he must continue to impress the lady, and her friends as well. And if he succeeded in this line, why surely he would become as popular as the sergeant. Promotion would be his for the asking. He had not the fiery whiskers of his colleague—his own efforts to grow mustaches were ridiculous—but he had his youthful charm and sandy eyebrows. To be sure, the ladies of the town would yearn to mother him and bake him cakes and so on.

"Mrs. Katherine Webster"—that was the name she gave. "Widow of a Liverpool luggerman. Now cook-general in the service of Surrey households." Pew had probed his memory and old notebooks for mention of this woman. But he'd drawn a blank. Perhaps she had not long been in the immediate area of Richmond. Mrs. Thomas had spoken of Teddington and a family called Mitchell. He'd check these details in due course, but he doubted any useful findings.

So he'd chosen to see this cook-general for himself. He would talk with Mrs. Webster about her antecedents, hurl quick-fire questions at her like his clever inspector. If she was genuine, her story would hold tight; but if she prevaricated, her lies would become apparent, and then he'd arrest and charge her for something or other.

By the time PC Pew reached Mayfield Cottages he was out of breath. He carried too much weight for his twenty-six years. He opened the garden gate and noticed the disorderly state of the rose bushes. Perhaps he might offer to replant the roses? Mrs. Thomas would then be well disposed toward him.

Adjusting his helmet and tightening the leather belt about his waist, the constable rapped the knocker on the front door. He stepped back a pace, slid on his earnest expression, and waited.

But it was Kate who answered the door. For a long time the constable and Kate just stared at each other, Kate sullen, the other very hostile. It was Kate who finally broke the silence. "Now who'd expect yourself t'be calling!"

"No, I don't imagine you're too pleased to see me, Mistress Lawler," said the policeman. His face had reddened, and two white angry spots had appeared on either side of his nose.

"It's none of your concern, mister!" Kate said.

"All thieves are of concern to me," Pew replied. He moved to pass into the house, but Kate barred his way. "Let me pass, Katty!"

"She's not in!"

"Then I'll wait for her inside."

Kate allowed him in, her eyes never leaving his face. PC Pew was a man she'd never liked, and his sudden appearance had come as a shock.

"You can wait down in the kitchen," she suggested in the hall.

The constable nodded. He didn't care how long he'd have to wait for Mrs. Thomas. He could amuse himself meanwhile by tormenting this Irishwoman.

They descended to the basement, and Kate put a kettle on the range. She'd try to be nice, but she doubted whether Pew would go away.

"Tea, or something stronger, Mr. Pew?"

The policeman removed his helmet, ruffled his short fair hair, and sat down at the table. "Tea will do. Five sugars." He watched as Kate made the brew and filled a milk jug from a metal churn. She poured him his tea and placed the sugar bowl beside him.

He took a sip and pulled a face. "Pshaw! You trouts all make rotten tea. Stew your knickers in it, I suppose?"

Kate took the chair opposite him. "Will ye be after tellin' Mrs. Thomas of me?" she asked.

PC Pew avoided her eyes—too black and piercing for his comfort—and added more sugar. "Tell her? Why, I've a mind to arrest you here and now!" he said as he stirred.

"You've not the right to do so, Mr. Pew."

The policeman looked up with surprise. "Not the right? You come to Richmond. You fail to notify us at the station. You are on ticket of leave. I have the right, woman!"

Kate shook her head. "Wrong," she said. "I come out last February, and I did full stretch. There was no ticket o' leave, mister."

The constable grunted. He wasn't sure of the true position.

The Kingston magistrates had given her twelve months in February '77. Perhaps there had been no license in her case this time.

"I suppose Mrs. Thomas knows about that business?" he asked.

"She does not."

"I suppose Mrs. Thomas knows about Miss Katty Lawler— alias Webb and Gibbs and Gibbons—serving an eighteen monthser before that?"

"She does not."

"Thirty-six cases of larceny from shops in Kingston, wasn't it? Sent you off to Wandsworth House on the fifth of May, if I remember right."

Kate made no reply, and the life in her eyes had died.

"And before that?" the constable persisted. "How many times has it been, Katty?"

"I was innocent!" Kate said.

"But of course you was innocent!" Pew was beginning to enjoy himself. "No one has ever suggested you was guilty! You were sent orf to spin for your good health, Katty. *I* know that, but does Mrs. Thomas?"

Pew was now prepared to brave her eyes, and was satisfied to find them moist and weak. Press on, he told himself. He'd get her blubbing yet.

"In and out of prison all your life, eh Katty? Long firm swindles with that fellow Strong; burgling people's houses with that fellow Strong; doss-house dodges with that fellow Strong. But in the end it's you what takes the rap, eh Katty? Never Strong! Not fair, is it, Katty?"

A single heavy tear ran down the woman's face. Pew studied her for a moment.

"God, you're an ugly crow!" He banged the table with his open hand. "But I pity you, Mrs. Webster—or whatever you call yourself these days. No, I really does." An idea was beginning to form in his mind, and he spoke gently. "Strong's the villain, I know that. And you and I could put it right. You just tell me as to how I find this laddie Strong, and we'll make things even. How about it, Katty?"

Kate lifted her head. "I've done with Strong," she said and sniffed.

"More's the pity then," said the constable, feigning indifference. "That means I'll have to tell your mistress *all* about you, don't it?"

Kate's despair became complete. Tears flowed freely, and the big woman groaned. "I thieved for the sake of me child!" She sniffled.

"Oh, your little lad?" the policeman said with a wicked smile. "I'd let him slip my mind. It'll have to be the workhouse for him, if you've no work nor lodgings."

Kate dropped the dirty handkerchief she'd been holding.

"Sblood be on your hands!" she screamed at Pew, so that he leaned away with alarm. "I'll see you blinded and in hell afore yer take me child!" and Kate began to rise from her chair.

The constable feared assault. He'd gone too far.

"Hold hard!" he said. "I wouldn't want that! But the parish might take that view. Now don't you go hitting me, Katty, or they'll throw away the key!"

Kate was trembling as she struggled with her rage. But his words had their effect. This mutton-shunter would throw the entire Calendar at her if she struck him. So she resumed her seat, bowed her head, and commenced to weep and wail again without restraint. Pew relaxed. He had no desire to be cudgeled by those bony fists.

"Just tell me the whereabouts of Strong," he asked softly and waited.

Kate retrieved and trumpeted into her fallen handkerchief. She was endeavoring to pull herself together. Was she going to break?

"He'd never have to know, Katty," urged Pew. "It'd be our secret. You and me and no one else."

"Are you a fair man, mister?" Kate's red eyes were on him.

"You know I am! There's none fairer!"

"Then I'll tell yer, Mother of God forgive me. And only for the savin' of me child, you hear?"

PC Pew nodded solemnly.

"He's not a local man," Kate went on. "He keeps this oil shop in Holloway. He comes to Surrey only in the line of business."

Pew was surprised. These facts did not fit in with his own inquiries.

"Rumor has it that you and he were living together in Acre Road, Kingston," he said.

"Strong's a clever one. I lived there, and he come visiting. But right now you'll not be finding him at all—unless you search the prisons." It was easy to lie to a man like Pew.

"He's in jail!"

"Aye. Doing a quarter stretch with hard."

"Where? When did this happen?"

"December. He comes up before a six-monthser magistrate at Clerkenwell, and now he's wearing the broad arrow. I hears he was calling himself Mitchell at the time."

PC Pew considered this information. If this was true, Strong was due for release this month. Pew could check the north London prisons in an official capacity. But his search for Strong was private and informal. Tracing Strong could take time.

"You telling me the truth, Katty?" he challenged.

"You gives me no choice, blind yer eyes!"

And the constable was convinced. But should this Irish vixen have deceived him . . .

"I'll be off now," he said, getting to his feet, helmet under arm. "If you have played me false, Katty, I'll be back to tweak your tail. Understand?"

Kate nodded, hiding in her handkerchief again. She was astounded that the policeman had believed her at all. But she knew Pew to be an ambitious man, of the kind ready to believe anything to his advantage.

"You'll not tell Mrs. Thomas?" she asked him.

Pew shook his head. Not yet. But when he had completed his investigations into Strong, he'd have to reconsider. It might then become a matter of duty to inform Mrs. Thomas of the fact that she was sheltering a tigress. Meanwhile, Katty Lawler had time enough to steal the silver.

Miss Ives, clipping dead branches from a small bush in her front garden, looked up to watch the policeman put on his helmet and walk down the path of Number Two to the gate.

"Morning, mum!" called Pew with a cheery smile, and Miss Ives gave him a nod of recognition. "Weather's turned chilly again," added the constable over the fence as he drew level with her.

"Nothing wrong, I trust," said Miss Ives, gesturing toward Number Two with a gloved hand.

"Wrong? Of course not, mum! Just routine. Mrs. Thomas asked me to step by and verify the credentials of her new housekeeper, that's all."

"And?"

"Mrs. Webster's all right, mum. And you can tell Mrs. Thomas that from me when next you see her." The humor of the situation made Pew grin broadly; never would he have imagined himself speaking up for Katty Lawler.

"I'm pleased to hear it," said Miss Ives, and she gave the bush a shake. "And it was well of you to take trouble on Mrs. Thomas's behalf, Constable."

Pew executed a quick salute. "No bother, mum. Always ready to be of assistance. Any problems, just you be in touch with PC Pew, mum." Another tick for me, reflected the policeman. One more step up Sergeant Rusty's ladder of success.

Miss Ives stared after the constable's retreating back before returning to the bush. How absurd it was, she decided, for her tenant to call upon the services of the constabulary in order to satisfy her qualms about a servant. Still, if it did make Mrs. Thomas happy—if it did ease her silly troubled mind—perhaps it was for the best.

II

Mrs. Thomas decided to be generous. The episode of the gypsies was to be forgiven if not forgotten. In the past Mrs. Thomas had pardoned her servants their various minor foibles, and a few days' grace should be allowed a new employee, during which a peccadillo might be overlooked. Naturally, all faults must be noted, and condign punishment follow any repetition.

But it was proper that small allowances be made when one considered lack of intelligence and general background.

In the case of Mrs. Webster, Mrs. Thomas concluded that the very coarseness and savagery of her ancestors were much to blame. Mrs. Webster was quick to anger and lose her reason. So she must be taught to manage herself without delay. Work— long and hard—was the answer. Prayer? Alas, no. Mrs. Webster had been born the slave of priests and idolators, and therefore stood beyond the reach of prayer. So honest toil it must be, from dawn to dusk, for six and a half days a week. Mrs. Webster could visit her child on Sunday afternoons. But she must be back on time.

"I attend church at the Presbyterian Lecture Hall at six," her mistress told her. "You are to be back at fifteen minutes before the hour, so as to mind the house whilst I am gone." And it was imperative that Mrs. Webster be punctual.

Lists were prepared with regard to the administration of the house. Mrs. Webster must not be wasteful with food or gas or coal. It was not necessary for either Mrs. Thomas or her general to have eggs or meat more than once a week. Butter was expensive and to be treated as a luxury. Both could look forward to a slice of seed cake on Saturday afternoons.

Sure, I'll soon be thin as a rasher of wind, thought Kate.

Cleaning the house itself required method. Since the state of a person's accommodation was a mirror of the mind, rooms and landings must be kept spotless. Soot from the fires tended to settle everywhere, even in the most unlikely places. Dusting should be treated as an art.

"Once you have done a room," came the advice, "pause, inspect, and do it all over again."

Laundry and clothing. Mrs. Thomas chose to make her own

bed each day, and it was not for Kate to enter the long bedroom without summons. The copper would continue to be heated by coal, and linen changed once fortnightly. There were irons in the basement which could be heated, and Mrs. Thomas liked her dresses pressed on Friday. No, there was nothing to justify the purchase of a uniform for Kate. She already owned two black dresses, and, provided she made good use of needle and thread, these were quite adequate. She was not required to wear an apron unless her mistress had visitors. It was most unlikely that Mrs. Thomas would have occasion to entertain, but if she did, Kate must ensure that her apron was properly starched.

And so the days passed, and Kate grew tidy and slim. Mrs. Thomas spoke well of her to Miss Ives and Miss Loder and regretted that she could never find it in her heart to compliment the woman herself. For Kate was still a maze of contradictions. She was quiet without being surly; she was eager in word but clumsy in deed; she was not impertinent, and yet she opened private drawers in the most inquisitive way; her cooking was careless and bad, but she was at least a "tryer"; she was also plain and ungainly, yet Mrs. Thomas had heard her singing in her room with a pleasing voice.

"You sing very nicely, Mrs. Webster," she said.

"I come from a land of sad songs, missus." Kate was happy to be praised.

"I too am fond of music, Mrs. Webster."

Kate agreed. She had heard her mistress play her piano. Kate's yen to master that instrument was revived.

"I was wonderin' if you'd show me how it's done," she asked.

"I beg your pardon?"

"The piano, missus. I was wondering if you'd teach me?"

Mrs. Thomas was somewhat taken aback. "I am not a French piano instructor, you know," was all that she could say. She did not add that it was not a servant's estate to be taught music by her mistress.

But she did allow Kate to clean in the drawing room during her practice hour each morning. And it was during one of these treats that a most unhappy occurrence took place.

It was after nine, and Kate's instructions for the day included a complete reblacking of the grate. The fire had been in regular use these past few days owing to the cold, and Mrs. Thomas ordered that the shine on the iron framework be restored.

Arming herself with brush and cloths, Kate knelt down by the chimney and set to work, while her mistress labored at the piano at scales in a minor key. Kate wore gloves, for the greasy blacking tended to impregnate the pores of the skin and defy easy washing. But the gloves were made of thin cotton and full of holes, and within a short time Kate could feel the blacking on her hands. She removed her gloves, intending to wipe her hands on one of the cloths by her side. To do this, she shifted her position, and in her awkwardness lost her balance, one knee banging against the fender and the other descending directly onto the pot of grate blacking. The pot was broken under her weight, and soon there was blacking on the fire surround and on the carpet. Kate tried to rub it off, but the more she moved, the more the shiny ointment spread. And all the while Mrs. Thomas tinkled at her piano.

"Bad cess to this!" Kate growled.

She attempted to stand up without moving the leg with black on the knee. But this was difficult, and she reached up to grab the mantelpiece for support. Her hand struck a china figurine, which came crashing down to shatter on the fender.

"The divil take it all!" Kate shouted.

Mrs. Thomas's monotonous scales came to an abrupt halt. She turned on her swivel stool to see what was happening. There was Kate, standing by the mantel and wiping a grimy hand across her brow, and Mrs. Thomas saw the pieces of the shattered figurine.

"My Dresden!" Mrs. Thomas left the stool to rush across. "My lovely Dresden!"

Kate glared at her. Her blood was up. She felt dirty and a fool.

"What have you done!" Mrs. Thomas challenged her.

"'Twas but a silly shepherd and his lass."

"It was best Dresden china, you stupid woman!" And Mrs. Thomas stamped her foot.

"It was an accident. I'll gum it together for you."

"You'll do no such thing. Don't you dare so much as touch it!" Mrs. Thomas was close to tears. Besides, the figurine was beyond repair.

Kate licked her lips. She had offered to make amends. What more could she do?

"I've said I'm sorry," she snapped. "Anyone can have a little bit of an accident."

Mrs. Thomas made no reply but bent down to pick up the head and shoulders of the shepherdess. "Utterly ruined! Look at it! Well, don't you care?"

Kate folded her arms and stared back unblinking. Her left nostril had begun to twitch, and her face was white.

"You are both careless and pernicious," Mrs. Thomas went on, unaware of the danger signals. "Worse still, you are obviously unable to admit to fault." She stopped short. Kate felt the urge to strike the face below her, and something of this desire was conveyed to her mistress—a look implacable and infernal

—and Mrs. Thomas shrank back from her servant. Like an animal, Kate took advantage of her fear.

"Yer mustn't be after talking to me so," she said very softly, advancing.

Mrs. Thomas found her retreat blocked by the armchair. She touched it for support, as if for reassurance. She was too frightened to speak.

"D'you hear me now?" Kate asked in the same dangerous tone. Mrs. Thomas tried to say something, to express assent, but she was only able to nod her head.

"That's well then," Kate managed, and her control was returning. "Now I'll be fetching a brush and pan to tidy up. You just be getting back to yer piano playin', missus." And she strolled clumsily to the door and out of the room. Outside in the hall she looked at her hands. They were shaking violently.

When Kate returned, Mrs. Thomas had not moved from the chair. Her face was flushed and she still trembled, but she was bravely composed. Her fear had turned into anger, but she was careful not to show it, and she moved away on Kate's approach.

"I am wondering, Mrs. Webster," she said as Kate cleared up the debris by the fender, "I am wondering whether your situation here is to your liking?" She spoke to Kate's back, and the other did not turn from her task.

"It'll do, missus."

The reply was offhand and lacked the menace of before, giving Mrs. Thomas added courage.

"I shall need you only until the twenty-eighth of February, Mrs. Webster." Mrs. Thomas chose that date for no particular reason. Kate continued to brush.

"I'll be off when you say," came the unexpected reply.

Greatly relieved, Mrs. Thomas tiptoed over to her piano and

gently closed the lid. Then she stole from the room, the swishing sound of hard bristles in her ears.

Her mistress gone, Kate stopped sweeping and sat back on her heels. Her thoughts were in a whirl and divided. She had anticipated instant dismissal, not respite for three whole weeks. She had come close to laying hands on the old lady. Mother of God be praised that she had held her back. Best if Kate stay away from Mrs. Thomas in the house; their contact led to mischief. Better still that Kate take her leave this very day?

No, that she would not do. Mrs. Thomas had not put her out for a reason both pitiful and strange. Mrs. Thomas was a-feared of her, of her own maidservant. For days she had used her ill —working her to the bone, following her around to pick at her efforts, denying her decent food or a chance for pleasure. Jeremiah-mongering all the time.

And then a bit of china gets broke, and Katty speaks up loud, and the little woman shrivels up like a Spanish onion. Kate smiled to herself. Scared as a bird she'd been, and all because Katty tells her to mind her tatur-trap. And if that was what was needed to keep the lady in line, then Katty could oblige. If Mrs. Thomas turned cross-grained again, Katty would stage another flare-up. For Katty was not unused to frightening people who gave her cause. Many was the wardress at the House she'd learned to mind her manners.

Kate picked up the head of the shepherdess, laughed, and popped it into her pan. Yes, she'd stop awhile.

ARKANSAS TOOTHPICK

I

In the days that followed, Kate and Mrs. Thomas were happy to avoid each other's company—Kate busying herself in the basement or out of the house, Mrs. Thomas in the drawing room or her beloved garden when the afternoons were sunny. It was as if a silent pact lay between the two, and no mention was made of either the Dresden figurine or Kate's impending departure.

Kate was allowed to do very much as she pleased. She could concentrate upon one household duty rather than another without hindrance or criticism; she was permitted to order groceries of her own choosing from Mr. Buller without reference to her mistress; she could, if she wished, do nothing at all. Life became tranquil, and there developed within Kate a feeling of being part of Mayfield Cottages. Indeed, so full of well-being did she become that Kate took the time and trouble to make contact with her uncle.

John Lawler, her father's brother, remained Kate's single tangible relation in County Wexford. He it was who had taught her how to read and write—long before she fell from grace and life was soured—and so it was to him she sometimes penned a letter. And she wrote to him on headed notepaper, a single sheet pilfered from the davenport. Uncle John would be much impressed to receive a letter from his niece written in ink upon blue paper with an embossed address. She was doing well, she told him, for she was Senior Housemaid at a mansion of "a titled lady of the land," with a dozen underlings "to boss about"; she was earning sixty sovereigns a year and "sporting it" with a Master Sergeant of Dragoons who "longed for to be her man"; and her condition had "much improved" since last she'd wrote, so that she'd soon visit Killane "with cash and presents for them all." It was a good letter, Kate assured herself, and bound to cause a stir at her uncle's little farm.

On Sunday Kate paid her usual call upon Mrs. Crease. The weather was misty but fine, and she took her son for a walk down the hill to the river, stopping to buy horse chestnuts from a vendor with a brazier. And they ran and chased an iron hoop until both fell down exhausted on the grassy bank.

"Are you happy with your ma?" Kate asked in a while.

The boy grinned and wriggled close.

"To be sure you are"—Kate shook his head by the hair—"and we'll be together again soon and for always." She stared upward at the bare branches of the trees and the swirling vapors. The extremities of the branches were sharp and grasped the air like fingers, fingers she had seen before, the fingers of girls in match or pen-grinding factories, fifty girls to a bench, windowless halls of gray brick, leather straps turning the machines—the sweat shops.

"Let's away," she said, pulling her boy to his feet. He'd be wanting his tea. "I daresay Mother Crease'll be making toast for you t'dip with." And they went off to the warmth of Mrs. Crease's kitchen.

It was after six when Kate took her leave and started home. She'd be late, but she had yet a call to make—on Mr. Thorpe, ironmonger, who stayed alive on Sundays.

His shop was large and in the High Street, and Mrs. Thorpe was in the process of closing when Kate arrived. But Kate spied her through the glass and tapped urgently.

"We're supposed to be closed," said Mrs. Thorpe as the door pinged open. Kate's face was not familiar.

"I knows that, but me missus needs a carving knife, she does, and she'll be in an all-fired rage if I return without."

Mrs. Thorpe was won over. "What kind does she want?" she asked, letting Kate into the shop.

"One that's sharp and handy." Kate began to search around.

"Good knives are hard to come by these days," the shop-keeper observed. "My husband says they use all the steel for bayonets now—to prick the Zulus."

Kate was looking for a standard carver, but her eyes fell upon a selection of knives displayed on a circular board above the kettles. The knife at the top was unusual.

"That looks sharp to me," Kate indicated.

Mrs. Thorpe hobbled forward. Spectacles hung on a thong about her neck, and she held them up to take a peep.

"Those! Well I don't know nothing about *them!* Mr. Thorpe placed an order with Sheffield and down they comes by mistake."

"The big one," Kate said. "That should cut all right."

"I daresay." Mrs. Thorpe strained to take the knife from its hooks. "But it's not intended, you know. It's not a proper carver."

Kate took the heavy knife from her hand. The blade was clip-backed, with a wicked point, whereas the handle was standard cutlery in German silver. She examined a floral design and some writing on the blade. "Alexander, Sheffield," she read. And "The Celebrated Arkansas Toothpick" was engraved along the length.

"What's this mean?" she asked.

Mrs. Thorpe shrugged. "Who's to know? Mr. Thorpe says they sent us a batch of hunting daggers by mistake. Had that one now for months. Can't sell it."

Kate thumbed the edge. Very sharp. And the blade had been polished in oil to a bluey glimmer.

"I'll have it," she said. "How much?"

Mrs. Thorpe did not know the price. But she remembered her husband's anger on delivery and was wont to hazard a guess.

"A shilling?"

"Ninepence," said Kate.

"Tenpence?"

"Ninepence, three farthings."

Mrs. Thorpe chuckled. "Very well, ninepence, three farthings." They were well rid of the beastly thing.

Kate pulled out her purse and took the sum from the housekeeping money. She had made herself a farthing on the bargain.

"I hope it does nicely for a joint," Mrs. Thorpe said as Kate was let out.

"Sure it'll cut most anything."

Kate turned off the High Street and hurried up the hill toward Park Road. A black horse was tethered outside the Hole in the Wall, still bearing funeral plumes on its head, and she crossed herself absent-mindedly. Somewhere the living were drinking with money made out of the dead.

As she had expected, Mrs. Thomas was waiting for her at the front door—coat on, bonnet adjusted, ready for church. A week ago there would have been a scene and much foot-tapping, but now circumstances had taken a change.

"I shall be late for service," was all her mistress said, and she bustled away into the night.

Inside the villa Kate continued to wear her coat. A solitary oil lamp winked in the hall—no fires, no gas—and it was cold. Kate went upstairs to her room by light of a candle taken from the usual box in the hallway, and the pine stairs creaked under her tread.

So cold was it in her bedroom, that Kate's breath came in a white mist as she pulled a shabby leather case from under the bed. Moth-holed clothing—clean but untidily strewn—was pushed aside, and she extracted what she wanted. A bottle of Allsop's ale and a small bottle of gin. She had taken beef extract at Mrs. Crease's and had a thirst for beer, but the chill in her bones—in her entire skeleton—was enough to justify a "chaser."

Kate sat on her bed, took off her bonnet, and swigged from the bottles alternately—one measure of gin to three of beer. The liquor warmed her, and she lit a pipe. Drink and the smell of tobacco. She began to long for the environs of a public house. Noise—it was noise she missed in this old dark house. Once nightfall came, it was like living in a tomb.

Strong, I forgive thee all! she shouted at herself. Strong was Jonah, but Strong was the man for an evening in the taproom.

Fill Strong with the right amount, and he'd sing out the catch-pennies better than any man alive—a fine old flare-up. Kate began to hum.

She finished the bottles and her pipe and hid the empties in the suitcase.

"Seven long years' transportation, down under in Van Diemen's Land."

She fanned the air to clear the smoke. "Far away from my friends and companions, t'follow the black velvet band!" She would go downstairs and have a prowl. She'd hammer the piano while the missus was out.

Kate felt her way into the drawing room and struck a match. She lit the wall light, the gas popping into flame, and turned it low. Mrs. Thomas seldom used this lamp. It was in a state of bad repair and it spluttered angrily.

"I wonder why she fears the brightness," Kate mused and began to look through the stacks of music in the canterbury. Many times had she done this since her arrival at the house, for the songs and pictures fascinated her—scenes of lovers hand in hand, of sailing ships and storms at sea, of palm trees and plantations. The pictures fed Kate's desire to visit other lands, to go out "foreign" to countries with exciting names. Californy and St. Louis, the Friendly Isles and St. Petersburg . . .

Kate put back the music and searched the room for something else to occupy her interest. China and glass in the cabinet were dull, and she had already examined the photograph of Mr. Thomas on the mantelpiece—a sour face in a silver frame. But the wellington chest was yet a mystery in its corner. Once Kate had opened the top drawer, only to be caught by Mrs. Thomas and ordered away.

The wellington was a series of button-handled drawers in

plain walnut, and Kate rummaged through each in turn. Balls of wool and knitting needles, a stone hot water bottle, and rubbish. The last drawer was stiff to open. Rolls of cloth—but something underneath—a book of sorts, large and leather-bound. Kate pulled it out. Morocco and brass-studded, big as a family Bible, and a catch secured it. Kate ran her hand over the bottom of the drawer in case the key had fallen out. Nothing. But the catch was old and weak, and Kate's strong fingers snapped it open. The book was not a Bible but an album of pictures—some drawn, some photographed—and it bore no title. Kate looked at the pictures and gave a little gasp. The more she turned the pages, the more incredible the sight that met her eyes. For the pictures were lewd and disgusting— naked women and little girls posturing in extraordinary ways and grinning at the viewer.

"Sblood, but 'tis a filthy thing," Kate whispered, turning the pages, guilty for looking. She snapped the book shut, flung it back into its drawer, and rubbed her hands down her skirts as if to cleanse them. She had seen certain things in prison, to be sure, but nothing of this kind.

" 'Tis a mortal sin!" Her voice was loud with indignation.

But what was the book doing in the house of a lady, a refined lady and a churchgoer? It could not belong to Mrs. Thomas. It must be the property of her dead husband, first or last. Kate had heard of Englishmen of gentle birth and good advantage grati-fying their murky desires with such material. It was said that even members of their Parliament collected most peculiar li-braries. Kate pushed the drawer closed with her foot.

And Mrs. Thomas compounded the sinfulness of it all if she allowed so vile an article to lie in her home. The book should have been destroyed upon the death of her husband. To maintain—to cherish—a memento of this kind was beyond forgiveness. Unless . . .

"Perhaps she is a sorceress!" Kate was enveloped in a sudden chill. Was it possible? Mrs. Thomas was left-handed. The British were a race of heretics, lost to Rome and lost to God. The British harbored gypsies; they believed in witches and warlocks and indulged in pagan rites to indulge their perverse carnal appetites. She had certainly seen evidence of this in Lancashire and in Essex, and had not Mrs. Thomas spoken of a connection with the latter county? She had. And Essex was a hive of devil worshipers. The mudflats abounded in men and women paying homage to Satan and his dark angels. This bleak house might too. Did her mistress really go to church? Well, perhaps she did. But hers was not a *true* church, just a rigmarole for Freemasons.

Kate wandered about the room thinking on these lines until her head reeled. She was not afraid, however. The wail of the banshee and the ghosts of the wronged did not lie in this house. Only blasphemy and a false faith.

She walked over to the gaslight, turned it down and out, and put a match to her candle. Holding the candlestick up high, she glanced around—at the flaked mirror over the fireplace and the shabby etchings on the walls. If there was only corruption here, it could not hurt her, and she hiccupped. She gave a short laugh —at herself. Too much Allsop, too much gin.

"Sure I'll be seeing hobgoblins next," she said.

II

Morning came with an aching head, and Kate was late with her attendance upon Mrs. Thomas. The porridge was badly prepared and cold, but her mistress voiced no complaint.

"Would you be minding if I takes myself off this evenin', missus?" Kate asked, drawing back the curtains.

Mrs. Thomas eased another lumpy portion of her breakfast onto the side of the plate and ruffled her bedclothes. Mr. Thomas had died on a Monday. Mrs. Thomas did not wish to be alone on that particular day of the week.

"I should prefer not," she said.

Kate drew back a curtain and fastened the loop. "It's for to see my little boy. He's sick," she lied.

Mrs. Thomas made a noise of concern. "Then you may go to him, of course!" It would be unthinkable not to let the woman go in these circumstances. Strange, however, that she wanted to visit him so late in the day.

"I bought the carver you was wanting," Kate interrupted her thoughts. "Cost me one shillen out of housekeeping."

Mrs. Thomas pointed to a small table. "Then hand me my purse, and I shall repay you, Mrs. Webster." Mrs. Thomas did not like being in debt.

Kate handed her the purse and watched as her mistress extracted a coin, noticing the rings on Mrs. Thomas's fingers.

"That's a dandy stone there," she observed.

"What? Oh, yes, it is very nice. A pigeon-blood. My late husband always chose me rubies."

"He was a man of taste," said Kate, thinking about her recent discovery downstairs.

Mrs. Thomas smiled. At times Mrs. Webster had the gift to please.

"He was a man of distinction," she said.

Who probably liked little girls to birch, thought Kate, and it was her turn to smile.

The day passed quickly, and Kate saw Mrs. Thomas infrequently. In the afternoon she remained belowstairs and diced some mutton for a stew. She used the new carver and marveled at its strength and sharpness. Hunting knife or no, the instrument was an excellent cutter of meat. The blade earned full satisfaction. And its purchase had brought Kate a profit.

Kate put the stew on the range to simmer. When it was done, she'd call Mrs. Thomas down for her evening meal. The old lady ate slowly but very little, and with luck Kate would be off before seven. A quick call to see her son, and then on to Hammersmith and the man called Strong.

Mrs. Thomas dined off a trolley in the drawing room, and Kate waited upon her with impatience. Every morsel chewed like the cud for benefit of the stomach.

"This meat is very hard," said Mrs. Thomas after a while.

"Then I'll speak with the butcher," said Kate.

Mrs. Thomas rightly suspected her servant's cooking rather than the butcher, but she said nothing. She could see that Kate was anxious to be gone and feared an outburst should she complain.

"I believe I've had enough," she said after two more mouthfuls.

"Then I'll be having your plate," Kate said and took it away. No offer of another course, and the trolley was rushed off with a clatter.

Mrs. Thomas heard Kate blunder across the hall and slam the front door. What an extraordinary creature she was! Literate and convivial or brutal and sullen according to her mood. The police had proved unhelpful, so she could take it that all was well. Nevertheless, Mrs. Webster could be frightening in her manner; Mrs. Thomas was glad to reflect that her servant would be leaving shortly.

III

Having visited her son and Mrs. Crease, Kate took the new District Railway to Hammersmith Station. The train lurched along the rails but Kate enjoyed the ride. She felt elegant in her straw bonnet and black coat with beaver trimmings; one of Mrs. Thomas's rings was all that she needed further.

The train drew into Hammersmith Station, and she got out and crossed the cobbled Broadway. The window lights shone through the river mist, and she could hear the noise of people from various public houses. This was life, a far cry from the somber atmosphere of Richmond. Here people sang and danced and talked. This was the beginning of the city itself.

Strong would be at the Rising Sun in Rose Gardens. Kate knew the locality well, though not this particular tavern. She was aware that Strong used the Sun often of late. He was wont to call there on a Monday; for the taproom was an auction for receivers, and Strong assessed the value of goods from their chatter.

As Kate walked in the direction of Rose Gardens, she considered the best way to tell Strong of Constable Pew's interest in his whereabouts. Strong would not be pleased, but better for her to inform him than let the man discover the worst from another source. They might call Katty many names, but never a copper's nark.

Rose Gardens was as Kate remembered it—a field of mud,

edged with thicket to hold in sheep, and surrounded by small workers' cottages. The public house was obvious in a far corner, a small building of uncertain date with bending walls. Old habit caused Kate to look about before she entered.

She went straight to the taproom, low-ceilinged and filled with a fog of smoke and a stench of vomit. Men and women sat on benches drawn up against the yellowed walls, and a child was wrestling with a dog on the floor. Kate peered through the haze for sight of Strong and found him up by the bar. He was sitting on the far end of a bench and speaking with the man serving behind the counter. Kate strode across and tapped him on the shoulder. It was the approach of a police officer, and Strong jumped.

"Not this time, darlin'," Kate said.

Strong swore, and the barman moved away.

"Well, aren't you pleased to see me?" Kate asked, and she barged a couple farther up the bench to make room for herself.

"What are you doing here, woman?" Strong found Kate's manner too bright and friendly.

"Come and seek out an old fox in his lair. Buy me a drink, Mr. Strong. I'm fair parched."

Strong shouted an order for gin. The measures served were small, and Kate looked at her glass with disgust. She could never understand meanness in a man, and Strong was surely mean. She drank her gin in a swallow and banged the glass down on the counter. "Threepennyworth twice over!" she called to the barman. He poured the drinks from a stone pitcher, and Kate glanced up at him—a long-nosed fellow with a light brown beard and a curious quiff. Natty dresser too.

"Who's he?" she asked Strong, jerking her head.

"Jack Church, the proprietor," Strong said when the barman was out of earshot.

"He fence for you?"

"Hush your tongue, woman!" Strong sipped his gin. "Yes, of course he do. One of the best. But he don't want the word got round, see?"

Kate continued to watch the barman. She had known most of Strong's associates. It hurt her vanity to realize this man had been kept a secret.

"Sure he's square, Mr. Strong?"

Strong trusted no one, not even Katty Webster, but Jack Church he considered to be "square." Then it occurred to Strong that Kate might be jealous, and he smiled.

"He's all right. Why?"

"I don't like his face."

"No?" Strong decided to trail his coat and make her angry. "And can *you* be trusted, Mrs. Webster?" In normal circumstances, Kate might well have reacted to his teasing, but she was thinking of Constable Pew and the confession she'd have to make. Better make it now, in a crowd and with drink taken, than later in a quiet moment to a sober Strong.

"You be the judge of that, Mr. Strong. I shot me mouth a day or so ago."

Strong looked at her but misunderstood her meaning. Was she in trouble again? Trouble followed Katty Webster about like a ripe smell. But it was of no concern to Strong this time, whatever she might have done.

"I was asked about you," Kate continued, and she jolted Strong out of his peace of mind. "A shunter from the village. He came to speak with me—a proper busnacking bastard. I knew him over in Teddington. He knows my record, and he knows about you. He's after you, Mr. Strong." Kate's eyes never left the barman, as if his every movement and mode of dress were objects of great fascination. She dared not look Strong in the eye.

"What did you tell him?" Strong's voice was close and fierce.

"That you'd changed your name to Mitchell. That you were picking oakum uptown. That I hadn't slapped eyes on you in three months of Sundays. And that I'd stick you with a pair of scissors if I did. He believed me too."

Strong relaxed. No harm done then. One thing you could say for Katty Webster, she could lie her head off to the law.

"This rosser, who is he?" Strong asked quietly, and Kate knew she was out of the fire.

"Just a pavement peeler with a nose on him—and an urge to see me spinning a loom on Bantry Bay."

"And you say he believed what you told him?" Gin dribbled down Strong's chin, and he wiped it away with the back of his hand.

"Ah, he's just a simple bobby, Mr. Strong. He'll be pesterin' after every man named Mitchell till past Good Friday."

Strong nodded. He put his glass on the counter. "Fill her up," he ordered the publican. Kate twiddled her own glass without success.

"I thought it right to speak out," she wheedled.

Strong ignored her. Some anxiety still remained, which Kate appreciated. But she was grateful to him for keeping his temper.

"You're riled with me?" she added.

"Who me? No. But I'm dampened and I'm scary. I don't like a hunt being started after me."

Now he was considering going to earth for a time, and one part of him told him to finish his drink and leave the bar right now, leave Katty Webster and her long mouth and her peeler friends. But he had work to do that very night.

"If you want to make amends, there is something you can do," he said to Kate.

"Sure. What is it, Mr. Strong?"

"You know some folks that live hereabouts," Strong said into her ear. "And I need a hideaway, somewhere to keep some stuff nice and safe."

Kate drew away. The only people she knew living in the Hammersmith area were a family she had not seen in more than five years, and by "stuff" Strong meant a cache of recently stolen property.

"What folk are these?" she pretended.

Strong looked at her sharply. "C'mon, you know who I mean. I've heard you speak of them a hundred times!"

"You mean the Porters?" There was no use in continuing to deny them.

"Yeah, that's them, the Porters. Live round here, don't they? Yes. Got a house, ain't they? Yes. Got space enough to stash some bits and bobs? Yes. And I'll make it worth their while, and see that they comes to no harm."

Kate was thinking of the Porter family—father Harry, mother Annie, sonny Robert and his brother, and the little girl Kate had cared for before she died. Those had been earlier and happier times.

"They live not far from here, on t'other side of the Gardens," Kate thought out loud. "I used to help Mother Porter with the washing. She took in laundry for a living then. Father was a painter. I liked them—they were a happy family until the tragedy—and they took to me. I'd care for the youngest, a little girl of three. Loved her like my own, I did, with her curly head —curls so tight and yellow they shone like goldspun, they did. I knew the Porters back in 'seventy-three. 'Twas after I'd left Mrs. Meredith's home for discharged persons that I come to meet them. Sure, I'd bitten Mrs. Meredith to the bone, and she flung me out without a farthing. But the Porters took me in and gave me work."

"Knowing that you was a jailbird, I suppose?" asked Strong.

"No, no! The Porters knew no such thing! They asked no questions, and I told no lies. They were respectable people, you see? They were—they still are, for all I know—and that's why we'll not use them for your swag, Mr. Strong!"

"I thought you wanted to put things right," Strong said.

Kate nodded. "So I does, but not that way. Why not try your little Mary? She'll take you in together with the crown jewels anytime."

Strong said nothing. Bad blood lay between Mary Durden and Katty Webster. Mary Durden would do anything to please him, it was true; but he dare not rely on that fast-talking hatter for so much as the time of day.

"You know I can't go down to her," he said.

Kate laughed. "Still spittin' pizen on account of me, is she? Poor Mary."

Strong was tempted to tell her that he was constantly amazed as to how it was a maid as fair as Mary Durden could envy as grotesque a creature as Katty Webster, but he held his tongue.

"Anyway, I don't see her any more," he said.

"Gettin' wise in yer old age, are you, Mr. Strong? She's not for you, as I've said before. Leave her to her hat-making."

"So you'll not help me with these people—the Porter folk?" Strong tried for the last time.

"No. Come on, man, don't look so! Take me back to yer drum and I'll give you a spot of pleasure if you want." This was true sacrifice, for the thought of Strong's grimy hands upon her had never been much to her liking. She offered Strong one of her small cigars, but he refused, sulking like a child.

"I'll be your spot of jam for tonight, Mr. Strong," Kate offered again.

But Strong's thoughts were elsewhere. It was now clear that Katty Webster's days as his bunter were over. She was no longer safe. She feared the prospect of further imprisonment too much. Worry for her child had sapped her vim. Pity, there had been a period when the woman had shown great fortitude, serving time for him without rancor, her mouth shut, always shut, about his very existence. Now she would not so much as lend him the use of her old acquaintances.

"Forget it," he said and began to rise from his seat. He could have said no worse a thing.

"Forget it!" Kate screeched, and other customers turned their heads to watch.

"Forget it! Why, you clapped-out son of a nigger whore-monger!" She had offered Strong her body and he had the nerve to reject her? "You hump of the divil, you pox-marked eunuch of a man, I'll have the bone of yer arse for me rosary beads!" And Kate stood and struck him across the mouth, a backhander that jarred his head. Then hands took hold of her, and Strong made good his escape.

"I'm sorry, Mrs. Webster!" he called from the door, respectful of her name to the last.

STRONG'S FRIEND

Outside the public house Strong paused and stood in the rain. He was half minded to return to the taproom, not to risk another blow from the irate Irishwoman but to make amends. Though what point was there in that? he asked himself. Her refusal to use the family named Porter had been final, and now his upper lip had begun to swell. So Strong huddled himself deeper into his greatcoat and strode off through mud and puddles in the direction of Brook Green Farm.

From the shelter of a twisted oak Police Constable Pew emerged and began to follow.

Strong walked quickly, and the roll in his gait suggested to the police officer that his quarry had once been a seafaring man. He was wrong in his conclusions, for Strong walked as he did because of a pistol ball still lodged in his right hip.

Pew maintained a steady gap of about fifty feet behind his quarry. It was not an accomplished tailing, and but for the present downpour Strong would certainly have become aware of the policeman's presence. But Strong's thoughts were on his stolen plate. The hoard was housed in Shepherd's Bush, in a shed beside a terraced cottage now derelict and deserted. He'd be there in ten minutes, then must he unload the silver from its boxes and place it in a sack. The sack would be heavy—he guessed in excess of thirty pounds—but to move it away and store it safely was of paramount importance. The shed was by no means secure. Anyone could break in and thieve the lot.

Strong had decided to shift the treasure to certain premises at the rear of a nearby music hall. The theater was small but popular. People would be coming and going, but Strong would not be observed in this rain. By God, he'd kill to preserve his rights over that silver. And he patted an inner pocket of his coat.

Constable Pew wore plain clothes. He was not officially on duty; in fact, he was out of his jurisdiction altogether. When he'd followed Katty Lawler that evening, and she'd taken the train to Hammersmith, he had been of two minds whether to continue the pursuit. Sergeant Rusty and their inspector could put him on the mat were they to learn the nature of this adventure. But Pew had decided to risk one energetic bending of the regulations; and if he caught this man Strong, his indiscipline would be forgiven. Then, by Jove, they'd hail him as a hero!

The man ahead turned off down a narrow lane toward the dark outline of a cluster of buildings, and Pew slackened his pace.

Good thinking on his part to spy on Katty Lawler rather than swallow her story and spend his time burrowing through prison records. Oh, he'd believed her at first, but then he'd used his common sense. Katty Lawler was incapable of speaking straight. And back there in the Rising Sun he'd been rewarded for his pains. The man he'd seen her talking to could only be the one called Strong.

As for Katty Lawler—or Webster or whatever—there was a price now for her to pay. He'd engineer her up before the Beaks or at the Slaughter once again; he'd ensure that certain valuables from the house of Mrs. Thomas were found upon her person, and he'd make the charges stick. Pew stepped in a puddle and instinctively kicked out angrily.

Strong heard the noise and stopped. Bending down, he pretended to tie his laces and took a backward peek. There was a man some forty feet behind.

Strong stood up and continued walking while his mind assessed just what to do. He stopped again, this time to fiddle with the other boot, and he saw his follower slow down. So it was a deliberate tail? No doubt about it, and Strong must put it to an end. Someone from the Sun, someone who had heard about his plate. But what action should he take? It was quiet hereabouts. The dwellings up ahead were inhabited by rats, not people, unless someone was abroad in search of scrap. Strong wanted no witnesses. He walked on without hurry. The nearer he came to his plate, the greater the risk. But how to do it?

Strong's fingers groped within the inner recesses of his coat. There it lay, smooth and cold to the touch, a treasured possession and the envy of various colleagues (although Mary Durden had hated it). It was made by a Mr. Reid of New York and called, according to the inscription thereon, "My Friend." Part knuckle-duster and part revolver, a pepperbox without a barrel, and a weapon as yet never used by Strong. Well, here came a chance to test the brute.

He would hit the man with the handle, which was kidney-shaped, with a hole to accommodate the little finger. Strong slid his own into the aperture. The round handle made a natural and deadly fit. The weight alone transformed his hand into a club. He'd break his follower's jaw and his nose, Strong decided, and he slipped into the hedgerow.

Pew was still deliberating upon the manner of his revenge when Strong executed his move. Daydreams took their toll, for when the policeman looked up the lane again, his suspect had disappeared.

Pew broke into a stagger and then a run, his eyes darting left and right. Then his heart jolted as Strong sprang out and seized him by the collar.

"What's your business!"

Pew struggled, but the grip on him was too strong. "What's your'n?" he squeaked.

Strong examined the man he proposed to bludgeon. Scared and young. Were they sending children after him these days?

"Best you say who sent you!" he advised. He would hit the youth only once in view of his age.

"I'm an officer of police!" piped Pew. "Surrender yourself to me without struggle!"

Strong stared and then laughed. "And I'm king of the Zulus," he said and delivered Pew an uppercut.

The policeman yelped and fell down. His hand went to his jaw and came away wet. He touched again, and the wide lips of a wound told him he'd been cut to the bone. Then he spied the silver lump in Strong's right hand, and he began to urinate where he lay.

Strong heard him and saw the steam begin to rise.

"Dirty little beggar, you've pissed y'self!" And his laughter echoed down the lane.

"I warn you!" began the constable, on his back like a turtle, and Strong's amusement died. He stepped forward and astride the downed man. Leaning over so that this expression could be seen, he raised his hand again to menace with his gun.

"See you here, you young pup!" He shook the weapon under Pew's nose. "I'll wallop you like batter if you don't—" But the pistol, brandished less than an inch from the policeman's nose, went off with a deafening report. A big blue mark appeared on Pew's brow, and giving a little surprised sigh, he fell back dead.

"God's hooks!" Strong muttered. "Bloody heck!" Blood and brains ran out over the mud. Strong looked at Mr. Reid's revolver, author of this sudden destruction, and the metal winked back at him. He turned the body of the dead man over with his foot, gingerly and with difficulty. He could see the skull smashed at the back. "He's snuffed it!" he said stupidly.

It had been an accident, of course. How was Strong supposed to know the pistol had a hair trigger, since he'd never fired it? This fellow Reid was a fool to put such a trigger on a gun that was also designed to be a knuckle-duster. Some gunsmith, some "friend."

But he'd best search the lad and remove any articles of identification. And do this quickly in case the shot had been heard. Strong began with Pew's topcoat, extracting money and a leather wallet. And in the waistband of the trousers he found an ironwood truncheon. "Hell's bells, what's this then?" On the body of the stick he read the letters V.R., and Strong dropped the truncheon as if he held a snake. And in the wallet was confirmation of his fears, a warrant card in the name of Police Constable Edmund Pew, Surrey Constabulary.

"A rosser. The geezer *was* a rosser!"

Pew, the name Kate Webster had given to the man who sought him. And now he was dead, slain by Strong. Every peeler in London would hunt him for what he'd done, and the law would hang him like a dog. But this need not be the case.

Strong began to examine the clothing of the dead policeman with meticulous care. A packet of cigarette papers and a white-brass whistle of stamped police issue. A dirty handkerchief and a key. Nothing else. All these articles Strong crammed into his own pockets, and the revolver was returned to its secret place. Time would pass before the body was found—maybe even weeks. And then it would be the discovery of yet another un-named corpse in a London lane. No identification—robbery or an act of vengeance would be presumed. A bullet wound, from an unknown gun of uncommon caliber held in an unknown hand. A victim who showed no trace of occupation or of origin —at least until the mortuary gave away the truth. And how long before that happened? Strong recalled a colleague, stabbed and flung in the Thames at Putney, who had not been identified for three full days. Say two for this shunter, just in case. Strong gave himself two days to disappear. Simple! He'd head east, off to Sunrise London and beyond the Temple Bar, into that labyrin-thine world of Yiddish folk and organ grinders. He'd go east as far as the marshlands if required. For they would never find him there—not Katty Webster, not pretty Mary Durden, not a cop-per born. Long gone, they'd say of Strong.

Strong retrieved the black truncheon from where it had fallen and pushed it into his overcoat pocket. He then looked about him for a suitable hiding place, a hideaway for both the policeman and his staff of office. Dense thickets grew to the right, a wilderness of unkempt hedgerow. Strong dealt with the truncheon first, flinging it by its thong into the bushes. The sound of the stick's disappearance brought from him a grunt of satisfaction; he'd once been bludgeoned by the truncheons of the police—blows to the face, knees, and elbows—and he reminded himself of that pain.

With Pew himself Strong was more gentle. He took the constable by the ankles and slowly dragged him over the ooze and into the undergrowth. The policeman was heavy, and Strong maneuvered the body with difficulty.

"Out of sight and mind," Strong muttered, inspecting the hedge from the lane.

TWO LADIES OF MEERUT

I

Striking Strong had been an error of judgment, and Kate had regretted her actions the moment her rage had cooled. Strong had never upped and left her as he had done that night, and Kate knew that he would shun her company for a while. You did not slap such a man as Strong, and it would take time to heal his injured pride.

But Kate would wait in patience. Strong might skulk in one of his many dens and curse her name, but Strong could no more stay away from Katty Webster than Katty Webster could resist for long his tempting her to commit further crime. He was part of her life, and she part of his, each bobbing up in front of the other without warning and usually when least needed. And that was why the likes of Mary Durden could never take Strong away from her.

Kate combined a visit to Mrs. Crease with a liquid lunch at the Hole in the Wall next day, staring insolently at Mrs. Hayhoe and refusing to be drawn into her gossip when the landlady made her usual approaches.

"That cook-general of Mrs. Thomas down the road is a bit

stuck up!" Mrs. Hayhoe complained to her husband behind the bar.

After leaving the public house, Kate strolled down to Mayfield Cottages, her mittened hands stuffed into her overcoat pockets. She was whistling a tune when she came up to the front gate, and she stopped at the sight of Mrs. Thomas, heavily muffled against the cold, pruning the hedge.

"Hello there, missus," she said, lifting the latch.

Her employer put the secateurs into their leather scabbard and came across.

"I have news for you, Mrs. Webster." Her voice was quiet, but Kate detected an air of excitement. "Yes, good news. We are to have the pleasure of entertaining visitors."

"Visitors, missus?" Kate was truly surprised. "Your relations, missus?" she asked. Kate knew only of a brother in Brighton.

"No. A good lady and her daughter, recently returned from the subcontinent of India. They are to stay with me as house guests. They are very well spoken of by the vicar." It was to the vicar that Mrs. Thomas had taken her plea for respectable lodgers, and her offer had been circulated among the parishioners. But it was not, she made plain, because of any need on her part for money. It was simply because she was of a charitable disposition and because of the size of her house. Rent would be kept to the very minimum.

Mrs. Thomas waited for her servant's reaction to this development.

"House guests, you say?" Kate repeated. She closed the garden gate behind her. "Now what would you be wanting with house guests, missus?"

Mrs. Thomas had rehearsed her explanations.

"Well, for a start, the villa is too large, and I wish to make use

100

of all the rooms. I have always maintained that the best way to air a room is to occupy it, and the box room upstairs is unoccupied. Do you not agree, Mrs. Webster?"

"No, I do not."

"And secondly, now that you are off and about so very often, I shall need the companionship of others—people I can talk to, and with whom I have something in common." Mrs. Thomas did not intend to be rude.

"I'll stick at home more often then," Kate said sourly.

"Gracious no. My *last* wish is to tie you in any way!"

"I said I'll stay, missus!" Kate began to pull off a mitten with her teeth.

"Now please don't fret, Mrs. Webster," she said. "Everything has been arranged. Mrs. and Miss Corbishly will be here this very afternoon, in time for tea." And she tilted her nose in a pathetic gesture of defiance.

Kate removed her other mitten, staring at her employer. This was a deliberate ploy on the part of her mistress, and one she should have envisaged. She knew that Mrs. Thomas had let off rooms in the past.

"I am sure we will all be most contented," said Mrs. Thomas, looking away from Kate. "My word! How this garden needs doing!"

Kate did not reply but stalked off into the house and slammed the door.

Mrs. Thomas enjoyed the sensation of both relief and triumph. Relief that there had not been another scene, triumph to think that the dreadful Mrs. Webster had at last been vanquished. Mrs. Thomas would inform the good Corbishly ladies of her servant's wiles and impertinences. Perhaps they would be able to advise her; perhaps she herself might be more courageous with the three of them in the house; perhaps the Corbish-lys were of sterner mettle than herself and would put the Irish-woman in her proper place.

II

Kate was summoned by gong to meet the ladies Corbishly and serve tea. And a formidable pair the mother and daughter transpired to be. Mrs. Corbishly, gaunt and yellowed by the plains of the Northwest Provinces, and with a definite attitude toward her inferiors; Miss Emelda Corbishly, at forty a mere twenty years her mother's junior, with hooded reptilian eyes and a harsh laugh.

I'll have mind to watch me tatur-trap, Kate thought with justification.

Having poured tea in the drawing room, Kate was bade stand by the window by Mrs. Corbishly and thereafter pointedly ig-nored. The conversation was of slipping standards of behavior and of India.

"The sepoy will never rise again," promised Mrs. Corbishly. "The colonel said as much before he died, and twenty years have passed."

"Papa blew them from the mouths of cannon for their crimes," added Emelda Corbishly, eating a muffin.

"Or hanged the Moslems in the skins of pigs," said her mother.

"What a fascinating life you've led!" enthused Mrs. Thomas.

Kate, listening from the curtains, looked from one to the other in awe. Mother of Sorrows, who were these people? And how was it that the genteel Mrs. Thomas could so obviously relish their tales of foreign barbarity?

"Webster!" Her name was suddenly called. It was Mrs. Corbishly, one finger crooked in the air. "Come here a moment, woman." Kate approached cautiously. "Your apron, Webster. It is positively *filthy.*" Mrs. Corbishly turned to Mrs. Thomas. "Really, you should not permit your staff to make so slovenly an appearance!" She looked at Kate again. "Have it clean and starched by dinner. Now off you go." And Kate was waved away.

Kate took extra care over the preparation of the dinner—a joint of beef with three vegetables—but her efforts went unrewarded. On the contrary:

"This meat is not cooked," said the colonel's lady.

"Nevertheless, my portion is burned," said her daughter.

"I feel I must apologize," said Mrs. Thomas, secretly pleased by the thought of what must follow.

"Apologize? Stuff and nonsense, my dear!" cried the colonel's lady, and she glared at Kate. "Well, Webster, what have you to say?"

Kate hung her head, her hands fidgeting behind at the tie of her freshly cleaned apron.

"Slapdash cooking, Webster, just won't do, will it? No! Fine waste of expensive food. I'd dock your wages if you were mine. Now you go below and make sure you don't ruin the remainder of the meal."

Kate muttered an excuse about the range and retreated, slinking from the dining room like a cur. Outside she paused to listen.

"Give her notice, my dear!" Mrs. Corbishly was saying.

"She is to leave on the twenty-eighth," replied Mrs. Thomas.

"Good riddance!" said Emelda. "I cannot abide the Irish. They're all the same, you know, and the women are worse than the men. We had plenty of hangers-on to the regiment. Always drunk or stealing or both. Papa could flog the men, but not their women, alas. You count your silver when she goes, Mrs. Thomas!"

Mrs. Thomas said something, but her voice was weak and timid, and Kate missed the words. But the remarks of the ladies Corbishly rang out loud and clear.

"An illegitimate child you say? Good grief!"

"Drinks and smokes, does she? We must put a stop to that! Let bread and broth be her diet forthwith!" And:

"Mrs. Thomas, you are too kind; your tolerance has verged on sanctity!"

Kate could gladly have rushed the trio and taken their withered throats in her hands.

When the dishes were cleared and washed, when breakfast had been laid, when hot water and coals had been deposited in the bedrooms, and when Kate was sure that all had at last retired, she went to her own room and took refuge with her gin. She lay on her bed fully dressed and drank from the bottle direct, and she gave Mrs. Thomas credit for her ingenuity.

No mortal could be other than afraid of the ladies Corbishly, late of Meerut (wherever that heathen place might be), and Mrs. Thomas had succeeded in poisoning their minds against her in one short day. With this dislike imparted, they would take up cudgels against Kate on her mistress's behalf—while Mrs. Thomas looked on, to smile or shake her head with shame for her erring servant.

I'd best skedaddle, thought Kate.

Leave the house, quit the district, anything other than three weeks of torment. But where was she to go? And what of her little boy with Mrs. Crease?

Kate got off the bed and inspected the contents of her purse. Three shillings and twopence, and a silver button. The trip to see Strong had seen to the rest.

Steal from the house? No notion struck Kate as more ridiculous. Steal a single thing with these three witches in the house! Not even Strong would have pressed her on this occasion. And what of Strong? Well, he was lying dormant in some unknown place, reddening his nose and sense of injustice with cheap alcohol, no doubt. No, she could not turn to Strong.

So she must brave it for as long as she could stand their devilry. She had promised Mrs. Thomas to be out by the 28th of the month, a promise she had never considered valid. But with the Corbishlys present, that promise might be made a reality. "Give her notice, m'dear!" Kate mimicked, flopping down on her bed again. She blew out the candle and stared at the dark. She could only hope that a substantial improvement in her conduct might lull the ladies of the house into forgetting her presence until the moment of the guests' departure came. And hope was not a virtue well known to Kate; hope had died ten years ago in Liverpool—and in the arms of "Captain" Webster, in the arms of Strong. But for three short weeks Kate, queen of misrule, determined to do her utmost to give satisfaction.

III

The days passed, and Kate worked hard and well. Much of her time she spent in the dank basement area, preparing food, boiling clothes in the copper, and making endless pots of tea for consumption by the two ladies of the Indian Empire. Kate would be called by bells located in a wooden box above the kitchen door and pulled by strings. And she would hasten to their bidding and pour tea, waiting close by for further instructions. Tea-drinking was ceremonial.

"In Meerut the colonel smoked a hookah with his tea," confided the widow of that august man.

"Is not that some species of pipe?" asked Mrs. Thomas.

"Pipe! My dear, it is the lordliest of pipes!"

And Kate suspected the use of narcotics.

"After tea," Miss Emelda addressed her, "Mrs. Thomas and myself will be taking the air at Richmond Park. It has been sleeting, and there will be slush about. Our shoes shall doubtless need cleaning. We shall leave them for you in the hall upon our return. Carry on, Webster."

When Miss Emelda and her mistress had departed, Kate went into the dining room to lay the table for dinner. Preoccupied with the arrangement of cutlery, she failed to notice the entry of Mrs. Corbishly.

"It is well to find you working," said that lady, and Kate started.

"I try t'please, missus."

"Do you? I wonder sometimes. No matter, you have much improved these past few days."

"Thankee, missus."

"Yes. What you need is discipline, Webster. You will find life easier when you learn to do what you are told when you are told —and without argument. Mrs. Thomas says that you are argumentative. Is that so?"

Kate wiped a fork with her apron. This woman reminded her of a senior wardress.

"I hopes not, missus," she said.

"I hope not too, Webster. Mrs. Thomas, in her kindness, has let things slide. But now my daughter and I propose to take you in charge. We shall give you your orders until we leave. Do you follow?"

Kate nodded and executed a clumsy curtsy as Mrs. Corbishly left the room.

"We shall give you your orders until we leave." Those had been her words. Until *they* left? Was it just a mistake? Had she not meant to say "until *you* leave"? Kate was puzzled but thought no more of it.

That very evening the mystery was revealed, and the knowledge gladdened Kate. The ladies were assembled in the drawing room and the gossip was of India, while Kate was brushing the dirty shoes in the hall. The door was open, and she could hear what was being said.

"We shall have to leave on Sunday, alas," boomed the familiar voice of Emelda.

"I'm afraid it has been all arranged," said her mother, who went on to speak of her husband's brother and the Port Authority on the settlement of Gibraltar.

"Uncle has promised us the dearest little house high up on the Rock," said her daughter. Mrs. Thomas was crying, "Oh dear, oh dear!" as she received this information, and Kate tiptoed over to hear better.

"Must it really be as soon as Sunday?" she heard her mistress ask in anguish.

"Our steamer sails with the tide on Tuesday. We must be

punctual. If we miss this ship, we will be forced to wait another month, my dear."

"Oh do please take a later vessel, Mrs. Corbishly!"

"No. We must leave as planned. My bones are too old to stand the cold of another English winter!"

And Kate returned to the brushing of the shoes with added vigor.

True to their word, the ladies Corbishly took their leave on the following Sunday afternoon. There was much fuss as to the destination of baggage and the hire of cabs; and the drivers, when they came, were lazy fellows, so that Kate was obliged to carry down the heavy leather trunks and bags herself.

Mrs. Corbishly stood at the foot of the staircase, ready to direct and disapprove.

"You are obviously very strong," she said as Kate brought down the last of the luggage.

Kate paused, an enormous trunk on her shoulder, one hand on the banister. She looked deep into the eyes of the colonel's lady.

"That I am," she said. "That I am because when I was a little girl I was diggin' ground as hard as stone for praties—lest me da' and mine took to starving."

"The Famine in Ireland?"

"And the years that followed 'forty-nine."

"We too had famine in India, Webster. I know what it's all about."

"Does yer, missus? Were you the ones short of food then?"

"You are grossly impertinent, Webster!"

Kate gave a short laugh and walked past bearing her load.

Mrs. Corbishly followed her with her eyes, a strange expression on her face.

Out in the street the drivers were lashing down the bags. Mrs. Thomas hovered near the foremost coach, washing her hands in the air, worry on her face. Soon they were joined by the ladies Corbishly, each carrying identical hatboxes and umbrellas. A large brooch on the breast of Miss Emelda Corbishly caught Kate's attention and fancy—a fine emerald set in pearls, and worth at least twenty sovereigns.

"We did so enjoy our little stay," Emelda was saying to Mrs. Thomas. "And we shall, of course, recommend your hospitality."

"Give our compliments to the reverend," said her mother.

Mother and daughter began to clamber up into the first cab. Mrs. Corbishly paused on the steps. She looked about her—at the house, at Mrs. Thomas, and then at Kate—and hard at Kate. Then she entered the coach and was joined by her daughter. A small wave of an unknown hand came from the window, and the cabs clattered off down Park Road.

Mrs. Thomas commenced to wring her hands again, her thin back bent in the cold.

Kate came up to her from behind. "Well now, missus," she said with a grim smile. "We're all alone again, are we not?"

A TERRIBLE PASSION

I

With the Corbishlys gone, the spirit of fear re-entered the heart of Mrs. Thomas. She spoke with the vicar at the conclusion of service on the following Sunday, drawing him aside to one corner of the porch.

"Lodgers," she said to him, "I must have lodgers." And she longed to tell him why.

"I'm afraid that I do not know of anybody at the moment." The vicar failed to notice her agitation—his mind was on the lead that was being stripped from the roof of his church by thieves, apparently at night.

Mrs. Thomas stepped out into the dark. As she did so, she gave a little sigh, and this was heard by Julia Nicholls—another elderly lady, another parishioner, and once a Saturday help to Mrs. Thomas.

"Evening, marm," said this worthy, and she made a bob.

Mrs. Thomas first looked vacant and then recognized her old employee. "Walk with me, please, Mrs. Nicholls."

They walked in silence for a time, and Julia Nicholls observed the stiffness in the other's gait. "Bad rheumatics, marm?"

Mrs. Thomas nodded. She noted that her old retainer's step was brisk. Perhaps Julia Nicholls could assist . . .

"Tell me, Mrs. Nicholls," she said. "Have you ever had occasion to meet, or to hear spoke of, a certain Mrs. Katherine Webster?"

Julia Nicholls sensed that her reply was of some importance to Mrs. Thomas.

"In what connection, marm?" she asked.

"She is presently in my employ. She is not local. She has been of late in Kingston."

Julia Nicholls knew of most people in the town and neighborhood. But a Katherine Webster?

"Can't say as I've ever heard of her, marm," she said at last, irked by her inability to help. And she wanted to help. Mrs. Thomas might have been a difficult employer in her time, but Julia Nicholls was of the older class of servant and had expected no favors. "Can't you tell me more about her, marm?"

"Only that she has a little boy, who is cared for by a Mrs. Crease who resides in Mitchell's Row."

"Ah!" Now Julia Nicholls was able to assist. "If your Mrs. Webster is on friendly terms with Sarah Crease, then you've nought to concern yourself about, marm."

Mrs. Thomas stopped. "Did I say that I was concerned?"

Mrs. Nicholls smiled. "I can tell, marm."

Mrs. Thomas began to walk again. It was wrong of Mrs. Nicholls to presume in this way—out of place. But Mrs. Thomas was nevertheless grateful for the reassurance of her words. Mrs. Nicholls had reached the same conclusion as her friend Miss Loder. Could it be that Mrs. Thomas was seeing menace where none existed?

"Thank you, you have been most helpful," she said.

111

Kate was in good humor, for she had spent the afternoon with her boy and she had also unearthed three twists of tobacco from a hidden recess of her valise. She was smoking in her room when she heard Mrs. Thomas come in and the slow footsteps ascend the stairs. They paused outside her door and then continued. Mrs. Thomas's door opened and closed quietly, and there followed the sound of bolts being shot.

The old lady chose to lock herself up at night.

Kate dampened her pipe for use on the morrow and drew a sheaf of very cheap paper from her apron pocket. A letter from her uncle in Killane had been delivered with the Sunday post. She read it for the fourth occasion that day, and this took time, for the writing was barely legible. Perhaps her uncle had deteriorated. She knew that sometimes in the old country a man would sink lower than a beast when times got hard. The loss of a goat or a cow could spell disaster. And the hand that wrote this letter was feeble. Poor man! Had the landowners taken all from him at last? With sudden anger Kate crunched up the document in her hand and stuffed it into a lower pocket of her flannel dress. Would that she had the means to make the old man's last years on earth a time free of troubles. Would that she could do as much for herself and her son.

Kate felt no inclination to sleep. She knew she could easily slip out of the house and call in at the Hole in the Wall, yet she lacked the energy. But looking around her garret of a room, she felt she must go somewhere. Very well then, she'd go downstairs and pick out a ballad on Mrs. Thomas's piano while that lady slept in her lock-up.

She took off her apron and went down. She didn't bother to be quiet, and the flickering light of the single candle she held caused her to stumble and blunder on the stairs. The devil welcome the noise—and bad cess to the old crone if she be awakened.

In the drawing room Kate shut the door and flipped open the lid of the piano. She placed the candle on the surface of the instrument, indifferent to the possibility of dripping wax. With her knuckles she struck a jarring chord on the keyboard. There was music on the rack, and she paused to take a look. A hymn. She read aloud:

> The rich man in his castle,
> The poor man at his gate,
> God made them high or lowly
> And ordered their estate.

"And bad cess to the likes of them too!" she said aloud and banged the piano hard. Slowly she lowered her bulk onto the piano stool. Finding a section of keyboard she knew by ear, she began to croon in Gaelic, picking out a single note here and there with accuracy and harmony. The song was sad and she sang it well; the passion in her voice filled the room. It was a song of love and death, and the pathos demanded a volume that she provided. She met the climax of the third verse full force when the door opened wide.

Mrs. Thomas in night attire and head-cap looked like a ridiculous ghost, and Kate greeted her appearance with wild laughter.

Mrs. Thomas had observed the trail of candle grease running down the side of her beloved piano, but she waited for her servant's mirth to subside before speaking.

"This cannot be, Mrs. Webster," she said in a small voice.

Kate closed the lid of the piano and stood up. She said nothing but continued to smile.

"You presume too much, you know," said her mistress.

The smiling silence prevailed.

"You are due to leave on Friday next, Mrs. Webster. All I would ask is that you behave in a civilized manner until your departure. It is not too much that I ask for, surely?"

The words were right, but the voice that spoke them uncertain.

Kate's cause of amusement changed.

"Not 'civilized,' am I?"

Mrs. Thomas looked away. "I was not simply being offensive."

"What now if I *take* offense, missus?" Kate ceased to smile. Did she detect a tiny quiver of the lower lip?

"And I *do* take offense," she pressed.

Mrs. Thomas now wished to flee the room. It had taken her many minutes to summon the courage to come down at all; now she desired only to be back in her bed, door locked and her face beneath the bedclothes.

"Then I apologize," she murmured.

" 'Then I apologize,' " Kate mimicked. "D'you think yer can be insulting and then 'apologize' and then expect no more of it?"

"I have intimated my regret, Mrs. Webster!" Mrs. Thomas felt the need for a glass of water. "What more can I possibly do? I am driven from my bed by your strange singing; I find you at my own piano; I see candle wax upon the marquetry. Is not all of this ample grounds for my vexation!"

Now Kate was truly hurt. What was so strange about her singing? This woman added injury to insult. But Katty must stay calm.

"Come Friday I'll be gone," she said quietly, hands on hips. "Come five days, and you'll not see the face of me again."

"Quite so. You shall have one week in lieu, of course."

Kate picked up the candle. The flame flickered close to her face, heightening lines and creases and the heavy bone structure. She walked past Mrs. Thomas, and her mistress leaned away.

Kate made her way upstairs without bothering to offer light to Mrs. Thomas. Within the last few moments she had resolved to seek out and steal every valuable contained in this house, to spirit away the most treasured possessions of the old woman, to find her savings, if she could, and leave her destitute, *and* to reveal knowledge of her husband's twisted mind within the Wellington. Then Kate would take "The Book" with her when she left. Should Mrs. Thomas expose her under any circumstances whatsoever, then Kate would point toward the owner and inheritor of that awful evidence of hell-deserving depravity. All this she would do, for no man or woman alive might criticize her singing.

II

Kate absented herself from the house on Tuesday afternoon while her mistress was lurking in her bedroom. The letter from her uncle had upset her, and she sought solace in the company of her son. As she stepped through the gate and into Park Road she met Miss Ives.

"Off to the shops?" Miss Ives asked.

"To see my little boy, missus."

Miss Ives raised an eyebrow, for she knew Kate's free time fell on Sundays.

"How is Mrs. Thomas?"

"Well enough, missus."

Miss Ives misunderstood her reply. "Not well? Why in heavens did you not tell me!" What was this dolt of an Irishwoman doing, leaving her mistress sick in the house and telling no one?

"No, no," Kate said. "She's not sick at all. I didn't mean that!"

Miss Ives sighed. "Well that's a relief. I really do worry sometimes about your mistress." She touched Kate's arm. "It's a blessing she has you to look after her, Mrs. Webster."

Kate was taken aback. Was not Miss Ives aware of the bad feeling that lay between them? Had her mistress divulged nothing? She watched as Miss Ives let herself into her own house. Evidently the landlady was ignorant of matters. Still puzzled, Kate walked the mile and a half to Mitchell's Row and Mrs. Crease.

Her son was playing on the doorstep with a wooden top and ran to greet his mother the moment she came around the corner. Kate picked him up as though the boy were made of feathers and entered the cottage.

"And where's Aunt Sarah now?" she asked her son.

He said he didn't know, and Kate went to the kitchen. The remains of a stew and some dirty plates marked their lunch, but there was no sign of Sarah Crease.

Kate took a fork and helped herself to some of the stew. She was hungry and—horseflesh or no—the stew was good. As she ate, her son picked up her hand and held it to his nose, sniffing and sniffing again.

"D'you like it then?" she asked him. It was some of Mrs. Thomas's lavender water, rubbed onto her hands to kill the

116

smell of cooking. "Well now, let's be off with us. I'll just leave a note for Aunt Sarah." She found a pencil on the dresser and scratched a sentence on the edge of a newspaper, propping up the message against the stew dish. "Now 'way with us, little man. Your ma's got a penny for you to spend and all!"

Hand in hand, they left the cottage and walked down to the river. The Thames looked brown and cold, and various small craft had been moored in groups, lashed together for safety. Across the water, rows of villas and small dwellings pumped evil smoke up into the sky. Beyond, toward the great metropolis, the air was gray and yellow, dirtied by the burning of more than a million coal fires. It was an ugly sight, and Kate compared the scene with memories of County Wexford, where the sky was light and the only smoke that of fresh-cut peat and wood. Again she thought of her uncle and his tenant farm. Perhaps his lot was even more terrible than she'd imagined; perhaps he lay dead of the fever before the hearth, rotten and shrinking in his leather jerkin; perhaps the "Crowbar Brigade" had beaten down his door and evicted him into a death from cold among the hedgerows. All things were possible.

She looked down at her boy and observed the thinness of his neck. He too was wasted, though Mrs. Crease had saved him from the rickets and stunted growth. But Mrs. Crease's stews and bacon sandwiches had to be paid for with money. Poor woman—and the saints bless her for what she'd done—but she was not a soup kitchen; and she had a half-pay husband to account for. And come the 28th, Kate must up her bags and leave. She could not dally at the house. Mrs. T would call the rossers, Police Constable Pew no less, and have her shifted. Unless . . .

They sat down on an iron jetty, and her son began to play with

117

a coil of rope. Absent-mindedly, Kate showed the boy how to fashion a hangman's knot.

. . . Unless she seriously carried out her intentions of the other night—ransacked the house of valuables and made quick passage to another part of the country. If caught, a long jail sentence lay ahead. But this time, for the first time in many a year, she would be acting alone, without the jinx of Strong. Strong would not even know about the deed. And she would quit London and the city's environments altogether and forever. Go north again, perhaps to Sheffield or Birmingham. To the latter town. She had never been there and would not be known. And she would have money this time, not the customary pittance presented to her in the past by Strong but a lot of actual money. She could change her clothes and her appearance, dress like a lady, dress her son like a young gentleman, use carriages, and purchase a first-class compartment on the Darlington line. She could sport a veil of black gauze and shut out her face, while rings of gold and precious stones would hide the calluses of her hands, and her large feet might appear quite dainty under the skin of snake or crocodile. Her boy would wear a velvet cap, or perhaps even a brushed-up topper . . .

Pipe dreams perhaps, but she was possessed and fearful of the alternative. Not for herself—*she* could manage the cruelties of her position and scotch them all with strong drink—but rather for her son, wide-eyed and trusting, uncaring and so utterly doomed.

"We'll be away now to spend your penny," she called to him, struggling to her feet. "A stick of treacle and a slice of currant cake it is for you!"

They strolled up the sloping fields to the market area. A good shop here—treacle toffee, bull's-eyes, and even hot potatoes.

Kate treated the boy and then herself to a potato, fumbling away the heat of it in her hands before tearing free the skin. As she ate, she planned. It would be best to turn over the old lady's house at a weekending, best of all upon a Sunday when she was at church. But Kate was committed to leave on Friday. An extension for a day or two. This she must obtain. She would speak with Mrs. Thomas upon her return.

III

Speak she did, and for a cavalcade of reasons, all rejected.

"I fail to understand," said Mrs. Thomas, who had been angered by her servant's absence.

Kate grew desperate. Unless she succeeded in her quest, she might be obliged to return later and burgle the woman—Strong's forte, not hers.

" 'Tis a bad day for the moving!" she said, a remote thought in the far reaches of her mind.

"Bad day? How is this?"

"The twenty-eighth be a Friday, missus. He died for the all of us that day!"

Mrs. Thomas put down her sewing and considered this answer. Friday. He died for us. Good Friday, of course.

" 'Tis only the extra two day I'll be wanting, missus," Kate pleaded.

"And this is because the Saviour died upon that day?"

Kate nodded and looked reverential. "He washed away our sins, He did. 'Tis bad fortune to be busy at such a time."

Mrs. Thomas was impressed. Easter was a period of sadness for herself. Mr. Thomas had died on Easter Sunday.

"Very well, Mrs. Webster," she said firmly. "But I shall expect you gone by nine the following Monday. Is that understood?"

Kate gave her the best of smiles. "To be sure I will, missus." And she curtsied—for the first time in more than a week.

Over the next two days Kate methodically took note of every portable and potentially valuable article in the house, from the jewelry she knew her mistress locked away up in the long bedroom to the solid brass rings on which were hung the curtains in the drawing room. The evening service at the Presbyterian Lecture Hall tended to last only under an hour, so within fifty minutes Kate must strip the villa and be gone.

But Mrs. Thomas, as ever suspicious of her servant, was carrying out her own observations. Nineteen times she had caught the woman fingering things or examining the hallmark on the silver. Yet, mistrustful as she was, it did not enter into her head that Kate had plans to rob her; the very reverse: she concluded that Kate took pride in the luxuries of the house, that Kate was loath to leave the comfort they provided, that Kate proposed to stay beyond the appointed time.

She *will* leave on Monday, wretched woman! Mrs. Thomas said to herself in the safety of her room.

But what if the woman refused? Supposing she just dug in her toes, offered more excuses, and stayed and stayed and stayed? *How* could she get rid of her?

Mrs. Thomas considered turning to her friend Miss Ives. She was certain that Miss Ives would not be afraid of the Irishwoman. But for that reason Miss Ives would, in all probability, laugh at her. Mrs. Thomas could hear her voice: "Just tell her to go, you silly thing!" Miss Ives would never understand that she lacked the courage to expel her servant on her own.

Of course, she could next visit her alarm upon her dearest friend, Miss Loder. But what would be the reaction of that good lady? Mrs. Thomas could foresee it now: "Be charitable, my dear. The woman has suffered much. Let her stay out the month!" Miss Loder was too pink and fat to be severe.

That left the constables at the police station. She might visit that nice young constable by the name of Pew. But would he help, was it indeed within his duty to help? Most likely not. He had been supposed to make inquiries about the woman and report any matters detrimental. And no doubt he had carried out an investigation, but he had not seen fit to divulge his findings to herself. That being so, one must presume that he had drawn a blank; and that being so, it was not for him to interfere with troublesome domestics. No, the police might consider her a silly old nuisance and send her away like a stupid child who'd lost his conkers.

And Mrs. Webster was suddenly being very kind, very considerate toward her: "Can I do this, missus?" "Can I do that for you, missus?" all day long. She sought to melt her heart. Mrs. Thomas mentally stamped her foot. Her heart would *not* be melted, she would *not* be swayed!

"She has no *right* to stay here!"

But Saturday came, and the position had not changed. Mrs. Webster prowled the villa upstairs and down in the manner of a large black cat, offering effusive endearments to her mistress whenever their paths should happen to cross. But the mouth and words did not tally with the look in her eyes, for that was hard and unyielding. Mrs. Thomas concluded that her servant anticipated her own fears and that she was forewarning her mistress not to press for a departure in two days' time.

Kate, on the other hand, did not recognize Mrs. Thomas's

concern. The old lady's ways were no more enigmatic than usual. And Kate sought only to mollify her mistress, to allay all suspicion of what she intended. It was only fair to be kind to the one you planned to plunder.

IV

Sunday came with a high wind and sheets of rain. Kate rose late and lit the fires in the kitchen and drawing room. Then she made her mistress porridge and some tea and carried the breakfast tray upstairs to her room. She had to knock long and hard before she was bade enter, but she found Mrs. Thomas already dressed and sitting at her dressing table.

"Put it down by the bed," came the order.

"You're up early, missus, for Sunday," Kate said as she was about to leave.

"I propose to go to morning service," said her mistress.

Morning service? What did this mean? Mrs. Thomas always went to church in the evening. Moreover, this change of routine would ruin her plans.

"But I shall also be going to the hall this evening," Mrs. Thomas went on. She was determined to spend as little time in the house as possible. But she also wanted to take the sacrament this morning.

"I'll be back in time, missus," said Kate, much relieved, and she left the room.

Mrs. Thomas was gone for an hour between eleven and twelve, and upon her return she ventured out into the garden despite the weather. The wind was threatening her beloved rosebushes, and she was determined to tie them back with string. In the little garden she lowered herself painfully onto her knees and set to work. She had misplaced her gardening gloves, so the thorns scratched her hands, but she didn't mind. Beneath her the soil was damp, clinging to her dress like glue, but again she didn't mind, though from an upstairs window a watching Miss Ives decided her to be a very foolhardy woman. Kate was watching too, from the drawing room, and a feeling of being looked at caused Mrs. Thomas to raise her eyes sharply. She did not see Miss Ives, but she did see her servant, face pressed hard against the windowpanes, and she gave an involuntary shiver.

Kate retreated from the window and went into the hall. She put on her coat and bonnet to go out for the afternoon. The old villa was exceptionally quiet and gloomy this day, and she yearned for the warmth and sounds of the Hole in the Wall. Even Mrs. Hayhoe's chatter would be welcome.

Kate smoked and drank at the public house until after one o'clock, when she ate a slice of pie and took her leave of the publican's wife. The wind had dropped but the rain persisted, and Kate wished she had brought along her mistress's umbrella. No matter. She was full of gin and ale, enough to brave any tempest.

She arrived at Mrs. Crease's, and the latter opened the cottage door. "Come on in then!" she cried. "My, you look bedraggled!"

Kate saw no sign of her little boy.

"He's upstairs with Mr. Crease," came the explanation. "The

lad's got the sneezes come on, and I thought it best for him to stay in the warm."

"He's not ill!" asked Kate, and Mrs. Crease smelled her breath.

"No. But I don't think he should be running about outside in this weather, Katherine."

Mrs. Crease did not care for Kate's drinking habits. And it was not fitting that a son be out with his mother in her present state.

"Come into the kitchen. You can have some hot broth."

Kate followed her and allowed herself to be sat down in the wicker chair by the fire. It was Mr. Crease's chair—the most comfortable in the house—and she closed her eyes. A sensation of spinning forced her to sit bolt upright. Nine pegs of gin on an empty stomach had taken their toll.

"Broth?" Mrs. Crease offered her a bowl.

Kate shook her head. She was not hungry, and she was warm and happy where she was. She allowed her body to relax, and she fought away the spinning. "My little boy," she said once, but Mrs. Crease told her not to worry. Kate heard her say that the child would be happily amused by his "uncle" upstairs. Reassured, Kate began to dream of other things, and soon she slept quite soundly. Mrs. Crease crept out of the kitchen.

When Kate awoke, the room was in darkness and the fire had died to a glow. At first she was unsure of her whereabouts, and she lurched out of her chair and around the room. Her head ached and her mouth was dry. She found matches and lit a candle. She went over to the pump by the sink, pulled the handle, and ran water over her face and mouth. She gargled and spat and combed her hair, retying the bun behind.

"Mrs. Crease!" she called, gathering up her coat. "What time has it, Mrs. Crease!"

A sound of footsteps in the hall, and the kitchen door opened. Mrs. Crease held a battered wooden clock in her hands.

"Five minutes to six, Katherine. But you can't trust the master's timepiece no more these days."

Five to six! "Why did you just leave me in the sleep of the dead?" Kate asked angrily.

Mrs. Crease smiled. She had tried to rouse her once. "You looked too fierce to wake," she said.

"Sblood, but I'll be late again!" Kate sped into the hall, adjusting her straw bonnet. "I must be off without delay. Kiss me darling for his mother, and say I'll call round later. I'll be back this evening, d'you hear?"

Kate had wanted to explain to Mrs. Crease that she must take her boy away that night, and she'd polished the tale she was to tell. Too late now. If she was to have that hour alone in Mrs. Thomas's house, there was not a second to be wasted.

"I'll explain the manner of things to you later," she said to Mrs. Crease. "No time now!" And she virtually ran out of the cottage and up the road.

Kate pushed open the door, and as in the past, Mrs. Thomas was waiting for her—although inside the house this time to avoid the wet. Kate observed that Mrs. Thomas wore her spectacles, and her face was very grave.

"It is after six," she said crisply. "This really is too bad!"

"I come as fast as I could," huffed Kate.

"You present one excuse or another whenever you happen to be tardy, Mrs. Webster. It is beyond toleration!"

Then be off with you to your heathen ceremonies, thought Kate. Why was the old crow standing here and fussing?

"Have you no shame at all?" Mrs. Thomas demanded.

Kate muttered an oath.

"I *beg* your pardon!"

"I said, 'Get you to your measly service!' "

Mrs. Thomas rose on her toes, so great was her indignation. But Kate didn't care. The longer the other stayed, the less time she had to search the house. "Now go along!" she repeated. "You'll be missin' the vicar's jawing!"

Mrs. Thomas came forward like an angry ferret, and Kate misjudged her movement for a possible assault. Putting out a hand, she placed it upon the older woman's chest and pushed her back so that she nearly stumbled. Mrs. Thomas uttered a frightened cry, and her bonnet slipped over her eyes, but she recovered her balance.

"Now get out, damn and blast your eyes, you carrion-headed daughter of Lucifer!" Kate roared at her.

Mrs. Thomas experienced a sharp pain under her heart and a blurring of the vision. Only an instinct for survival forced her from her frozen state and out the front door into the night.

The rain drove into her face until her hat was sodden and her hair tangled, but she did not pause—not even to open her umbrella—until she came to the porch of the lecture hall. She passed through and brushed against the figure of a woman— Julia Nicholls, shaking water from her unfurled umbrella. Julia Nicholls was surprised to see her former mistress—surprised to see her for a second time at church that day, and surprised to find her late for the service.

"Mrs. Thomas . . ." she began.

The other reached past her and turned the heavy iron latch

of the door. At close quarters Julia Nicholls observed her face to be unnaturally flushed and saw her mouth moving excitedly and without words.

"You all right, marm?" she asked.

"What's that you say? Oh, hallo, Julia! Yes, I am very well, thanking you; but I am exceeding late, I fear!" The reply was garbled.

"We both of us be that, marm," said Julia. There was no need for her mistress to apologize.

"Yes, yes! I'm afraid Mrs. Webster was most unpunctual. I'm afraid I had cause to reprove her!"

"Serve her right, marm. Now you just come in out of the wet."

"Yes, yes! But . . . you see . . . she flew into a terrible passion when I did so!"

Julia Nicholls held open the church door and stood aside. So that was it? She'd ticked off her servant and had been given a spot of the lip for her pains. Julia Nicholls recalled the many times she herself had felt that urge. Strange that Mrs. Thomas had taken it so hard.

The lecture hall was packed, and the minister was holding forth in the pulpit. Julia Nicholls expected Mrs. Thomas to proceed unabashed to her usual seat at the end of the pew directly beneath the pulpit. But she didn't do so. Instead she simply flopped down in a solitary chair close to the church door, and there she remained, water dripping off her clothing, while Julia Nicholls found a vacant place in a back pew. From this position she was able to keep an eye on the woman. Clearly Mrs. Thomas was most agitated. Her mouth still trembled, and the hands on her lap twiddled incessantly while her eyes darted about the church as if suspicious of every occupant.

127

The minister completed his sermon, and the congregation rose at his request to repeat a prayer. Mrs. Thomas began to stand up with the rest, but as she did so she slipped forward in a stumble, saving herself by grasping the wall. Her bonnet slid from her head to hang at the side of her neck by its ribbon. Julia Nicholls left her seat, alarmed in case her former mistress was seized by a fit. "You're not well, marm," she whispered when she reached her.

"Not well? Yes, I am very well indeed, thank you! But I think I'll sit just the same!" Words spoken out loud, so that various heads turned to stare.

Julia Nicholls resumed her place but maintained close observation. If Mrs. Thomas was seized again, she might fall to the floor and injure herself.

But what of Mrs. Thomas herself? *Her* thoughts ran strange and wild. She was filled with a dread of Mrs. Webster and of her villa. She shrank from the prospect of ever returning to that place. Her fears went beyond the few hard words spoken so recently. Her fear was something intangible. Breeding and reason told her that she could never seriously fear a simple serving woman, but in terror she now was. What was she afraid of? Not of further hard words surely? If the woman was saucy, it was her right to give her immediate marching orders. True, she had failed to dismiss her in the past. But Mrs. Webster was to leave tomorrow in any event. . . . Fear of bodily harm being caused to her by the woman? The idea was preposterous! It was an offense punishable with the utmost severity for a woman of her station to lay hands upon her mistress. Mrs. Webster must know that, unless she was an imbecile, and an imbecile she certainly was not. And yet she'd had the temerity to push her in the hallway, to push her quite hard, to push her nearly to the ground, to literally *hurl* abuse at her, to call her a "daughter of Lucifer" no less.

Mrs. Thomas closed her eyes and prayed. She prayed to her God for His reassurance; she prayed to both her late husbands for their protection; she prayed to St. George for fortitude. Her prayers, like her thoughts, were muddled, and she confused her messages to those above. Aware of this, she repeated her prayers with more deliberation and fervor, until she was happy that they must be understood. Then she allowed herself a period of quiet anticipation, so that even Julia Nicholls marked her calm.

Mrs. Thomas was waiting for some sign—for a definite indication, a lightening of her heart—to prove that she had been heard. She concentrated in this manner for many minutes, relaxed in both mind and body, until she achieved the tranquility of a semi-trance. And a spirit of great resolution entered her brain. Her timidity died away, and she experienced a dawning of auspicious equanimity. Her troubles were relatively trivial. She could look down now upon recent events as if from a height, personally uninvolved and unthreatened. Her prayers must be answered! A wonderful warmth ran over her body, and her hands ceased to shake. She opened her eyes and smiled. She gave a little giggle, which astonished Julia Nicholls. And then Mrs. Thomas left her chair and went to the church door. Her mind continued to race, but it was pacified. Her mind was also made up. She would return to Mayfield Cottages and face the ghastly Mrs. Webster, face her like a true Christian, face her as Sir Guy had faced the heathen host; and her tongue would be her lance, and her Right would be her shield; and Mrs. Webster would quickly recognize the Power she possessed and quail before her like the Serpent, hide her head with shame and slink away. . . .

129

Mrs. Thomas opened the door and left the church. Her footfall was steady and brave. Not once did she pause or falter on the journey home but stepped along quite gaily with her umbrella held up high. For not only did the Power within her push her along, but something quite uncanny and irresistible seemed to draw her with supernatural hands toward her house.

V

The gas was lit in the hall and the front door slightly ajar. Mrs. Thomas felt no lessening of her resolve, but she was surprised to find Kate Webster standing by the drawing-room door, as if she had been waiting for her to arrive.

"I see that you are still up and about, Mrs. Webster," said Mrs. Thomas. She closed and locked the door and took off her coat. Kate said nothing, but, immobile as a statue, watched through half-shut lids.

"I would have thought you'd gone to bed," Mrs. Thomas went on. Her tone was conversational but cold. She rattled her umbrella and began to furl it carefully. "I think it best if we both repair to our rooms now," she said. "We shall review the situation on the morrow."

Still Kate made no move.

"Well, I'm inclined to go upstairs even if you are not!" Mrs. Thomas started to walk past Kate.

"I just knew you'd be back," Kate breathed.

"Pardon? What did you say?"

"I said I *knew* you'd come back." Kate eyed her strangely, as if she had never seen her before.

"Of course I came back! This *is* my house, don't you know!

I *live* here, or have you so forgotten?"

Kate shook her head slowly and with wonderment. "I willed it, and you came!" she said as quietly as before.

"You did what? I fail to follow—"

"I said I *willed* you to return here!"

And so she had, with her head in her hands, until the effort was exhausting.

"Stuff and nonsense!" cried Mrs. Thomas and began to mount the stairs. She kept her eyes away from Kate, for some of her earlier courage had started to drain away.

"Not so," Kate said and moved out of the doorway. "I say I made you."

Mrs. Thomas turned on the stairs. "I shall not argue with you, Mrs. Webster. Now I bid you good night."

Kate came after her quickly and with her face intent. "You don't believe me then?" she insisted.

Mrs. Thomas ignored her and continued up. Only when she reached the landing did she become aware that Kate was still behind, following closely. Kate's breath came in short gasps. She was angry. She had spared this woman her property—her precious rings, her plate, her clothes. And now she was being called a fool and a liar once again.

"Please leave me alone, Mrs. Webster," said her mistress on the landing. The light was poor up here, and Kate's dark figure loomed. "I shall see you tomorrow morning."

Kate mistook the cold control of Mrs. Thomas for contempt. "I'm not leavin'," she said.

Mrs. Thomas paused, one hand on the handle of her bedroom door, her keys in the other. "God give me courage!" she murmured.

"What's that you're saying?" Kate snapped.

131

Mrs. Thomas took a deep breath, and raised herself as high as she was able. "I said, You *shall* leave this house tomorrow, and you shall leave without a Character from *me!*"

"Not so, missus. You see, I've got the measure of you and yours!" Kate laughed, a false sound.

"What are you saying, woman?"

"The book. I knows about the book below!"

"Book—what book? What is this?"

"Your husband's book of nasties that's a-lying with its sin in the bureau in the parlor. Now don't you be telling me you know nothing of it!"

Mrs. Thomas thought for a moment. Then she understood. The woman was referring to Mr. Thomas's five-year diary. How dare she poke around in something quite so private!

" 'Tis a filthy, evil thing!" Kate spat at her.

Mrs. Thomas peered at her, trying to read her expression, trying to understand. "What are you saying?"

"I'm sayin' that your man's roastin' meat in hell, that's what I'm a-sayin'!"

"That diary is locked. It has always been locked. There is no key. How—"

"I broke the lock, you eejut, and took an eyeful!"

But Mrs. Thomas still failed to comprehend. She herself had never inspected the contents of that diary. She had never learned the nature of what lay within. Never would she have presumed so upon the privacy of Mr. Thomas. This woman, on the other hand, prying about, poking into drawers . . .

"You go too far this time, Mrs. Webster!" she said. "I do believe you may well have been overinquisitive. How do I know that you have not been actually stealing!"

"I've stolen nothing!"

"We'll let the police be the judge of that."

Kate's throat tightened. "The police?"

"Yes, the police! I propose to call them here tomorrow! If you have been honest, then you have nothing to fear."

Police Constable Pew. Her record exposed. Odds and ends that might be lost, now presumed stolen. Arrest. Interrogation. False testimony. Charged, trial, prison.

"You'll not do that, missus," Kate said thickly and stepped toward her mistress. She was prepared to plead on bended knees, to beg forgiveness yet again for the things she'd said to Mrs. Thomas. The latter sensed rather than saw the effect of her words.

"Oh yes I will!" she said triumphantly. "I shall call upon them after breakfast!"

"Oh no, missus. Oh no!" And Kate began to shake her head slowly from side to side. She came up to Mrs. Thomas without rush or indication of what might have been passing through her mind. Indeed, she had no particular intent, only a desire to be reassured that Mrs. Thomas did not mean what she said.

"Oh no, missus. Please, missus!" And she gently took hold of her employer by the collar, pulling her this way and that.

"Let go of me this instant!" Mrs. Thomas started to say, but Kate cut off her words with a hand across her mouth.

"Please tell me no, missus," Kate repeated. She lowered one arm and took the keys from the other's grasp. Still holding Mrs. Thomas around the face, she unlocked the bedroom door and pushed both their bodies through. It would be nicer to discuss things—to sort the problem out—in the lady's bedroom.

"Now can I let you go, and can we speak awhile, missus?" Kate asked, slackening her grip. "Please don't you call out. Miss Ives next door might be thinking there's a panny going on!"

Mrs. Thomas reached up and with a squawk pulled Kate's hand free of her mouth. Her heart was pounding, she could barely speak, so Kate gave her time to recover.

"I shall see that . . . I shall see that you are prosecuted for this," Mrs. Thomas said at last.

With a cry, Kate pounced upon her. "I'll shut your garret!" she shouted and struck out at Mrs. Thomas with her right hand. The keys were still in that hand—seven heavy keys on a brass ring—and they opened the flesh of Mrs. Thomas at the temple in a single ragged wound. "Now you got me in an all-fired rage!" shouted Kate and hit the woman again, the keys causing a deep laceration across the nose and cheek.

"Help! Mercy! Murder!" squealed Mrs. Thomas, but her mouth was full of blood and she was already falling to the floor. She fell badly and heavily and began to crawl away toward the door. Kate was now weeping in her anxiety and regret as she watched Mrs. Thomas gain the door and pull herself out onto the landing. Kate was thinking of four years' penal servitude and that when she came out her little boy would be ten years old, for there could be no ticket of leave allowed for what she had done now. *She* had done? Bad cess to that! She had been *forced* to do it. Mrs. Thomas had *made* her do it—the fault lay with Mrs. Thomas! Sobbing, Kate ran out onto the landing and stood over the stricken woman. The latter turned her head up and looked into her eyes. A reproachful look, like that of a wounded animal. Kate's sobs changed into a low wailing. This woman had now destroyed her, this woman who had succeeded in taking her from her son.

"By God, but I'll smash you to smither's ruins!" Kate cried. She bent down and scooped Mrs. Thomas up in her arms. Her body was quite light, and she didn't struggle very hard, not even when Kate held her out over the edge of the banister. Only when Kate let go did she utter a tiny moan. Then she fell twelve feet to land on her side in the hall below.

Kate stared down for a long minute or so, wiping her nose on her sleeve, wondering what to do next. Had she killed the old lady? And did she really want her dead? She thought not; she had desired only that the woman be punished. She looked at her hands. She was still holding the key ring. There was blood on the keys and upon her cuff. She dropped the keys. She must see if Mrs. Thomas was still alive. She walked down the stairs quietly and with care, her eyes on the body in the hall. Perhaps Mrs. Thomas wasn't really dead at all. Perhaps she was pretending. Perhaps she was only unconscious. Kate approached the fallen woman with caution and knelt down. She sought her pulse. Nothing. One of Mrs. Thomas's feet was strangely twisted, almost back to front. Kate listened for the sound of breathing. Nothing. Then she turned her mistress over, saw the ruin of the face and staring eyes, and knew the truth.

"May God have mercy on her soul," she mouthed, and she crossed herself.

AT THE DEVIL'S DINNER HOUR

A silence reigned in the house, broken only by the occasional creak of a floorboard or window frame. Kate was sitting on the hall chair, keeping vigil over the body. How long she stayed in this position she was never able to judge, but she fancied she saw strange shapes among the shadows and heard whisperings from the nooks and crannies. Her thoughts were divided, one part infusing in her an overwhelming lethargy, the other demanding immediate action. The last eventually prevailed. She could not just sit and wonder at what she had done; she must brace herself and get rid of the corpse—hide it, tuck it away in some secret place before the break of day. It was the striking of twelve bongs by the hall clock that finally forced her from her chair.

She picked up Mrs. Thomas, and carrying her over her left shoulder, made her way down the short flight of steps to the basement area. In the dark she traced the shape of the kitchen table and laid the body upon it. Then she lit two candles and paused by the door. In life, Mrs. Thomas had been very small; in death, she reminded Kate of a large doll. Kate inspected her

136

hands and her clothes. There was blood on both. Quickly she went to the sink, pumped water, and rubbed her hands together with distaste. She was sponging her apron when she experienced that curious feeling that she was being watched. She turned around quickly. Mrs. Thomas was watching her from the table with one eye, a dead fishlike eye, and with a singular slant. Kate began to shake, but she was determined to brave that eye. She walked over and bent down to face it. The eye had grown a film, but it was still the eye of Mrs. Thomas— obdurate and complaining even in death.

"I shall feed you to the fishes," Kate said with hatred.

She realized the menace of the body. If "they" should find the body, Kate was doomed. But if "they" never found a body, no crime could be proved to have been committed. As far as Kate was concerned, every homicide required a corpse. And of a body, the head was surely the most important part; only the head could really identify the rest. And of the head, the eyes themselves were of the greatest significance. Had she not read how the eyes reflected the last moments of the deceased, how by looking into the eyes one could see the face of the slayer?

To simply conceal the corpse of Mrs. Thomas was too dangerous—no guarantee that the body would not be unearthed someday, if not soon. Therefore Kate must ensure that Mrs. Thomas would never ever be found.

Kate went to the kitchen dresser and opened the long drawer. A cluster of knives and sharpening rods. The largest of the knives she recognized. She took it out and felt the edge. "Arkansas Toothpick," read the blade.

Kate pulled out a second drawer. In it, she knew, lay a short hacksaw, good for cutting bone. The saw was there, and something else. A gentleman's razor with a bone handle. Kate had used the razor from time to time to pare her corns. It was strong and deadly sharp. Kate opened the razor. It was bright save for a streak of rust near the top of the blade. There was also a small dent in the edge. No matter. The razor would be invaluable.

Taking the knife, the saw, and the razor, Kate approached the table and Mrs. Thomas. She placed the articles on the table with a clatter. Close by was Mrs. Thomas's left foot—the one so badly twisted. Kate touched the foot, gingerly at first, and then started to waggle it about. Then steeling herself, she took off the shoe. The foot was delicate in its stocking but callused on the sole. Kate was surprised to see no sign of bunions or of corns. She let the foot fall and stood back a pace. Well, if she must do what she must do, then she was well advised to do it properly. This was no time for weakness.

Kate made her preparations with speed and care, as if for spring cleaning. She lit a hand lantern and placed it on the dresser for better light; she assembled every bucket and container and stood them in a row on either side of the kitchen table; she collected as much linen and sheeting as possible and heaped them in a corner; she covered up her dress with three aprons, one tied close to her neck; then she rolled up her sleeves and stripped Mrs. Thomas of all her clothing, quickly and without looking, for the sake of decency.

Mrs. Thomas's head, with those incriminating eyes, she cut from the trunk with the razor, using a sawing motion when she came to the vertebrae. Once free of any connecting tissue and skin, the head rolled backwards and onto its side, and there Kate let it remain for the time being.

Severing the limbs from the trunk required more effort, and the use of both the hunting knife and the hacksaw. Hoping that the human body might be dissected in the same manner as a

138

fowl, Kate began by attacking the major joints—the knees and the elbows. But Mrs. Thomas was arthritic, and the work was harder than Kate had supposed. Finally she decided that it was quicker to saw through bone itself, above the elbows and just below the knees. And so the cheerless basement area was filled with the sounds of the hacksaw and an occasional grunt of exertion from Kate. The hands and the feet she removed with ease, slashing with the knife, slicing with the razor. The twisted foot she divided from the leg high up on the ankle, and when the foot fell from the table to the floor, she kicked it out of the way.

And so only the trunk remained, slightly obscene in its present state, almost inhuman. But to Kate this was the part of the body that once housed the Soul. True, she knew the Soul had gone long since; and she had been taught that once the Soul had departed, a body was little more than a carcass of common meat. It was therefore essential that she cast from her mind any thought of sacrilege. She opened the stomach with the hunting knife and reeled back at the sweet stench. Holding her breath, she ripped and cut with particular ferocity, all the while intoning a silent prayer. And when she could stand it no longer, she turned away and vomited into the sink. She realized her strength was failing; she must do something else for a while.

So she lit two fires—under the copper in the annex, and in the grate of the stove. Once they were burning well, she returned to her work on the table. She tried to imagine that all this meat, all this blood and slime, came from an animal and not from a person made in the image of her God. And to some extent she succeeded with her illusion. She set much of the flesh into the copper and filled the great bowl with water. It occurred to her that boiled flesh might be difficult to identify as human, and so she added more and more flesh to the pot. Other portions she popped into the stove, and a new and sickening smell joined that of the entrails and stomach contents. So she picked up the latter in her hands—blue snakes and worse—and placed them upon the fire, so the odor might become as one.

Once again her determination wavered, and she was sick. She would put as much of the loose flesh as possible into the copper, including a limb or two. She would fill the copper up and leave it to boil until all the water was gone. At least in the copper it was out of sight.

Brown paper. She recalled a store of wrapping paper tucked away behind the larder door. Kate fetched the roll and spread it out upon the floor. Pieces of meat and limb she carefully wrapped up in the brown paper, tying the parcels up with a ball of gardening twine from the dresser. She made neat packages and reviewed the result with satisfaction. Butchers in the town wrapped their wares in such fashion. The final quantity was not large, but Kate realized she had packaged only a single thigh. She would need more of the paper eventually for the contents of the copper.

Still prominent on the table there remained the head and a hand. Kate picked up the hand, very white and heavily veined. The ring finger sported a small dress ring and two keepers, all in gold. Kate pulled the rings away and put them by the sink. Then she tossed the hand back onto the table. The head of Mrs. Thomas still lay on its side, a mass of gray-white hair, the shriveled neck gaping under the jaw, half an inch of spine protruding. Kate took hold of the head by the hair; it was heavier than she expected. Blood had dried on the face, and the features now resembled a mask. The eyes, mercifully, were closed at last. Kate put the head down. Her knees were wobbling with shock and fatigue. She was thirsty, but she dared not drink in case there followed another bout of vomiting. She licked her lips and sat down on a wicker chair. The head lay directly before her, facing her; the head lay in the same place where once Police Constable Pew's arms had rested. Kate shut her eyes and allowed her chin to fall forward onto her chest. A gray light had entered the basement; she was aware of it and knew it must be morning. She should be up and about her task, which was by no means finished. But she lacked the will. It was cold, and she hugged herself about the upper arms. Then she slept.

THE BLACK CARPETBAG

I

An insistent banging from above roused Kate from her dreamless sleep. She sat bolt upright, and she froze as her vision adjusted. Memories flooded back, and she uttered a cry. The head and the hand on the table, the gore at her feet and splashed about the walls, the hunting knife with a piece of gristle adhering to the edge.

More banging from upstairs. The front door, someone was demanding entry. The police come to arrest her? Kate left her chair, and her shoes stuck to the floor as she went over to the bottom of the stone steps. The banging stopped, and she listened intently. What time was it? She sifted among Mrs. Thomas's clothes bundled on the flagstones and extracted her watch and chain. Two minutes past twelve. Exhaustion—a total weariness of both mind and body—diminished Kate's natural fear of the caller at the house. If it was to be the police, then let them come and find the worst; if it was not the police, then she'd brave it out and shoo them off. Kate slowly climbed the steps and crossed the hall to the front door. Pulling back the bolt, she opened the door about ten inches and peered out bleary-eyed.

"Mrs. Thomas in?" asked a voice.

Kate looked at the speaker—Mr. Deane, the local coal agent. What was the likes of him doing here on a Sunday? But of course —it was now Monday.

"Mrs. Thomas?" repeated the coal agent.

"Not in," Kate said huskily.

"Can you tell me when she is likely to be back then? It's about her order."

"I don't know."

"I see. Well, give my compliments to Mrs. Thomas. Tell her when she arrives that Mr. Deane called."

Kate said nothing and slammed the door.

"Bad-tempered puss!" muttered Mr. Deane.

Kate stood with her back to the door, anticipating the man's return for some vague reason.

Mr. Deane walked slowly away. Mrs. Thomas had been specific about her order for coal, and she had been told that he would call upon her that Monday. Was the old lady becoming forgetful?

Outside the gate to Number Two, Deane stopped. Another customer, Miss Ives, was in her garden next door. He resolved to speak to her.

"Morning, mum! You haven't seen Mrs. Thomas, have you?"

Miss Ives came across the small lawn to her gate. "No. Have you tried her door?"

"Yes, but there's only this servant woman, and she says she's out. Mrs. Thomas was insisting that I called today. And at twelve on the dot."

Miss Ives raised her eyebrows. This was typical of her friend these past few weeks.

"Call back later, young man," she advised. "I'm sure Mrs.

143

Thomas is about." She had seen washing on the line; from her own kitchen she had heard the copper being used; she had observed breakfast things uncleared through the dining-room window of Number Two. She had also noticed something else.

"Tell me," she said, "do you smell something peculiar?"

Deane sniffed, but he had a cold and shook his head.

"Then it must be my imagination! But all morning, particularly when I was in the back garden, I could have sworn there was this most unusual smell."

Deane tried the air again. Nothing. "Can't say's that I can smell anything, mum. Maybe it was breakfast that was being cooked. Maybe something took on fire?"

Kate waited behind the front door until she was confident that Mr. Deane had gone. It was a bad moment. The local tradesmen were an inquisitive breed, forever looking through windows or peeping through letter boxes. But when the coalman failed to return after five minutes, Kate felt safer.

She made her way back to the basement with dreadful reluctance; it was as if her boots were filled with lead. The hand lantern had gone out, and the kitchen lay in a gray gloom. The table, the floor, and part of one wall were streaked black with congealed blood. In the far alcove the copper continued to hiss and bubble.

Ignoring the sight of so much carnage, Kate boiled a kettle on the range and made herself a cup of tea, wishing that she had brought down some rum from her room with which to lace it.

She drank her tea standing, watching the head and the hand and other grisly relics as she did so. What of the head? She considered the copper. No. Better to burn the head in a fire. The fire under the range was still hot and burning well. She put

144

down her cup and moved quickly. She picked up the head by the hair, leaned forward in a crouch, and swung the head at the range opening. Her aim was poor, and the head struck the edge and fell back to the floor with a dull thud. Kate cursed and stepped away in case the head rolled against her feet. At first she dared not touch the head again, but desperation overcame her fears and she grabbed it by the hair once more. This time she pitched it carefully into the glowing coals and pushed it with the poker, holding it into the fire, face upward. Flames flickered around the head, and there was a fizzling sound. "Burn, burn," Kate willed the head. The features of Mrs. Thomas were well illuminated by the flames. Suddenly, as if in answer to Kate's frantic urging, life itself entered the head. The hair rose up in a sheet of fire like a ghastly halo; at the same moment the mouth dropped open and the eyelids flew up, so that for an instant Kate was staring straight into the eyes of Mrs. Thomas. Kate dropped the poker and screamed, falling to one side in a near faint. Now lacking the poker pressing it into place, the head tumbled out of the grate and lay smoldering on the tiles, hairless and charred. Kate's breath came in sobs as she scuttled away across the floor to hide in a corner, as frightened as a child.

Minutes passed before Kate could restore her mind to sensible thought. But one aspect she knew was of paramount importance—she must complete this work before it was too late. To dally would be fatal.

So she got herself up from her crouch and ran past the head and out of the kitchen. Great blundering footsteps took her up the steps, into the hall, up the stairs, and into her own bedroom. Quivering hands pulled her bag from under her bed, searched and found her gin bottle, and raised it to her lips. She drank half the contents of the bottle without a pause and until her throat and stomach burned. She recovered her wind sitting, bent double, on the edge of her bed; then she drank again, with the same desperate action, until the bottle was empty. She knew she'd soon be very drunk and prayed she'd not be simply sick. But she might not be drunk enough for what lay below. More liquor was required. She delved into her bag again and swigged down the remnants of some rum, sweet and horrible after the gin.

There was no Allsop's, so her supply of drink had gone. But she remembered a bottle of barley wine left by Mrs. Corbishly. It was in the drawing room, and she hurried down. She found the wine tucked away behind some plates in the china cabinet. The bottle was three-quarters full. She pulled out the cork with a hard twist and drank. Wine was not to her taste, and she doubted its power, but at this moment she'd imbibe turpentine if that was what was required.

And so Kate became drunk, and she even strummed the keyboard of the piano in her new-found fortitude. She looked at the carriage clock on the mantel, but it had stopped, so she had no idea of time. Then she went upstairs and fetched a pail of water and a scrubbing brush from Mrs. Thomas's bathroom. There were bloodstains on the landing and in her mistress's bedroom. All these spots must be wiped away, and she began to clean the telltale areas with as much care as she could muster in her present state.

When this was done, Kate took the pail with fresh water down to the hall and scrubbed the floor where Mrs. Thomas had lain in death. When the water had turned quite red, she refilled the pail and continued thus until the boards met with her approval. Only then did she return to the basement area.

The head lay as it had lain before—monstrous, and as if daring her to approach. And indeed its presence transfixed her in the doorway. There she stood, motionless for all the alcohol in her veins, while the copper roared in the alcove. But in the event, the rum and the gin and the wine served to give her an angry determination. Running forward, she kicked the head hard against the dresser, jolting from its mouth a plate containing two false teeth. She stooped and picked up the plate, examining it with curiosity. In her society lost teeth were not replaced in this way, and she had never realized that her mistress wore a plate. But she'd keep the teeth—perhaps they were of value—and she put the plate down on the corner of the sink.

Being of a mind to do her best while her courage lasted, Kate worked hard in the basement area for more than an hour—heaping flesh and bones into a tidy pile to await wrapping in the brown paper, washing down the table and the floor, adding fuel to the copper. By the table she discovered the twisted left foot and placed it to one side. She had forgotten it till now, and she was to forget it again.

When some semblance of order had been established, Kate reviewed the scene and was well satisfied. She had earned herself a break, she decided; she would take herself away, out of the house. Besides, she was sobering up and saw the need for further fortification.

So she put on her bonnet and coat and walked up to the Hole in the Wall. It was three o'clock, and the afternoon skies had cleared enough for an occasional glimpse of the sun. Kate was pleased. The washing on the line would have a chance to dry.

Mrs. Hayhoe was serving behind the bar. Kate placed with her an order for gin.

"Meant to be out shoppin' for the lady, are you?" Mrs. Hayhoe asked her slyly.

Kate nodded and drank standing at the bar.

"Bet she don't know you're in here, love," said the landlady.

Kate shook her head. "As before," she ordered again.

Mrs. Hayhoe poured another measure. "She at home then?"

"That she is."

"Playing her piano, I'll suspect?"

"Sleeping."

"Ah! Now that's convenient for you."

Kate made no comment, finished her gin, paid, and left the public house. She could no longer stand the chatter of the land-lady and was fearful lest her own answers or expression give cause for suspicion.

She walked in a westerly direction until she came to a beer shop, small and secluded and known locally as Fletcher's. The shop was empty when she arrived save for a man with a sty serving at the counter.

Kate drew out her purse and bought two bottles of stout.

"And a half of your gin too," she said as she handed over her money.

"Don't sell gin here. Not allowed to," said the man.

Kate pointed to the curtain hanging behind the counter. "It's kept back there, and I'll be having half a bottle."

She was in no mood to argue, as the man could judge from the tone of her voice, and he retreated toward the rear regions of the shop. When he returned, Kate took the bottle from his hand and examined the contents. Bad liquor this—worse than the poteen—but good enough for the effect it had.

"How much?"

"One shilling."

"We'll make it sevenpence—and count yourself in luck."

The man took the money gratefully; his profit was in excess

of 300 per cent, and it was not for him to care if his gin made this woman blind.

When Kate returned to the house, darkness had fallen. She entered boldly, in case of watchers at the house next door. She feared most of all a sudden visit by Miss Ives. Inside she lit lamps in the hall and drawing room, drew the curtains, and clattered about most noisily before she adjourned to the basement. In the kitchen she lit the lantern and stoked the fires under the grate and copper. It occurred to her to talk to herself in different voices—to try to carry on a normal conversation between her mistress and herself—and she talked of cooking and provisions, of the leaky state of the roof, of the coal agent, and of many other things. And all the while she drank her beer and still-gin in turns and worked upon the body.

When every limb and section of the trunk was either boiled or mutilated beyond identity, Kate packaged the remains in convenient lots and searched for a suitable container. She found nothing of that kind in the kitchen, so she went up to the hall and began to look around the house. She was in the dining room, poking about a cupboard, when a soft rap on the front door interrupted her efforts and caused her to stand very still. The knocking was repeated, and she inched her way along the wall to the bay window. Drawing back a fraction of the curtain, she looked out. On the doorstep stood a lady Kate had never seen before, staring up at the house, toward the long bedroom above the porch—Mrs. Thomas's room. Then she turned away and walked briskly up the path to the garden gate and was gone. With beating heart Kate endeavored to recall the face of the visitor, but to no avail. The woman was a total stranger.

Kate went upstairs and into the long bedroom. The woman

at the door had looked at the window of this room as if she had known it to be Mrs. Thomas's room. Kate noted that the curtains here were drawn too, so perhaps the caller had imagined Mrs. Thomas to be sleeping.

Kate also saw her mistress's bonnet, bloody and crumpled, lying on the floor. She picked it up, turned out the gaslight, and left the room. She *must* find a trunk or box for the body downstairs without wasting further time. She went to the spare back room and unlocked its door with Mrs. Thomas's bunch of keys. It was very dark, and Kate had trouble finding the candle fixed to a bracket on the wall. She struck a match, lit the candle, and looked around. The room was bare and dusty, and without a sign of recent use by the Corbishlys.

In one corner, upturned on an end, stood a deal box. Kate went across and opened the lid. The box was as deep as it was long and stuffed with old newspapers. Kate pulled the papers out and found a shabby velvet hat at the bottom. Perhaps the box was intended for hats, battered and plain as it was. Anyway, it would suit her purpose, for it was both strong and roomy.

Beside the box lay a bag. Kate picked it up, brushing off dust. The bag was made of a coarse black material, with a double handle in leathered wood. Kate had heard such bags called carpetbags. This one was large enough to be useful.

Kate put the carpetbag into the deal box and shut the lid. The handle of the hatbox was worn—too fragile to support the weight it carried—and Kate lifted the box by its sides, hefting it up upon her shoulders to carry it downstairs.

In the kitchen she lowered the box and took out the carpetbag. On her way downstairs she had reached what she considered a canny decision. She would not place all of Mrs. Thomas in any one container, but rather she'd distribute sections of her body here and there. And in particular the head.

"Slife, but I'll see to that!" Kate muttered. Having successfully assaulted the head with her foot, she now cursed it for the terror it had caused her.

She'd reserve the carpetbag for the head—with its eyes and brain and tongue—and deposit it far away from the body of Mrs. Thomas, far beyond any chance of reattachment.

Kate stepped up to the kitchen table with the carpetbag. As she did so, her boot crunched down onto something soft and yielding. She looked at her feet. Her mistress's foot, the twisted left foot, lay beneath her under her heel. The ankle was gray and distinct, the flesh curled and greasy at the point of severance. There was a jut of white bone, holed in the center and red with marrow.

Kate picked it up; the foot was quite silky in her hand, so that she felt the urge to squeeze the flesh. She placed it upon the dresser ledge and turned her attention to Mrs. Thomas's head.

Kate was able to take hold of the charred and hairless head with more distaste than fear. She popped it into the carpetbag and closed the top. Then a thought crossed her mind, and she opened the bag again, retrieved some of the brown paper from the floor, and crammed it into the bag so as to cover up the head. The catch on the carpetbag was weak, and it would not do for it to spring open suddenly outside the house.

And for the next few hours Kate made good in the basement area, scurrying hither and thither until sheer exhaustion again made its claim upon her. When she could no longer bear the pace of her activities, she blew out the lantern and returned to the upper house. She would sleep in her bed this night and restore her strength for the morrow. As she undressed, certain plans began to formulate in her mind until her thoughts crystallized into the inception of one very clever idea. It would require great courage on her part, so she was forced to admit to herself, but its successful execution would guarantee for her a proper reward for her recent troubles. Indeed, Kate decided her plan so brazen as to be ingenious.

II

When Kate awoke on Tuesday, she instantly began to revise her plan of action for the day even before she left her bed. Her mouth was dry and her eyes stung, so that she longed to seek the oblivion of sleep again; but she couldn't afford to do this. It was after eight by her mistress's hunter, and she had much to accomplish in the next few hours.

She dressed herself in a black silk dress often worn by Mrs. Thomas on her local calls. The fit was tight and the dress much too short, but Kate was determined to look elegant. And to this latter end she poked about in her mistress's jewel case, selecting three rings and two guards for her left hand, a plain gold signet for her right, and a French cameo to pin at her breast. She examined her hands critically. Large and rough-skinned they might be, but at least the fingers were long and slender. Mrs. Thomas's hands had been small and creased and stumpy.

But her efforts to put on a pair of her mistress's shoes were unsuccessful. The shoes she chose—dark brown cayman—were tough and unbending, and they pinched her toes and heels so painfully that she was obliged to abandon them in favor of her customary boots.

"The woman had the feet of a fairy," Kate said to herself. And then she remembered the twisted foot downstairs.

She must dispose of that foot without delay. No need to open up the hatbox and tamper with the parcels. She could hide the foot by itself. But where? She dared not bury it—any dog might sniff it out. No, if the rest of her mistress was due for a watery grave, let the foot accompany the corpse.

Kate brushed her hair and pinned it up with grips. She walked down the stairs and across the hall slowly, her eyes looking for any telltale traces of blood. At the frame of the door of the kitchen she espied a spot and rubbed it away with her thumb.

In the kitchen she brushed her teeth at the sink and washed her hands and face in cold water. She filled the kettle and put it on the range. The iron surface was cool, so she bent down and looked at the grate. The fire was dead beneath a mound of white ashes. For the sake of tidiness she chose not to relight the fire and sacrificed her morning tea. Anyhow she felt no desire to eat.

The foot—she must not forget the foot.

It lay where she had left it. Kate picked it up in a sheet of newspaper; she recalled the feel of this foot the night before and did not wish to touch it again. She wrapped it up, placed it in a household shopping basket, and went up to the hall for her coat and an umbrella. She opened the front door to take stock of the weather and found, to her surprise, that a light sleet was falling. She returned to the coat stand and exchanged her topcoat for a waterproof cape—a garment favored by her mistress when gardening. She had left the front door open, and she started violently when a voice suddenly addressed her.

" 'Ello there. I was hoping you'd be in!"

In the doorway stood a girl of fifteen or sixteen. She wore a woolen cap, and the tip of her nose was red with cold. Her face was familiar, but Kate did not identify the owner at all. As she made no reply and showed no sign of recognition, the girl took a step forward into the hallway.

"Ye'll not come in here!" Kate barked.

The girl stopped. "I've only come about the roof," she complained.

"The roof?"

"Yes. Miss Ives says to tell Mrs. Thomas she's got some men what's coming to fix the roof."

"What men? What's wrong with the roof? Who are you anyway?" Kate's questions came like bullets from a gun.

"I'm Mary, miss. From next door—Miss Ives's 'prentice girl. She sent me round, she did. Said some slates be loose, and they needs some fixin', all because of this snow!"

Kate could see that the girl was unhappy at her treatment. She must be calm and make amends.

"Oh yes!" She gave the girl a wan smile. "Sorry, girlie, but the water's not coming in at all. We've been inspecting, you see; we're having people in tonight. More of missus's would-be lodgers, I'll suspect. So me and the missus took a look. Do you follow me, girlie?"

Mary grinned at the other's change of tone. "I saw a notice for lodgers in the window yesterday, miss. Is that why it's gone?"

Kate knew nothing of any advertisement for the lease of rooms, but she nodded.

"Well then, I'll be away," said the girl.

"That's it, girlie. And you just tell your missus that all is fine and dandy here!"

The girl departed, and Kate sighed and shut the door with

relief. The eyes of children were sharper still than those of tradespeople.

The foot. She must remove the foot. She'd give the girl ten minutes or so and then set off. She'd take the foot to some distant place and not to the river. Twickenham—she'd go to the rough land outside Twickenham, where only fox and badger made their home, and the foot would be free from early discovery.

So in a quarter of an hour Kate braved the elements and set off for the Richmond omnibus depot, shopping basket in hand.

She took the coach to the outskirts of Twickenham, got off, and then retraced her route to an empty spot called Crop Hall. It had ceased to snow, but a high wind howled and bent the branches of the trees around her, while a party of rooks swirled in the sky and mocked her with their cries.

Soon she was tramping a narrow path across the wasteland, and she observed that sections had been fenced off and tilled as allotments. If the land was worked after all, then this meant people. But she doubted the presence of humans here at this time of year or in this kind of weather, and she was full of confidence when she stopped to dispose of the foot. Over a broken fence she saw a stretch of unturned earth, neglected and choked with weeds and scrubby bushes; in the farthest corner was a mound of compost and manure. She took the foot from her basket and removed the wrapping paper. Holding the foot by the heel, she drew back her arm and hurled it onto the far side of the dungheap. Such a resting place showed little respect for the dead, she admitted, but nothing could be worse than what she had already done to the body of Mrs. Thomas.

She returned by omnibus to Richmond and Mayfield Cottages, intent upon the execution of her plan.

"Did you see Mrs. Thomas?" Miss Ives asked young Mary without turning from the upstairs window. From her front bedroom she had just seen Kate return, suddenly appearing out of the afternoon gloom, shopping basket in hand.

"No, mum. But I spoke to her housekeeper, I did," said her apprentice.

Miss Ives nodded and drew the curtains. Mary was polishing at the dressing table, caressing a tortoiseshell-handled mirror with a piece of shammy leather. "You say you mentioned the roof ?" Miss Ives asked.

"Yes, mum. And her housekeeper said that she and Mrs. Thomas had already looked to it."

"Looked to it?"

"Yes, mum. Inspected it like. The housekeeper woman said it's not leaking no more." Mary put down the mirror and commenced work on a matching hairbrush.

Miss Ives considered it strange that her friend had anticipated the workmen. But perhaps this Mrs. Webster was something of a carpenter—good with her hands. She also wondered why it was she had seen nothing of Mrs. Thomas over the past two days. It had happened before, of course, this sudden withdrawal into the house by her tenant—almost a form of religious "retreat" from the outside world. No doubt that was why Mrs. Webster was in and out all the time, coping with all the household needs on behalf of her mistress, as well as repairing the leaking roof. It was good to see Mrs. Webster so busy. It was good that she was so versatile.

III

Robert Porter had been in the employ of Mr. Young for six whole months now, and he yearned for something better. He found little excitement in the trade of house painter and dreamed of being a soldier. Mr. Church, the publican, had been a soldier with the Eleventh Hussars—or so he'd told young Robert and so the lad believed—and Mr. Church was a fine and upright man with more than ten years' service under his belt. Yet Mr. Church, who had fought real battles in the campaigns of India and Africa, chose to forsake the blue and gold and woolly fur of the Hussars to run a drinking house; this was something Robert could never understand. Were such a chance of adventure offered to *him*, he would never abandon it to slop out beer for nights on end. But alas, fate played young Robert a shabby trick, for at sixteen years he was barred from accepting the Queen's shilling.

Robert Porter was thinking about his future as he reached the door to his father's house, so he paid scant attention to the tall well-dressed lady about to tap the knocker.

"And you must be Bob," said the well-dressed lady. "How are you, Bob?"

Robert stared at her. It was nearly six, and too dark to see her face clearly.

"You'll not remember me too well, Bob. But it's as Kate you knew me once." The voice was cheerful. "Now do us a favor and let me in, young man. I'm next to perishin' out here!"

Robert opened the front door with his key and ushered her

in. The woman looked about. "Well, I'd say it's not much changed."

At that moment Robert's mother came out of a room to the side.

"Kate!" she cried. "Is it really you!"

"Ah, that it is, mother!" And the two women embraced. Mrs. Porter was an emaciated woman of about fifty, with frizzy close-cropped hair. She was beside herself with pleasure at the sight of Kate Webster.

"And how is it with you, mother?" Kate asked her as they separated.

Mrs. Porter gave a sigh. "Not well, Kate. These bones are getting old."

"Then I'm here to bring you cheer, mother; come for chitchat and a spot of tea."

Kate removed her—Mrs. Thomas's—cherry-ornamented bonnet.

"It's been a long time, Kate." Mrs. Porter wagged her finger. "Where've you been?"

"Ah, now that's a story for the telling, mother. Made myself good these past few years, I have. Married me a gentleman, I did. It's Kate the layabout no longer."

"Married? And your husband?"

Kate looked at her feet. "Dead, God bless the man," she murmured and crossed herself.

A hand touched her arm gently. "And your little boy?"

Kate brightened. "Kickin' well, the little darling! Why, he's six years old now, mother!"

"Come into the parlor. Leave your bag in the hall," Mrs. Porter insisted, and Kate followed her into a small front room furnished in pine and chintz, bag still in hand. "Now sit you down and tell me all, Kate. My, but you're a one! Married!" And Mrs. Porter clapped her hands.

"Stanley was a good man, mother, but too old for me, if I tell the truth. He passed away not long ago, did Stanley Thomas."

"And now?"

"Stanley left me well provided."

"But where have you been living?"

"Up north." Kate licked her lips. "I'm down, you see, on account of my inheritance. I've been left a spot of property, mother. I've been doing a perusal this very day—down in Richmond Town. A little house that my Auntie Mary says in her will is to be mine. And finding myself in a town so close to mine own darling mother and father Porter, I takes the notion to pay this call. God forgive should I fail to do such a thing! I'll not forget those so dear, however great my fortune!" And she flashed the rings on her fingers.

Mrs. Porter smiled at her old friend, happy for her improved condition. Kate of old had been scruffy and indolent; only her natural kindness and good humor had endeared the Irishwoman to herself and her husband—humor at the pressures imposed upon her, and kindness toward their little girl so long dead. But here was Kate quite different: dressed like a lady, almost genteel.

"Father will be home soon," she said. "And he'll find a bottle once he knows you're here, Kate!"

Kate turned to young Robert, who was standing at the mantelpiece feigning interest in the conversation.

"Fine boy you are, Bob! Why, I'll guess the girls be onto the tail of your shirt these days!"

Robert blushed and shifted his feet. He remembered Kate now: the big dark-haired woman who had mothered and nursed

159

his little sister many years ago, until the Porter house was smitten sour with the tragedy of her death. He recalled that this Kate had shown him tricks and told him jokes as well. He thought he'd liked her.

"Bobby's working like a good boy now," said his mother with pride.

"That so? What you doing, Bob—aside from courting the fillies?"

"I paint."

"You paint? What—pictures?"

"Walls and that."

"Walls! Now there's no satisfaction in that, young man. Tell me, what d'you really want to do with that manly frame of yours?"

Kate observed the boy's discomfort with pleasure; she liked to tease young men in the hope that they'd speak out against her.

"There's no harm in what I do!" snapped Robert. "Although I wish to join the army, and I can't!"

Kate giggled. "Well spake up, Bob. And you've the right to put this old meddler in her place. But tell me now, how bes it that you can't wear the uniform?"

"Father says no, and so I'm stuck with . . ."

His words dried up as the parlor door opened. A thickset man came in, cap in hand and dressed in a canvas overall—Henry Porter—and Kate rose to greet him.

"Hello, father."

Henry Porter looked from Kate to his wife and back again. Then he smiled through blackened teeth.

"By God, it's Kate!" He grasped her hands. "I'll swear I'd never known had you not spoke first!" And he stood back while his wife told him of Kate's arrival and new-found circumstances, muttering, "That so . . . that so?" as the tale was told.

"And now for a proper handsome tea," said his wife as she finished. "An egg, Kate. You'll have an egg?"

They went in a procession into the rear room and took seats around an oval table. Kate brought her black carpetbag along with her and set it down at her feet. Robert Porter took his place beside her. Looking down, he noticed that the bag had fallen open to disclose a bundle wrapped in coarse brown paper.

Mrs. Porter retreated to the kitchen, later to emerge with a plate of bread and butter, tea, and boiled eggs. These she distributed among her family and Kate, but she did not eat herself.

"No appetite, mother?" Kate asked of her.

"No. I'm too weary to eat a morsel."

Kate unbuttoned her coat and produced a half flask of whisky from inside. "Here, mother. Have you a drop of the crathur—true Irish comfort for your ailments."

A glass was fetched, and Mrs. Porter drank a tot.

"I'd prefer a glass of ale to this here tea," Mr. Porter said, his eyes on the whisky.

"Fine man you are!" Kate cried. She drew out her purse and counted off a shilling. "Robert, now you nip off to the nearest House and buy a jar of beer and half a pint of juniper juice for your daddy and myself."

Robert took the money and did as he was bade.

"This is very grand of you, Kate," said Mrs. Porter.

Kate beamed; she enjoyed being generous. " 'Tis a little celebration, mother!"

"Tell us more about your house in Richmond, Kate," said Mr. Porter. It had become apparent to him that Kate had cash to throw about. He'd observed the hunter and chain across her waist when she'd opened her coat, and a finer "souper and slang" he'd never seen.

" 'Tis fully furnished and all in trim," she replied. "I tried to let it off in apartments but without success. Now I'm wondering whether or not to dispose of the place for good and all."

"To sell it!"

Kate nodded. "Me da' in Wexford's not long to live, you see. I'm minded to go back and care for the old fella." She was thinking about her uncle, and had referred to him as her father purely on the spur of the moment.

"You always were a goodly soul, Kate," said Mrs. Porter. She was at the sideboard, and Kate watched her as she brought a large platter to the table. On the platter lay a ham, and when she pulled away the cloth that covered it, Kate was nearly ill. The fatty ham with the protruding bone was a dread reminder.

"And I shall be needing your help, father," she said, looking away quickly, and trying to control her rising gorge.

"Anything . . . anything."

"Well, for a start I'll want an honest man to take the furniture for a fairish price before the gypsies bust in and steal the lot."

Mrs. Porter laughed. "You never did like gypsies, did you, Kate?"

"No, and my view's not changed to this day. They are the bane of decent people, mother!"

Young Robert returned with the beer and gin. "I sent Elsie for it," he said and put some glasses on the table.

"Elsie?" Kate inquired.

"A lass who lives with us," Mrs. Porter explained. "She pays her rent by doing jobs around the house. I'm not fit to—"

"Here now, mother!" Kate said and filled a glass to the brim with neat gin. "You drink this down this instant!"

Mrs. Porter did as she was told, and Kate refilled her own glass.

Mrs. Porter gave a sigh and slumped back in her chair. "I think I've had enough," she said. "I think I'll take me to my bed and rest."

Kate did not attempt to deter her. She would be seeing much of Mrs. Porter over the next few weeks, and her immediate designs required only the services of Henry Porter—or young Robert.

When Mrs. Porter had gone, Kate turned to father and son. "Will you get me this man about the furniture as soon as possible, father?"

"I'll see to it myself this very evening, Kate."

Kate grunted. "Then you'll be hearing from me tomorrow, father," she said. "In the meantime, do you think I might be after borrowing this fine strapping son of yours to help me shift this bag as far as Broadway Station?" She pointed to the carpetbag.

"Yes, see to it, Bobby." Mr. Porter glanced up at a small clock on the wall. He felt the urge for a stroll himself. "I'll come along with you, Kate," he added.

They all got up and went into the hallway, where Kate put on her bonnet. Robert held out a hand for the carpetbag. Kate clipped the catch hard into place and gave it to him. Robert was greatly surprised at the weight of the bag but said nothing.

"I'll come with you as far as the Angel," Mr. Porter said outside in the street, and they walked along Rose Gardens side by side, while Robert brought up the rear, pulled over to one side by the heavy bag.

As they walked, Mr. Porter asked Kate the odd question

about her recent Richmond inheritance, and she made him polite reply. But her mind was elsewhere. This must be the same Rose Gardens as Strong's Rising Sun. There was no sign of this public house, and she was confused.

"Is there a house called the Rising Sun hereabouts?" she asked.

"There is, further up." Mr. Porter pointed. "Why, d'you know it?"

"No, but I've heard tell of it."

"Ah!" This snip of conversation had fed Mr. Porter with an idea.

The trio came to Hammersmith proper and passed the shops to the corner of Bridge Road near the river, the road that led to Hammersmith Bridge and, beyond, to the village of Barnes. The lights of the Angel were plain to see, and they stopped as a figure came out of the public bar and waved with a loud "hullo!"

For an instant Kate thought it to be Police Constable Pew—the same height and build—and she jumped nervously.

"It's my other boy, Willie," said Mr. Porter, surprised at her reaction. "Here, Willie! You'll not remember Mrs. Kate."

Willie shook his head. Kate recalled the youth as a fourteen-year-old boy; he was much changed with age.

"What you got there, Bob?" Willie asked, pointing at the carpetbag.

"I dunno—it's Mrs. Thomas's—but I thinks it's full o' lead." Robert looked at his father. "Will you have it for a bit?" He lowered his voice: "I needs to give my snake a hiss, Dad."

Mr. Porter took the bag from him. "All right, boy. You be off then. There's one round the back of the Angel. Willie and I'll take Kate into the public for a glass; you'll find us there."

While Robert went in search of the lavatory, Kate and the others entered the public house. Kate and Willie sat at a table, and Mr. Porter ordered beer at the counter.

"So you haven't seen Ma and Pa for some time?" Willie asked.

"No. I've been away. Your father's very kindly helping me out over some property I own."

"Oh yes? What's that then?"

Kate watched with distaste as the young man picked at a pustule on his chin.

"A little house in Richmond," she said.

"A house, eh? Then I expect he'll get John Church for that."

Kate thought the name was familiar.

Mr. Porter returned with three pewter tankards. They drank in silence until Robert appeared. Then his father finished his drink and got to his feet. "C'mon, let's go somewhere else. I can't stand this boozer. Let's away to the Oxford by the bridge." He gave the others barely time to finish their drinks and hustled them out into the road.

But Kate was content. She looked at her watch—time enough to do what must be done and for her to catch the Richmond train.

In the street Willie shook her hand and took his leave, and Mr. Porter carried the carpetbag while son Robert trailed behind. It was now very dark, and the cobbles glistened under the occasional gas lamp.

"I shall have to leave you for a few minutes," Kate said casually as they neared the Oxford and Cambridge public house. She could see the gray iron ramparts of Hammersmith Bridge a short way off. "I've arranged to see this friend over the bridge in Barnes, you see? To give him this bag you're so kindly bearing for me."

"Oh?" Mr. Porter sounded surprised. She had said nothing of such a meeting before.

"Well, have something afore you go," he said. "It's a cold night and becoming colder."

So they all went into the private bar of the Oxford and Cambridge and chose a window seat.

"My turn, I think," said Kate and produced her purse. She opened it quite boldly for all to see the sovereigns and crown pieces within. Four pounds, fifteen shillings, and a threepenny bit had she found in the house before leaving for London. Mr. Porter was duly impressed by this sight of her wealth, and they drank Irish whisky.

"Well, to be off and away with me now," Kate said, wiping her mouth with the back of a gloved hand. "Gimme the bag, Bobby."

Robert handed up the carpetbag, and Kate took it easily.

"Who's this friend o' yours across the water, Kate?" asked Mr. Porter.

Kate gave him a wink. "Now you'll not be after asking a lady the ident'y of her gentleman friends, would you, Mr. Porter?" She gave a laugh and was gone.

A thin blue mist was rising from the Thames as Kate reached the foot of Hammersmith Bridge. To the right an odd lantern shone among the boathouses of the Mall.

She advanced a few feet cautiously, but there was no one about. The bridge appeared to be deserted. She could hear the lapping of the water far below, and the smell of the sewage was strong. She quickened her pace. She would traverse the bridge and wait awhile on the far side. It might be that there was a towpath on the Barnes side. If so, she must be sure that nobody was there.

Across the bridge, Kate peered into the foggy gloom, to the left and to the right and back again, and listened. No suspect sight or sound. The bridge was as still as a graveyard.

And yet she waited—paused under the struts and supporting cables for a full ten minutes—to satisfy herself that she was really alone. The foot and the dungheap had been a different matter, with only the birds to bear witness; a proud bridge across a busy section of London's river was, however eerie, a public place much frequented. How could she be certain that no drunken waterman lurked in the shadows or under the approaches to the bridge?

"Courage!" she told herself and began to walk the causeway.

At the very center of the bridge Kate stopped. She lifted the carpetbag so that it rested on the top of the guardrail. She looked down, but the water was lost in the darkness. Then she gave the bag a hefty push and it fell from sight. Silence . . . a splash . . . and silence. It was done. At least some of it was done. More remained, much more, much worse.

A VETERAN OF THE ASHANTI WARS

I

When Kate rejoined the Porters at the Oxford and Cambridge, father and son were deeply engaged in conversation, and she stood beside them unnoticed for a time.

"When ye've finished jawing, perhaps ye'd be fetching me a drink," she said at last.

Mr. Porter came to his feet and gave her his chair. "You weren't long," he said.

"My friend didn't show," Kate murmured.

Mr. Porter went up to the bar, and son Robert turned to Kate. "If your friend didn't show, then where's your baggage, Mrs. Thomas?"

Kate cursed herself for a fool. "I left it in the public house on t'other side," she said.

"Which one is that then?" Robert's questions were quite innocent, but he wasn't giving Kate time to think.

"Less of your queries!" she snapped. "Now where's that drink o' mine, for the love of—"

But Mr. Porter returned with a glass of whisky. Kate took it

168

from his hand, and drank it back in one, even before the man could sit down.

"Another of the same, father," she said, holding out the tumbler, and Mr. Porter made off to the bar once more. Old Katty Thomas liked her liquor.

While he was away, Kate was watching Robert, trying to read his face for a sign of suspicion. But his expression was bland. She peered into the boy's own glass. "Gin is it?" Robert nodded.

" 'Tis not fitting for a lad to be drinking spirits," she said.

"Only sometimes. When father buys!"

"Which leads to most times. Many's the man I've seen baned like a rat by the stuff. You lay off, you hear?" And she drained the contents of his glass.

"But you drink yourself, Mrs. Thomas!" came the protest.

Kate laughed. "Aye, that's a fact. But I got reasons a-plenty for doing so. You got no reasons yet. They'll come, I'll wager, but not yet. And in the meantime a lad of your age should be courtin' every lassie from here to Hampton Court, instead of wasting ye money and ye strength on the devil's brew."

Robert did not answer. His father was coming back.

"Father," Kate began as Mr. Porter took a chair. "I was wondering if ye'd be doing me a favor. Will you loan me your lad to fetch me home to Richmond? I'll stand his fare, of course. And I also swear he'll be back with his honor intact—and that's resisting temptation for yer!"

"Why surely, Kate." Mr. Porter grinned. He put a Woodbine in his mouth and flicked a match with his thumb. The match head broke off and flared under his thumbnail, and he yelled with pain. A familiar smell of burning assailed Kate's nostrils. Her gorge rose, and she immediately held her glass of whisky

169

under her nose. Young Robert observed the look of fear and revulsion on her face with interest.

His look did not escape Kate's notice.

"You arright now, father?" she asked quickly. Sudden fright caused her to mispronounce.

"Bugger me, but that smarted!" Mr. Porter sucked his thumb.

Kate's hand went into her coat pocket. "Here's something to distract you," she said and pulled out a leather cigarette case. It was monogrammed in silver on both sides, and she opened it. "Feast ye eyes on this lot," she said. Four rings fell out upon the table—diamond, emerald, ruby and an opal, all set in gold.

"Me sister's," Kate explained as Mr. Porter examined each in turn. "Me sister Mary. Dead of the cholera, God bless her!"

"They're wondrous fine!" Mr. Porter said with awe, poking the rings with his finger.

"Then choose one for mother," Kate urged.

Mr. Porter gazed at her and sadly shook his head. "I couldn't, Kate. It wouldn't be right. They're your family, after all."

"So they're mine t'give!"

Mr. Porter inspected the rings again. He was sorely tempted. "No," he said finally. "Thankee, Kate, but no."

Kate shrugged her shoulders. Some people she'd never understand.

"I'll show you me family to alter your decision," she said. She burrowed into her pockets again and drew out a set of browned photographs. What reck it would be to produce the private album of Mr. Thomas, she thought.

"That's me." She handed Robert a tiny disc photograph.

Robert stared at the picture and then gave it back. "Not much like you," he said.

"No. Would you believe the mischief of the man who fired the

170

powder! I'm prettier, ain't I, Bobby?" She pushed the cigarette case and the rings toward him. "Now you just be minding these for me, will ye? Slip 'em in your pocket."

But the youth drew her attention to his jacket pockets. "Not big enough, Mrs. Thomas."

"Then you take these instead," Kate insisted and handed him a bunch of keys. "Don't lose them now. They're for the door to me house."

Robert wondered why he was being asked to carry her possessions, but since his father did not comment he didn't either.

"Another drink, Kate?" suggested Mr. Porter.

"Nope!" Kate patted her chest. "I'm filled to the gills, father, and your boy and me must be on our way." Moreover, there was more to be done that night.

They rose together, the men putting on their coats.

"I'll walk with you as far as the District," Mr. Porter said and took Kate's arm. The Royal Oak lay close by the railway, and he saw no reason why he should be temperate.

They walked back to the Broadway, and at the station Kate released herself and turned to him. "I mean what I say about the rings," she said. She looked at Robert, who came up from the rear. "You persuade him, Bobby."

But Mr. Porter shook his head and his son looked down at his feet.

"Then promise me you'll speak to mother of them?" Kate added. The Porter family were kindly folk. They made her feel at home in their company. But she could see that Harry Porter had made up his mind. "So be it!" she said. "C'mon, Bobby, let's away to the lair of this lonely widder woman!"

They talked little during the journey to Richmond, and Robert was happy to be silent. He decided that he liked this Mrs. Thomas. She was easy and she spoke her mind, but no malice lurked behind her words. She was also generous. She had struck good fortune and now she wished to share it. He felt his father's refusal to accept a ring had been ungracious and inspired by stupid pride.

The train drew into Richmond amid a cloud of steam, and they got off. Kate walked ahead, through the ticket barrier and up the main road, a position she maintained during the long walk to Park Road. The streets were silent and dark, and the gaslights yellowed a river fog.

Park Road was smaller and less grand than Robert had envisaged. He noted the public house and wondered how many hours Mrs. Thomas whiled away in that establishment.

"Here we are then," Kate said and opened the gate of a tidy front garden. Beyond stood a tall but narrow house, semi-detached and in darkness. Robert followed her up to the front door. "Have ye got the keys?"

Robert handed them over, and Mrs. Thomas turned the lock three times. Robert was impressed by this security and anticipated a mound of treasure within.

"Hold fast till I find a light," Kate warned in the hall. She lit a wall lamp and pointed to the drawing-room door. "You best wait in there, Bobby."

They both went in, and Robert shuddered with the cold while Kate lit the gas. "You're near to perishing," she observed. "I'll fetch you something warming."

When he was alone, Robert took in his surroundings. This was only a small house, but far larger than his home in Hammersmith. The room smelled of age, and he found the atmosphere strange. But that was to be expected. As he understood it, the house had been unoccupied for quite some time.

Kate returned and handed him a glass of milk.

"I don't like milk," said Robert.

"Drink it down. It'll build up yer bones."

Robert drank, gulped, and pulled a face. "What's in it?" he protested. "Tastes all funny like!"

"Just a drop o' rum to warm your gut."

"But I don't like rum!" Robert put down the glass on a little desk.

"You put it down," said Kate. "You see, we've got to go out again, Bobby. I just remembered something very important." She waved a hand, and Robert saw that it held two pound notes and some booklets. "My aunt's," Kate explained. "And I've promised to give them to a friend."

"What, tonight!"

Kate nodded. She knew she was being clumsy, and this boy was not the fool he looked. But she must press on regardless.

"A promise is a promise, Bobby. I got to meet this fella on Richmond Bridge at eleven o'clock, and time's running short. There's also this box I want for you to carry."

Robert shrugged and finished his rum and milk. He set down the glass on the top of a piano.

"Not there!" Kate swept the glass away. "You'll make rings on it!" She gave Robert a booklet. "Here, you count up what it says inside." And Kate left the room again.

Robert studied the book. It was a building society savings book. It didn't strike him as odd that it was in the name of a Mrs. Julia Martha Thomas.

"Sixteen pounds exactly," he announced on Kate's return.

She was lurching under the weight of a square deal box bound with cord, and Robert rushed forward to help her lower it to the ground.

"Careful, in God's name!" she gasped.

"What is it, Mrs. Thomas?"

"In the box? Oh, bits and bobs for my friend."

"And we're to hump it to some bridge?"

"Aye, to Richmond Bridge—not far." She began to inspect the knots of the cord.

"Do you always meet your friends on bridges at the dead of night?" Robert asked.

Kate looked up sharply, but then she laughed. She had no answer to his question. "Well then, let's get it done with," she said.

Together they left the house and bore the wooden box through many streets and lanes until they came to the wide road leading to the bridge. The ground fell away sharply on either side. The Thames was flowing fast this night, the river rushing its banks. Robert could see the lights of a barge twinkling on the water.

Thirty feet from the bridge Kate stopped. "I can't see me friend," she said, "but I reckons he'll be along in a jiff."

They gained the bridge and walked across to the far side. At the last recess, by a seat carved into the stone balustrade, Kate halted again.

"Put it down," she said quietly. "You go on, Bobby. Me friend will be here directly as arranged. Then I'll catch you up."

Robert did as she bade. But as he released his grip on the cord, Kate took hold of his hand. "This fella I'm meeting is someone special," she said. "So get you out of sight and sound, you hear?"

Robert set off obediently. He had no wish to spy on lovers, and he secreted himself in a clump of rhododendrons at the side of the road. From here he couldn't see either the river or the bridge, and he turned up his collar and waited quietly. Somewhere in a wood a night bird called and was answered. Mrs. Thomas's rum had warmed him for a time, but soon Robert began to shiver.

And because everything was so quiet, he heard the sound of a splash, quite distinct, from either below the bridge or from the vicinity of that barge he'd seen. As he strained his ears, a figure suddenly walked past his hideaway—a tall man dressed in black, who paused and looked about him. Mrs. Thomas's lover? Had he forsaken her? Was the splash from the river the sound of Mrs. Thomas's body—shunned by the man she loved—flung from the heights in an appalling act of self-murder? Young Robert imagined all of this in a panic, so that he sprang from his leafy nook, past the startled man in black and onto the bridge.

"Are ye always this crazed at night!" whispered a voice from the lee. It was Mrs. Thomas, and her face was furious.

"I thought—"

"Ye thought nothing at all, ye batty fool!" She seized his arm above the elbow and rushed him over the bridge, muttering things he could not understand.

On the road, she released his arm. "Let's away to the station before you miss your train," she said more calmly, and he fell in behind her. He suddenly wondered what had become of the box. The man he'd seen didn't have it, nor did Mrs. Thomas now. Robert wanted to ask of its whereabouts, but the back of the woman he followed was stiff with disapproval, and he held his tongue.

In ten minutes they had gained the station. The booking hall

175

was dark and deserted, and Kate went in, to reappear almost immediately.

"'Tis shut, and the last train is gone," she informed Robert with a frown. Some traps and hansoms were assembled in a corner of the station approach, and she guessed their owners could be found in the cab office. "I can't afford the money for a cab," she said, assessing the likely fare to Hammersmith. "You'd best return with me to Mayfield and stop the night."

"I'm due at work at six!" protested Robert.

"Boo to that!" Kate sounded more friendly and slid her arm through his. "Your painting can wait, and I'll stand you breakfast in the morn."

So Robert began the long trudge back to Mayfield Cottages without further argument. Whatever the casual charm of this large lady, her fiery temper counseled caution.

II

Robert Porter, painter's lad, lay beside Kate in Mrs. Thomas's fourposter and dreamed of scarlet tunics and the whip of bullets about his ears.

Kate Webster, murderess and impostor, lay on her side and stared at the dim outline of the long bedroom. Past tears and past fear, she yearned only to wash the blackness from her soul, to expiate her guilt.

The youth near her snored on his back, short snorts and snuffles, like a pig. Kate was tempted to crimp his nostrils together and put an end to this racket. She was also tempted to wake him properly, so that she might lie in his arms, entangle herself in his limbs, lick his ears and kiss his eyes, fall asleep in sorrowful comfort. He wore a borrowed nightshirt, the late Mr. Thomas's, no doubt, but she could feel the warmth of his body against her back. Never had she desired the security of a man's embrace more.

But young Robert was not yet a man. Kate deliberately reminded herself of his youthful features. How could she seriously consider imposing herself upon him! To do so—perhaps even just to think of doing so—was in itself a hellish manner of sin. The boy would misinterpret her need for solace as an offer of her body; and doubtless he would randy over her furiously until, rejected, he would slink away, hateful in his humiliation. She could, of course, give him all. To the devil for such a notion! The lad was young and virgin, and entitled to a love of equal purity. Kate herself was foully soiled by men like Strong. She could not do it, though she so desired.

She heaved herself out of bed, and the boy made an angry sound in his throat. When she was sure he was still sleeping, Kate moved across to the double window. She drew aside the velvet curtains and looked out into the small rear gardens of this house and the one next door. A pale moon flitted through the clouds, and the trees and bushes of the gardens had acquired a soft and waxen hue. The lawns were white with frost, and she was glad that dawn had heralded. She let fall the curtains and stood immobile in the darkness, listening for she knew not what, torturing herself with her imagination. But the only sound was of the sleeping youth, and Kate went over and clambered unwillingly into bed.

It was Robert who woke her shortly after six, and he did so with difficulty, wrenching her mind away from curious disjointed dreams.

"I must get back!" he kept saying.

"I'll get you sumpin' t'eat," Kate muttered and stumbled out of bed. She pulled on Mrs. Thomas's dressing gown, and Robert followed her downstairs to the basement. The range was dead.

"I'll get some wood," the youth volunteered and looked about the kitchen.

"No!" A thought had roused Kate from her torpor. "Leave it. I'm sorry, but ye'll have to make do with milk." The ashes of the grate contained things Kate did not want inspected. She must hurry and clear them away.

"I still don't like milk," Robert grumbled.

But Kate ignored him, pouring the milk into a teacup. It was thick and creamy, and Robert drank it down. It was very cold and eased the dryness of his throat.

"You made me tight last night," he said, watching Kate cut bread. "I've got a head and a half this morning."

Kate turned from the dresser and held out bread and butter on an earthenware plate. "Eat this, and ye'll feel better. I'll get together some things for your mother in the meantime." And she wandered around the kitchen filling a basket with various foods and the remains of a joint of beef. "You fetch these to mother," she said when she had finished. "And tell her I'll be along later this morn."

"You stopping with us then?" Robert asked.

Kate placed the basket on the table. "'Tis so arranged, Bobby."

Robert chewed on his bread. It was stale. Mrs. Thomas staying with them? He could recall no such plan. But the woman was welcome, provided she didn't ply him again with milk and rum.

He finished his meager breakfast, and Kate escorted him up to the hall, handing him the basket of provisions at the door.

"Ye'll get a train easy at the station," she said, patting his shoulder. "Tell your ma I'll be over shortly with more supplies." Her voice was weary, her face unnaturally pale. This woman drank too much, was Robert's decision.

Kate arrived at Rose Gardens at midday. She had occupied the morning hours by assembling as many useful articles as she could find about Mayfield Cottages, and she now carried two hampers filled with oddments ranging from bed linen to an india-rubber plant from Mrs. Thomas's bathroom.

Mrs. Porter opened the door and was surprised to find her thus laden.

"Dearie me, what have you there!"

Kate stepped into the hall and put the baskets down. "Things for you, mother. You know Katty pays her way." Her eyes rested on a little girl of five or six hovering behind Mrs. Porter. "Now who have we here?" asked Kate.

"Oh, this is Mildred. She's my youngest—born after you went away to become a rich woman, Kate. Say hello to Mrs. Thomas, Mildred!"

Kate went down on her knees. "Mildred is it? Come to Auntie Kate, little one!"

Mildred extracted her thumb from her mouth and hid in her mother's skirts, one eye fixed on Kate. The latter took out her purse and extracted a coin. "For Mildred," she said and held out a shiny new penny piece. "C'mon, child, take it! You can ask yer ma to buy you bull's-eyes!"

Mrs. Porter gave her daughter a light push, and the child took the penny.

"You're the very fount of kindness!" Mrs. Porter said to Kate.

The latter stood up and straightened her dress, Mrs. Thomas's autumnal arrangement. "But you're looking very weary today," Mrs. Porter added.

Kate sighed. "So much to do in Richmond, mother. Did Robert get home all right? Good. He missed the last train, you see, and we couldn't get a cab for love or money that time of night!" She lied because she was ashamed, ashamed because she could have afforded him the fare, and because of those certain thoughts toward the boy.

Mrs. Porter picked up the hampers. "Come and have a nice cup of tea," she said and led Kate and her daughter to the rear of the house.

"Has father had any luck with a broker?" Kate asked her in the kitchen.

Mrs. Porter used a poker on the range and put on the kettle. "He did say something this morning, yes. He thinks our grocer, Mr. Brooks, will know what to do. But you ask father yourself when he gets back this evening."

Mrs. Porter made the tea in a china pot, and when she turned she saw that Kate and her daughter were holding hands.

"You see! I knew she'd like you!"

"Me and kids get on dandy," Kate replied.

III

Kate slept well at the Porter house, upon a settee in the front parlor, wrapped in a sheepskin rug. She was roused by the sound of Mrs. Porter preparing breakfast for the men and boys, and she dressed quickly to lend a hand.

The sons came down first. William acknowledged Kate and

his mother with a nod, but Robert took his seat at the table in silence.

"Where's ye manners, boy?" Kate asked of him.

Robert mumbled something without looking up from his plate. Kate leaned across and tweaked his ear, so that the youth called out in pain. "That's better!" he was told. "If you were a son o' mine, I'd take a strap to ye!"

Mrs. Porter chuckled as she sliced a loaf. It was good to have Kate Thomas about the house. Her boys liked her enough, but she judged Kate instilled a holy terror in their hearts.

Mildred was next to arrive. She slowly opened the door and poked her head around—and was seized immediately by Kate and hoisted up into her high chair. Before the child could speak a word, Kate was spooning porridge into her mouth.

"What ruddy time is it!" Mr. Porter made his entry scratching an armpit, tousle-headed and unshaven.

"Late!" said his wife, pointing to his congealing eggs at the head of the table. "You're always late when you've been on the beer!" Her husband had not returned from the Rising Sun until after midnight. Accustomed as she was to his habits, his wife was not prepared to accept them. "Where was you this time?" she demanded, although she knew the answer.

"Playin' crib at the Sun." Mr. Porter lowered himself into his chair and rubbed his eyes.

"With that man Church, I suppose?"

"Of course! He runs the place, don't he?"

Mrs. Porter sniffed. "Don't like him," she said.

"What? Oh, Jack's all right, woman . . . when you gets to know him!"

"*And* he was in the army," added son Robert gravely.

"And he's a good businessman," intoned son William.

Mrs. Porter looked at each of her brood in turn. "But he's sharp," she said. "Too sharp by 'alf. He'll cut himself one fine day, you mark my words!"

"Horse plop, woman!" said her husband, eating furiously.

Mrs. Porter, however, folded her arms defiantly and shook her head. "I knows a wrong 'un," she said quietly. "And Jack Church is as about right as a thirty-shilling piece."

Now to all of this Kate had listened attentively, her hand holding the teaspoon an inch or two away from the reach of Mildred, until an angry protest from the child returned her to the task in hand. John Church . . . the Sun . . . Strong's friend. Jack Church, auctioneer for the proceeds of crime—the one person who might be able to tell her of the whereabouts of Strong himself.

A loud banging on the front door sent Robert Porter scurrying off. "It's the *Gazette!*" he shouted as he left the room. "I asked Bill Doggro to drop one by!"

"Another recruiting campaign," grumbled Mr. Porter. "Telling lies to catch young fools."

His son returned, immersed in the pages of a cheap newspaper, and resumed his place at the table. "They says there's going to be more fightin' with the Zulus," he said solemnly after a while.

"Who says?"

"Them Afrikanders down in Nattle land."

"Nattle land? Never 'eard of it! Bloody heathen places you read about these days!"

"Hush, father," admonished Mrs. Porter. Bad language was forbidden in her breakfast room.

But William had been staring at the front page of the newspaper held by his younger brother, and he suddenly snatched the *Gazette* away from him.

"What's this then!" he announced to the company at large. "Another 'orrible murder!" and he began to read. " 'Yesterday morning, Mr. Henry Wheatley was driving his coal cart along Barnes Terrace, close to Barnes Bridge, when he spied a large wooden box in the water, apparently stuck in the low-tide mud. Mr. Wheatley stopped his cart and went to examine the box. He managed to pull it ashore, and cut the ropes securing the box. The wood was apparently rotten, for the box fell into pieces, revealing its terrible contents—parts of a human body—' "

"Gimme back my paper!" Robert interrupted.

"Shut up, Bobby." His father waved him quiet. "Go on, William."

" 'Mr. Wheatley, unable to believe his eyes, at first assumed the flesh to be butcher's meat, but a closer inspection confirmed the dreadful truth, and he reported his finding to the Barnes Constabulary.' " William paused to note the excited faces of his family. " 'A surgeon (name withheld) being summoned, the headless torso appeared to be that of a woman. It is not yet known who the deseased'—no, *deceased*—'might be, nor how long this box had lain in the water with its awesome secret. One opinion is that some of the flesh had been cooked!' "

"What's that?" asked Mr. Porter.

"Cooked, Father. But it says here, 'At the moment, the police are not prepared to comment.' "

"Is foul play suspected?" asked Mrs. Porter.

"Don't be silly, woman!" said her husband. "Of course it is! This is a case of murder!"

Kate Webster stirred Mildred's porridge reflectively, her

eyes on Robert Porter, and made no comment. She looked at the youth quite boldly, but he was fussing for the return of his newspaper. Plainly he was more interested in the prospects of a South African insurrection than in local events.

"I say it's one of them practical jokes," William was saying. "You know, those medical students at the 'orspitals at it again. They're always leaving bits of cadaver lying around to cause a fuss. They stuck an 'and on a lamppost up Piccadilly way over Christmas. They steal the bits from the mortuaries and just fling 'em around like."

"*I* wouldn't like *my* body left about the place if *I* was dead!" observed Mrs. Porter.

Her husband shook his head, rubbing the bristle on his chin. "No, no, no. You don't get torsos—whole torsos—bobbing up in the Thames. I still says it's a case of murder." He swallowed down his tea. "And I must be off. Can't sit 'ere talking all day." He got to his feet and belched. "I'll see you boys at the shop." And he was off and away before his wife could remind him to shave.

Robert was next to leave, and Kate casually picked up his newspaper. She read the passage about the finding of the body for herself, and then so as not to seem too interested in it, turned to other columns within the pages. First she read that a certain Sir Bartle Frere was inclined to dismiss the Zulu insurrection as mere "nigger-thunderings," but then another article —short and tucked away at the bottom of the page—arrested her attention.

"Hammersmith Body Finally Identified," claimed the headline. "Savage murder of young policeman," it added. "The ragged and bird-pecked body found last week proximate to Brook Green Farm has at last been identified as that of Police

Constable Edmund Pew, late of the Surrey Constabulary. This dread discovery was made by the constable's own mother—Mrs. Deidre Pew of Willesden village—only last Saturday, and awful confirmation has been provided by the finding of the constable's truncheon in the same rough ground that has guarded its fearsome secret over these past few weeks. Footpads and foul murder are suspected, for the wretched constable's skull had been cruelly shattered by an assassin's bullet, and his purse or wallet has never been recovered. Enveloped in alarm and the utmost despondency, the Teddington Police have yet to unveil the mystery of their so-lamented colleague's untimely death, for we understand that the officer was not upon any known mission which trespassed into the Hammersmith area, and that he was attired in common apparel when he encountered his demise. The Editor and staff of this, our newspaper and yours, do offer humble condolences to the mother of this spirited limb-of-the-law. A Service is to be held at Teddington Chapel at 11 o'clock precisely, Thursday next, when it is expected that Inspector Dowdell of Richmond Station will represent the Commissioner."

There's one I know who'll not be attending, thought Kate. She should be cheered by news of her tormentor's death, but she was not, and she felt only grief for his mother. At any age, under whatever circumstances, how bad it must be for a mother to lose her son.

"Terrible, ain't it?" said Mrs. Porter, who'd been watching her.

Kate turned her mind back to the river discovery and nodded slowly. "Aye. 'Tis the work of the devil himself."

Yes, Satan may well have entered into her being during those long strange hours in the basement. But the killing of Pew was the work of no devil. Strong, she decided, it could only have been Jack Strong. The constable must have been onto his coat-tails, and Strong must have felt cornered. And Strong cornered would be dangerous, with or without his gun. But he must have lost all reason to *kill* the silly copper. He could have blackjacked him from behind and not be seen. Yet who was Kate to talk about self-control?

Mrs. Porter was still watching, and she determined to swerve any interest away from the box in the river. Kate turned to William.

"Willie, your ma's kindly consented to visit me place in Richmond, but I'd also be glad of the opinions of a canny young man such as yourself. Can *you* come along too?"

William was duly flattered, but he shook his head. "Work," he explained.

"Well, what about this evening, after ye've done for the day?"

William thought it over. He'd arranged to meet a friend for a game of dominoes. But that could wait.

"Yeah, I'll come," he agreed. "I'll be back home come six. We could go then."

"God bless ye! I'll be waiting here for your return." Kate wiped Mildred's mouth. "Now, mother," she said to Mrs. Porter, "I'll be givin' you a hand with all this clutter." And she began to clear away the breakfast things from the table, even singing a little ditty for the benefit of young Mildred.

IV

"I forgot me keys and we can't get in," Kate said to William, turning out the pockets of her coat.

William tried the front door for himself. "Any other way?" he asked.

Kate stepped back onto the gravel path and considered each of the front windows in turn. She had aired the long bedroom only the other day. Perhaps she had neglected to secure the window catch.

"Up there." She pointed. "And you should find a ladder by the side of that wall."

William went to the right-hand wall of the house and retrieved a worn and unsteady ladder of about twelve feet in length. The wooden rungs were crumbly to the touch.

"You sure this is safe?"

"If you're brisk, and don't be dancing a jig on it. Here, let me hold it for yer!" Kate helped him place it against the house and held the lower section. William climbed up gingerly, slid open the bedroom window, and disappeared into the inside. Moments later he was down to let Kate in.

Lamps were lit, and Kate showed William into the drawing room. "You nip in here while I go fetch us a bottle. You can light the fire if you're so minded."

When she returned with a flask of gin and two glasses, William was over by the fireplace, inspecting the photograph in its silver frame on the mantel.

"Mr. Thomas?" he asked.

So it was, but Kate shook her head. "Me father. The one I am t'care for."

"He looks very much a gent," said William.

"And so he is. He was in the government service, you know. But he's on half pay now." She handed him a measure of neat gin.

William put the portrait back and drank while his eyes

roamed around the room. He knew little of the value of household effects, but he imagined the furniture here would fetch a few pounds.

"Did Father speak to you of Mr. Brooks?" he asked.

"He did. We're going off to see the man this very night."

"And if he's not interested, there's always old Jack Church," William said when he'd finished his appraisal.

"Aha! Yes, your friend Jack Church."

"Queer smell down 'ere," commented William in the kitchen.

Kate was arranging various articles on the table—petticoats, tablecloths, nightdresses, antimacassars and napkins—and she didn't reply.

"Must be the damp," William added to himself.

Kate finished what she was doing and patted the pile of linen. "There! I'll have your mother wash these for me. Then we'll sell them for a bob or two."

William helped himself to more gin from the bottle on the dresser. "Who lives next door?" he asked, jerking his head.

"A little old lady," Kate replied. "Nice, but"—she tapped her temple—"a wee bit soft in the head."

William drank in silence while Kate continued to fuss about in the basement area. But time was passing. He checked it with a pewter timepiece secured to his waistcoat by means of a piece of string. Glory be! He'd been here for more than an hour, and been doing nothing save stand about and drink. She had asked him to put a value on her property; she'd asked him for his "expert" opinion. But really she'd asked him nothing, and he wondered at the purpose of his visit at all.

"Well," he said and swallowed his gin. "If you'll not be needing me any more, I'll be off home, Mrs. Thomas."

Kate looked across at him from the vicinity of the copper. William observed that she had been rewhitening the surround.

"Not at all," she called. "Thankee for ye company, Billie boy!"

William went upstairs and let himself out of the house. If he hurried, he might yet enjoy that game of dominoes with his friend. "Bloody waste of time," he muttered as he half walked, half ran in the direction of the railway station.

From the window of her front room, Miss Ives saw him leave and pass under the light of a streetlamp, and she was puzzled.

They had gone in search of Mr. Brooks—Kate and Henry Porter—and the man could not be found. They had called at his shop off the Broadway, and they had scoured various public houses known to be to his liking, but to no avail. So they sought solace in several pints of beer themselves, finally returning to Rose Gardens arm in arm, and slightly tipsy.

"Sho we'll get Jack Church!" Henry said when they reached the Porter house. In the hall he swayed and held on to the wall.

"You're as full as an egg," Kate told him.

"Sho are you, you great big woman you!" And Henry Porter placed his hand over her left breast.

Kate smacked his hand away and laughed. "Be off to ye bed like a decent man!" she said and dragged him to the foot of the staircase. She bundled him up a couple of steps and then returned to the parlor door, waiting for the man to reach his bedroom safely. The sound of shrill arguing broke out, and Kate knew he had found his wife. With a small smile she went into the room that served as her bedroom.

She removed her coat and bonnet, flopped down on the settee, and hauled the rug up to her chin. She wanted to undress, but she was physically and emotionally spent. She blew out the candles and closed her eyes, but sleep continued to elude her as before. She thought of Mrs. Crease and her little boy, of the hills and vales of County Wexford, of the new wealth at her disposal, of her Uncle John in Killane, and of the few pleasant memories she had acquired in thirty years of life. And she thought of Strong. It could be no coincidence that Pew had met his end in a part of west London much frequented by his quarry. The murder of the young policeman still shocked her. Snuffing a copper was against "the rules" as Kate understood them—rules taught to her by all and sundry, including Strong himself. And for *Strong* to pull the trigger, of all people! Over the years she had grown to believe the man as cautious and as cunning as a fox. Why, Strong had never suffered for a single crime himself. He'd let others do so, and usually his Mrs. Webster. She bore him no ill will, however, She admired Strong, who had the ability to slip away unnoticed, to slide past the tentacles of evidence. And good luck to him for that. But now he was toying with the gibbet; every bluecoat from here to Barkingside would be employed to track him down, and she doubted he'd get refuge from the underworld. Strong had now become no better than the man they'd hanged up north last month—a lunatic with the features of a Barbary ape—John Ward or Charlie Peace or something.

Kate's mind roved away to consider the years of their acquaint. Strong it was who had induced her to quit the service of Captain Woolbest in favor of his dreary oil shop. Strong it was who had seduced her there and used her in his "long firm" swindles—buying up goods on credit from a bogus shop, selling them off cheap, and closing shutters before the suppliers could close in with their demands. But Strong's plans had gone awry, and they'd removed themselves in haste to Kingston, she with a bulge in her belly that might have been her cracksman's or any one of his friends', for by now she'd acquired that fierce necessity for drink which led her so often into further crime and the beds of other men. The birth of her son, by candlelight and without nursing, was followed by Strong's rejection of her—a jilt that lasted for more than a year. Stealing to feed a small mouth. Wandsworth Prison—the "corrective" wing—another resentful inmate being taught an unskilled trade by indifferent instructors. Release with Strong waiting in his cart. More crime, more prison—until she'd told him no, and sought out the Mitchell home. Her endeavors at that house to curry appreciation, but always Strong lurking and whispering in her ear whenever she ventured out. She'd tried to stick by her resolve—let nobody say otherwise—but in the end he'd drawn her forth like a limpet from its shell, and so she'd fled Teddington and found Mrs. Thomas.

Kate's mind ventured little into what had occurred thereafter. She pressed the knuckles of her right hand against her teeth. But memories took her down into that basement whenever she began to doze, and she forced herself awake again. Dawn found her still staring at the ceiling.

She rose with the weak sun, and put on one of her late employer's dresses, as usual straining to get it on. She washed her face and hands in the kitchen and cleaned her teeth with her fingers. She drank cold tea left over from the day before, found the keys to Mayfield Cottages on the sideboard, and escaped the house before the Porter household stirred.

She caught the first train to Richmond and was at Number Two by eight o'clock. She immediately went below to make herself some breakfast. The meal revived her. Wake up, wake up! she told herself, for she had tasks to perform. Mrs. Porter was due to visit here at midday. Mrs. Porter would inspect the house with a womanly eye. Mrs. Porter would wish to see all the rooms, with their chests o' drawers and wardrobes full of clothing. Mrs. Porter was bound to pay great attention to the kitchen quarters. Accordingly, all areas *must* be spick and span, without the faintest hint of telltale blood.

But as it transpired, Kate had little more than an hour before a knock on the front door heralded the arrival of Ann Porter.

"Slife! but you're early, mother!"

Mrs. Porter entered regally. "Well, we woke and found you gone," she said. "And seeing how you forgot your keys last time, I made haste to bring you down your purse." She handed Kate Mrs. Thomas's brown silk purse. "But I see you've got your keys after all."

"You'll have a bite t'eat?" Kate asked, closing the door behind them.

"I will. I've fed the boys but not myself as usual. What's that?"

From outside, from Park Road, there came this treble voice calling to the neighborhood. Kate opened the front door, and they both stepped outside to listen.

"Supposed murder, shocking discovery!" announced the voice, getting nearer. " 'Uman remains in a box! In the Thames! Shocking discovery!" and into sight came a newspaper lad hawking his bundle of sheets.

"Not another one," Mrs. Porter said wearily.

Kate chuckled and shrugged her shoulders. "I expect that's only a catchpenny. But we might as well have one for the fun of it. Hey, boy!" She beckoned to the news vendor, and he came up the garden path.

Kate unclipped her purse. "How much?"

"Two for a penny, miss."

"One for ha'pence then." And Kate executed a swift exchange before the lad could protest.

In the security of the hall Kate read the broadsheet through twice. "D'ye want to see it, mother?" she asked Mrs. Porter. "Looks as if we've a pack o' cannibals running loose hereabouts!"

But Mrs. Porter declined. "There's some that likes these things, and there's some that don't," she said. "I don't."

They went down to the basement where Kate seated her guest, made her tea, and gave her bread and jam. From her position at the kitchen table, Mrs. Porter took in her surroundings. The floor and walls were spotless, but she noticed the heavy staining on the table—dark stains that had obviously defeated all attempts to scrub them off. The range was clean, but she detected the remains of a fire in the grate. And the same applied in the case of the copper over in the alcove. The surround was freshly done, but the grate had certainly not been cleared.

"I see you've been doing some laundry," she remarked to Kate.

"What's that, mother? No, I have not."

Mrs. Porter pointed to the copper.

"Oh, that!" Kate said a little nervously. "Why, that's just some bits o' linen I've been disposing of!"

Mrs. Porter drank her tea. Her eyes wandered to the dresser, and rested on two jam jars on the ledge. They appeared to be filled with fat—dripping, perhaps, although darker in color than might be expected. Mrs. Porter was close enough to reach out and take hold of one of the jars.

"And what have you here then?" she asked, sniffing the contents.

"Dripping!" Kate said quickly, thoroughly alarmed. Why in the names of the saints had she left those lying around?

"Not beef surely?"

"No. Goose fat."

"Goose, you say? Don't smell much like goose to me, dear!" Mrs. Porter did concede that the greasy texture of the fat *might* be consistent with that of fowl, but the odor was quite different; she was quite unable to place it.

"An especial kind of goose," Kate was explaining. "Different. They breeds 'em up in Richmond Park. I thinks they call 'em Rooshen geese."

Mrs. Porter accepted that dripping made from the carcass of a Russian species of goose was quite without parallel.

Thereafter Kate maintained a close eye on the other as she ate her breakfast. Without further queries or inspections.

When she'd finished, Kate said, as sweetly as she could, "Mother, I was wondering if you'd be doing me a little favor?"

Mrs. Porter licked a finger. "Why, surely, Kate."

Kate sat down opposite her. " 'Tis me little lad. He's stopping over now with Mrs. Crease, but I'd be a sight happier were he with yourself, seeing as how I'm now staying in Hammersmith. I've not had time t'see him for days and days, and I'm pining something awful for his company. I'll pay you for the service, of course."

Mrs. Porter, a kindly soul and at her happiest in the company of as many children as possible, was delighted by the request.

"Of course. You bring him up to us just as soon as can be," she said. "But I'll not take your money. Wouldn't dream of it, Kate."

Who is that woman? thought Miss Ives as Mrs. Porter left the house next door. She took note of the latter's coat and bonnet from the parlor window—a clean and well-pressed coat, but shabby after much wear, not a lady's coat by any means. Nor was the face of the wearer that of a lady—an honest open face, perhaps, but with the rough scrubbed features of the working class. Surely not a friend of Julia Thomas? she reasoned. And not a tradeswoman either. Miss Ives knew most of the shopkeepers who called at houses in this street. Who is that woman? she wondered again as she withdrew from the windowpane.

Mr. Porter filled his pipe from a tobacco bowl on the mantelpiece and struck a match by running the head up the seat of his trousers. Kate watched and wondered if he'd fire his breeches as he had done his thumb.

"You reckon you can trust this Church, father?" Kate asked him when his pipe was going.

"Jack Church? Yeah. Been a pal of mine for years!"

And a pal of Strong's too. Kate marveled at the naïveté of Henry Porter.

"When does I get t'meet him?" she asked.

"Sunday lunchtime. I'll take you along to the Sun so's you two can get acquainted."

Kate nodded. Sunday would be soon enough. She then took stock of the furnishings in the Porters' parlor. Not much, and nothing good.

"I'll be pleased for you and mother t'take something for yourselves," she said. "A chair or table, perhaps?"

Mr. Porter dampened his pipe, and muttered his thanks. It was not like taking her jewelry.

"You can make your choice when you come down to Richmond tomorrow," Kate went on. "In the meantime, I was wondering if you'd be doing me a little favor?"

"What's that then?"

"This." Kate took Mrs. Thomas's dental plate from her pocket. "I found it at the house. It must have been me auntie's. I think I'll sell it. It ain't no good t'me. Is it worth anything at all, father?" She tossed the plate to Henry Porter, who caught and examined the article. Plates and false teeth always had a value. And these two artificial teeth were set in gold—not much, but gold all the same.

"We'll flog it to Charlie Niblett," he said.

So they went to Niblett's shop off King Street, and Kate watched through the window while Porter made the sale.

"Here you are," he said when he came out and handed her the money. Kate counted the cash and returned to him a shilling for his trouble. Inside the shop this minor transaction was entered in a ledger: "One worn dental plate (lower jaw); two teeth—gold: 6s-0d."

V

Church sat on his customary stool behind the bar, well pleased with himself and the world at large. Maria, his wife, had cooked for him an excellent Sunday lunch of roast pork and cabbage. His new suit of tweed matched perfectly his old and favored deerstalker. He had managed to secure the hiring of a longboat for the river picnic. And, best of all, Georgy Woodbridge, secretary to the Oak Slate Burial Club, had only last night assured him of his candidacy elect as president. Life was seldom so tolerable, and he helped himself to a glass of port by way of celebration.

Church checked his watch. Twenty past one. The bar was full of folk dressed to their best, and trade was brisk.

"Mornin' Doggro," he said and took an order. As he poured the beer, Church reflected that it had taken him nigh on eight years to build up his business here, to transform the premises from a beggars' ale shop into a well-known tavern. Respectability, it was true, had yet to come. But Church was in no hurry. Come it would, when he could afford to lose a slice of present custom and eschew their slippery offers.

" 'Ow's Mrs. Doggro?" he asked without much interest, and he paid little heed to Mr. Doggro's answer, smiling and nodding when he guessed it right to.

Eight years! A positive age. And what a desperate time had it been before he'd put his chances into the Rising Sun. There was "the year" in everybody's life, Church reasoned, the year when all things went wrong. And 1856 had been "the year" for Jack Church. He'd put his cash—and other people's—down on a natural winner, and when the jockey hit a fence and not the finish, they had called it fraud. He'd tried to pay them back, begged for time, but they wouldn't listen. And his judges had given him the choice of fat or fire—two years in the jail at Colchester or ten at Her Majesty's disposal. He did nine in all, taking her shilling at Soho Square back in 1857. The Bengal Regiment and then the Eleventh Hussars. That absurd fracas with the rebellious sepoys and then the Ashanti fuss on the west coast of Africa. White man's grave, they called it, miles of stagnant jungle and mangrove swamps. Yellow jack and blackwater fever killed off more men than ever did the niggers.

"Yes, Freddie lad? One glass of satin coming up!"

197

For the umpteenth time Jack Church blessed his brother Job, who'd bought him out before his bell was tolled.

"Thankee, Freddie boy!" Church took the silver crown and weighed it in his hand. Money—only a man with money was free in this life. Money back in 1856 would have saved him from the army. Money in 1866 had spared him from a Snider bullet. Then the humdrum role of gentleman's servant—four years' drudgery up in Pall Mall. But four years of thrift, and with his savings the purchase of this pub. Crikem Jiminy, but he'd done well! And Jack Church intended to stay on top!

"Hello, Jack." The call of his name interrupted his daydreaming.

Henry Porter, his odd-jobber and painter, together with young Willie and a tall, striking woman Jack Church had never seen before. Or had he?

"Henry, old fellow. How's it then?"

"All the better for three pints quick, John."

Church grinned through his beard and pulled their ale, still watching the tall woman.

"This is Mrs. Thomas," Henry Porter said, and Church nodded to her. To his surprise, the woman stepped up to the counter and touched his arm.

"Don't yer know me, Jack?" she said. " 'Tis me, 'tis Kate!" As if they had been long acquainted. "I was an old neighbor of the Porters some years back," she went on. "Surely you've not forgot?"

Church noted the Irish accent. Many of his old comrades at arms had come from Hibernia.

"That's as may be," he said but shook his head. He did not remember her as a friend of the Porter family, and yet her face was vaguely familiar. It was not a face easy to forget. He put the tankards before his customers.

"Mrs. Thomas has a spot of business as might interest you," Henry Porter was saying. "Come into a spot of property down in Surrey, she has. Bibs and bobs and furniture she wants rid of. What say you, John?"

Church listened with cautious attention. Henry Porter did not deal in tainted goods as far as he knew, so this must be a straight deal.

"Always open to a decent offer," he said. "But you'll see how I'm up to my ears at the moment." He gestured toward the crowded bar. "Why not pop round dinnertime tomorrow? It'll be a sight quieter then."

Kate Webster did not contribute to the men's chatter now or later, content to bide her time. Only when Church was truly ensnared in the execution of her grand plan would she divulge her association with the man Strong. Then Church could tell her of his whereabouts.

"I think John will help," Henry Porter said in a low voice when the publican turned away to serve another.

"I'm grateful t'yer, father."

COMINGS AND GOINGS

I

Having engaged the services of John Church, publican and other things, Kate saw him next day as arranged. But the bar was as crowded as before, with Church slaving like a demon behind the counter, in company with a small freckle-faced woman.

"It's a boat race," Church explained to Kate and Henry Porter. "Best if I nip over to your house tomorrow evening. What's the address again? Number Two Mayfield Cottages, Park Road. Got it! Righto then. You can expect me around five, five-thirty!" And he rushed off to serve another customer.

Outside the public house Kate turned to Mr. Porter. "Who was the woman behind the bar, father?"

"Maria, John's missus. I should have introduced you."

But Kate was less interested in Mrs. Church than she was in the earrings she had noticed that lady wearing. Opals set in gold.

"Do you want me down when Jack comes?" Mr. Porter asked as they began to walk back to his house.

"No, father. I'll manage on me own."

Tuesday came, and Kate journeyed down to Richmond in the early afternoon. Church was an unknown quantity, and Kate deemed it well to make certain preparations—to supply him with a list of household effects against her own reckoning of their worth, and to have ready several bottles of strong drink with which to soften his brain and loosen his tongue.

Church came punctually at a quarter past five.

"Just in time for a spot of refreshment," Kate said as the other stepped into the house. "Tea or gin 'twill it be?"

Church removed his deerstalker and smoothed his hair. He was already assessing the contents of the hall. "You on your own?" he asked.

Kate nodded.

"Then I'll indulge this once. 'While the cat's away,' what? Gin it is, Mrs.—er—Thomas."

Kate took his hat and cape. Ridiculous clothing for a ridiculous little man, she decided. She showed him into the dining room. He could go ahead and value the plate and silver while she fetched the bottle.

When she returned, John Church had opened the canister of cutlery on the dining table. He was examining the markings of the spoons and forks with an experienced eye, and he began to cluck with mock disappointment for her benefit. Kate noticed that his mouth, partially obscured in his sandy beard, was small and red. A weak and fussy mouth.

"Your gin, sir."

Church checked her pouring with a "Tch!" and sniffed his glass before he drank.

"It's not wine, you know," Kate said.

Church frowned slightly, vexed that this coarse peasant of a woman should see fit to mock him. "And *this,*" he countered, holding up a spoon, "is not silver!" He flung the spoon back into the canister. "None of these are silver. Just plate, I fear, and not very valuable."

A light footfall made him stop and stare past Kate to the door. "Who have we here then?"

Kate turned. "My son," she said. She had picked him up from Mrs. Crease upon arriving at Richmond.

"He's up late," Church commented. "And I find children tend to interfere with business deals." Church did not care for children any more than children cared for Church.

"You've none of your own perhaps?" asked Kate.

"On the contrary! I have a lad of six, and a right little pest he is too!"

Kate detected no trace of humor in his voice. "Well now, let's to work," Church went on. "I've spent the whole morning at the licensing committee and I'm tuckered out." He produced paper and pencil and began to jot down the contents of the dining room. Whenever able, he took the opportunity to pull a face or make an adverse comment.

"Well, that lot's done," he said finally. "Where do we go now?"

Kate led him to the drawing room, and as he passed through the doorway, Church cannoned into her boy.

"Push off, you little basket!" snapped the publican.

Kate said nothing. She lifted the lid of the piano and tinkled the keys.

" 'Tis a fine piece," she said coldly.

Church grunted and inspected the inlay. This piano *would* look well in the new private bar he was planning at the Sun, a place where ladies and gentlemen could gather of an evening. But he didn't show his feelings.

"Unhappily, not of a very good make," was his professional opinion.

Kate knew he was lying. " 'Tis worth all of fifteen pound," she said quietly. "And I know that for a fact. It was a favorite with me aunt."

"In that case, again unhappily, your aunt was mistaken," returned Church. He strolled over to the mantelpiece and took down the silver-mounted photograph. "Your husband, Mrs. Thomas?"

"Me father, Mr. Church."

"An imposing face, if I might make so bold!"

"He's a solicitor up in Glasgow. He's old and in bad health, and I'm soon away to keep house for him."

"A lawyer? My word!"

Kate knew Church would be impressed—his kind always were. "Yes," she said. "And he'll be interested in what I gets for auntie's pianoforte, Mr. Church."

The veiled threat was duly absorbed by the publican, and he moved on in his valuation.

"May I?" He pulled out the top drawer of the wellington chest of drawers. Kate assented without thinking, and Church began to rummage around, one drawer after the other. At length he came to the bottom drawer, and stood up holding that large and curious book, once the property of Mr. Jonathan Thomas.

"God's blood!" Kate leaped forward to snatch it from his grasp. The book fell to the floor and opened, face upward, and Kate stamped her foot down to hide the pictures.

"Well I never!" cried John Church, startled by the other's wildness. But he had failed to catch a glimpse of the illustrations.

"Sorry," Kate murmured. She picked up the book in such a way as to prevent him seeing inside. " 'Tis me family Bible," she explained and tucked the book under her arm. "I didn't want it touched."

"Funny way to treat the Good Book!" Church said, recalling that huge pounding foot across the pages.

"How much for the chest o' drawers?" Kate asked of the wellington.

"Two pounds." Church sniffed and stepped back to take another look. Kate's son had come up close behind, and he again nearly fell over the child.

"Hey you! You just beat it while grownups are busy!"

The boy ran to his mother, and Kate held him close. She was angered by the man's attitude to her, to the furniture, and now to her greatest treasure of all. She felt the urge to seize him by his beard and give him a good shake, but she kept control.

"I'll take him downstairs," was all she said. "You carry on as ye please. There's the three rooms up the stairs. The doors ain't locked, and you can use the lamps down here. You just come and go as you will. You'll be finding me and me boy down in the basement when ye've done." And she left the room with her son.

When Church presented himself in the kitchen, the list in his hand was long, and he said it was complete.

"I'll just take a peep down here." And he started on the various kitchen utensils and the dresser.

"Ten bob for this," he said of the dresser. "Hey, what's the stink down here!"

Kate had hoped the smell had gone; indeed, she hadn't noticed it herself that afternoon.

"I left something on the boil," she said.

"Phew, it's a darn sight worse than that! You sure your brat ain't disgraced himself?"

Kate's son had long been trained, by both herself and Mrs. Crease, but once again she held her tongue.

"Anyway, here's your inventory." Church handed her his list.

Fifty pounds he was offering, fifty pounds for all the furniture. Church licked his rosy mouth in anticipation.

"Seventy, Mr. Church." Kate put down the list.

"Seventy! Why, I've been overgenerous as it is . . . in view of your recent bereavement."

"Seventy pound, or ye've been wasting your time an' mine."

Church saw that she could not be moved. And if he pressed too hard, he might well annoy her and find himself driven from the house. He further realized that the furnishings were worth at least a hundred pounds on the Hammersmith market, probably more.

"I tell you what, Mrs. Thomas," he said with great unction. "Seeing as how I'll have to pay for the removal van, I'll give you sixty pounds for *all* of what I take, plus the chandelier in the hall."

"Seventy."

"Sixty-five?"

"Seventy."

"Sixty-eight?"

Kate nodded. "Sixty-eight it is, but I want it all in gold, Mr. Church."

"In *gold!* Odds bods, d'you think I carry that much money around in gold!"

"No. But you can get it, can't ye?"

John Church pulled out a sharkskin wallet. "Will you take these?" he asked and offered two five-pound notes. Kate held them close to the beam of the lamp and examined the watermarks.

"They'll do on account," she said. "But have ye got any gold on you?"

Church produced his watch chain from his waistcoat. Attached to the chain was a silver sovereign case, from which he released eight coins. Kate licked her lips at the sight of them.

"All I've got on me," the publican explained.

"They'll do for the time being," Kate said, carefully putting the notes and the sovereigns into her purse. Never in her life had she so much money of her own.

Church recognized the greed in her face. Hers was not the reaction he might have expected of a solicitor's daughter.

"But I'll be wanting no more paper money or any bills of exchange, Mr. Church," Kate added.

Church readjusted his watch chain and replaced his wallet. "I'll get 'Enry Weston fetch your chattels up to 'Ammersmith," he said. His suspicions of Kate were increasing by the minute. Her manner—her haggling, even her physical appearance—did not match either her mode of dress or her apparent inheritance. Where *was* it he had seen her, or her very double, once before?

"You say you're from Scotland?" he asked her as they climbed the steps to the hall.

Kate paused midstride, one hand upon the dark brickwork. She wondered if the shiny surface might have hidden from her some solitary smudge of blood.

206

"I did not," she said, moving on. "I've said nothing of the sort."

"Oh? I must have misunderstood you."

"I said me father's up in Glasgow, that's all."

John Church unhooked his cape from the antler horns of the coat stand and slipped it on. Kate held out his deerstalker for him. "What's this fool thing for?" she asked. She'd seen this kind of hat, she thought. Gamekeepers sometimes wore them.

"That's my titfer for the races," said Church with pride. "Cost me a guinea it did."

Kate shook her head sadly. There was no counting the ways people had for wasting their money. Church—receiver, publican, skinflint, and now a racing man. It was time for her to tell him more of what she knew.

"Strong likes the horses too," she said mildly.

Church stopped buttoning his cape to stare at her. So *that* was how he knew her face! He'd seen her with Strong.

"Who's Strong?" he asked, a croak in his voice.

"A fella well known t'both of us, Mr. Church."

For the second time that evening Church realized this woman could not be bluffed.

"Strong's no friend of mine," he said, "just a customer at my pub."

"To which he brings his ill-gotten gains for yourself to dispose of, Mr. Church. 'Tis no use pretending with me, man. Strong's told me all." She handed him his hat. "Now you be off fixin' things with this fella Weston." She was laughing at him, cheap little crook for all his airs and graces. She opened the front door. "Will I see ye tomorrow?"

John Church put on his deerstalker as he stood on the doorstep. It was raining gently, and he released the flaps of his hat to tie them under his chin. The sight of him now, all beard and tweeds, amused Kate the more. "Well, Mr. Church?"

"Yeah, I suppose so. I'll be down sixish to stack the furniture. I'll ask Harry Porter to lend me a hand."

Kate chuckled. "Why not ask Strong?"

"Haven't seen him for some time," came the reply.

Kate wasn't sure whether to believe him. She doubted whether Jack Strong would have informed this man of the shooting. But perhaps the publican had heard something along the thieves' grapevine. No matter, she could put him to the test tomorrow when he came. Meanwhile, she must take her little boy back to Mrs. Crease for his supper and his bed.

"Bye now," she said to Church and closed the door.

She returned to the basement in search of her son, calling his name in the funny voice she reserved for children. It had been wonderful having him with her again. His presence had the effect of reducing the dismal gloom of the house, of shutting from her mind the dreadful memories of the past few days.

"Come along, you little pixie," she called. "Come to ye poor old mother and give her a kiss before she cries."

She found him lurking in the alcove, half hidden behind the copper, and they staged a grand reunion. Soon they would be across the seas and as free as the mountain goat. Perhaps they would cross over an even wider stretch of water, over an ocean itself? Kate disentangled herself from the boy's embrace, and sang him a snatch from "My Love Is in Amerikay."

II

Confused and irritated, John Church was of a mind to forgo any further association with Mrs. Katherine Thomas, a lawyer's daughter who nevertheless rubbed shoulders with Jack Strong. How was it that she knew such a man? Church should have been braver. He should have taxed her about it immediately instead of allowing himself to be dismissed without so much as a smidgen of explanation.

Yet Henry Porter, who had known Mrs. Thomas for several years, spoke well of the woman. He'd asked Henry many questions that very evening of the Tuesday, and the answers had been satisfactory. Of course, he hadn't mentioned the existence of Strong to Henry, but nothing he'd been told implied a criminal connection between this woman and any person living or dead. Henry confirmed that she was mysterious in her ways, coming and going over the years, but *he* was obviously prepared to accept that she'd been the wife of a Mr. Thomas of Birmingham, that she had inherited a house in Richmond, and that the furniture was hers to sell.

The power of profit being as compelling as it was within the soul of John Church, the publican accordingly resolved to overlook the unexplained features of the subject and to concentrate himself upon the possible amount of cash for his pocket.

"Never masticate over the making of money" was one of his dictums.

And so it came about that Church paid a call on Kate again next day. He came in company with Henry Porter, who bore witness to the debt of fifty pounds owed Mrs. Thomas and assisted in the portage of a quantity of plate, carried in a square basket to the clubroom of the Rising Sun to await disposal.

"This will make us a tenner and more!" enthused John Church, and Kate marked the use of the word "us." She said nothing, however, for that afternoon she called at Mrs. Crease's and removed her little boy from that lady's care. She had to lie, of course, promising her great friend that she would visit her again as soon as possible, and all the while she cursed herself for this deceit.

"God speed you back to Mr. Crease and me," said her friend, eyes streaming.

"Sflesh, darling, we'll be back before we're gone!"

Such falseness to so steadfast an ally was beyond redemption, and Kate had wept in turn at her wickedness as she walked away, her son's small hand clutched in her great red raw-boned one. "I'd fain be struck down fer what I done," she addressed his curly head.

So Kate was not prepared to argue with John Church over the commission on a sale of plate. Her natural greed had been momentarily displaced by her sense of contrition. Not even Mrs. Porter's "I'll mother him like my own" served to raise her spirits.

Now, Mrs. Thomas in a silent mope about some private matter and Mrs. Thomas forbearing to threaten him with the name of Strong instilled into John Church a new confidence, and he made preparations for the removal vans, ordering the Porter family about without mercy throughout the Thursday and Friday.

"Those curtains will go well in my clubroom," said he. "That carpet I'll have in my bedroom. Roll it up, Harry! Look sharp, Bobby!"

On Saturday he introduced a Mr. Henderson, greengrocer and Daedalean dealer in doubtful property, to inspect "what was in the offing."

"You'll come boating with us tomorrow, Mrs. Thomas?" asked Church, very benevolent. "Willie Porter, my wife and her daughter, and maybe some others?"

Kate agreed. Better Church in sight than out of it.

"Racing and boating, that's the life for me!" Church went on, checking the sacking tied between the dining-room chairs. "I likes it down here in Richmond too. Last time I was here was to see the Shah of Persia." He turned to Mr. Henderson. "You remember, Joseph? When 'is Highness went to see the botanic gardens out at Kew?" Mr. Henderson shook his head, not recalling this particular occasion, but Church prattled on about the various merits of touring royalty until Kate became impatient.

"The moving of all this stuff," she said, pointing at the stacked furniture, "what day's it to be?"

"Tuesday morning, ten o'clock on the dot. It's all fixed up with 'Enry Weston."

Satisfied, Kate took her leave of the two men and went down to the basement area. She made herself a mug of cocoa and remained in the kitchen until the men above called out their farewells and left the house. She would follow them in about twenty minutes, for she had no desire to travel in their company. With Church alone maybe, but not with the stranger Henderson. Why was Church dragging so many people into their business? Hoards of people milling about the house was a sure way to attract attention, worst of all, the attention of Miss Ives next door. It was dark when Kate let herself out of Mayfield Cottages, and her feeling of ill ease persisted.

211

Sunday came, and Kate gave her son breakfast before the Porters raised themselves from their beds.

"When do we have this outing with Mr. Church?" she asked Mrs. Porter when she came down.

"Noon. He's got a craft over on the south bank, and says to meet him there."

Kate looked toward her little boy. "I'll not take him," she said. He might fall in the river and drown; he might be sick on the water; he might catch cold, for it was blustery weather.

"I'll watch out for him," Mrs. Porter offered. "You won't get *me* in a boat, I can tell you! No, I'll be minding your lad and my Milly while you're gone, Kate."

This arrangement suited Kate, and she helped Ann Porter prepare eggs for the men upstairs.

As it happened, the excursion on the river was a pleasurable event. John Church, Willie Porter, Mrs. Church and her daughter, and a youth named Ambrose were all in high spirits, so that Kate relaxed and added her own brand of good cheer to the proceedings.

"We'll moor at Mortlake Fields and have a bite to eat," suggested Church, very much the skipper in command.

As the rowboat pulled in, Willie Porter made to leap ashore and fix the line. But his foot slipped on the bow plate and he tumbled into the muddy water, drenching those on board with the splash.

"Aarrh! A sea monster!" shrieked Ambrose as Willie's form dragged itself up out of the slime.

"Aarrh! The answer to the Barnes mystery!" echoed John Church.

They rocked the boat and roared their appreciation, all except Kate, who was quietly smiling to herself. Then a hand helped her onto the bank. It was Church, still grinning, a straw boater perched on the top of his head. Kate brushed down her skirts.

"And just what is this Barnes mystery?" she asked calmly.

But Church was being distracted by the others laying out the rugs and putting out the food from the hamper, so that she was obliged to tug his sleeve. "The Barnes mystery, what's that, Jack?"

"You'll find the pork pies under the napkins," Church called without turning to her. "What's that, Kate? The Barnes mystery, you say? Oh, that!" He gave her his attention. "Why, that's the chopped-up body they found in a box round 'ere! Sort of cooked it was."

It was as Kate had expected and no worse.

" 'Twas the prank of medics, or so they say." She laughed.

Church's smile faded. "No prank," he said. "Bloody murder, I'd say. And whoever done it will swing, I'd say."

Kate pulled a face as if unconvinced and walked off to where the rest of the party had laid out their picnic. She sat down upon the grass by Willie Porter, who served her pie and onions and a tin mug filled with ale.

"You're mucky as a pig farmer," she told him.

He moved away and his place was taken by Church. They ate together in silence, watching Willie's endeavors to tidy up his clothing. Kate finished her pie, leaned back on the grass, put her hands behind her head, and closed her eyes. So they had dubbed it the Barnes mystery. Clearly, the head had not yet been found. Nor would it ever be found. The carpetbag would have sunk to the bottom of the river, would have embedded itself in the ooze. Until they found a head no identification of the trunk and limbs was possible; so the Barnes mystery must

213

surely remain unsolved. Confident, Kate turned to where Church was sitting. The others were out of earshot, but she spoke softly. "Where's Strong, Jack?"

No reply, so she cocked open an eye. Church had heard and was looking down at her. There were crumbs in his beard around that prissy mouth.

"I don't know," he said. But worry showed in his eyes.

"You lie to me, Jack."

Church licked his lips. The pink of his tongue was of a paler hue than that of those lips. Kate judged that Church was anemic.

"Why do you lie?" she insisted.

"I don't. I swear to you I don't! If I knew, I'd tell you, s'help me!"

"Hush, man! Not so loud!"

But she believed him at last, and no more was said.

When they had eaten, the party romped together on the riverbank, Kate with Church's daughter. Then they clambered back into the rowboat and the men pushed off with their oars. Kate sat in the stern, Church's daughter on her lap. As was her custom when she was content, Kate sang the little girl a song.

"Once I was a waterman, and lived at home in ease,
 But now I am a mariner who plows the angry seas:
 I thought I'd like see ferrin lights, so bid my love adieu,
 And fixed as cook and steward boy, on board the Kangaroo.
 Oh, over many a ferrin sea I went, and to many's the ferrin shore,
 And many's the ferrin present unto my love I bore.
 There were tortoises from Tenerife, and toys from Timbuctoo,
 A Chinee cat, a Bengal rat, and a Bombay cockatoo."

She laughed and hugged the girl, pulling her plaits.

"What's ferrin?" asked the girl.

"Ferrin? Well, it's ferrin, that's all!"

"She means 'foreign,'" Willie Porter explained with slight contempt.

"I was in Bengal," Church put in. "And I've been to Bombay and all!"

Kate looked at him and winked. "Indeed, you are a man of many parts, Jack Church," she said.

"*And* I've sailed by Tenerife." Church was not to be deprived of a chance to regale an audience. "Went out to Indiah in summer 'fifty-seven in a three-master troopship, down the coast of Africa and round the Roaring Forties. Been to the Gold Coast too." And so he continued until they reached Hammersmith jetty. But Kate wasn't listening. She was staring over the gunwale into the greasy river water. Indiah—pronounced in the fashion of Mrs. Corbishly. An evil old broiler, that one. Would that it had been she who had been parceled off into the Thames and not Mrs. Thomas. A spasm of regret overcame Kate, so that she gripped the child closer and a heavy tear ran down her face.

" 'Tis a fine life that you've led by all accountin'." She sniffed at Church when she found the boat party looking at her with surprise.

III

Miss Ives had been busy—with the decorating of her hallway, with the early planting of some shrubs in the garden, with the sudden turn for the worse that had overtaken her frail mother.

Miss Ives had been too busy to notice how little she saw of her friend and tenant, Mrs. Thomas. But at last the comings and goings at the villa next door had attracted her attention. Who *were* all these men? They were not tradesmen of the town; they were not acquaintances—surely?—of Julia Thomas; and their continual calling at Number Two was not only unseemly but actually slightly suspect.

So upon the Friday Miss Ives was prompted to inch aside the lace curtains of her front parlor and to start a surveillance that day and the one that followed. Sunday's inactivity allowed her to rest awhile, but the peace also gave her time to think it over —to think back, to attempt to place noises and faces and snatches of conversation she had seen or heard over the past eight days or so. For example: Julia's maidservant had been very busy last Monday and Tuesday—hanging out washing at an unusually early hour, cleaning all the windows of the house, yet permitting breakfast things to remain uncleared upon the dining-room table. (Miss Ives had stolen a glimpse through her window on her way to shop.) And the back window to Julia's bedroom had been left open, wide open, over both Tuesday and Wednesday (a day when the weather was particularly inclement). And had she not heard the voices of both men and women while doing the tapestry in her workroom, voices that had droned on until past ten of the evening? Was it on Tuesday or Wednesday, or even on Thursday? She really couldn't remember. No matter. She was certain that *someone* had been tinkling the keys of Julia's pianoforte, not a thing Julia would choose to tolerate at so late an hour. And she was certain about a man she'd seen only yesterday, a man with a shock of hair, perched upon Julia's stool before Julia's davenport, writing in a notebook, a *very* coarse and common man indeed. She had seen him over the fence in her back garden.

That lumpish maidservant she had seen often, of course. Barging in and out, calling in a raucous voice to others in the house, carrying away parcels and panniers whenever she left the villa, bedecked with a nasty flashy pair of cheap gold earrings. How *very* strange it was.

Resuming her place of observation the next day, Monday, she saw the maidservant (what was her name again?) and the man with the vulgar dress of hair pay a short visit to the house. Miss Ives missed their leaving, for her agent had called with a fresh quotation on the price of paint for the hallway. But it was on Monday that she recalled the endless use of the copper and the noisome odors in the air of a week ago.

Lying in wait early upon the Tuesday morning, she noted that the maidservant was first to arrive (Mrs. Webster, she had remembered, the Irishwoman with an illegitimate child). Anxious to exchange words with Kate, Miss Ives rushed from her point of vantage, out of the house, and down her front path. But the surly maidservant had simply scowled in her direction and entered the villa, banging closed the door. Miss Ives returned to her house in a huff.

"I shall certainly speak of her to Julia when next we meet," she vowed.

And when two large horse-drawn vans clattered to a halt outside Number Two, Miss Ives confidently expected Julia Thomas to emerge from her retreat within. But she failed to appear. Men poured out of the vans and went inside, ushered in by the Irishwoman, and sounds of banging and scraping escaped the open door.

There were other sounds—of laughter, male and female. All morning it went on, and from time to time people would leave, walk up toward the junction and toward the Hole in the Wall (an establishment of whose custom and very presence Miss Ives did not approve). With great reluctance Miss Ives withdrew from her spying for lunch, but she denied herself her customary nap and returned to the front parlor at two o'clock, just in time to witness the loading of a chest of drawers onto the larger of the two vans.

Bless me, that's Julia's lowboy! she thought and sped into the hall to put on her coat. So furniture was actually being removed from the house. Why? Julia had said nothing to *her* of quitting her tenancy.

She opened the front door and went into the garden. A man in a cloth cap and overalls was lounging against her neighbor's fence, and Miss Ives hailed him.

"Pray tell me what is happening, my good man."

Henry Weston took his pipe out of his mouth. "Moving for Mrs. Thomas, mum."

Men passed, carrying a washstand.

"I was not aware that Mrs. Thomas was moving," said Miss Ives. "Where are you taking everything?"

Henry Weston shrugged. "Up to London." Then he caught sight of Kate standing just beyond the doorway of Number Two. "There's Mrs. Thomas now," he said. "I'll go fetch her over." And he went across to the front door.

Miss Ives did not wish to converse with her friend Mrs. Thomas over a garden fence like a commoner, so she retreated to her own doorstep and waited for the other to come.

But it was not Mrs. Thomas who cautiously came up the path; it was that Irish maidservant, Mrs. Webster. Each looked hard into the other's face. Miss Ives found Kate's expression both defiant and alarming.

"Miss Ives, is it not?" Kate said eventually, nervously grinding her teeth. "Is it me you wish to speak with?"

Miss Ives composed herself. "It is not. I should like a word with Mrs. Thomas about all of this." She indicated the vans.

"The furniture is sold," Kate replied. "Mrs. Thomas has sold it all up. Mr. Weston's having it away to Ham'smith." She was unable to pronounce the latter word in full.

"So I have been informed, and I say I want to consult your mistress."

" 'Tis all in order. I can show you receipts," came the stiff reply.

"I don't want to see any receipts; I want to see Mrs. Thomas!"

"She's not here, missus."

"Not here! What do you mean, 'not here'! Where is she then?"

"I don't know, missus."

"Why? Has she taken up residence elsewhere?"

Kate said nothing and looked down at her feet.

"Well, what *is* her new address? Can't you give me her new address?"

Kate lifted her head. Her mouth was turned down and surly. "No."

Miss Ives might have considered Kate's attitude as simply irksome had it not been for the troublous guilt that showed in her face—the face of a difficult child caught stealing jam in the pantry. Miss Ives resolved to say nothing more to her but to report her churlish manner to her mistress in due course. She turned on her heel and went into her house, shutting the door in Kate's face.

But once inside she again considered the strangeness of Kate's mien. If she still worked for Julia Thomas, then why not divulge her whereabouts? If she no longer worked for her friend, then what was she doing here, shipping off the contents of the house? Miss Ives was certainly not one to pry, but did it not become her bounden duty to Julia Thomas to make check upon her servant's extraordinary activities? Miss Ives put on her bonnet. She would go and see her agent, Mr. Frobisher, who helped manage and advise upon her leaseholds. Mr. Frobisher lived only a short distance away and would be at home and pleased to counsel her. Taking an umbrella in case it rained, Miss Ives left her house. She locked the door behind her, in view of the strange company next door, and set off at high speed to see her agent. She hoped that Mr. Frobisher might be good enough to return with her to Mayfield Cottages and question the Irishwoman further.

"'Oo was it then?" John Church asked Henry Weston. Church was in his shirtsleeves, despite the cold, and hefting the button-back chair out of the drawing room.

"Woman next door," said Weston. "Asked for Mrs. Thomas. Sent her over, but the woman next door acted all funny. Didn't hear what they was saying, but I reckons the woman next door don't care for her or us none. Shut the door on Mrs. Thomas, she did."

"How's that?" asked Church, but he already knew. In that instant it dawned on him what was happening, and the revelation pleased him not at all. Mrs. Kate Thomas might or might not be Mrs. Thomas, and it didn't matter a fig. What *did* matter was the fact that Mrs. Thomas was not entitled to be doing what they all were doing at the moment—namely, stripping a house bare of its contents for a quick sale.

"There is something wrong," Church said to Weston, putting down the chair in the hall. What he understood to be wrong was this: that he and his friends had been tricked by this Mrs. Kate Thomas into lending their services in a "lodger fraud," that Mrs. Kate Thomas was no more than a tenant of this furnished house, and now she was engaged upon an act of grand larceny, involving all of them up to the hilt. "We'd best fetch the goods back out of the van!" he cried, pulling down his shirtsleeves. "That bitch has led me astray! She's welshed on me!"

Henry Weston did not grasp the reason for his colleague's panic, but did as bade, unloading the vans rapidly one after the other, until the hallway of Number Two was stacked high with assorted furniture and bedding. And all the while John Church muttered curses concerning the treachery of women.

Kate heard and saw from the top of the staircase, and knew.

"So you're opting out?" she said to Church when he caught sight of her.

John Church mopped his brow with a polka-dot handkerchief, a brow wet from both exertion and fear.

"I want no part of this!" he snapped.

Kate came down slowly. The very worst was happening, but she was calm.

"You're in it, Jack," she said at the foot of the stairs.

Church stared at her with hatred. It was true. No police officer, no court of law, would believe him to be an innocent tool. The police had never liked him, his ways, and his success in running the Rising Sun; had they not tried to bar his liquor license only last week? And Kate Thomas knew the man called Strong. It grew blacker the more he thought upon it! Damn and blast, she'd shop him to save her own skin.

"There's one way out," Kate said.

"What's that then?" Any idea was welcome to Church at that moment.

"I'll skedaddle. I'll be off and away, and no one will be the wiser."

Henry Weston looked on stupidly. "What's up then?"

They ignored him, testing each other's eyes, and Kate was the stronger.

"Where to?" asked Church.

"Scotland."

Church nodded. The sooner he was gone from here, the sooner could he think for himself; the sooner he was rid of Kate Thomas, the sooner could he marshal his thoughts.

"Take these," Kate said and threw him two dresses draped over her arm. "Get yourself lost of them." She picked her way through the piled furniture and past him. Church saw that she still carried a bonnet box and a black dress over the other arm. "I'll go back by District. You take the vans," she said, and Church marveled at her poise.

"Shall I see you up in Hammersmith?" he asked, hoping that this would not be so.

Kate shook her head. She had no further use for a man so obviously just a braggart and a coward.

"You're safe, Jack Church," she sighed. "Zoodikers, but you're a man quick to turn a person up!" She ran a pin through her hat into her hair. "Take care, Jack. One fine day you'll get yourself disliked." And she marched out of the door with a stately bearing.

IV

The sea was rough, and the swell forced Kate to come up on deck to be sick for a second time. Her mouth foul with the taste of bile, she steadied herself against the rail and watched the black and fluffs of white of the waves below. She thought of her little son, battened down with others below, and prayed for a glimpse of dawn to show itself on the horizon.

As she listened to the pounding sea and stared out into the darkness, she took stock of her present situation. It had been a hasty flight, ill prepared and without funds sufficient to carry her farther afield. But it had been time to cast aside hope of profit, to leave behind persons and places she had known before. To have dallied might have been fatal. With Jack Church sniveling and Miss Ives playing the bloodhound, Kate had mustered her son and her resources and taken to her heels. Like old King James, she had been obliged to ride her white horse as far from the site of battle as the saints would allow. And the very rate of her departure! By cab from Richmond Station to the Broadway and to the Rising Sun, the collection of a bonnet box and a loan of money from Mrs. Church —not much, a half-sovereign and some silver from the till. And from the public house to the home of Annie Porter to collect her son. Young Robert had sensed the urgency but asked no questions, dressing her boy in his knickerbockers and best green jacket. Then the wild rush to the Metropolitan station in a hansom, the train to King's Cross terminal, followed by the long journey up to the port of Liverpool. Familiar sights and smells on the docks, but no time to waste with memories, and she had been fortunate to find this coal ship about to sail. The anchors weighed, the first mate found blankets for her son. He lay within them now, half dead with fatigue. But his mother still had over fifteen pounds in gold and paper money tucked inside her purse. She would breakfast him as soon as landed, pack him tight with food. Then south

223

they'd go, to County Wexford and the quiet safety of Killane.

Yet Ireland, of course, was British, a miserable pocket of Empire, much chastised by her Mother Queen for speaking loud or pointing pikes or concealing rent amid the rafter straw. And Ireland—place of Lawlers, kings, and heroes—had shown little truck for her when first she'd sinned, at sixteen years, against the might of law. Now she bore on her brow the mark of Cain, had perpetrated the most ultimate of crimes. Would her own protect her from the jaws of leonine justice?

But she'd be with her uncle on his boggy farm, and she determined not to advertise her presence abroad. She would avoid the market town and shun the public houses and stay away from Mass. In the latter respect she anticipated little difficulty; Kate Webster had not set foot within a church or taken Holy Sacrament for nigh on eleven years.

PART

2

THE ARM OF OLD MOTHER
ENGLAND

I

Returning to Wandsworth had required much pluck of Strong, and he fumbled nervously with his keys to gain access to the oil shop. Once inside, the familiar smell and silence gave him courage, and he lit a lamp on the hall dresser. The premises were small and plain—once built to house a canal man's family—with small rooms to left and right of the hall. Upstairs lay a long loft, used for storage, and reached by a short stairway with a rope banister. Strong took the lamp and climbed the seven steps. Habit told him where to avoid the rotten timber and how to slide open the trapdoor at the top. Within the attic a breeze from displaced roof tiles stirred the flame of the lamp and made the shadows dart. But Strong was unperturbed; he knew what it was he wanted, and he found his professional cache hidden beneath a pile of sacking in one corner. A brassbound trunk, the leather green with mildew, he opened to reveal a mass of ironmongery and five velvet pouches. The tools of his trade—and gold. He crammed his money into various pockets, surprised and reassured by the weight, and then began to select various tools with care. Picklocks, wire cutters, and a set of drill heads in a canvas bag. Best Birmingham or Sheffield steel every item, and they had cost him several pounds on purchase. Too good to be wasted, hence his return to the shop.

Strong's claw-hammer coat had been specially made, and he secreted his gadgets within unusual pockets sewn into the lining. Heavy as a gladiator, he shut the trapdoor to the loft and descended the rickety stairs. A last look around—to the rooms on either side, now dusty with disuse—and he blew out the oil lamp. A final sniff of the oil still lingering in various jars, and he let himself out.

Strong's donkey and trap were waiting, and he climbed aboard and flicked the reins in one motion. As the cart clip-clopped away and into the rapidly falling fog, Strong decided that his mode of transport had outlived its usefulness. Besides, there were those who knew him to be a vendor of coal oil.

He'd abandon the trap at Wimbledon Common and release the donkey onto some waste ground. He could kill the beast, of course—or could he? He dare not use his gun for fear of the report. And how did you cut a throat as large as that of a donkey? Strong decided that the animal must be spared its life and allowed to roam. Donkeys were not like dogs, after all; they did not follow their masters. Strong lashed out with the reins again. A strange feeling always came over him when he thought of dogs.

Katty Webster sometimes reminded him of a dog. Not a gentlemanly dog, not one of those West End poodle dogs from France or those yappy hairy creatures with ribbon between their ears. Katty Webster recalled something different, something big and black, one minute whining about her pup, next minute snarling and biting. A common alley cur.

"Charlie, come to my house; 'ad some bread 'n' jam. Stole me mammy's pudden; stole me daddy's ham," he sang quietly into the pea-green smog.

Yes, Katty Webster was a black dog all right. But she'd turned mangy, and her bunting days were done. He'd leave her be now. Isn't that what she wanted? Leave her be with her brat—his brat?—what did it matter? Perhaps she'd take up with an honest lad in due course, marry herself a navvygavvy or brewer's driver. Perhaps she'd settle down and become respectable.

But she'd left her mess on his doorstep, had she not?

"Bad cess to *you*, love!" he shouted, but his voice was lost in the mists.

Turned gammy, she had, bitched him up.

"If pa kills ma, who kills pa?" he tried to sing again. "Marwood! Marwood!"

II

John Lawler was with his pig, scratching her bristly back with a stick, when the trap arrived. Being a man of nearly eighty years, he did not hear the hoofs of the pony clopping into the yard, and it was Kate's call that attracted his attention. But his eyes were as poor as his hearing, and John Lawler saw only three blurred shapes sitting atop the trap.

"Uncle, it's me!" Kate cried again. "Don't ye know yer own long-lost niece!"

The old man put down his stick and stumbled over. Kate saw that he had aged beyond recognition, his face crisscrossed with lines and broken veins, his hair and eyebrows white instead of the blue-black she remembered. He was bent with a hump too, unshaven, and his smock was tatty.

Kate climbed down from her seat and put an arm around him. He smelled of manure and porter.

"Sflesh!" she said, "but you're an old fella now."

"Is it Katty?" he asked, without believing. "Is it really Katty?"

"Aye, that it is. And with her son, and the lot of us over from England just t'see you."

John Lawler uttered a little cry and kissed her on both cheeks. Then he stepped up to the trap, peered at her son, and patted his head.

"Did yer get me letter, Katty?" he asked, turning.

"That I did. And I've bided by my promise, Uncle. And we're here to stay, if you'll have us."

"Have yer? Have yer?" the old man repeated. "Why, I'll die of grief should you try to leave." And he helped Kate carry her bag and boxes into his cottage.

The farmhouse was much the same as Kate recalled. A tiny cottage—one room below and two above, reached by a steep and rickety staircase—with whitened walls, three feet thick, and a roof thatched with rushes. It had been built long before Cromwell gave its occupants the choice of hell or Connaught.

Kate pulled back the sacking on the single window of the downstairs room to let in light.

"Begod, but this'll take some cleaning," she said, looking about.

Her uncle laughed and shook his head sadly. " 'Tis been hard since your Aunt Mary died," he said.

Kate climbed the stairs and deposited her baggage in the vacant bedroom. There was only one bed, broken and leaning, but she was content to share it with her son.

"You've been living here on your own?" she asked John

Lawler when she returned downstairs. He was making a poor attempt to light a fire in the gigantic cross-beamed hearth.

"Aye, I have. But I have only now me pig and me goat and me Mary, and I can manage the three."

"Mary?"

"Me cow, named after your aunt. 'Tis fitting to keep a name in the family." He looked up. "And what's the name of your son, Katty? Yer told me in your letters but I clean forgot."

Kate told him his name.

"Now that's a poetical name, to be sure," said her uncle. "Fit for a priest or a president."

Kate made a noise of agreement. She would be happy here with John Lawler. Her little boy would be happy. And she would stay with her uncle until he joined his beloved Mary in the Killane churchyard. Then, perhaps, she would reconsider thoughts of the American continent. In the meantime she must pay off the trap driver and put her uncle's house into some semblance of order.

"Tell me about London town," John Lawler asked over supper.

Kate's son was in her bed above, and they were alone, and the old man was too excited by sudden company for sleep. An expression of his gratitude, a stone jug of poteen, stood on the table between them.

" 'Tis a terrible place," Kate told him. "Dirty streets, dirty fogs, dirty houses, and people—more people than you'd scarce imagine."

The old man nodded. "So have I been informed. Work?"

"Only gutterling jobs for the likes of us."

The old man poured her a stiff measure from the jug, content that he had stayed on his patch of farm and not followed so many others back in 1849.

"Tell me of your dead man," he said.

"Upped and left me for another three years back, and died a short while after—may his black soul rest in peace." Kate crossed herself.

The old man nodded again. Better not to question her about her husband, this mariner called Webster, for he could see that the memory pained her still.

"And what of my family?" Kate asked him.

The old man frowned and thought. "Not here, no more. Yer sisters all a-married and moved west. I know not of your brothers. Dick, I believe, went off for to be a soldier. I alone am left of your name and race, my girl."

Kate decided this an opportune moment to tell her uncle her conditions for remaining in his house. She did not wish to lie to him, but she had no option.

"Uncle"—she touched his hand—"I must speak with you. When himself died, he died insured. Not much, minding you, but sufficient to last the boy and me for a while. But I don't wish for others to have the knowledge of it, see? If certain folk find out, they'll be calling on me and saying, 'Katty this,' and 'Katty that,' and begging me to help them out. I'd like to help, Uncle —Mother of God, you knows I would—but I can't. And I've got to be thinking of me boy. I'll pay you for me keep, of course."

John Lawler put his free hand over hers and shook his head. "Not a word will I breathe, Katty. I swear it. But folks'll find out you're here, for sure; there's no way of stoppin' that!"

"But you won't tell them who I am, or that I'm from England?"

"No. And what *shall* I tell them?"

"That I'm from Glasgow. That I'm not a Lawler. That you knew me father, and that he sent me here to care for you."

"Someone might recognize you, Katty."

"I won't be stepping round for a time. Not to the town, nowhere. And I've changed a bit in sixteen years."

"Mass time?"

"No church, Uncle."

"No Mass! God save us, girl. You're sacrificing much for the sake of money!"

Kate smiled a bitter smile, but she did not laugh lest she offend her uncle.

"I'll have the father come visit you here," the old man reassured her after a moment.

"No! I mean no, Uncle. Not even the priest's to know."

"Not even Father Brannigan? Why, he it was who baptized you, Katty! And *he'll* not be after stealing your savings."

Kate stood up and corked the jug. "Not even he, Uncle. At least not until I tell you." She towered opposite him, waiting for his undertaking.

"So be it, Katty," he said with a sigh. "You are indeed a strange one, and you must be very, very rich!"

Kate walked around and helped him from his chair. With an arm about his narrow waist, she took the candle from the table and escorted him up to his room. She took him inside, put the candle down, and started to remove the leather stock from his throat.

"Come, come, girl," he protested. "I'll not have thee strippin' me, niece or not!"

But she ignored his objections, and made him take off one filthy layer of clothing after the other, until he stood unhappily in a set of verminous underwear.

"It's a bath for you tomorrow, me fine old man," she said. "And it's me who'll be doing the bathing of you—with the hardest, stiffest brush I can lay me hands on."

The old man wailed, but she pushed him toward his narrow cot with shrieks of laughter. She now had two men to nurse— one old, one young—and specters of the past momentarily flitted from her mind.

III

The days ran into a week and more, and Kate reorganized the cottage, the farm, and the daily living of her uncle with pleasure and alacrity. While her child skipped beside her, she mended the leather hinges of the door, cut a fallen tree into firewood, tended the livestock, and trained the goat to forsake his chompings in the potato patch. John Lawler, overawed and grateful, either looked on idly or made fleeting excursions into town to buy provisions with his niece's money. It was a cheery time, and the color returned to the cheeks of both mother and son.

Only with the sinking sun did Kate's high spirits wane. With the darkness came nights of dreams and visions. And talking to the old man, whose talk was limited, did little to lighten the joyless evenings. He would take himself off to his bed once he had supped, so that she was obliged either to sit alone and intoxicate herself in silence or creep upstairs and lie beside her little boy while her thoughts raced and remembered what lay beyond the Irish Sea.

A short distance down the rocky road to town was Power's Inn, no more than fifteen minutes' walk from the farm. Kate had seen the tavern when first she came, and she began to yearn for a glass of honest ale or Yard of Satin gin rather than the fiery poteen she'd been drinking.

"I'm going out," she told her uncle one Friday evening. "For a walk."

And she walked as near to Power's Inn as she might dare, admiring the lights at the windows and the occasional sounds of laughter from within. She searched inside her pockets for her clay pipe, to find it left behind, and this final annoyance served to shatter her resolve.

"The divil take it!" she swore and marched up to the tavern.

Faces turned to eye her as she walked in through the door, faces she had never seen before, with expressions ranging from blank indifference to mild interest. Power himself was behind the walnut bar, a bear of a man, with yellow beard and hair tied back with a black ribbon.

"Porter." Kate smiled at him and put down a penny.

Power served her in silence, and she drank with her back to the rest of the room, studying the rows of bottles beyond.

Then a slight figure joined her at the bar. "Would you like a chair?" The voice was silky. Its owner was a small man in his early thirties, with frizzed-up hair and a long and narrow nose. Kate shook her head and drank again.

"I'll be beggin' your pardon, miss," the man went on, "but the rule of the house is that ladies sit when drinkin'."

Kate looked at Power, and he nodded his endorsement of this rule.

Kate took her glass and sat at an empty table, ignoring the little man. But he was not to be discouraged and followed her over, drawing up a chair without invitation, a tot of amber liquid in his hand. He leaned forward so that his face was only inches away from Kate, and she observed him to have a pronounced squint.

"Is it at old Lawler's place you're stopping?" he asked. "I heard there was a fine, handsome woman such as yourself staying there." Though Kate didn't answer, he went on: "Me name's Keogh, Johnny Keogh, though me friends call me Corky. You can call me Corky if you wish. Are you old man Lawler's long-lost daughter, perchance?"

"I am not."

The little man pulled a face. "Shame on me!" he cried. "Of course you could not be his daughter, for you are far too young a woman. You are surely his granddaughter!"

"I am surely not."

"Aha!" He leaned back in his chair. "A woman as mysterious as she is beautiful."

Kate laughed despite herself.

"My name is Mrs. Webster," she said. "I'm over from Scotland to care for John Lawler. Me father and he were pals."

"Aha!" The little man turned in his chair and addressed the room at large. "This is Mrs. Webster, from Scotland, come to attend upon John Lawler in his old age. The very milk of human kindness!"

Greetings were murmured at Kate, and some of the men raised their glasses.

"Then buy her a drink, Corky!" someone shouted.

Corky Keogh took Kate's glass, got to his feet, and made a small bow. He reminded Kate of some kind of rodent, but he had charm and she was susceptible to charm. So casting caution aside, Kate allowed herself to be entertained by Keogh and his friends. Soon beguiled by beer and good companionship, she satisfied their kindly curiosity with a host of tales about her recent life in Glasgow. When she left Power's it was after midnight, and she was quite tipsy.

"If you're bold enough to down the beer, you're bold enough to take the Sacrament," her uncle told her on Sunday. A deeply religious man, he could not tolerate such backsliding.

Kate helped him fix his collar, and she brushed his suit about the shoulders—his Sunday suit of heavy broadcloth and unearthed by Kate from the bottom of a chest.

"Not yet, Uncle. Not yet."

John Lawler glared at her over his shoulder. "Not yet, you say? You were in a hurry to partake of a jar or two, but Holy Communion is less important, is that it, girl?"

Kate stayed calm and patted his cheek, feeling its stubble. "You've missed a bit shaving, Uncle," she said. "In future, I'll be doing yer shavin' for you."

The old man grumbled as Kate led him from the cottage to his donkey cart, but Kate knew that he'd soon forget. Would that she could accompany him; would that she could see Father Brannigan; would that she could confess to him.

Returning to the farmhouse, she took a missal from the window shelf and opened it. Half the pages were missing and the remainder yellow with age and damp. Her uncle never read this book. He had difficulty with all but the simplest construction of words, but she would read it now to her little boy. There was no need for the sins of the mother to be visited upon the son.

IV

The night was fine, clear and starry, and a warm breeze sang down from the surrounding hills. The song of the blackbird, thrush, and linnet had died, but an owl was challenging the neighborhood from a nearby wood as Kate came out of the cottage, pulling her shawl around her. A dry night and a Friday night. Power's would be packed with farming folk, and O'Mara was bound to have brought along his fiddle. There would be singing and dancing until the small hours, and Kate was eager with anticipation as she tripped along the path to the inn. If asked—and they were all bound to ask—she would certainly sing for them, and she hoped Corky Keogh had come with his recorder. And the songs she would sing for them would be sad, with a beauty to match the night. She would sing for them till dawn if they so desired.

Power had lit a lantern outside the entrance, and Kate paused to scrape the mud off her shoes with a stick before making her entrance. She wore Mrs. Thomas's best black dress, her cayman shoes, and carried her evening bag. She had brushed her long black hair with care that evening and pinned it into a bun with a pair of tortoiseshell combs. She considered herself "as pretty as a picture" and bounded into the tavern with a jaunty air.

Power was there in a freshly laundered shirt, and a fire blazed fiercely in the hearth. Rows of glasses lined the bar, waiting for their owners, and pots of fresh wild flowers had been scattered among the tables. Clearly, a fine party was at hand. But, for the moment, the only customer was an ancient and haggard crone, drinking porter in her favorite corner and muttering into her tankard. Kate was mildly surprised.

"Where are all the boys then?" Kate asked Power, stepping up to the bar.

Power shrugged and began to pour her a pint.

"O'Mara, Corky?" Kate asked.

Power replaced the jug of beer on its shelf and handed Kate her glass. "Not come," he said.

"They'll be along," Kate reassured herself as much as the publican and sat herself down at a central table. Power disappeared from sight to a cellar off the bar.

"Me da's been dead sixty year," the crone informed Kate from her corner. Kate nodded and smiled. Time passed.

"Me ma said for me always to wear blue," added the crone. "Said it matches the color of me eyes."

Kate agreed with her, watching the door.

"They transported me da'," the crone said suddenly, tapping the stone floor with her stick.

Kate tut-tutted.

"Buy me a drink!" insisted the crone in a furious voice.

Kate got up and went to the counter. "Mr. Power," she called, and the man emerged from the shadows. "What does she have?"

Power filled a half-pint glass from a wooden cask. "The cheapest."

"Make it a pint," Kate said. Where was everybody? She took the crone her drink—to be poked with her stick.

"What's that for?" snapped the crone.

"For you, mother." Kate smiled.

"I'm not your mother. Get away, you brazen hussy!"

Kate retreated and resumed her seat, her back to the angry crone.

After half an hour Kate guessed that something was wrong. She did not have Mrs. Thomas's hunter, but she put the hour as past seven o'clock. In normal circumstances the tavern would be packed by now. Yet Mr. Power had not noticed anything amiss.

Kate looked toward the bar. Power was there, polishing glasses, his face bored. Perhaps there was a fair in town? Yes, that must be it! Everyone had gone into Killane to celebrate some occasion. While Kate sat here like a lemon! Kate finished her drink with a laugh at herself.

She left her table and handed Power her empty glass. "Night to you, Mr. Power!" Of course, she could not go into Killane. She felt sad to be missing the gaiety. She dearly loved a fair. No matter, she would come here again tomorrow night; she would have O'Mara jigging with his fiddle until the strings melted with the heat.

Kate was quite sober when she reached John Lawler's cottage, and she vowed to compensate this frustrating evening with the assistance of several tots of the old man's vicious poteen. A light was burning downstairs. The old fellow was not yet in bed. Good, she could bear a bit of company.

She lifted the latch and went in. Three candles had been lit on the table, and her uncle was sitting at the far end. He looked up as she came in but said nothing. And then Kate caught sight of the other man.

He too was seated, away from her uncle, on the long bench, and he got up slowly. Kate observed him to be wearing a long blue cloak fastened at the throat by means of a silver chain. In his hands he held a hard flat-topped felt hat. His face was long and grave, with mutton-chop whiskers, and now he looked at her uncle inquiringly. The old man nodded and then buried his face in the crook of his arm upon the table.

"My name is Roach," said the man. He pronounced it "Roash," and Kate took him for an Ulsterman. A sound of sobbing came from her uncle. The stranger picked up a candle and held it high, inspecting Kate.

"Mrs. Webster is it?" he said. "Roach—Royal Irish Constabulary."

Kate felt her stomach turn and her legs weaken. She couldn't speak. None of this was real.

"You answer this description," Roach went on and handed her a slip of brown paper. "And I think your real name is Lawler, and that this man"—he jerked a thumb at her uncle—"is related to you."

Kate looked at the piece of paper, but the words were meaningless. Her eyes couldn't focus. Roach took it from her.

" 'Wanted,' " he read, " 'wanted for stealing plate, et cetera, and supposed murder of mistress. Kate, aged about thirty-two, five feet, five to six inches high, sallow complexion, slightly freckled, teeth rather good, prominent. Usually dressed in dark dress; jacket rather long and trimmed with dark fur around the pockets; light brown satin bonnet; speaks with Irish accent; and was accompanied by a boy, aged five, complexion rather dark, dark hair. Last seen at Hammersmith.' " Roach folded the notice and put it in his overcoat pocket. "Are you this Kate? Are you from Hammersmith, London? Apart from the clothing, this description matches you." His voice was harsh and unemotional.

Kate just stared from him to her uncle and back.

"Your uncle—if that what he be—has refused to say anything about you to me. But I've been upstairs. Your boy still sleeps. And you told a man named Keogh that your name is Kate Webster. What have you to say?"

Kate looked up. "Nothing, sir."

Roach stepped closer. "My advice to you is to say nothing. But you must come along with me." His eyes were as hard as pebbles.

"Where to?"

"To Killane and thence to Enniscorthy. You are wanted by the London police. They'll be here tomorrow. Come!" He put out a hand, and she drew away.

"I'll not come without me boy!" she said with a snarl, and Roach realized he had a potential tigress on his hands. He thought for a moment. It was contrary to normal practice, but this was a case of murder and the responsibility of the British.

"Very well," he said. "Fetch him down, but no tricks, mind."

Kate turned and climbed the stairs with leaden feet. This was still another nightmare from which she would soon awake.

She gently shook her son awake. "Up," she said. "You and your mother are going on another little adventure."

She dressed the boy and took him downstairs.

"Will he be all right?" Roach asked. No pity in his voice, just a desire not to be inconvenienced.

"Have I no time to pack me bags?" Kate asked.

Roach shook his head. "Just bring along enough for you and him for the night. Your property will be picked up here tomorrow by my men."

Kate understood. The Boys of the Crowbar Brigade—the R.I.C.—they would tear the cottage apart to find the evidence they wanted. Suddenly, Kate felt resigned. She went over to her uncle. His head was up now, and his eyes red from the tears he'd shed on her behalf. He was a good man, and she pitied him.

"Fare thee well, Uncle," she said as brightly as possible.

"Is it true, Katty?" The old man's voice quavered.

"Not a word of it. Believe nothing you hear. It will all be lies and slanderisings."

John Lawler tried to get up, to embrace her, but she held him down. A shock of this kind could kill him for sure. If it was slaughter the police desired, then it was enough that they killed her alone.

"I'm ready when you are," she said to Roach.

IF PIERCED BY THE ARROW OF
WOE

I

They put Kate and her son in a small detention room and left her there for a night and a day, providing three simple meals and a bucket of coal for the fire. The men of the Enniscorthy police station were reluctant to handle her case and treated her with polite indifference, acceding to her demands but anxious for true authority to arrive from London.

That authority came in the form of Inspector Dowdell of Scotland Yard, a friendly man with straggling mustaches and a bright smile. He had come via Dublin, in which city he had been joined by Inspector Jones. Dowdell examined the property and possessions retrieved from John Lawler's farm before introducing himself to his charge.

It was eleven o'clock in the evening when first he saw Kate in her cell. She took him for a doctor rather than a policeman when he stood in the doorway.

"Me boy can't sleep," she said at once.

Inspector Dowdell crossed the room to the mattress upon which her son lay. He felt his forehead for signs of fever. But the boy's head was cool.

"Prrps 'e's 'ungry?" he ventured. He beckoned to the turn-key. "Get the lad a bit of bread and some cocoa."

"Cocoa?"

"All right then, tea!"

The turnkey retired, and Dowdell turned to Kate. "Sits ye down, miss," he said gently. He took off his checked cap and produced a notebook from within his cape, and Kate realized he was a police officer. He then took out a stiff card and held it up for her to see.

"It's my card," he explained. "My name is Dowdell—Inspector or Mister, whatever you wish—and I'm here to fetch you back to England. Sorry." His apology sounded sincere.

"Me boy?"

"I can't say just as yet. Anyone 'ere who can care for him?"

"No."

"And your uncle's too old, of course."

"That he is."

"So you admit to being his niece, and true name Lawler," he said quickly, jotting down this discovery in his notebook.

"I admit to nothing!" Kate was angered by his trick.

"But of course not, miss! And very sensible too, if I might be so bold!" He allowed himself a slight smile. "Say nothing if you don't want to," he added gravely. "If you do, down it goes in this little book, and I gets to repeating it later. Understand? Good. Now, nonsense over, I'll tell you why I'm here and why you are taking a sea trip home. Hold hard now! Let me finish. You will be charged with the murder of one Mrs. Julia Martha Thomas of Number Two Vine Cottages, Richmond, in the fair County of Surrey."

"Mayfield Cottages," Kate put in. "They changed the name just afore I arrived there."

"Aha! So you further admit that you were in the employ of the late Mrs. Thomas!" Dowdell had used the old address deliberately. "And," continued the inspector, "you will be further charged with the larceny of certain property—to wit, furniture —from the said address."

Kate opened her mouth to speak, but the inspector stopped her. "Now shut your trap, you silly woman!" he said. "Don't you realize that this is a *capital* charge!"

Kate kept silent. She liked this man; he was not a mutton-shunter like Pew.

"That's better for the both of us," the inspector said. "Well, I'm off. I'll see about your lil' lad's supper for you. And I'll see *you* again in about 'alf an hour. Got to drag you up before a beak, it seems, to get the right to jack you away. Typical, bloody typical!"

And off he went, apparently without concerning himself about the security of Kate and the open cell door. But a few moments later his head popped around the jamb.

"And watch out for my colleague, Inspector Jones," he whispered. "He's Welsh, and not a man to be trusted." A wink, and Inspector Dowdell left again.

They took Kate before the magistrate, who read the warrant and formally remanded her in custody for transfer to England.

"You say she is accused of murdering her employer?" he asked the inspector. "Has the body been found?"

"Most of it, sir," came the reply, and the magistrate winced.

Dowdell and Jones came for her at eight the next day with two uniformed members of the Irish Constabulary, and together they traveled to the railway station in a police vehicle.

Kate watched the busy streets from the small wired window, but not a single glance of interest came their way. Roach was there at the station to meet them, to exchange documents with Dowdell and finally resign all responsibility for the prisoner. Kate spoke only to her son, who was cheerful and excited at the thought of yet another ride on a train, and the various police officers did not attempt to engage her in conversation.

The Dublin train was crowded, the bare wooden coaches jammed tight with people and livestock, so that a great commotion was to be heard along the length of the platform.

"To the last carriage," Roach rasped to Dowdell, and they were escorted to the end of the train, to an ordinary coach coupled onto the guardsman's van. A second class compartment, with upholstered seats, was reserved and empty.

"Sit between Mr. Jones and myself," Dowdell advised her. "Your lad can sit by you." And he leaned out of the window to speak with Roach until the whistle blew and the train began to shunt out of the station.

Kate leaned back into the seat and stared at a fluted mirror on the opposite wall. She tried to think who might have told the police about her.

"Mr. Dowdell," she said, and he was all ears in an instant. "Tell me this. Is there any person in custody for the murder?"

Dowdell looked surprised. "Yes, you are, miss!"

"No, I mean in London?"

Dowdell became wary. "I don't know if I can answer that question at all," he said.

Kate sniffed. "Well, there should be!" she said after a deliberate pause.

The two policemen said nothing. They were afire with anticipation, and Kate inwardly laughed. Very well, she'd give it to them: "It is very hard that the innocent should suffer for the guilty."

Dowdell's notebook was again in his hand as if by magic, but Kate taunted him with another bout of silence, and the train chugged along.

"I hope you're not puttin' the blame on an innocent party, miss!" the inspector said to coax her.

"I can only tell you the truth of things," said Kate. But she then commenced to tell her son a long and involved story concerning a pixie and a crock of gold.

"I shall tell *you* a story too, when I'm so minded," she said to Dowdell at the end.

"Not another fairy story, I trust."

"No. 'Twill be the truth I'll be telling you, sir."

They reached Dublin at midday, and a cab was engaged to transport them to the police station in Chancery Lane, behind the castle.

Kate played with her son in a converted storeroom until the inspectors came for her at seven. They proceeded by police van to Westland Row Station for a train to Kingstown, where their ship was berthed, and Kate gazed once more from the window at passers-by in the evening gloom.

"I see that they know nothing of me," she said to Dowdell.

A short laugh. "They do in London, miss, rest assured they do!"

At Kingstown the ship, a steamboat of doubtful reliability, was delayed by the weather. A wind was up, and the waves punished the quay, so they retired to the office of the dockside police and customs men, where they were fed broth and fried eggs. Kate's boy fell asleep on her lap, and a blanket was borrowed to cover him up. Soon all were asleep, gathered around a hissing iron fire in the center of the shed, and there they remained until aroused sometime later with news that their ship was ready to battle the seas.

"I shall be sick," said Kate as they mounted the gangplank. So she was taken below to a cabin strewn with charts and instruments, where they gave her a basin and left her alone. Her son still slept, put on a bunk by the sailor who'd borne him aboard, and Kate stroked his head when her retching was done.

A knock on the door, discreet but demanding, and Inspector Dowdell appeared. He sat down at a brassbound desk and moved compasses and sextants aside to make room for his elbows. Then he leaned with his chin in his hands and stared at Kate. He too was unwell, but he had his duty to do.

"The story?" he asked.

Kate left the bunk and came over. She tried to move a chair by the porthole but found it screwed to the floor. Dowdell got up and offered her his at the desk, perching himself on the edge.

"Well?"

Kate looked at his hands. "Where's yer little book then? I want for this to be in writin'."

Dowdell shook his head. With the pitch and the roll of the boat, he could not hope to pen a solitary line of sense. "I'll remember what you say," he said.

It was Kate's turn to refuse. Her statement had to be exact, otherwise no statement. Dowdell must not let this opportunity slip.

"Tell you what I'll do," he said. "You tell me now, and I'll get it down when we're home. Then I'll read it over to you for your approval, to sign it yourself if you want. What about that?"

Kate considered his suggestion.

"Will I get a lawyer?" she asked suddenly.

"You will."

"But I've not the money, man."

"It's murder. You'll have your lawyer for sure."

"I done no murder!"

Dowdell tugged at his mustache. "I know. But you say you know who did. Help me, and you help yourself."

Kate drew out a pouch of tobacco and her pipe and put them on the desk before her. She dared not smoke, however, much as she cared to.

"D'you know of a man named Church?" she asked.

A nod.

"Then you know the man you're after. Church killed her. At least I think so; I didn't see him do it. Was it he who told you where to find me?"

"No. We found a letter from your uncle in a dress." Dowdell's voice did not reveal the turmoil of his thoughts. So Church *was* in on it, after all. "Go on."

"Church has surely tried to come off zeb and lied to you," Kate said quietly and with conviction. "He gives me no choice but to tell you all. He's been the ruination of himself."

And she proceeded to tell Inspector Dowdell everything that she would have him believe.

"How much of that can you remember now?" she asked him when she'd finished.

It was a tale Dowdell would not forget.

"All of it. It'll be wrote down when we gets to Lunnon." He tugged nervously at his mustache again, twiddling the waxed tips. "But let me just understand this right, miss," he went on. "You say that you have known Church for nigh on seven years;

that Church comes round to Mrs. Thomas and suggests that you and he give her some noxious substance, poison her unto death, and then do a bunk to America; that you sensibly refuses, but that next day he's already done it when you get back from seeing your boy; that he threatens to serve you the same with a carving knife if you don't go in on his plans; that—"

"He said he'd stab me with it to the handle," Kate interjected. "I was fairly fainting with the fear!"

"Yes, I dare say you was. That Mrs. Thomas was lying half dead on the mat in the passage of her house—"

"And groaning piteously, sir."

"And groaning piteously, yes. And that you were taken to Mrs. Porter's by Church. And that all of this happens on Monday, March third?"

"I swear it is true!"

"And that next day, having met with Church in the street, you arrange to meet him at a hotel near Richmond Bridge."

"I took along Bobby Porter for me own safety," Kate insisted.

"But you went alone into this hotel. You met Church. He gives you the keys to Mrs. Thomas's house and orders you to fetch a box from there, with young Porter's help, and bring it to the bridge, to leave it on the bridge?"

"To be sure," Kate said. "I asks him, 'What are you going to do with it?' and he says to me, 'That's me own business,' but I did as I was told. Bobby and I went to the bridge. Bobby hung back a bit, but I put the box on the bridge. A tall man came along, told me to be off after Bobby. I left, then I hears a splash."

Dowdell grunted. "Who was this tall man?" he asked. "Ever seen 'im before?"

"No, sir."

Another grunt. "And the carpetbag. You say you were told to

251

bring a carpetbag away from the house as well?"

"Aye, that is so. Bobby had it with him."

"What was in it, d'you know?"

Kate swallowed. "No, sir. At least, I was told it was only books and meat, sir."

"Meat, you say?"

"Indeed, sir. Excuse me, sir, but I think I'm going to be sick again!" and Kate ran for her basin.

II

They disembarked at Holyhead and took a fast train to London, Kate now strangely silent after her long talk to Inspector Dowdell. Throughout the tedious journey across England, Dowdell went over all that she had said. He had interviewed the Porter family—as had Inspector Pearson, his associate back in Richmond—and he had questioned the Churches. Could this woman be right about what she said? Or was it a devilish attempt to involve an innocent man? Church was a slimy rogue, by all accounts, a profiteer who had evaded prosecution many times in the past by guile. A toady, a liar, a cheat—yes to all of those descriptions. But was he really a *murderer?* Two aspects of his charge's version of events troubled the inspector sorely. A photograph and a printed card, the face and name of Church, had been recovered from the Lawler farm among her possessions; and, more significantly, had not Robert Porter made mention of a "tall man" passing by him on that night upon Richmond Bridge? Inspector Dowdell would talk with Pearson, suggest a direct confrontation between the Irishwoman and the man she accused.

"Will you be arresting Jack Church?" Kate asked him an hour or so from the outskirts of London.

"You call him Jack, do you?"

"Aye. We've been pals for years, remember."

Not according to the publican. He had told both Pearson and Dowdell that the woman was a total stranger to him. And Church referred to her as Mrs. Thomas. If an atom of Kate Webster's tale were true, then Church was an accomplished actor.

The train pulled into Euston at last, hissing and roaring, clouds of smoke billowing out of the funnel. They got off and hired a porter for their baggage, while Inspector Jones carried the potential exhibits found at the Lawler farm in his official grip. Dowdell wondered whether to handcuff his charge, but decided to forgo it in view of the presence of her child. The boy was still happy, obviously unaware of his mother's plight, and Dowdell did not want a wailing infant on his hands.

A Black Maria—a two-horse carriage of blue with V.R. depicted on the sides in gold—was waiting in the station forecourt, and they climbed aboard amid stares from other passengers and railway personnel.

"Not the first time you've been in one of these, eh, Kate?" Jones said when they were all inside.

"Mrs. Webster to you, young fella," Kate replied. "No, I've been in a 'Virtue Rewarded' before, as well you know."

Dowdell said nothing, but he was thinking of Kate's criminal record. He had been provided with a copy at Scotland Yard. Burglary, shoplifting, receiving, and one case of drunk and disorderly. But no hint of violence, nothing to equate with murder.

It took more than an hour to reach the police station at Richmond, and a sudden terror possessed Kate as they dismounted from the cab. Pew! What if Police Constable Pew had been part of this investigation?

Inspector Dowdell didn't notice the change in her expression, for he had now to perform a duty he had been dreading throughout the long passage from Ireland.

"Come inside." He showed Kate through a door in the yard. "Inspector Jones will take your boy off now for a bite to eat. I expect the nipper's famished." He made light of it, and Kate was deceived.

Dowdell led Kate down a narrow passage of whitewashed brick and into the charge room. As they came in, a middle-aged woman dressed in gray got up from a chair and approached. Kate recognized her uniform. A prison wardress.

"This is Mrs. Webster," Dowdell said to the woman. "I shall give her into your custody in a moment. No, please don't go! I would prefer for you to remain." He turned to Kate. "Your child, Mrs. Webster," he began, and he saw the fear enter into her eyes. "I'm afraid your boy cannot go with you. Regulations, you see. It would be quite impossible." Kate drew back from him. Her face began to twitch, and the prison wardress moved closer. "Your son will be well cared for, I promise!" But Kate was at him, clawing his face and kicking out in every direction. The prison wardress took hold of her arms, only to be hurled to the floor, and it was Inspector Dowdell, using all his strength, who pinned her against the charge-room wall, trying to calm her with words. "He'll be all right. You'll see him again tomorrow—I shall arrange for him to be brought here—but meanwhile you *must* be sensible and brave!" Slowly the life seemed to run out of Kate, until she slumped down into a sitting position, too weary either to continue fighting or to weep.

The prison wardress picked herself up, cursing foully. "You'll charge her with assault!" she said to the inspector. But he was paying her no attention, and she had to repeat her demand.

"Have you no children of your own?" he asked. Had she no pity? He put out his hand to help Kate to her feet, but it was ignored. He retrieved his hat from where it had fallen. He too was tired. He must leave his charge to the tender mercies of the wardress. At the door he stopped and looked around. "Be kind to her!" he ordered.

III

Kate passed the night in the Wandsworth House of Detention, a night without rest and full of thoughts only for her little boy. She felt, however, that Dowdell was a kindly man and that he would be true to his word.

In the morning a police van took her back to Richmond, and Inspector Dowdell was waiting in the charge room with another uniformed police officer whom he introduced as Pearson. Dowdell sat at a table, a pile of paper before him, ink and pen to one side.

"My boy?" was her first inquiry.

"He'll be here at eleven. You'll see him then. In the meantime . . ."

"Where did they take him?"

"He is being cared for by the parish. They'll make all the arrangements, and he'll be safe."

Kate then took the chair pulled out for her and folded her arms. She must concentrate now on her statement about Church.

"I have known John Church for near seven year now, having

first got acquainted when I was living two or three doors from him, at the Porters'. He used to take me out to London, and to various public houses." And so she went on, while Dowdell dipped his pen and scribbled furiously.

"You say that he stabbed Mrs. Thomas at about teatime on Monday, March third?" asked the inspector called Pearson.

Kate nodded. "While I was out seeing me little boy. I never laid a hand on Mrs. Thomas, and had nothing to do with the murderin' of her. But I knew Jack Church had done it. And all the money left in the house was a five-pound note and thirty shillen. This note I changed at the fishmonger's in Richmond. Church and Porter were with me at the time." She paused and added, "I intend for to tell the whole truth, as I don't see as why I should be blamed for what Church has done."

"You are wise to tell us everything," said Dowdell.

"I wouldn't accuse my greatest enemy of anything wrong, let alone a friend," Kate replied, "which Jack Church has been to me up till now!"

Inspector Dowdell stopped writing and wiped his pen on a cloth. "Then I'd like you to meet your greatest friend," he said and beckoned toward a constable standing by the charge-room door.

When John Church came in, he looked about inquiringly.

"Hullo there, Jack!" Kate said.

"Do you know this woman?" Pearson asked Church.

"Why yes, it's Mrs. Thomas." But Kate was so haggard and disheveled that he went on: "At least I think it's she."

Kate laughed. "C'mon Jack now! 'Tis me, Katty Webster. Stop putting on a quare line of talk, man!"

Dowdell came from behind the table, Kate's statement in his hand. His face was grave when he spoke.

"Mr. Church, I just want you to listen carefully to this, to what Kate says." And he began to read everything Kate had told him in the last half hour, pausing to study Church's reaction from time to time.

"And now I must warn you not to say anything—anything at all—unless you want to, Mr. Church," he concluded. "Inspector Pearson is bound to write down what you say, and it could be used in evidence. Do you follow?"

But Church was laughing, laughing until the tears ran into his beard, and Dowdell frowned at such levity.

"This is a serious matter," he warned.

"No, no, no," Church said when capable of speech. "Why, the lying woman, how *can* she say that about me? I know *nothing* of her!" He was about to add more when Pearson touched his sleeve.

"Follow me," ordered the inspector, and Church was taken from the room still shaking with laughter.

Kate caught Dowdell's eye. "What about him?" she asked.

Dowdell resumed his chair at the table. What indeed? At the moment his colleague was charging John Church, publican, with the murder of Julia Martha Thomas and with stealing various articles of plate and silverware recovered from the Rising Sun. They had no alternative. The Barnes mystery was far from solved.

"Do you wish to add anything to this?" he asked Kate, picking up his pen and dipping it into the inkwell.

Kate thought she'd embellish her version. Wasn't she supposed to be the maligned party? The innocent must always be outraged and ready to speak.

"I can tell you *this,*" she said. "Church it was who wanted me to help to fetch the furniture away. He then asked that Henry

257

Porter do the valuing, which he does, at fifty pound. And between 'em they fixes things to sell, and beguiled me on a party on the river, nice as pie and a-hoping that I'll mind me tongue, the devils! Then we come to the day we tried to fetch away the property; I was at Mayfield in the afternoon, and the vans come up, all arranged, so t'speak. And out comes Miss Ives from next door, and speaks she to the carman, asking who and what for Mrs. Thomas's furniture be going. And Church gets himself into a rare old tizzy, asking me to step round and ask the old lady if rental still be owing from Mrs. Thomas. For to calm her down, you see? But Miss Ives ain't fooled at all, not at all! So I tells Church as how she's got the eye on us, and Church says to me, he does, that he thinks Miss Ives might be nipping off to call the police. And such a terrible anguish in a man you never saw! Church is near to wetting himself like an infant in the cradle! So he instructs that I be off with meself." Kate paused. "But he gives to me his portrait, he does, and his address!"

Dowdell nodded. "Go on," he said.

"Well, so I'm off as told. To Hammersmith for me boy and a loan of cash from Mrs. Church—now there's a drinking woman for you!—and thence to me uncle's farm in Wexford, where you retrieved me from my misery."

Dowdell lowered his pen. He'd been able to take down very little of this owing to the rapidity of the telling. And he wanted more detail if possible.

"Mrs. Webster—may I call you Kate? Thank you. Kate, I must get this down on paper. Now you just tell me about it all once more—and slowly please—and you mustn't mind if I interrupt so as to clear up anything I don't fully understand. Do you follow me? Good! Now let's start again. You say that Mr. Church wanted to know how to get the furniture away?"

He took a further statement, checking Kate whenever she spoke too fast and putting odd queries when he failed to comprehend a point. Kate gave him all that her powers of imagination could muster, finishing with an explicit account of foodstuffs brought from the house, having decided to prove herself at least a conscientious manager of the Thomas household.

"Well?" asked Pearson, when Dowdell had done and Kate had been allowed to visit with her son.

Dowdell sighed and looked at a clock on the wall. Noon. He could be with his family in time for lunch if he could get away.

"You've charged Church?" he asked.

"Yes." And Church had prevailed with his lunatic laughter to the end.

"She admits to being an unwilling accessory after the fact," said Dowdell.

"You believe her?"

"No. I think she was party to it all the way along."

"And Church?"

"He too. No man laughs when accused of murder, do they, Fred?"

Pearson looked uncertain. "What about that fellow up in Sheffield last month? *He* did, and he was a butcher."

"Old Charlie Peace, you mean? Yes, that's true. But Charlie was no Church."

"What about this other business from that part?" Pearson ventured. "Young Pew."

Dowdell nodded. What indeed? Pew had been his case—on his files with the stamp of top priority—until only a week ago. "The commissioner—lord and master, mine and thine—has taken him away from me," he told Pearson. "London's sending down a mob from Westminster to ease that bobby's restless soul."

"Glad they're treating it so important," said Pearson with satisfaction.

But Dowdell laughed. "Beggar that!" he said. "I figure Pew's just a simple copper who got himself ramps by wandering astray out of the line of duty! Someone tries to roll him. He puts up a fight, and that someone pulls a pop. No, no black edging or raised truncheons for PC Pew—not so much as a mention on the force's scoreboard." The look of sadness on his colleague's face made Dowdell continue. "Once a bobby takes off his uniform, he becomes no better than a loaf. Ramp a loaf, and that's murder simple. Well, you can't dress up the corpse to make it look otherwise, can you? And PC Pew was acting the loaf the night he died. How can we show otherwise?"

"Maybe he was acting undercover?" suggested Pearson, full of hope.

"Naugh! Least, not to anyone's knowledge."

A brief silence followed, with Pearson clasping and unclasping his hands.

"One day we'll have us a plainclothes mob," Dowdell reassured him.

"To be called a bunch of spies, I daresay!"

Dowdell shrugged. "Perhaps. But in the meantime I'm obliged to forsake young Pew and concentrate myself on what is left of Mrs. Thomas."

"More important than a copper, eh?"

Dowdell saw no reason to delude the other. "Of course. *She* was a respectable lady of the town, wasn't she? She paid her rates and bills, and she had friends with influence in the parish.

Compared to that lady, PC Pew was fourpence to a guinea piece."

A thought struck Pearson. "They bothered when it was Charlie Peace," he said. Did the murder of a police officer only become grave when the assassin was notorious?

"Leaving Charlie to Mr. Marwood, Fred," Dowdell said, "who do you have in mind for Clay Pipe Kate? She'll need a lawyer."

Pearson knew most of those solicitors prepared to take on work of a criminal nature, and his mind flitted from one firm to another. Kate Webster was Irish. Very well, let she have the services of a fellow countryman.

"I'll suggest O'Brien," he said.

"And Church?" asked Dowdell. He wanted both parties fully represented. Time would be saved, reputations spared, and a quiet gentility promised when the case came before the Richmond justices.

"Church has stolen silver sufficient to hire the House of Lords," said Pearson.

IV

Kevin Fintan McGreevy O'Brien was a quiet and austere man, long of face and body, with a quick and desperate walk. He had left his native Clonmel more than thirty years ago, and his acceptance as a practicing solicitor of the British Supreme Court had been a long and painful business. But the London police and prison authorities had grown to like him, to send him work, hopeless cases in particular.

And now they had presented him with his first capital case,

a murderess. He was unhappy as he turned off the Wandsworth Road toward the Female House of Detention. Normally the state did not render its funds available to assist the poor in criminal matters, pursuing a policy of polite helplessness should application be made. But a case of murder could be different. Interest in the so-called Barnes mystery had heightened once the description of the woman had been circulated. "Big and freckle-faced," said one newssheet. "Of immense proportions, possibly a negress with a whitened face," said another. "Rumored to have talons caked with gore," cried a third. Mr. O'Brien was very worried by the prospect of representing such an ogress. But she was Irish, and he was Irish and therefore duty-bound to do his utmost.

The remand prison was an obscure building set in a side road under a mass of elms and plane trees. O'Brien, who had never been there before, paused to examine the exterior. A workhouse once, he judged, and before that anything from a temperance house to a brewery.

The prison door was small and cut into a wooden wall. He tolled the iron bell outside it. The door was opened, he showed his credentials and was accepted in. He was shown across a quadrangle and down passages until the door of a cell was flung wide and his presence announced loudly by the wardress.

Kate Webster sat on a stool by her palliasse; she rose slowly to greet him. O'Brien's head nearly touched the cell's ceiling, and he was obliged to stoop as he came forward. He took Kate in from toe to head, noticing the scuffed boots, the dusty black dress, the pallor of her skin in contrast with the dark hair and eyes. This woman looked more fifty than her said thirty years.

"My name's O'Brien," he said. "Please sit yourself down. I've been appointed your lawyer. And we must have a chat."

262

"The inspector said that you'd be comin'," said Kate. "How is he?"

"Mr. Dowdell? Very well, I think."

"No, not *him*. Me child. How is the boy?"

She had not heard for three days. Promises had begun to be broken.

Dowdell had warned O'Brien of this single love in the woman's life, and the solicitor was prepared.

"Well. He's been transferred to the village of Sheen, to an orphanage there. He is thriving."

"Thriving, you say? No child o' mine can *thrive* in an orphans' home. And he's not an orphan, is he?"

"Sit you down, Mrs. Webster," said O'Brien. "Now hear this. Your lad is better cared for where he is than in a parish home —where he could be put. Do you understand?"

Kate nodded and resumed her stool. O'Brien opened his leather bag and took out a notebook, some sheafs of foolscap, and a bundle of stiff white paper tied with a red ribbon. He looked about for another chair. There was none, so he sat on the palliasse, paper on his knees, his long legs splayed out across the brick floor.

"I have your statement made to Mr. Dowdell," he said.

" 'Tis true, every one word of it!"

"They don't think it contains everything though," said O'Brien. Dowdell had expressed his views, and O'Brien saw no reason not to pass them on to his client.

"They say Church has an alibi for the third of March, something to do with a burial club to which he belongs. And your Mr. Porter says that it was he who introduced you to Church, and not until a short while ago. What have you to say about that, Mrs. Webster?"

263

" 'Tis a lie!"

"Why should Porter lie?"

A good question, to which Kate had no answer. Unless . . .

"I'm not wanting to involve Henry Porter," she said, but she knew that she had no choice now other than to implicate him.

"Very well," O'Brien said. "But you just think about it, for your own sake. Meanwhile, I want you to tell me as much about yourself as you can recall. Everything, from the moment you came over to this country."

And he spent the next hour prising details from Kate. Some of what she told him was the truth.

When Kevin O'Brien had gone, Kate thought things over. Strange that they should provide her with an Irish lawyer. Perhaps his fees were lower? No matter. O'Brien was an educated man, and she was confident that he would do his best for her. And she was glad that he had informed her of Church's alibi. Silly of her not to have anticipated such a possibility. So Church was wriggling free, and he had Porter on his side. Poor luckless Henry! But now she was bound to unite him with Church. Not as a murderer but as an accessory. She would do it carefully, so that they would not actually prosecute him. Her only concern was to pin down Church, spread confusion, and raise doubts about her own role. It was wicked to spin such a web of lies. But her peril was great, and she hoped God would forgive her this once.

April marched on, but still Kate held back her exposé of Henry Porter. O'Brien pressed her to speak up whenever he visited the House of Detention, but Kate, experienced in the courts, resolved to hold her fire until the last possible moment.

"On Wednesday we are before the magistrates," O'Brien told her.

"Will I get to see me boy that day?"

They had brought him to visit her twice at the House, but she knew Dowdell would try to have him at the court if permissible.

"I will speak to the inspector," said O'Brien. "Now, are you going to tell me what you know about Henry Porter?"

Kate laughed and shook her head, and her solicitor gathered up his things to leave. "I can only urge you to reconsider," he said and rang for the wardress to let him out. Instinct told him that he'd rue the day he'd been assigned this case.

Wednesday came, and they fetched Kate from the House at eight, taking her to Richmond in a hansom. Dowdell had charge of her, for she was his responsibility whenever removed from prison. Dowdell had anticipated the wave of popular ill feeling now directed against his prisoner, so he had used the hansom; a Black Maria attracted attention and invited trouble.

But a notice had been placed outside the red brick courthouse listing the proceedings of the day. It carried Kate's name for all to see, and a large crowd was gathered at the court when they arrived.

"Sblood!" said Kate. "Have they all come here for to see our Katty?"

Did Dowdell detect pride in her voice? "They're not in love with you," he warned and pulled down the blinds on either side.

Angry shouts announced their presence, followed by boos and hisses, and pebbles rained down upon the hood of the cab. Dowdell leaned forward and prodded the coachman in the back. "Hurry it up, man! Get into the quad!"

The reins were lashed against the horses, and the cab shot

under an arch into the courtyard. Police constables closed the gates in the face of the mob.

"Will they serve Church the same?" asked Kate as she was helped out of the cab. So she didn't know? Dowdell was surprised. He'd assumed O'Brien must have told her about Church. "I don't think so," he replied, and they went into the courthouse by the side door.

Kevin O'Brien, dressed in black, a white cravat at his throat, was waiting in the jailer's office.

"Where's Jack Church?" Kate asked him. "I was hoping they'd cuff us together nice and cozy!" She was looking forward to the terror in Church's eyes when they were stood in the dock side by side.

O'Brien looked at Dowdell and then at Kate. He'd have to tell her. "Church is not being prosecuted," he said. "He has been released from custody. He is to bear witness against you."

The smile faded from Kate's face, and her mouth turned down into a dangerous curve. But she stayed calm. They had believed Church's alibi, then? No, Harry Porter was the one they had believed. Bad cess to that, for now she would have to speak of his role to Inspector Dowdell.

"I will tell you all," she whispered to O'Brien. But a cry from the door leading into the courtroom interrupted them. The case of Regina versus Webster was called on.

V

Cut into the brickwork of the wall was the inscription "Molly Lawson, mother of eight living, five dead," and Kate felt for the past occupant of her cell. She turned to Kevin O'Brien. "You've asked for Mr. Dowdell?"

O'Brien confirmed it. But he wanted her to tell him first; he didn't want her tale told straight to a police officer. For all he knew, her new statement might be as disastrous as her first two.

"And why did the court adjourn so quick this morning?" Kate asked. She had been charged, a lawyer had outlined the case for the Crown and then asked for a remand to the seventeenth of the month. She had been in and out in a flash.

"They obviously aren't ready. Their scientists are still looking at things."

Kate was interested. "What sort of things?"

"Well, I suppose the body—or what they've found of it."

"And what have they found?"

"Bits and pieces. A foot has been recovered from a manure heap, but they don't think it part of this case."

Kate could reassure them. But they hadn't yet discovered the head.

" 'Tis a terrible business," she said without any conviction her solicitor could detect.

"They call you a monster," he said. "The things they say get worse and worse." Kate made no comment, but her expression encouraged O'Brien to go on. "The townspeople hate you, Mrs. Webster. Shall I tell you what they are saying now? They say that you tried to sell two jars of dripping just after Mrs. Thomas disappeared, that you hawked them around, and that the dripping was the fat from the cadaver of Mrs. Thomas. A lie, of course. But that's what they say. And if this prejudice continues, I shall have to apply to have your case transferred to another locality, out of London altogether!"

Kate was thinking about the jars of dripping. Only Mrs. Porter had seen those jars—if her memory served her right—and she had *never* attempted to sell them. The thought was as disgusting as the slander vile.

"*Who* speaks these things?" she asked.

"Oh, people in Richmond and Hammersmith. There is a woman who minds a tavern—"

"Mrs. Hayhoe?"

"Is that her name? Well, I understand that she is behind much of what is being rumored. You have made enemies, Mrs. Webster."

Yes, it would be Mrs. Hayhoe of the Hole in the Wall. Well could Kate imagine that tongue wagging night and day to whomsoever would be prepared to listen. But the tale of the dripping was downright evil.

Dowdell finally came, and Kate watched as he brought out paper and that familiar pen and inkwell. O'Brien stood to one side, anxious lest Kate say much that could later be disproved.

"I want for you to know the *true* way of things," Kate began.

But Dowdell held up his hand to stop her. "We must wait for Inspector Jones," he said. "He must be here to witness whatever I write down." And so they waited until a rattle at the cell door heralded the arrival of the second policeman. Jones, who looked disgruntled at having been brought all this way for possible testimony, gave Kate a disapproving nod and positioned himself at his colleague's elbow.

"Carry on," said Dowdell.

Kate began to walk slowly up and down the cell, collecting her thoughts, mustering her imagination.

"On March second, when Jack Church pulls me into the house, I hears this cough in the back room, and I falls down inside against the chiffonier by the door. Upon recoverin' myself, I spies Henry Porter standing on the mat at the front-room door."

"Just a minute," Jones interrupted. "Do you say this was on March *second?* On the *Sunday* now?"

"Aye, that it was. I made me a mistake before. It was the Sunday, sir."

"Carry on," said Dowdell, but he gave Jones a meaningful look.

Kate indulged them for a full half hour, prattling on, acting out the roles of herself, Porter, and Church in what she fully believed to be her convincing best. It now transpired that Henry Porter had been in the house with Church at the time Mrs. Thomas was obviously done to death, although he had pretended to pay a call after Kate herself had been hauled in by Church. Both Church and Henry Porter had gone off into the rear room, from which Kate had heard this ominous cough —a death rattle? Then they had taken her to Hammersmith, and she had spent the night at the Porter home, frightened and helpless. Henry Porter had gone out again, left his house, for she had caught him when he returned. Where had he gone? She didn't know that answer, but the inference was plain—to help butcher Mrs. Thomas. And had he not admitted to her on the morrow that he'd been down to Richmond as she'd suspected? Had he not plied her with drink throughout the afternoon and evening in order to lower her powers of resistance, to make her more amenable to the demands of these brutal men? And she had been sent off to Richmond that very evening, with young Bobby Porter, to meet with Church at the Richmond hotel.

"Which hotel?" asked Jones.

"Hartley's," Kate said quickly. She knew this hostelry to be close to the river.

"Carry on," said Dowdell.

In the hotel she had been given more to drink and then packed off with the Porter boy to Mayfield Cottages. Her instructions from Church had been explicit. In the back room she would find a corded box and a large black carpetbag. Between them, she and Robert were to bring the bag and box to the bridge. Robert was to be sent off, while Kate alone brought the box and handed it over to "a man who'd be waiting for her."

"Who was this man? Ever seen him before?"

"No, sir. But he was tall and dark."

Like her story, O'Brien mused.

"Carry on," said Dowdell.

This man had taken the box from her, and both she and Robert had heard a loud splash.

"What about the carpetbag?" asked Jones.

"Bobby had it, sir."

"Ever see what was inside?"

"Yes, sir. A great big family Bible and some mate."

"Some what?"

"Mate, sir. Mate."

"Meat," Dowdell explained without looking up from his writing. "What kind of meat, Mrs. Webster?"

"Ordinary mate, sir. There was books in it as well. Seven, I think."

"Thank you. Carry on."

She went back to expand, adding details as they came into her head, and Dowdell was forced to scratch out entire sentences and rewrite. She had found a carving knife, she said, and a large iron saucepan filled with water. And traces of blood, evidence of floors having been scrubbed, and brown paper under the sink with odd marks on it.

"Where was Robert Porter?" asked Jones.

"Oh, I forgot. He spends the night at the house on account of the last train being gone."

And she had made Porter's son a bed in the same room as herself.

"And I finds this saw," she added. "I forgot to mention the saw."

"Carry on," said Dowdell wearily. He too had found a saw in the house.

"It used to hang in the kitchen by the range fireplace. But two days later I finds it in the wash house, by the copper."

"Did you move it, or leave it there?" asked Dowdell.

"I left it where I finds it," answered Kate.

Not true, thought Dowdell. He had retrieved this saw from under the draining board of the sink.

"Any marks on it?" he asked.

"Yes, like the carver, streaky sort of marks. Blood."

Not true. There had been such marks on the knife, yes. But none on the saw.

But Dowdell allowed her to move on to the following days and the eventual attempt to remove the property. In this respect, Kate was less at variance from her first statement, except that Porter was a party to what took place.

"What did Porter say—if anything—when Miss Ives started asking questions?" asked Jones.

"Henry? Let me think. Yes, I remember now! Jack Church says to me to give the lady the shun, whether bills be owed to her or not. But Harry Porter gets a-frighted and says to me, he

271

does, 'No, if we can do it on the quiet, do it. The thing is not being found out.' *That's* what he said, sir."

"And Church? What did he say to that?"

"Let me see! Yes . . . he says to us, 'There's only us three selves that know it.' "

Kate added further conversation with regard to the various butchers used by her late employer. Then suddenly her recitation faltered and came to an end. Jones was waiting, his notebook out, and O'Brien straightened up from lounging against the cell wall, anticipating the mind of the inspector.

"Why didn't you tell us this when first we interviewed you?" said Jones.

"She didn't have the benefit of my advice at that stage," put in O'Brien.

"I would rather the lady answered for herself!"

O'Brien stepped up to Kate, her protector at law. "You have not so much as cautioned her," he said to Dowdell. Then to Kate: "Say nothing further, Mrs. Webster, I beg of you!"

Kate shrugged. She was tired and bored anyway, unimpressed by her own limitations. Her story had been poorly rendered, and the fault lay with her.

"I'll now read out what I've written," said Dowdell.

When he had finished, the three visitors to the cell were looking away from one another. O'Brien knew from the start that his client's tale was false. Read over in Dowdell's lugubrious tones, it now *read* false.

A silence followed, broken only when Kate lowered herself down onto her palliasse and began to croon, gently at first, but rising to a strange and savage wail. The men listened to her words embarrassed. Only Inspector Jones felt contempt.

"Oh, fly to these arms for protection,
   If pierced by the arrow of woe,
   Then smile on my tender affection,
   Mo cailin deas cruidthe na mbo!"
   [My pretty girl milking the cow.]

MINE ELM IS GROWN

I

Mr. Valantine Brown, for the Treasury, offered no evidence on behalf of the Crown against John Church, and he was discharged. And Church's reception at his public house that afternoon had been a memorable occasion. Cheers and friendly catcalls had been his greeting, and he had been obliged to stand a general round of drinks to mark his appreciation of so many well-wishers. "Good old Jack!" and "We knowed you never done it, lad!" and "They'll hang 'er from a rope like a capon!" had called the voices of his customers and new-found friends. Nevertheless, after he had borne the cost of that initial flow of alcohol, custom had boomed for the Rising Sun.

But Jack Church was angry. The police—that Inspector Pearson in particular—had been hard on him with their insinuations. Arrested and deprived of the chance to make a proper explanation, he had been incarcerated at the police station like a common vagabond. Nor had either Pearson or Dowdell apologized to him for their gross error of judgment.

And the true author of his ill treatment was that Webster woman! How had *he* been supposed to know she was her mistress's butcher? She'd certainly put him on the spot! It was well and good to sack a house of its contents as an act of simple theft, but then to discover the true owner *murdered!* Jack Church was never to forget the moment of his charging for that crime.

He now plotted his revenge. He knew he was going to be called to give evidence against the Irish she-cat. Good. He'd embellish his testimony to her detriment whenever possible. But could he not do her a worse mischief?

It was on the Sunday that Church recalled Kate's old relationship with the man called Strong. He said nothing to his wife, but Church put it about among certain customers that a visit from this particular gentleman would be welcome—and might be profitable. And his tapping of the underworld drum did not go unrewarded.

Although nobody could disclose the present whereabouts of Strong, Jack Church learned of the existence of a young lady, a prostitute and occasional bunter, by the name of Mary Durden. It seemed she lived in London Street, in Kingston, where she "ran shop" as a straw hat and bonnet maker. And Church's informant—whose name does not matter were it even genuine —assured the publican that this lady of the streets knew Strong, had known Mrs. Katherine Webster, and loved not either.

Accordingly, Church armed himself with a bottle of gin and absented himself from his tavern and his family to pay a call upon the lady at the given address.

He was well received, the more so once liquor had been taken and he had given Mary Durden his version of events concerning Kate.

"So you see as how she's tried to fix me, Mary," he concluded. "And she'll try again, I'll wager, unless the truth about her be known. And the 'ole truth, mind."

Mary Durden—porcine and of very little brain—grinned.

"You knew the woman," Church went on. "Hated her very guts, from all accounts. And now we know she's done an old dame to death for the sake of a few bob! By God, she oughta swing for this!"

Mary Durden, remembering the rough passage she'd received from Kate, wanted to help this persuasive man. But she couldn't see herself as being of any value. "What can *I* do?" she asked.

"You can tell the police things about her."

"What sort of things, mister?"

"Well, suppose I ask you one or two questions about her, and you answers yes to what I say. Could be you'll remember something interesting about Kate Webster. Shall we try it out?"

The girl agreed.

"Righty-o then! You've known Mrs. Webster about four years? Yes? Say yes, Mary!"

"Yus."

"And you saw her last in February, on Shrove Tuesday, which I think was the twenty-fifth of February?"

"Yus. But where did I see her, and why did I see her then, mister?"

Church refilled her glass. "You saw her here, at this cottage, because you were poorly and she came to visit. Right?"

"Yus."

"And she tells you—on Shrove Tuesday, remember?—as how she was going up north, to Birmingham. She said she was to see about some property her aunt had left her in a will. No, it wasn't a will. It was just an ordinary letter. This aunt had sent her a letter saying that all her property was to be for her when she passed on."

"Who? Mrs. Webster?"

"No, the *aunt,* silly! The aunt said that Kate was to have all she owned, her gold watch and chain, her jewels, everything."

"I didn't know Mrs. Webster had an aunt," Miss Durden said, puzzled.

"She hasn't, you muttonhead!" Church chewed on his beard with exasperation. "But she *told* you that she had . . . and that this aunt had left her all her belongings!"

"When? Mrs. Webster never told—"

"Yes she did. Last Shrove Tuesday!" Was not Church wasting his time with this idiot?

"Ohh, I see. Last Shrove Tuesday. Yus, so she did."

"That's better! Now, Mrs. Webster was all excited about her aunt, laughing and talking. She actually bought an 'at off you. Paid two shillings for it."

"My hats don't cost two shillings, mister!"

"This one did. Now, Mrs. Webster also told you that her aunt had left a will, which was in a drawer with her jewels. She told you that, didn't she?"

Miss Durden thought for a minute. "You said just now, mister, that there weren't any will, that her aunt had sent Mrs. Webster a letter."

Church sighed, got up, and walked about the room. Patience, he must have patience.

"Now listen. True, her aunt had sent her a letter. But there was also a will—to be found in a drawer with the jewelry. Understand?"

"If you say so, mister."

"No, no. *You* say so. Kate said this to *you,* told *you* about the aunt, the will, the furniture, the jewels, and what 'ave you. Last Shrove Tuesday—pancake day. Remember?"

277

"Ohh, yus."

"Good, good! And just one more thing, Mary. Didn't she also tell you that she was now living in Richmond?"

Miss Durden sipped her gin, frowning again. "I don't know," she said. "I never saw her, did I?"

Church came over and sat down. He placed his hands on the girl's knees and looked her in the eye. This was going to be a lengthy business, he could see. But he would persist until the other actually believed that what he suggested to her had really taken place. He'd stay all night if necessary.

Once Miss Durden had been tutored to Church's satisfaction, he bade her volunteer her information to the Richmond police. She was not to mention his visit to her shop, nor indeed even his name, and he felt confident that she would not let him down.

The police, Church was sure, would be most interested in what this latest witness had to say, for all their prejudices and stupidity. They would be interested because, if Miss Durden was to be believed, a new and more ghastly light was being shed upon the case of Kate Webster. Murder in a fit of rage was one thing, even when followed by an act of hideous dissection. But murder premeditated, planned days before its actual execution, and, one could equally assume, preparations made for the disposal of both the body of Mrs. Thomas and her property—such a crime was beyond conception. Society would react with a cry for vengeance, the state would be forced to heed that cry, and Kate Webster, cause of Jack Church's recent scare, would be made to suffer the full penalty of the law.

Church was too cautious an individual to congratulate himself at this early stage, but he felt safe. His part in helping the woman remove her employer's goods had been dishonest because he *had* realized something to be amiss. But the police no longer treated him as a potential receiver—that charge had been withdrawn with the other—and Mr. Valantine Brown, for the Treasury, had been quick to assure the Richmond magistrates that Church was a man "used and accused quite monstrously." Church remembered those words.

"But for his prompt action, the mystery of this matter might well be as yet unsolved," had said the Treasury lawyer of Jack Church to the justices.

Yes, the publican was pleased with himself. He'd been spited by a madwoman, later to be cheered as a hero. He had become famous and brought custom to his business. And now he had enlisted the services of Mary Durden, a witness in his vendetta so deadly that this evil-minded Irish witch must surely perish. "They'll hang her from a rope like a capon," someone had shouted in his bar. So much the better if they did.

II

Kate had expected the hostility of Church's evidence, and she took it calmly, shouting out, " 'Tis false, you scoundrel!" only once during his testimony. But neither Kate nor her solicitor had envisaged the calling of Mary Durden before the magistrates.

"What's she to do with it?" Kevin O'Brien had whispered to her in the dock.

"Nothing, nothing at all," replied Kate.

But the lawyer for the Treasury startled them both with the questions he now put to the lady, and Kate was as amazed as

O'Brien was horrified by the answers she gave. Inspector Dowdell sat at the police officers' bench and didn't know what to believe.

"No questions," said O'Brien when his opportunity to cross-examine arose. What could he ask her without proper instructions from his mysterious client? How dare he suggest anything to Miss Durden? Her replies might well damn his client still further. He must wait for the trial proper, when he had engaged a barrister and matters were being canvassed before the jury.

"I'll now read over your evidence for you to sign," said the clerk of the court when O'Brien sat down. The magistrates' clerk was old and thin and paid scant attention to the horrendous facts which had emerged over the past few weeks, an indifference not shared by the justices themselves or the multitude thronging the public seats.

"You are a hatter, and you have known the accused some four years. You saw her last upon the twenty-fifth day of February, 1879, at your house. You were unwell at the time. The accused told you of how she intended to visit her aunt in Birmingham, in order to inspect some property her aunt had bequeathed to her. The accused made mention to you of a letter she alleged she had received from her aunt, instructing her as to the whereabouts of a gold watch and chain and divers jewelry. She said that her aunt had left her everything. She added that it was her contemplation to travel unto the City of Birmingham that very evening. She implied that such furniture as might be left to her she would sell for cash. She intimated that the jewels might be unearthed in the drawer of an unidentified bureau. The accused stopped at your residence for approximately one hour and then left. She was cheerful, if not actually exhibiting signs of exiguous perturbation. Is that correct, madam?"

Mary Durden nodded stupidly. She was sure that she had not said those very words—many of which she did not understand —but if this gentleman said she'd said them, then who was she to argue? The lawyer from the Treasury smiled; he'd encountered the pomposity of this particular clerk on a previous occasion.

Kate looked at her solicitor. But he was hunched over his papers, and her demanding stare brought no response. In fact, Kate might have been alternately gratified or concerned had she known the worry of his mind.

The Treasury lawyer was on his feet. "The Crown shall have the medical evidence tomorrow," he told the chairman of the magistrates. "I apologize for not being able to adduce this today, but you will appreciate, sir, that there have been certain complications."

The senior justice of the peace rose to his feet, glad that an early end to the day might allow him to return to his business. He delivered Kate a baleful stare and indicated to the policeman by her side that she might be removed. Then he and his two colleagues stalked off behind a curtain to the rear.

"Well?" O'Brien asked her, back in her Wandsworth cell.

"I didn't get to seeing me boy," Kate replied and sat herself on the bed. She had been assured yesterday by a message from Inspector Dowdell that her child would be at the courthouse this morning.

O'Brien looked unhappy. It was about the Durden woman he had asked his question, and now his client fussed over her offspring.

"I shall see what can be done," he said. "Now tell me what

281

you know of Miss Mary Durden."

"*Miss* now, is it? So he finally skedaddled!" Not that Mary Durden had ever been married to Strong.

"And who is *he?*"

Kate flapped a hand. She could not divulge the name of Strong to anyone, not even to her legal adviser. Too dangerous.

"You must help me to help yourself," O'Brien went on. "So you *do* know this woman and her husband? Tell me about it, I beg of you."

Kate pondered a while. She mustn't involve Strong by name, perhaps, but there lay no harm in casting a shadow.

"The man she lived with's called Rafe. He never was her real fella. He fancied me more than she. He used to take me out. She got jealous, and he upped and left her. Now she's mean as a cat toward me. Now she's tellin' lies." And privately Kate did wonder why Mary Durden had sworn falsely against her. She'd not seen Mary Durden since . . . A long time, anyway.

"Her man and me'd go to the Three Tuns," Kate continued. "Don't you want to write this down, Mr. O'Brien?" Normally her solicitor noted everything she said.

O'Brien shook his head. "Later," he said. "After your committal, when I've had a chance to look at every prosecution statement. Then I'll want your comments in full for your barrister."

"I gets a barrister, does I? And just who'll do the paying of the likes of him?"

O'Brien pulled the bell by the door. "Never mind about that, Mrs. Webster."

They waited in silence for the wardress to arrive. As the door swung open, Kevin O'Brien turned to Kate. "Meanwhile, I'll find out about your little boy. I shall see you tomorrow, Mrs. Webster. Good night."

Next morning the usual crowd of ill-wishers greeted Kate's arrival at the court, and police with truncheons drawn stood in a ring around the archway to the yard. Kate was oblivious to the yaas and boos, her mind set upon the promised meeting with her son. But when she and her escort passed into the rear of the building, Dowdell was waiting with a sorry expression, and Kate knew the worst.

"When then? When will I see him?" she asked the inspector, her manner crisp but controlled.

"The Home says tomorrow afternoon."

O'Brien, standing nearby, felt pity tinged with an element of annoyance. His client's child was proving to be a direct interference, and there was much work shortly to be done with regard to her defense.

They moved into the courtroom and took their various seats, rising when the magistrates filed in, sitting again to hear the Treasury lawyer call a series of witnesses who could deal with the body of Mrs. Thomas. Kate found interest in only one—a Mr. Henry Wheatley who had discovered the deal box lying near the Mortlake shallows. His tale was a story she had heard before, and then she recalled it as having been recited by William Porter and later read by herself in the newssheet. For the rest, Kate could think only of her missing boy; she could imagine the courtroom empty but for her child and herself, playing seek and hide among the oaken benches while the sun streamed in through the stained glass windows overhead. Then someone called for "Dr. Thomas Bond," and her attention was recaptured by the Christian name. For a moment she had thought Mrs. Thomas summonsed into their presence.

"You are a Fellow of the Royal College of Surgeons?" the

Treasury lawyer asked a man with a Balaclava beard.

"I am," said the doctor, assembling notes on the shelf of the witness box. He was short and stout and middle-aged, and Kate saw that he wore those clever gold-rimmed spectacles halfway down his nose.

"On March the twelfth," he went on, "I examined portions of a human body at the mortuary in Barnes. These consisted of the upper part of the chest and ribs, the heart—with part of the right lung attached—the right shoulder and right upper arm, the left upper arm in its entirety, and a right thigh—cut off below the joint—and the right lower leg cut off from the thigh at the knee." He looked over his glasses at the court. "The right foot had been cut off at the ankle—a clumsy amputation, I would say—and the foot was missing at this time." Dr. Bond sounded hurt and deprived but soon picked up enthusiasm. "I also examined part of a pelvis, with uterus attached, and a *left* foot severed from the leg at the ankle joint. The softer parts of the body had been hacked, and the bones sawn in a crude fashion."

"You say in a crude fashion, Doctor?"

"Yes. Without any anatomical skill whatsoever!"

"Was there anything else unusual about the remains?"

"Indeed there was, sir. They were dry, shriveled, and of a brown texture. No decomposition had occurred. I took the view that much of the body had been boiled."

"Cooked, you say?"

"No I do not. I said *boiled*, sir. Flesh is cooked to be eaten; and it is not for me to say that this body was to be eaten. Accordingly, my choice of word is carefully chosen—and it is *boiled*, sir, *boiled!*"

The Treasury lawyer ignored the rebuff. "Did you later examine a second foot, Doctor?" he asked.

"I did. And it had not been boiled."

"Did it belong to the same body?"

"I should say so." The doctor was careful again.

"Did you also examine certain fragments of human body brought to you in a box by the police?"

"I did. Some bones—a piece of left thigh bone, a fragment of the small bone of the left leg, the small bone of the right arm, the hand bones of the right hand, some bits of pelvis, and some fragments of the spinal column. All had been burned to a cinder, sir."

The Treasury lawyer turned to the magistrates. "The latter were found in the two grates at Mayfield Cottages," he said by way of commentary. He returned to the doctor. "No head? You examined no head?"

"I did not!" came the indignant reply. Dr. Bond did not like headless corpses; they were untidy.

"But are you able, Doctor, to come to any conclusion as to the person you examined?"

"Yes. She was dead." And a titter ran around the courtroom.

"She—the deceased—was a woman of about five feet in height, and aged about fifty years!" said the doctor, glaring at those who deigned to find him funny.

The Treasury lawyer came to his rescue. "Did you also examine a pot containing fat?"

"I did. I understand it was scraped off a copper by the police."

"Yes. We will hear about that in due course. But what kind of fat was it that you examined?"

"Just fat. The kind one might expect to be produced by boiling any flesh. Black and greasy."

"Human fat?"

"Or animal. It had been in contact with the copper, you know." Dr. Bond was not prepared to be subsequently proved wrong by some meddlesome second opinion.

But his last observation was missed by his audience. The latter —bench, bar, and spectators—were all staring at the dock. The prisoner had hunched forward with her head between her knees and was uttering strange noises—a mixture of a cough and a retch. Kate was unaware of the warder's hand on her shoulder; she saw again the pieces of Mrs. Thomas described by the doctor, and in her nostrils she could smell again the horrors of that night.

"What ails the woman?" Dowdell asked Kevin O'Brien when the court adjourned for a few moments.

O'Brien shook his head. No doubt it had been the hearing of what had happened to his client's employer. The solicitor himself had been disgusted. But, if Kate Webster had been also disgusted, was she in fact responsible? O'Brien did not accept that a murderess might be disgusted by the details of her own crime.

"I don't think she did it," he said to the inspector, and the other looked at him to see if he was joking. No. O'Brien was serious.

"Then who did, sir?"

O'Brien lit a cheroot. Who indeed? Church was in the clear, and so was Henry Porter. The police had been at pains to ensure that both alibis were unassailable before using the men as witnesses.

"I'm not saying Mrs. Webster isn't an accessory after the fact," O'Brien said helplessly.

"But an accessory to *whom,* sir?" persisted the inspector.

"I don't know," O'Brien said.

III

On April 16 the magistrates committed Kate for trial at the Central Criminal Court, and the proceedings at Richmond were concluded.

There was an air of satisfaction among the public as Kate was led from the courtroom for the last time, and no insults followed her through the door to the cell passage. What had been the private scandal of Richmond had suddenly become of national interest and importance. All London would now be concerned with the savage murder of Mrs. Julia Thomas by her cook-general, and matters would arrive at their natural conclusion far away in the busy City itself.

In the jailer's office Kate stopped and spoke to Kevin O'Brien. "Can I see me boy now?"

O'Brien looked at Inspector Dowdell, who nodded.

"He's in the clerk's room. I'd best fetch him out of there before the clerk returns." Dowdell did not imagine the clerk of the court would be too pleased should he find a criminal's child lurking in his private quarters. But there had been nowhere else to put the lad.

The inspector returned with Kate's son, holding his hand as if the boy were his own, talking nonsense to him while they walked.

"Where can they be alone?" Dowdell asked the jailer as Kate flew to the child.

The jailer looked unhappy. "Dunno rightly. Ain't got no catering for kids, sir." So Dowdell took the initiative and pulled open the iron door leading to the cells—tiny cubbyholes arranged in a row and facing a narrow drain which served as the communal lavatory.

"Put them in one of those," he told the jailer.

" 'Fraid that's not allowed, sir," came the reply. "Them's men's cells, sir."

"That doesn't matter." Dowdell could see no sign of any occupant. "Open one up and let them in."

The jailer took his bunch of keys from a hook by the door and unlocked the nearest cubicle. All of this was unorthodox, if not against regulations.

"They can only 'ave five minutes," he grumbled to the inspector.

Dowdell waited until Kate and her son had disappeared into the cell and the door was locked on them before he spoke. "They can have just as long as they like," he said quietly.

"What's that, sir! Oh no they can't! Why, it's more than my life's worth!" But Dowdell hushed him and drew him away from the area of the cells.

"Listen to me, man," he said to the jailer when they were with O'Brien. "From now on Webster's in prison proper, and there she stays until her trial. And in prison proper she gets to see her lad about once a fortnight, see? Once a fortnight if she's lucky, and that makes for an unhappy mum, see? And she'll be up for trial at O.B. in about six weeks. That means she sees her lad about three times before they ships her up to Newgate for the duration of the trial. And at Newgate nobody, but *nobody*, gets to see their kid or anybody else at all. And that makes for a *very* unhappy mum. So today we let her see her boy to her heart's content, because that heart's soon to be bust apart, man. See?"

But the jailer did not see at all. Here was a woman as good as proven guilty of as nasty a case of homicide as he could recall, and here was the peeler in charge of her case behaving as soft as a girl. They said the Webster woman was a whore and a witch, a sentiment with which the jailer was prepared to agree; and you did not show kindness to the likes of such a person according to his set of standards. Nevertheless, an inspector of police was still an inspector.

"Okay, sir," he said grudgingly. "But do us a favor? 'Ave her out of there by dinnertime."

Dowdell and O'Brien both looked at their watches. The jailer's time limit gave Kate Webster just under half an hour.

Following her committal, the authorities at Wandsworth Prison removed Kate from her old cell to another, a larger and cleaner room. A window set high up in the wall was without bars, but it had no sill from which she might jump and injure herself, and the small square frames were of thick opaque glass so that she could not look out upon the yard below. The door was of wood and iron, and the Judas hole could be operated only from without. And well operated it was, this spy hole, for Kate was watched at frequent intervals both day and night.

On the Sunday evening, Kate was visited by the governor of the prison, Captain Colville, a shy man of military bearing who found little to say to Kate, and she had little to say to him. With the governor came the matron, who tried to look reassuring but failed to hide an obvious awe of Kate.

"Would you like to have the chaplain visit you?" Captain Colville asked his prisoner when about to leave.

Kate shook her head. She had no use for Protestant pastors.

"Father M'Enery is a Catholic padre," the governor added, reading her thoughts.

What kind of prison was this house? Kate wondered. Men mixed with women, and now a Catholic priest.

"I shall send him to you," said the governor, and they left Kate alone.

Kate stood up and pulled her skirts into place. They had taken her comb away lest she use it to cheat the hangman, and she was obliged to tidy her hair with lick and hands. But, she now reflected, she was fortunate they'd left her hair at its present length. In some prisons of her past experience heads were cropped close to combat lice; sometimes heads were even shaved to ridicule. Wandsworth Prison might be a grimmer place than the Wandsworth House of Correction, but it seemed as if in some ways it treated its inmates benignly.

Kate's attempts to improve her appearance went unrewarded, for no Father M'Enery showed himself that night, nor in the week that followed. Only Kevin O'Brien came, as worried as ever, and armed with scrolls of parchment paper.

"These are for the brief I must get together for your barrister," he explained.

"Me boy—when do I get to seeing me boy?"

O'Brien ignored her, hoping that she would not repeat the question and knowing that she was bound to.

"I am very concerned about the first statement you made to the police," he said. "It doesn't tally with the second, and I feel much to be missing. You must trust me, Mrs. Webster. I must have your confidence!"

"Are they treating him well at the Home?" asked Kate.

"Of course! Now, tell me who else was involved in the property removal. Did this man Weston have anything to do with Mrs. Thomas?"

"Has he clothing sufficient for his needs? I'd hate for the little fella t'be cold at nights."

"I'm sure that the Home will provide him with everything, Mrs. Webster. Now, what about Henry Weston?"

"They're not being cruel to him on account of meself, d'you suppose?"

"Heaven forbid! Henry Weston?" O'Brien was desperate, but he knew that he could never concentrate his client's mind while she was thinking about her child. Her own peril—any desire to save herself—had become submerged by a mother's consideration, and O'Brien wearily began to tidy up his papers.

"I shall see you again on Monday," he said to her, tying the pink tape around the roll. Perhaps if she could see her boy over the weekend, her mind might be put at rest as to his well-being and he would be able to extract the information he desired.

Kate watched her solicitor pull on his cloak and pick up his cane. She had not seen him with a stick before, and she inquired after his health.

"Rheumatism," O'Brien explained, and Kate thought of Mrs. Thomas.

"I'm sorry, sir, if I've not been helpful," she said.

O'Brien gave her a bitter smile. Perhaps he was getting old, perhaps five years ago he would have been able to force the truth from his client. But perhaps it was the very nature of her crime that made him hold back from pursuing the truth too fiercely. At that moment O'Brien realized that he was unfit to be involved in a case of murder, and a murder of this kind in particular. The sooner he engaged the services of a barrister the better.

He banged the door with his cane and waited for someone to come and let him out.

IV

The weeks passed, and Kate didn't see her little boy and Kevin O'Brien didn't obtain coherent instructions from his distracted client. While Captain Colville was at pains to point out that—as far as he and his prison were concerned—Kate might see her child upon any Sunday afternoon, the governing body of the orphanage concerned did not relish the idea of a six-year-old under their care visiting its mother now incarcerated in a proper prison. The detention wing at Wandsworth had been one thing, but the block in which Kate had of late been housed was another. The very coarseness of both the surroundings and the convict inmates might upset the child or, worse still, cause him to feel important and thereby exercise an unhealthy influence over other children at the Home. Captain Colville tried to reason with the governing body, but they were adamant in their decision. It was not normally their custom, or their misfortune, to have in their charge the infant of a possible murderess, and it had been necessary for the body to lay down a specific policy. And the policy henceforth to be adopted in cases such as this was simple—no visits.

Having learned of this final decision, Captain Colville was at odds as to how he might break the news to his prisoner. A report from the Clerkenwell jail and a confidential letter from the governor of the Wandsworth House of Correction both stated that Katherine Webster, alias Lawler, alias Webb, and alias

Shannon, could be an extremely violent and troublesome re-sponsibility—under any name.

"Foul-mouthed, defiant, and subject to ungovernable fits of rage," said Clerkenwell of Katty Shannon, alias Webster. "Cross-grained, no respect for discipline, and surly," said the House of Correction of Lawler, alias Webster. As a result, Captain Colville requested the attendance of Kevin O'Brien in his office. An unprecedented meeting, in the governor's experience, but desirable under the circumstances.

"I am pleased that you have come," he said. "May I offer you a small glass of Madeira?"

O'Brien accepted the drink and waited for the governor to resume his seat behind the desk, wondering just why he had been summoned.

Captain Colville placed the tips of his fingers together and studied the solicitor before speaking. "Awkward customer, I would imagine," he said at last of Mrs. Webster.

"Her case is not uncomplicated."

"Yes. Well, I'll come to the point, Mr. O'Brien. I fear that the powers-that-be at her child's orphanage will not permit any more visits. I think that they are being unreasonable, and I have said as much. But there it is."

Kevin O'Brien nodded. He'd had his suspicions, which were now justified. "How has she reacted?" he asked Colville.

"She has not yet been informed. This is a matter of the utmost delicacy. Hence my invitation for you to come and see me."

"I know that she yearns for her child," O'Brien said. "In fact, she speaks of little else." He did not think it wise to inform the prison governor as to his difficulty in obtaining worthwhile instructions from his client.

"Physically, I am told that she is quite well," Colville said. "She eats well, she sleeps well, and she enjoys her daily exercise in the chapel garden. I do not want her to become debilitated by the receipt of bad news." Nor did he want his prisoner tearing up her cell or assaulting his staff.

"Then have the orphanage change its mind!" said O'Brien.

"Impossible."

"Then how am I to assist, Captain?"

"Couldn't you speak to her, reason with her?"

"You mean break the news to her."

"No, no! That is my responsibility, and a duty I shall perform. But when I have told her the worst, couldn't you ask her to be patient?"

"'Patient'? A woman facing the executioner is deprived of her child, the only thing she loves, and you ask her to be 'patient'? Really, your choice of word is most unfortunate, sir!"

"She will also have the comfort of the chaplain," said the governor quickly.

"Aha, a chaplain! And where is he? Has he seen her yet?"

"Alas no. Father M'Enery is at present attached to the Newgate jail and cannot be with us until the end of the month."

"Then procure another priest."

"Priests are not 'procured,'" said the governor, as a matter of revenge. "And very few are authorized to visit a prison."

Kevin O'Brien grunted. In this country priests were papish and papists were invariably Irish—and the Irish, like himself, were suspect. He finished his wine and rose.

"I shall do what I can," he told the governor.

"Capital!" said that worthy.

294

Fearful of Kate's reaction, Captain Colville took along with him the prison matron and a cohort of warders when he visited her in her cell. He explained the decision of the orphanage and his own subjugation with languid regret. There was nothing he could do; rules were rules.

But Kate didn't respond in the manner anticipated by the authorities of Clerkenwell or the House of Correction. To the governor's pleasant surprise, she uttered only a pitiful moan and fell in a semi-swoon upon her bunk, weeping copiously, refusing to be comforted by the matron, but raising not a finger to anyone. Grateful, Captain Colville took his leave as quickly as possible.

When they had gone, Kate turned on her side to face the wall. The scratchings of past prisoners formed a network on the bricks, but she examined them without interest, aware only that they had passed unnoticed until this instant. The words of the governor rang in her ears, and she attempted to put a fresh interpretation on them, to discover some meaning other than the obvious. And when her imagination failed her, she took to weeping again.

Then her howling came to an abrupt stop.

"No more visits until you are removed to Newgate," the governor had said. (And it was not a deliberate attempt to raise a false hope.)

Until Newgate! Mr. O'Brien had said she was bound for that prison once her trial was listed in the Calendar . . . and she would not be long in Wandsworth. So it would be like her appearance in Richmond again, with Inspector Dowdell bringing her boy to the court to see her. Kate recalled the joyous time spent with her son in that tiny cell. She got off her bunk and rubbed her eyes, which strayed to the cell door and the Judas hole, and those behind it let the disc slip into place.

"Zoodikers!" Kate yelled as she spied the movement. In one quick movement she was at the door, and she spat into the aperture. "Be off with yer, you poxy sons of harlots!" There followed the sound of scurrying feet.

Later that evening Captain Colville was informed that his charge had taken to using vile language and had attempted to assault two prison officers in the most disgusting manner. No action was taken, in view of the circumstances of this particular prisoner's case, but Captain Colville duly entered an account of the incident in the official record.

V

The brass cartridge case had been fired only once, but Strong detected a small flaw on the lip. He examined it carefully under the light pouring in through the skylight. He was annoyed. He had only five cases in all, and it was virtually impossible to obtain more. He put down the case and picked up a bag-shaped gunpowder flask and began to fill the spent round in accordance with the measure set on the nozzle of the flask. Then he remembered the cigar in his mouth and put it out. You did not smoke when pouring powder.

While he'd been working, he'd been thinking of Kate Webster. He had read of her arrest in the *Police Gazette*, of course, and he judged the tale it told as unlikely. Katty was many things, most of them bad, but she was not a killer. Moreover, had he not seen her himself shortly before the date of the alleged murder? Hadn't she refused to bunt for him—wasn't she trying to go straight? If Katty Webster had abandoned larceny simple, Strong could not see her resorting to homicide.

The cartridge case filled with powder, Strong pressed home the lead conical bullet, pushing hard with his thumb until the base of the bullet was firm against the charge. Lastly, and more complicated, he inserted into the top rim of the case a thin percussion cap. He cursed this complex ammunition and the day the pin-fire gun had been invented. One day he'd furnish himself with a simple Colt.

But if *his* pop was tricky, what of Kate Webster's plight? Bits of boiled body bobbing up in the Thames . . .

"Irish stew," he said with a laugh.

But the aspect of the case that amused him most of all was the accusation leveled against Jack Church. Incredible! Must have given Church a turn—old snake in the grass—turned his whiskers white.

"Crazy woman!" he muttered. For Katty must have taken leave of her senses to put a finger on Jack Church. Curiosity tempted Strong to leave the filthy garret in which now he lived, to head west and watch events at closer hand. He could tap a few channels to find out how the Irishwoman was faring in Newgate—if that's where she was. But reason warned Strong to stop where he was. He might himself be sought. He had heard nothing since the shooting. He didn't even know if he was on the run, a bad state of affairs with which he could take no chances. So tucked away, within the shadows of St. Paul's, he bided his time with his pistol, always expecting the rap of truncheons on the door.

Strong inserted the loaded cartridge into his "friend" and poured himself a rum. As he drank, he began to smooth the metal framework of the gun. Caressing the weapon had become a nervous habit of late, so the knuckle-duster grip was worn and shiny.

Bloody gun, bloody copper! he thought. Had it been his fault his pop had gone off so easy; was it his fault that mutton-shunter had jacked it in? Now here he was, east of the Griffin, a rat in a possible trap, forced to color his meerschaum with bad liquor. Then a sudden thought came to him.

"Blow me down, she wouldn't!" he said aloud.

Oh yes, she would, his brain told him. If she put Jack Church in it, she might also name *him* as a culprit. She'd chosen Jack Church first because he was there and handy; but now Church was in the clear she'd look about for someone else. And who better than himself? He'd wriggle out of that, of course; but if she mentioned that shunter Pew, the rossers might add two to two, and bingo! they'd have him nailed, nailed as tight as a vat of Malmsey wine.

"I'll put the shutters up for good," he vowed into his drink.

And so he would. He'd go underground. He'd stay here for just one more week and then go south into the countryside. Maybe raggle-taggle with the gypsies in Kent for a spell, maybe turn tar on a coaster for the duration of the fishing season. Maybe anything. But one thing for sure, he'd court no more old haunts and habits, and he'd stay away from everyone.

"Slife to her too!" he cursed Kate Webster. "I hopes she mounts the cart!" Affected by the rum, Strong stretched back in his chair and cast his eyes upward to the roofing beams of his attic room. His mind turned to cobwebs—all that money he'd made on the plate and which he couldn't spend—and to murder.

"I love Charlie. Charlie was a thief," he mumbled tunelessly.

"Charlie killed a copper. Charlie come to grief. They caught Charlie, hung 'im on a rope. Poor old Charlie, hadn't got a hope!"

And he topped up his glass with the rum.

"His name is Strong," Kate told O'Brien, "and he's the worst-est man alive."

Her solicitor hurriedly took the detail down in his notebook. "And?"

"Could be *he* can help me," she said.

"How?"

"Could be he'll be saying he was with me when Mrs. Thomas died."

"And was he with you?"

Kate made no reply.

"Very well," said O'Brien unhappily, "let us assume that he was. Will he come forward?"

Kate shrugged. "I know not." But the absurdity of the suggestion caused her to smile: Strong surrendering himself to Inspector Dowdell with a "I know it will cost me a trip to the gallows, but I've come to tell lies on behalf of my beloved Mrs. Webster!"

"Is he the father of your little boy, Mrs. Webster?" O'Brien had a tidy mind. Someone must have fathered the child.

"He was." True or false, Kate did not care.

"Where can I find him?"

"I know not." True.

"Would the police inspectors be able to assist?"

Kate laughed out loud. Not now, not if Jack Strong was on the run for murder. No police officer in England could track him down. Hence the safety in giving her solicitor his name, even if he passed it on to the authorities. No doubt the cracksman had laid drag scents in every direction other than the one which led to him.

"I see," said O'Brien. "But are you sure he can really be of service to us, Mrs. Webster?" Nothing could be so fatal as a false alibi.

Kate shrugged again and sighed. She had mentioned Strong to her lawyer to please him, to give him something to scribble onto all those sheets of blank stiff paper. No, Strong was gone, and she could think of no one else useful in her cause. Even Sarah Crease was now to be used by the prosecuting forces.

"Think, think!" urged O'Brien.

PUTTING ON A SHOW

I

The days passed slowly for Kate, and she became sluggardly in both mind and body. She ate the stews they served her and walked the perimeter of the chapel garden in a lingering manner, so that some who did not know her might have misinterpreted her ways for sleeping sickness or even dignity. In truth she had become at last fully conscious of her awful position.

She longed for the end to her nightmare nearly as much as she longed to hold her child, but not quite. The question of her fate now lay beyond any manipulation on her part, although she felt sure that Kevin O'Brien would eventually steer her to safety. As for her boy, she was now aware that she had wronged him grievously. No woman was fit to call herself a mother who, in failing to protect herself, failed to protect her infant. Her statements as to Church and Harry Porter had been stupid in the extreme, and she had been reckless with regard to other matters.

All this must change. Henceforth she would not seek to sprinkle blame hither and thither in times of panic. She must act responsibly, use every guile at her disposal, to save herself and so her child. She could not tell her solicitor the full story, of course. She would *like* to do so; she would certainly tell the truth to all were she given a single hint that by speaking up she might be saved a trial for murder. But nobody came to bargain for the truth, and Kate resolved to hold her tongue.

In the meantime she could do this: Behave herself within these prison walls, strive to create a good impression, even rehearse the way she'd act her part when she came up for trial. Perhaps they would grow to pity her condition. O'Brien was not unsympathetic; the governor, plainly embarrassed by her presence in his prison, had shown compassion; and even the hard-eyed matron had been merciful toward her that dreadful day when they had informed her about her son. Yes, they surely pitied her.

And when it came for her to stand in answer for her crime, alone and humble in the dock, a jury of her peers would be watching. Not a solitary judge—a jury. But Kate had no experience of jurors. Over the years, whenever she had found herself called to book, she had always pleaded guilty—to be lectured and be sentenced by a black-robed recorder of quarter sessions. But this time, she reasoned, the coin was turned. Her court was to be the Central Criminal Court, a court of assize, a grander place by far. And no "thirteenth juryman" (as Strong had called a biased judge) would consider her case. She would be tried by ordinary men, from collar makers to costermongers, and they would treat her fair. They too would pity her; but for Fate, could it not be their mothers, wives, or sweethearts persecuted in her place? They would be studying her smallest movements, and she knew she would not fail her child.

Strong had told her once that at Old Bailey a mirror was positioned above the head of a defendant so that his demeanor could be seen from every angle. If this was true, well and good. For Kate would practice hard these next few weeks to achieve that quiet nobility expected of an innocent person. She would not tell O'Brien of this plan; she would surprise and please him on the day.

With this thought in mind, Kate set herself upon her stool and stared ahead at the cell door with straight-backed concentration, and there she remained until the strain on her lumbar regions forced her to find her bed.

Kevin O'Brien walked into Court Four—a drab and boxlike room paneled in dark oak—and tiptoed over to the table reserved for clerks and solicitors. On the bench sat Mr. Commissioner Kerr, black-gowned and red-faced, listening with impatience to an elderly barrister's plea in mitigation of sentence. The barrister spoke in a series of clichés, and O'Brien gathered from his words that his client had just been convicted of counterfeiting. O'Brien hoped that this was not the Mr. Frith whose whereabouts he now sought, and he looked at the other barrister appearing on behalf of the Crown.

"I suppose ye'll be gettin' ter the nub of the matter-rr presently," said Mr. Commissioner Kerr, tugging the lobe of his right ear. Both his irritation and Scots accent were very marked.

Defense counsel's voice trailed off, and O'Brien understood him to be saying that he was unable to help the learned judge any further.

Mr. Commissioner Kerr picked up his quill and scribbled in the book before him. Then he looked across the court at the man in the dock. "Noo, I would think not, Mr. Iverson," he said to defense counsel but staring at the prisoner. "Ye've said what yer can, and a mite more besides; yer client may be as perplexed as I, but I daresay he's not ungrateful. Stand up, Franklin!"

Kevin O'Brien watched the convict, flanked by warders, prepare himself for sentence.

"Yer-rr a wicked, wicked laddie," the commissioner said. "But I'll no waste words on yer-rr. Utter-ring sweated coin's nigh on treason, mon. Yer-rr what we call a 'smasher,' Franklin. And wunce a smasher-rr, ever a smasher-rr. Seven years!" Mr. Commissioner Kerr rose from the bench and retreated through a door even before the prisoner could be spirited below.

With the judge gone, Kevin O'Brien approached his Mr. Frith.

"Mr. Frith? My name is O'Brien. Your clerk said that I might find you here."

The barrister looked up from his papers. He was young, thought O'Brien, but he did not look as blatantly incompetent as the wretched Franklin's lawyer had sounded.

"Your clerk told me that you have had a chance to read my initial instructions in the Webster case," O'Brien added.

A look of recognition crossed Frith's face. "Ah, yes!" he said. "So sorry, you had the advantage of me for a moment. Yes, I have read it, only last night. Dreadful business, Mr. O'Brien, dreadful business!"

O'Brien nodded grimly. Now he would have to find a quiet place—in counsel's chambers or within the Central Criminal Court—to discuss the problems presented by Mrs. Webster, and to inform the learned Mr. Frith that, as yet, he had received no indication of what her possible line of defense might be. He could only pray that the learned Mr. Frith might show initiative —present him with a spate of questions he could put to Mrs.

Webster, demonstrate the way to break down the woman's show of good-natured silence.

II

June—a wet and humid month—came to an end, and upon the last day, a Monday, Kevin O'Brien journeyed once more to see Kate at Wandsworth Prison. He observed that her traditional dress of black had been exchanged for light blue, and he was pleased that this time she did not immediately harass him as to visits from her child. In truth, Kate's preparations for the day she was to face the jury had preoccupied her mind, so that now she had a faraway look, and her movements were stiff and unnatural. And when he informed her that the important moment had finally arrived, did he detect her relief at this news?

"Your trial starts on Wednesday," he told her when both were seated. "You will see your counsel, a Mr. Frith, tomorrow, when you are transferred to Newgate. At present I have only engaged the services of Mr. Frith; but I am still hoping to have Mr. Warner Sleigh leading him in due course." Finding a senior barrister either willing or available to handle her case had proved to be almost impossible, and even at this late hour he could not guarantee the presence of Warner Sleigh.

"I gets two lawyers, does I?" asked Kate. She supposed that she was to sound grateful, but she really wanted Kevin O'Brien alone on her behalf, not men she had never seen or heard of.

"Indeed you do. If Mr. Sleigh is not available, your trial will be adjourned until I can find someone else. The court is bound to show us favor, for a law officer will be leading for the prosecution."

"A what?"

"A law officer—the Solicitor-General, Sir Hardinge Giffard. And I imagine that he will have at least two junior counsel with him as well."

So she was to have two barristers, Kate thought; the other side were to have at least three, including someone very important —a knight and a general. "Slife, but they're puttin' on a show for me!" she said in wonderment.

It occurred to O'Brien that perhaps she found the strength of the team against her inequitable. "We have a very fair judge," he said. "Mr. Justice Denman."

"Will I have t'speak for meself?" Kate asked.

O'Brien shook his head. "Not a word. Mr. Sleigh will ask all the questions and say what must be said. You just have to be quiet—well-behaved—and leave it to him."

"I *shall* behave, sir!"

"I'm sure you will, Mrs. Webster. Your junior counsel, Mr. Frith, says that the medical evidence in the case must be attacked. If the jury can be made to doubt that the body found is that of Mrs. Thomas, the Crown will have no case."

"I know nothing 'bout such matters!" Kate said.

"Of course not. But that is why you must be quiet during the trial. No outbursts, mind?"

"I swear it, sir!"

"You became overexcited at the magistrates' court," O'Brien said, remembering how she had shouted at Church.

Kate read his mind. "But that was John Church fibbing like a fool!"

"Mr. Sleigh will be given the opportunity to question Church," her solicitor explained. "He will endeavor to show Church up for what he is."

"I want him punished!" said Kate, banging her fist into the palm of the other hand.

O'Brien let out a sigh. "You still insist that your statements to the police are true then?"

Kate, realizing that she had slipped yet again into her wild denunciations, did not reply.

But O'Brien persisted: "Are you still blaming Church and Mr. Porter?" And he waited for Kate to comment.

"I will leave that to your Mr. Sleigh," she said after a while. Let her advisers do as they willed; for herself only total withdrawal could prevent her blunderings.

"Well, you will see him tomorrow afternoon at Newgate—should he be free to represent you. You will also see Mr. Frith. I shall be there, but I want you to answer whatever questions either of those gentlemen put to you. Time is now very short, and you have been laggardly—to say the least—in providing me with facts. I beg of you not to persist in your dilatory ways, but to speak up before it is too late to make amends."

Kate followed O'Brien to the cell door.

"That's a nice frock you wear," he said suddenly.

Kate beamed with pleasure. So it was, a dress borrowed from the stock left at Wandsworth by a prison visitor. She had begged Captain Colville for a change of clothing, and great had been her surprise when this dress had been provided.

"I have it until tomorrow," she told O'Brien. "The wearing of it is for seeing me boy!"

Kevin O'Brien opened his mouth but did not speak. What could he say? That she would see no one other than her lawyers once she left this place? That there could be no question of a visit from her child at Newgate? O'Brien wondered just who—

from stupidity or malice—had raïsed the hopes of his client in this cruel fashion. He suspected the incompetent Captain Colville.

That evening they took the blue dress from Kate and returned her own black gown. Kate did not protest or question this sudden change of heart on the part of the authorities, although she thought their conduct strange. Her black dress, however, had been cleaned and pressed, and someone had been good enough to replace a missing button and mend a tear in the seam. They gave her also her dark bonnet, the one in shiny black straw with a shot silk ribbon. Kate would have preferred another garment and another hat. She was about to specify exactly what she wanted when she remembered that those of her choice had been the property of Mrs. Thomas.

III

They took Kate to Newgate Prison in a prison van drawn by four horses. It was a large van, big enough to accommodate ten or twelve prisoners, but Kate shared it with only one officer and another woman criminal. No words were addressed to Kate during the journey from south of the river to the City of London, and Kate said nothing.

No crowd was at the prison to greet the van, and they took Kate off through a labyrinth of stone-walled passages to reach the small room which was to serve as her accommodation throughout her trial. For the sake of convenience, this room was adjacent to the courthouse, so her removal from cell to courtroom and vice versa might be accomplished without delay or contact with other capital offenders.

At two o'clock in the afternoon Kevin O'Brien arrived with two well-dressed men.

"Mr. Sleigh. Mr. Frith," introduced Kevin O'Brien, and for the next hour Warner Sleigh quietly took Kate through her statements to Inspector Dowdell. It soon became apparent to Sleigh that this woman would say anything but the truth, and that her only hope lay in his creating a fog thick enough to befuddle the jury, to blind them by raising unanswerable questions, all the while hoping that neither the court nor the jurymen themselves would interpret his chicanery for what it truly was. Warner Sleigh did not care to employ such tactics in normal circumstances, but wasn't the case of Mrs. Webster abnormal enough to justify an artificial defense?

"Well?" O'Brien taxed him when they had taken their leave.

"I think she is guilty," said Sleigh simply.

O'Brien felt disappointed. He still had faith in his judgment that Kate was certainly involved but that someone else had done the worst.

"I can attack the identification of the corpse found," Sleigh went on. "I can present our client as a kindly mother of a little boy, as a person incapable of such barbarity. I can hint at this fellow Church being the real culprit, with Mrs. Webster little more than a hapless tool in his bloody hands. All of this I can—and will—do to the best of my ability. But, Mr. O'Brien, can you seriously envisage our twelve commoners being hoodwinked into an acquittal? Never! Not with old Denman doing his courteous deadly best, not with Hardinge Giffard running the opposite side. Our only consolation lies in the fact Mrs. Webster herself will never be questioned. Why, that woman lies with her eyes as well as her tongue!"

309

"No fault of yourself, sir," Frith said to O'Brien. He had seen the latter's unhappy expression and took it to mean a sense of failure.

O'Brien turned to the younger barrister and nodded his gratitude.

"Will she be troublesome during the proceedings?" Sleigh asked O'Brien.

"No, I think not," said the solicitor.

But cause trouble she did.

At first they thought she was joking when she requested to see her boy, and she thought that they were being mischievous in their refusal. So they sent for the governor—Major Griffith—to explain the regulations and expose the fiction of Captain Colville's assurances.

"But he promised me, the bastard son of a he-goat!" Kate screamed at them in her cell.

"That I cannot believe," said Major Griffith for a second time, although he knew Colville to be capable of any foolishness.

"Ye calls me a liar, does you! You fuzzy-faced length of tripe!"

Major Griffith, who was proud of his mustaches and conscious of his great height, thereupon ordered Kate to be forcibly restrained upon her bed—a wise move, for in another second Kate would have been at his throat.

"You must learn to behave when under *my* charge," the major warned her as his officers gripped Kate's arms and pushed her back. "I keep an orderly establishment, and there are others here who face great torment. I will not tolerate any breach of the peace, you understand?"

But Kate was not concerned about *others* in this building. She knew only that she had been cheated, and now she wanted vengeance. Unable to tear at the governor's face, she chose the nearest alternative—her own. With a great effort, she broke one arm free of an officer's grasp and clawed at her cheek in a frenzy. Her nails had been kept short at Wandsworth, but the strength of her fingers compensated to some extent, and soon blood ran from three deep scratches. She also attempted to gouge out an eye, but the prison officers were quick and pulled her hand away.

"Fetch the M.O.!" shouted Major Griffith in panic. "Tell him to bring ether!"

By now the tussle on the bed had become more violent—with Kate as anxious to injure her two captors as herself—and both officers yelled out in pain as either tooth or nail found its mark upon them. One of the officers drew back his fist to hit her, only to be restrained by the governor's "No. For God's sake, *no!*" Major Griffith could not have this wildcat appearing in the dock tomorrow with her eye blacked.

At last the medical officer and reinforcements arrived. Three on the bed became six or more, and a pad was clamped over Kate's nose and mouth. She bit at the cloth, tasting the ether, but her struggles soon diminished as her will and limbs lost their power. The medical officer watched her face for excessive contortions and slid open her eyelids once her bouncing stopped. He removed the pad and stood aside, gesturing for the prison officers to let go their hold. He glanced at the governor, still hovering on the outskirts like a witness to an accident.

"She'll sleep now and wake with a headache," he said. His tone was curt, since he had no more respect for Major Griffith than had the latter for Captain Colville. The major tended to be less upset by an execution than he was by the slightest rowdyism within his grotesque catacomb of dungeons.

311

"Well done, I say, M.O.!" cried Major Griffith, now daring to step closer.

The medical officer held the ether pad loosely in his hand. "M.O.? My name, sir, is not M.O.," he said. "My name is Dr. Wynter. Kindly call me doctor, or Dr. Wynter, or just Wynter. I do not address you by a series of absurd letters; please forbear to do so when speaking to me."

He pointed to Kate's unconscious form. "This woman, I understand, faces her trial for murder on the morrow. That, I daresay, is something of an experience neither you nor I shall ever suffer." He stared up the governor's tall form with cold assessment. "You, Mr. Governor, have as much a task to fulfill as I. I shall attend upon the health of such unfortunates, whereas you are paid a substantial salary to look upon their mental welfare. I don't know what caused this lady's outburst, but—since you are here and fretting famously—I must assume you have been party to it. She has injured her face in your presence; if that be so, in all probability she will attempt to take her life. Should she succeed in so doing, you will be responsible and you must bear the consequences of as adverse a report of what I have seen tonight as I may choose to pen."

He looked meaningfully at the open-mouthed prison officers scattered about the cell. "Gentlemen all, I wish you a very good night!"

Major Griffith, who was used only to sycophantic staff, shared the astonishment of his prison officers. This Dr. Wynter was new to him. "Who is that man?" he asked of his most senior officer.

"Dr. Wynter, seconded to us from Wandsworth Prison, sir," came the explanation.

IV

They were obliged to rouse Kate with a shake at half past seven, and she woke with a dry mouth and an aching head, unsteady on her feet and unable to eat so much as a spoonful of the porridge they provided.

Kate washed her face and hands in the customary bucket, and at eight o'clock the cell door was unlocked to let in a stout red-faced wardress.

"Ye been sent t'spy on me, I'll wager," Kate said.

"Spy? Not a bit of it, lass. I'm here to see you made comfortable, that's all." The round blue eyes looked hurt, and Kate relented a fraction.

"This porridge is cold and lumpy," she said, pointing at the tin plate. "But I'd fancy a cup o' tea."

The wardress, who was called Milly, nodded, pulled keys on a chain from her overall pocket, and opened the door. "I'll see what I can do," she said, and she was gone.

A cup of tea produced by the wardress had revived Kate considerably by the time they took her from her cell at five to nine. They did not manacle her wrists, and she was allowed to walk at her own pace, the wardress at her side, to Court One of the Central Criminal Court. The passage they trod was underground and ended at a single iron-covered door. This door led onto a short flight of wooden steps that rose into the area of the dock itself; and at precisely one minute before nine o'clock Kate found herself looking out upon the courtroom.

Court One was large and airy, paneled in dark wood, with a

forest of oaken benches running along either side, like pews in a church. Straight ahead, set high above the well of the court and the dock, was the judges' bench, a series of boxlike tables, four big chairs upholstered in black leather behind, a palladium of wood carved into the wall bearing the royal coat of arms. It was a grander room than Kate had ever seen before.

She looked about the dock for the mirror Strong had spoken of but could not find it, and her attention strayed down to the well and benches of the court again. People were milling about —some in robes and wigs, some carrying heavy books and bundles of documents, some filling the inkwells or sharpening quills. These busy people chattered among themselves, and great was the hubbub, but not a one so much as glanced up at Kate in the dock. The stout wardress called Milly put a hand on Kate's arm and bade her sit down.

After a minute or so the noise died down, and Kate saw that some people had left the court while others had taken their places on various benches. One bench, to the right of Kate, remained empty.

Then she spied Mr. Warner Sleigh and Mr. Frith. They were talking earnestly to three other bewigged lawyers, one of whom wore a shiny gown—a burly man with a snub nose and sporting thin brown side whiskers. The lawyer in the shiny gown spoke in the main to her Mr. Sleigh. A tall barrister, with a beard like an Assyrian and without mustaches, was speaking to Mr. Frith. None appeared to be arguing, all appeared to be on friendly terms. Kate's eye passed on to the massive table occupying much of the well of the court, and seated there she saw both Inspector Dowdell and her Mr. O'Brien. She waved nervously at the latter, but he was testing writing sand in the palm of his hand, and her wave was returned by Inspector Dowdell. Perhaps *he* could talk to people about her son?

Three sharp raps on a door to the left of the judge's bench, and everyone fell silent while the lawyers scuttled to their respective seats. All were ordered to stand as liveried dignitaries marched in, followed by a judge dressed in red and ermine. The dignitaries bowed to one another, to the lawyers in their pews, to the world at large, even, so it seemed, to Kate herself. Then the dignitaries retired through that same door, and the judge took his seat. The judge looked old, but not unkind, and Kate was surprised to see that he wore only a little wig on his head, not the huge kind with bloodhound ears she might have expected of so very important a legal gentleman. But she admired his robes, with the white gloves, a posy of flowers held in his left hand, and the white fur trimmings. The judge fiddled for a bit and then put on spectacles to peer about at everybody, sometimes nodding, sometimes smiling. He did not smile upon Kate.

Another lawyer sitting directly below the judge now came to his feet and demanded the presence of a jury in a loud voice. Kate leaned forward eagerly as the twelve who were to try her were marched to that empty bench. The lawyer under the judge—the clerk of the court—called out their names and told Kate that she might object to any should she so choose. Kate looked toward her Mr. Sleigh, but he was whispering to the lawyer in the shiny gown, and each juryman took the oath upon a Bible unchallenged. Many of the jury couldn't read and had to mumble the words of their undertaking after an usher, a man who plainly delighted in this exposé of the illiterate. But Kate was pleased that some of her peers were simple beings; they were like herself. She felt they would give her justice.

Kate was standing at the rim of the dock before she realized she had obeyed the command to do so, and now the clerk of the court addressed her in a lofty tone.

"Katherine Webster, is that your name?" On the indictment in the clerk's hands were listed Kate's various known aliases, but the clerk saw no reason to put them to her. "Is that you?" he repeated.

"Yes, sir."

The clerk did not really hear her words, but he'd seen her lips move.

"Katherine Webster," he went on, "you are charged with the willful murder of Julia Martha Thomas, within the County of Surrey, on or about the second day of March, one thousand eight hundred and seventy-nine. How say you—are you guilty or not guilty?"

Kate shook her head, and the clerk entered her plea as one of not guilty.

"Let the defendant be seated," said the judge, and a chair was pushed under Kate so that she remained in the forward part of the dock.

The lawyer in the shiny gown came to his feet and rested his hands on a beige-topped lectern before him. He looked at the judge.

"Yes, Mr. Solicitor," came the cue.

"May it please your lordship. Members of the jury, in this trial for murder I appear on behalf of the Crown together with my learned friends Mr. Henry Poland"—he indicated the man with the Assyrian beard—"and Mr. Smith"—and he indicated a very youthful barrister to his rear. "The accused—Mrs. Webster, as I shall in future call her—is represented by my learned friend Mr. Warner Sleigh, together with Mr. Frith."

Kate approved of the way in which her own lawyers had been introduced to everyone.

"The deceased—the lady the Crown say was murdered by this defendant—was a Mrs. Thomas, and she lived at Number Two Mayfield, or Vine, Cottages, in Richmond, Surrey. She was a lady who had attained the age of fifty or sixty years. She had twice been married, and she lost her second husband in 1873. She also had a little independence of her own. . . ."

And so the Solicitor-General went on—to outline Kate's employment with Mrs. Thomas, the disappearance of that lady, the reappearance after six years of Kate at the Porter home, the involvement of John Church, the interruption by Miss Ives when the household effects were being removed, Kate's flight to Ireland, her arrest, and the making of two statements to the police.

"This matter being investigated," he said of her accusation of Church, "that happened which rendered it hopeless for the prisoner to persevere in her statement, for—most fortunately for Church—the *third* of March was fixed upon by the accused as the date of the murder. And Church was able to establish most conclusively that during the whole of that evening he was engaged in a sick and burial club, the Oak Slate Society."

Kate looked at the jurors. They were listening attentively, but their faces betrayed nothing of their thoughts.

"Up to this point," the Solicitor-General was saying, "she had not pretended to implicate Mr. Porter. Then it must have occurred to her that Mr. Porter was able to give evidence against her. And indeed he has, and will again. He can describe her visit to his house, state the damning fact that she described herself as Mrs. Thomas, and say how his son was used to help her carry the box to Richmond Bridge—a box, the Crown say, which held the remains of the real Mrs. Thomas." He paused. "So we have the fact that Church was able to establish an alibi. This in itself rendered it necessary for the prisoner to change her tale; and, accordingly, with a wonderful astuteness that probably over-reached itself, *another* statement was contrived—in which you will find that the date is changed. We are back to the second of March for the murder, which, as I invite you to conclude, is the real date of the murder of Mrs. Thomas." The barrister named Poland handed him a printed document, and he read to the court Kate's second statement. When he had finished, Kate saw that several members of the jury were looking at her in a curi-ous fashion. She returned their gaze haughtily.

"Some people do not understand the meaning of the term 'corpus delicti,' " the Solicitor-General was saying. "They 'En-glish' it—if you will forgive me—to mean 'body of the defunct.' But that is no translation. The words mean 'the fact of an offense having been committed.' And what have we here? Human re-mains—female remains—are found in a box. That box came from the house of Mrs. Thomas, who has disappeared. Charred bones are found in the kitchen grate and in the copper grate. Mrs. Thomas, last seen alive on March second at seven-thirty in the evening, has never been seen alive since. And on the facts that will shortly be put before you, members of the jury, you will have no difficulty in coming to the conclusion that the person who exercised dominion over that body, and disposed of it, is the prisoner at the bar; that the person who affected and claimed dominion over the deceased's effects, who took posses-sion over them and treated them as her own, is the prisoner at the bar; that the person who was in possession of a black bag, which has since disappeared, and only *she* can trace, was the prisoner at the bar; that the person who was the *only* other at the house was the prisoner at the bar; that the *only* person who absconded was the prisoner at the bar; that it was she who made

318

two statements quite inconsistent with each other, and which can in some respects be absolutely proved to be false; and that all the circumstances do point, as dumb witnesses, against the prisoner at the bar." The Solicitor-General turned to consult with Henry Poland, to ask him whether he had missed any point of importance in his opening address. The other shook his head, and the Solicitor-General looked up at the jury again.

"You may ask yourselves this," he said. " 'How could a woman, not very old and not very young, have contrived at such a ghastly plan as this?' Well, members of the jury, the Crown cannot burrow into the mind of any person accused of crime; far easier would it be for us to fathom the depths of an ocean than to reveal the innermost secret thoughts of a fellow human. But this the Crown does say: that this was a *planned* murder. For you will hear that on Shrove Tuesday, on the twenty-fifth of February last, the prisoner did say to a female friend, by the name of Durden, that there was shortly to be a change and an improvement in her condition and circumstances."

Kate began to stir angrily in her chair, and the wardress Milly grew alarmed. She leaned over and spoke into Kate's ear. "Don't do nothing silly, lass!" And Kate allowed herself to go limp again.

"So this Durden woman was told of how the prisoner lived at Richmond, holding good employment as a housekeeper, but also of how she was going soon to Birmingham to settle some property left to her by her aunt. And the prisoner went on to say that this aunt of hers—entirely fictitious a person, of course, members of the jury—had left to her a gold watch and chain, and other things including her furniture. The prisoner added that she intended to sell this property, and that she fully expected her aunt to be dead by the time she herself got to Birmingham. Now, all of this was said on the twenty-fifth February, and Mrs. Thomas, we know, was alive on March second. The Crown says that these lies were told by the prisoner to pave the way for that which was afterwards to follow."

And now the Solicitor-General was closing his address to the jury.

"So if you are satisfied, members of the jury, that the act by which Mrs. Thomas lost her life is traced to the hand of the prisoner at the bar—or to her procurement—then she is the person upon whom lies to be proved everything in mitigation or excuse. And if none such existed, then she is guilty of the offense with which she is charged. And if you are satisfied with the facts, it will be your duty to say so by your verdict." He picked up a bundle of depositions and turned to the judge. "My lord, I shall call first Inspector Wells. He simply produces a photograph of Number Two Mayfield Cottages, and various plans . . ."

V

Thursday came and went, and Kate preoccupied herself by sitting up straight and poker-faced to impress the jury. Her rigid position may have left the jury unmoved, but it did not escape the attention of the judge, who ordered that a cushion might be provided to ease the obvious strain on the prisoner's back. Kate allowed the feather bolster to be adjusted by the attendant Milly and then nodded at his lordship.

"Thankee, yer honor!" she said in a clear voice, and she was treated to a blink of recognition in return.

Young Robert Porter was nervous under Warner Sleigh's cross-examination but not hostile to suggestions made.

"He has been most favorable to us, I think," said Sleigh to Kate at the end of the day. "He has agreed that you showed kindness toward his late baby sister many years ago, and that you were to be regarded as a true friend to his family. This is most gratifying." Neither Warner Sleigh nor Kevin O'Brien went on to opine that the testimony of both Harry and William Porter undid much of the good.

"What of Jack Church?" Kate asked them.

Her lawyers looked at Milly, sitting in a corner of the cell.

"God's zebs, but she's all right," Kate assured them. "She's a biddy fine an' fair to me." And Milly smiled her pleasure.

"Tomorrow," Warner Sleigh said. "He is in the box first thing tomorrow."

Kate grunted. "He'll try to present himself a square one," she said after a while. "He's not, you know. He's so crooked his hair don't curl right. Ask him about his past, sir. He'll deny all things, I dare suppose. But the deceivin' man of him will show through his denialin'."

Sleigh and O'Brien exchanged glances. It was O'Brien who spoke. "You have told us how to cope with Jack Church. Can you now tell Mr. Sleigh what he is to ask of Mary Durden?" He offered Kate a cigar from his case. Kate looked at Milly, who nodded, and then accepted her solicitor's match.

Kate blew out smoke and shrugged. Some things were beyond even her powers of invention. "Just lies," she said. "Just lies."

Warner Sleigh was cautious in his approach to John Church. He took him through the details of his alibis for the second and the third of March, through his first meeting with Kate, and through the circumstances surrounding the removal of Mrs. Thomas's property. He was cautious because he was aware that Mrs. Church and Henry Weston would follow Church in giving evidence, and he hoped that the three might contradict each other in some salient way. When they did not, he knew that he must beg the court's leave to cross-examine Church again at a later stage.

But on the Monday morning they called Mary Durden to speak her piece, and Warner Sleigh fully appreciated that his client's case had set foot on unknown and forbidding country-side. In his instructions from Kevin O'Brien, Mr. Sleigh knew only this: that Mrs. Webster had been overfamiliar with this lady's husband at a public house called the Three Tuns and kept by a Mr. Parker.

"You say that you have known Mrs. Webster for four years or more, madam?"

"Yeh, since before she went into Mr. Mitchell's service in Twickenham."

"I suggest that you have not always been on good terms with her, but that the two of you fell out?"

"Oh yes? What about?"

"Over your husband and Mrs. Webster consorting together at an alehouse called the Three Tuns?"

"What you gettin' at?" asked Miss Durden, thinking of Strong.

"You caught Mrs. Webster and your husband there together on two occasions, did you not?"

"I never did!"

"Perhaps it was another public house, the name of which has slipped your mind?"

"Never!"

"Well, I suggest that this is so, and that you were jealous of Mrs. Webster?"

Miss Durden laughed shrilly and fearfully. "I don't know who told you that, sir," she said. "But Mrs. Webster was never about with my husband."

Warner Sleigh sat down. What more could he do? He knew neither what to ask nor the way to ask it.

The judge gave Warner Sleigh leave to recall Church in the early afternoon.

"I want to ask you some questions about your past, Mr. Church," Sleigh began, and Church became immediately unhappy.

"What was your surname before you enlisted in the army?" If Church was the criminal Mrs. Webster suggested, he might have changed his name a time or two.

"My father's name was Church, as far as I know."

"As far as you know? Perhaps you can tell us your mother's name?"

"Body."

"So at least you are sure of your mother's name. Let us move on then. You have not always been the owner of a public house, have you? No doubt you have had lowlier employment in your time—say as a simple barman?"

"I might have been before I joined the army."

"*Might* have been?"

The judge tapped his pencil to attract Church's attention, and his face was very severe. "Just attend to me, if you please!" he said. "You will be in great peril of an indictment for perjury if you tell us any falsehood or suppress any fact within your knowledge."

323

Sleigh continued. "Were you ever in a situation as a barman?"

"I might have been."

"Were you, or were you not—on your oath!"

"I might have been."

The judge gave an audible sigh and threw down his pencil. "Do you seriously mean to say you do not know?"

Church's thoughts were racing. What were they getting at? Did they all know about his "troubles" back in 1856?

"I may have been," he conceded.

"Where, in London?"

"Yes, I was in London."

"We know you were in London, but were you in a public house?"

"I might have been."

"Working as a barman?"

"I might have been."

"Where in London?"

"I cannot recollect."

"Do you mean to say—upon your oath and before the gentlemen of the jury—that you do not recollect?" And Sleigh looked up at Mr. Justice Denman.

"I might have been," said Church yet again.

"Don't say that any more!" snapped the judge. "Now, upon your oath, *were* you a barman or not?"

"Yes."

"Have you ever been in prison?" Warner Sleigh pounced.

"Before this case?"

"Before this case."

"Not to my knowledge," Church said quietly. Had this lawyer a record of his misdeeds tucked away within his gown or somewhere?

"Not to your knowledge. I shall repeat my question, Mr. Church. Have you, or have you not, been in prison before you were arrested on this charge?"

"No."

"And that you swear?"

"Yes." Why didn't the lawyer produce the proof *now?*

"A moment ago you said, 'Not to my knowledge.' "

"I spoke too rapidly."

Church was staggered to find this answer accepted, for the lawyer went on to ask him other things not connected with his past. Church soon realized that they did not have his crime sheet available, if they knew of it at all, and that the lawyer's questions had been mere shots in the dark. Shots aimed by Kate Webster over there. Jack Church stared balefully at the dock. Twice she had tried to drag him down, and twice she had failed. Jack Church was overcome with a feeling of triumph. Now the lawyer for the Crown was asking him something. . . .

"You went into the Eleventh Hussars in 1860, and purchased your discharge in 1866. Have you got *good* discharges, Mr. Church?"

Church straightened himself. "I have, sir!"

"He has already told us that," put in the judge. "They are not evidence."

Jack Church blinked at the Solicitor-General, but he did not dare look up at the judge. Silly old fool, he thought, always interrupting on the side of bloody Katty Webster. . . .

Late afternoon, and shafts of light poured into the court from the glass panels in the roof. The Solicitor-General was reading Kate's statements to the police in full, and his voice was tired and bored. Both Warner Sleigh and the judge were writing—

Sleigh his closing speech to the jury, the judge a summing up of the evidence he would have to deliver tomorrow. Mr. Justice Denman did not enjoy his task. He was apt to dislike all cases of murder—the more so where the accused was of the opposite sex—and the facts of this particular homicide were unpleasant in the extreme.

The Solicitor-General announced that the case for the Crown had formally come to an end, and Warner Sleigh came reluctantly to his feet once more. "The defense call no witnesses," he told the judge, adjusting his gown.

Mr. Justice Denman nodded. He then looked at the silver watch he always placed on the bench before him. It was after four o'clock. "Do you wish to address the jury now or in the morning, Mr. Sleigh?" he said. "If—having regard to the lateness of the hour—you would prefer to leave it to the morrow, I'm sure we will all understand."

But Warner Sleigh could see no advantage in delay. More time could not add to the little he had to say. Since a law officer was prosecuting, the Solicitor-General had the right of last word. Let *him* speak then tomorrow; let Sleigh speak now and send the jury away to their homes and beds with the arguments for the defense still ringing in their ears.

"I shall address the jury now, by your leave," he replied. "And I shall not be long."

Nor was he long. His speech concerned itself primarily with the question of the identity of the body found in the river, the reliability of Church and Porter as witnesses, and the consequences of a conviction.

Later in his speech he said, "What of the disposition of Mrs. Webster? We have heard of her undoubted love for her child. Mrs. Crease has described her as a kind and good-hearted creature—did she not watch and attend upon Mrs. Crease's husband when he was laid up in bed? And now you are being asked to send this woman to the gallows!"

And later still: "Let me deal with the evidence of this man Church. How impossible it was for me to obtain from him any information as to his antecedents. Is it not terrible that a man can go into that witness box and so unblushingly perjure himself before his fellow man? And upon that person's word, to a great extent, hangs another human being's life!"

The testimony of Mary Durden? She, said Mr. Sleigh, was simply mistaken.

At last Warner Sleigh could think of no more to say, and he knew his role on his client's behalf was ended.

"If there have been shortcomings on my part," he said, "I can say this in all humility: I had the papers in this case only a few short hours before the matter came to trial. Only *you*, members of the jury, are the bulwarks of safety between this accused and an unjust conviction. Upon *you*—and you alone—lies the power of sending this woman to the gallows, or preventing a miscarriage of justice. And so I leave Mrs. Webster to you, to my learned friends for the prosecution, and to my lordship, safe in the assurance that she will receive justice."

Milly obtained brandy for Kate that evening. She expected signs of great strain to show themselves on her charge's face, but there were none, and she was relieved. "Soon over now," she said when Kate handed her the emptied glass.

Kate had been thinking. "Tell me, Milly," she said casually. "When is it that they'll never hang a woman?"

It took a time for Milly to comprehend what Kate's question

327

implied. "When she's quick with child," Milly said eventually.
"As I thought," said Kate. "When she's quick with child."

VI

Sir Hardinge Giffard was not a man impressed by forensic dramatics, and he eschewed any style approaching a passionate appeal when he came to address the jury that Tuesday morning. Although he was polite to Mr. Warner Sleigh, he accused him of both exaggerating and inviting the jury to cast aside their common sense. And having pulled apart those arguments raised by the defense, he quietly told the jury to find their verdict according to right and truth.

Mr. Justice Denman had a harder task, for it was for him to paraphrase to the jury every important piece of evidence heard from every important witness over the past five trial days, and to do so without a show of bias or his own personal feelings. Kate listened to what the old man said, because something of his manner reminded her of Uncle John Lawler—not his face or his voice, but something, nonetheless. He had a large and crooked nose, which he sniffed whenever he paused, and the longer he went on the more often were the pauses and the sniffs, until Kate found herself anticipating the exact moment when both would occur. But he made it clear that the jury could accept Mrs. Thomas to be dead, and that Kate knew she had been murdered.

"You have got to consider all the circumstances," he told the jury after a sniff. "Twice did the accused allude to something like a violent death. First she said that Church had told her 'he had done it,' and later she did say, 'I know nothing about the death. I had no hand in murdering her, but I know that he did it.'"

Kate did not enjoy these references to her statements. Nor did she care for this observation by the judge: "I feel it my bounden duty to protest against the use by learned counsel for the defense of certain intimidating words—namely, that you will be sending the prisoner to the scaffold should you give your verdict as guilty. That was unfair of Mr. Sleigh. Nor is it a true thing or a just thing. You must give your verdict according to your consciences. You have nothing to do with the consequences!" Another pause accompanied by sniffing.

"The statements of the accused," he then said, "what of them? They amount in substance to this—that, either on the second or on the third of March, Church murdered Mrs. Thomas; that the accused had no part in that murder; but that under duress or intimidation was obliged to conceal it until at last he sent her off, and so it was that she went off to Ireland. Now, gentlemen of the jury, is that like the truth? Does it consist with facts that are proved? If it really *does* consist with facts that have been proved, why, of course the accused ought to have full benefit of the statement; and *if* it leaves on your minds any reasonable doubt as to whether Church committed the murder and she was really only a mere accessory after the fact, helping him to get rid of the body and so forth, she is not guilty of murder, and ought not to be so convicted."

The tone of the judge changed to signify regret, perhaps sadness itself, as he added, "But if on the other hand you are driven to an irresistible conclusion—by looking at the two dates fixed by her, by looking at the evidence of the prosecution, by looking at the evidence of Robert Porter and other witnesses who corroborate that boy—if by looking at *all* these things you come to the conclusion that this murder cannot have been committed except either by her alone or by someone in concert with her, you will have to find her guilty of murder."

What was the meaning of all those words? Kate wondered.

What else can I tell this jury? the judge asked himself, vowing to avoid any further trials for murder for the duration of this session.

"The issue of the case is now entirely for you," he finished. "If you are satisfied beyond all reasonable doubt that this accused is guilty of murder, you will say so. But if you entertain any *reasonable* doubt about it, you will then acquit her and say she is not guilty." He closed his notebook and put away his spectacles. But he noticed that Warner Sleigh had bobbed up again.

"Mr. Sleigh?"

"Would your lordship explain that the accused cannot be convicted as an accessory after the fact," said Sleigh.

"I have said that distinctly!" The judge was testy; it was past five o'clock, and he was tired.

A court usher now assumed the role of a jury bailiff, swearing an oath to keep the twelve hidden in some "quiet and convenient place," and leading them off through a door at the side of the courtroom. When he and his fold had gone, all rose for the judge to make his exit, and Kate was taken down the dock steps to the warren of underground passages.

Milly was with her, and they were shown to a small circular chamber. There was no window, the light coming from a grille in the door, and a thick plank of teak served as a bench on which they might sit.

"Cup of tea, lass?" Milly asked Kate, who nodded. Milly called out their request through the grille, and a voice answered from far away.

"So many important people," Kate said to the wardress when she returned to the bench. "You'd not think they'd be havin' a general and a lord all on account of old Katty!"

Milly realized that she was making reference to the Solicitor-General and the judge. "The judge is not really a lord, Kate," she said. "They call him 'my lord' and 'his lordship' in court because he's meant to represent the Monarch himself." Or so Milly had read somewhere.

Kate looked at her. "But we haven't got a king, Milly. We got ourselves a queen!" Later she asked, "Why don't they call the judge 'his ladyship'?"

Milly had no answer to this question, and a warder came bearing two mugs of tea.

"How long will they be?" Kate asked of the jury.

"No telling, lass. It could be hours and hours." And there was silence as they sipped tea. Kate endeavored to concentrate upon one thing at a time—upon the queer shape of this cell, upon her child, and upon the past six days—but her mind wandered until she was thinking of nothing.

"What d'you think they'll say?" she asked of the jury again.

"Who knows, lass. Perhaps they'll find you innocent."

That Kate doubted now. But she was not without all hope.

"Will his lordship sentence me to death?" she asked. Milly detected no fear in her voice and was able to reply. "Them's just words, lass. Just words." She remembered an experience of her own and saw fit to relate it. "I was at a court out in the country once," she said. "It was in front of Mr. Justice Hawkins—the hardest man alive—and there was this girl found guilty of killing her baby girl. And when Judge Hawkins passes sentence, he refuses to put on his black cap—although the sheriff tries to make him—and he says the words so quiet that none can hear them; and he tells this girl that she's to pay no heed to what he says anyway. And that girl never did get hung."

At twenty-five minutes past six a tramp of feet announced that they were to return to the court above, and Milly squeezed Kate's hand. Four male warders flanked them as they mounted the wooden steps to the dock, and Kate saw that all were assembled in the courtroom—lawyers, clerk, and jury—except the judge himself. But Kate had only just taken her seat when those three sharp raps announced the arrival of the latter.

Mr. Justice Denman, representative of some long-dead king, sat down and refused to look at anything other than his hands. At his side a chaplain stood, called over from St. Sepulchre's church nearby should the verdict be the worst.

The clerk of the court and Kate alone were standing as the foreman of the jury was invited to his feet.

"Gentlemen of the jury," the clerk asked of him, "have you agreed upon a verdict, and do you find Katherine Webster guilty or not guilty of the willful murder of Mrs. Thomas?"

The foreman looked toward the dock and then sharply away when he encountered Kate's pleading gaze. "Guilty," he said.

Kate uttered a little cry and would have fallen but for Milly's supporting arm. The male warders closed in.

And now the clerk of the court was speaking to Kate. "Katherine Webster, you stand convicted of willful murder. Have you anything to say for yourself why the court should not give you judgment according to law?"

Kate opened her mouth, but nothing happened. She cleared her throat and tried again, and when she spoke the words just tumbled out, addressed to the judge but garbled, so that he was forced to crane his head and pull a face.

"I am not guilty of murder, my lord!" she said. "I have never

332

done it, my lord! When I was taken into custody, I was in a hurry. And I makes this long statement against Jack Church and Harry Porter. I am very sorry for doing so, my lord. And I want for to clear them out of it." She paused, and the eyes of everyone were on her in the silent court. "And another thing!" she cried after a moment's thought. "And another thing, my lord! The man who is guilty of all of this is not in the case at all, nor never was. Therefore, I don't see why the likes of me should suffer for what other people have done! Y'see, there was a child put in me hands in 'seventy-four. And I had for to thieve for that child and go to prison for it, which can be brought to yer lordship. Anybody can tell it round Kingston, or Richmond too! Therefore, 'tis the father of that child who's been the ruination of me since 'seventy-three—up to this moment. And *he* is the instigation of this, and *he* was never taken into custody! I have cherished the man up to this minute, I have! But I do not see why I should suffer for a scoundrel who has left me after what he done!" And Kate commenced to whoop and cry.

Mr. Justice Denman, eyes still downcast, began to mumble. A black cloth had been placed on top of his wig by an unseen hand from behind his chair.

"Prisoner at the bar. After a very long and painful inquiry, and after powerful advocacy on your behalf, and all the assistance that could be given to you by a zealous and sympathizing attorney, you have been found guilty upon what—even in the absence of what you have now told us—I should have ventured to say was irresistible testimony of the crime of willful murder. You tell us now—er, for the first time—that you were instigated to that crime by someone who is not in custody and whose name is not before us, and you have made some reparation at this moment by exonerating from all charge two persons who—it was not impossible—might have been sent to the scaffold upon the statement you made against them, coupled with circumstances which it was hard for them to explain. So far, I think, all will feel that the result of this trial is in one respect satisfactory. But, though you put it to me that you ought not to suffer because *another* instigated you to this crime, this cannot be a consideration which will warrant me for one moment from hesitating to pass upon you the sentence of the law." He dared look at Kate for a moment, as if asking her forgiveness.

"Indeed, I have no option," he continued. "My duty imperatively demands it, and I must do it. Whether your statement now be true or not, only God can tell! After so many false statements, as you have made, it must not be assumed to be true as a matter of course. *If* it be so, it is no excuse for you; because, in point of law, you have been proved guilty of the crime of murder. And indeed that very statement shows the justice of the verdict of the jury."

What was he saying now? He had lost the thread of what he had intended to say. God spare him from cases of this kind!

"I say no more. I do not wish to hurt your feelings by saying a single unnecessary word. But it is my duty to pass upon you the sentence of the law."

A square card was placed before the judge by the same hand that had covered his head with the black cap.

"The sentence of the court is that you be taken hence to the place where you were last confined, and thence to a place of execution, where . . ."

The judge's voice fell so low that only those beside and behind him could hear the final words.

"I am with child!" Kate shouted across the court.

A muttering broke out from the various benches, and Mr.

Justice Denman looked up in alarm.

"What's that you say?" the clerk of the court asked Kate.

"In God's name, I am with child," Kate repeated, her voice less sure.

The clerk and the judge exchanged words. This plea had not been anticipated; now they must follow a certain procedure. No one present believed the prisoner's claim for a moment, but Justice must be seen to be done, done by calling a panel of matrons to examine Kate in private, in the presence of a prison doctor, to establish how genuine was her claim. The clerk of the court was angry—angry with Kate, and with himself for being unfamiliar with the proper process.

"Let the prisoner stand down and be escorted to the jury room," he ordered.

Kate turned to Milly. "Will ye come with me?" she asked.

But Milly declined. "Why are you torturing yourself?" she said.

DIMAS

I

Captain Colville was none too pleased to receive the notorious Kate Webster into his safekeeping once more. He had the report of her trial at the Old Bailey, and he had a letter enclosing the observations of Major Griffith of Newgate Prison. But he was less concerned about the complaints of the stork-legged major than he was with the weeks ahead. Kate Webster stood condemned to death, and his prison had no death cell; Kate Webster was to be executed by Mr. Marwood at a date not later than the 29th of the month, and he had no gallows. Kate Webster had a six-year-old son, whose upbringing was now to be the responsibility of the state.

So he had converted into a suitable cell a large room near the infirmary—space enough to house both the convict and any officers necessary to maintain the peace. In due course a shed must be built for the hanging.

But in the meantime Captain Colville was determined that the last days of this unfortunate woman would be as tolerable —to her, to him, to his staff—as possible, and he made contact with Father M'Enery without delay.

Father M'Enery, a native of County Cork, was widely used by the Prison Service in the Greater London area. A man of robust health and ready wit, he was able to withstand the sometimes obscene receptions afforded to him by the prison fraternity, and he had become over the years more a cheerer than a savior of souls. And when he came to Captain Colville's office that Tuesday night, he was as lively as the governor had ever seen him.

"So they've dumped the Ghoul of Richmond on *your* doorstep, have they, Captain?" he said, flopping into the only comfortable chair in the room.

"You'll see her, Father?"

"But of course. Every day until the end, provided you're sure she won't want me for her last breakfast."

"She's pining for her boy," said Colville.

"Then she can't be all bad, Captain. No chance of a farewell, I suppose?"

"None."

"Most men have hearts," said the priest. "But put them together to form an officialdom and they have none!"

The governor agreed, but didn't say so; one didn't voice criticism of one's masters. "We have a wardress with her now," he said. "But she seems to want someone by the name of Milly."

"Then find Milly."

"I have tried. But it seems that our Milly was attached to Newgate only for the purposes of the trial. And now Milly has been removed to Holloway for other duties."

Father M'Enery blew his nose and thought for a moment. Then he grinned. "I have someone for you," he said. "From the Sisters of Compassion, in Hammersmith. Sister Madeline is just the person for your woman."

337

"Your woman too, Father."

"Ah, yes. My woman too!"

Kate ate slowly but hungrily, breaking the blued potatoes with a spoon, mashing the halves, and sopping up the gravy around the edge of the tin plate. A stew of barley, potatoes, and the occasional shred of mutton, cooked in a greasy fluid, but edible nonetheless. Bread and jam, without butter, for pudding, all washed down with the inevitable mug of weak tea. Yet her fare was better than what others got within these rectangular walls, for she had been allocated a Category A number. She was somebody special in Wandsworth Prison.

She was finishing her evening meal when the outside bolts slid back on the door. It was the wardress who never spoke to her; she was with somebody else—a priest.

"Good evening, Katherine," he said. "Will you spare me a moment of your time?" Kate knew his accent. This must be the Father M'Enery of whom somebody had spoken. She wondered whether she was supposed to fall to her knees and kiss his hand. No, you did that to bishops. Was her Faith so far gone that she had forgotten even that?

"Bless me, Father," was all she could say.

Father M'Enery motioned for the wardress who never spoke to leave them alone.

"My name is M'Enery," he said. "But you can call me anything you choose. Can I call you Katherine? More pretty than Kate, I've always thought!" Kate pushed a chair toward him. She would have preferred a visit from Kevin O'Brien, but the priest was company enough.

"You'll be after hearing my confession, Father?" she said.

"No, not unless you want me to." He inspected the room.

338

"My, but you're well off in here, don't you know! Like a hotel room it is!"

He watched Kate nibble her bread and jam. The cell smelled of the stew, but he was acquainted with prison smells far worse than stew.

"What you want is a friend," he told her. "We can't get you your Milly—more's the pity—but I can get you another nice lady. What do you say, Katherine?"

Kate's mouth was full, but she nodded.

"Sister Madeline, one of the Sisters of Compassion—from your part of London to boot!"

"No nuns," Kate said through the bread. Memories of childhood flooded back.

"Well, she's not an *ordinary* nun, you know! Not one of those who made life a hell for *both* of us back in the Old Country. Sister Madeline's different, you see. She'll make you laugh, tell you tales fit to split your sides. You like to laugh, don't you, Katherine? Yes, I can tell that. And I'll tell you what." He leaned forward confidentially. "Just because *you* can't see your little boy does not mean that *she* can't. Why, Sister Madeline could wangle her way into a cardinal's bedroom, given such an unholy desire. And then, of course, Sister Madeline will be able to tell you how the little fellow's faring. How say you now, Katherine!"

He had Kate laughing, and he knew he had won. First victory to Mother Church, he mused. More important things could wait.

"Well, there it is," he said, rising. "I am off without ado to see Sister Madeline, and—*if* I can prevail upon her not to visit the cardinal this night—I shall send her sleuthing after your child. You shall hear from her tomorrow." He beat a tattoo, almost a tune, on the cell door and turned to Kate again. "Can you tolerate another visit from me, Katherine?"

Kate consented gladly; she would see anyone who had news of her son. All the misery of the past two days had been washed away by the visit of this priest.

Kevin O'Brien came next morning. Much as he had been angered by Kate's pregnancy hoax at the last moment in court, he had been impressed by what she had said to Mr. Justice Denman prior to sentence. She had justified his suspicion that another, a man, was concerned with the murder of Mrs. Thomas. Warner Sleigh had not been so impressed. "Bah, that woman will lie whenever it suits her purpose!" Sleigh had said, and his junior endorsed this view. But both Warner Sleigh and Frith were finished with the case. Only he, O'Brien, remained to carry her cause still further. There was no court of higher jurisdiction to which they might turn, but there was the government itself, in the person of the Home Secretary. And Kevin O'Brien entered her cell full of optimism.

"You must make another statement," were his opening words to Kate.

Kate was at a table reading of her trial in the pages of *News of the World*. She put the paper down and smiled. "I'll be hearing of me boy this day," she said.

O'Brien took off his bowler and sat himself on the bed. "Another statement—telling the truth about this other man," he repeated.

"What other man?"

"Concentrate, woman!" For the first time O'Brien was sharp with her. "The man you told the judge about on Tuesday."

So her words had not been unheeded? Kate could not recall

now exactly what she'd said that grim afternoon. She remembered only the embarrassment in the judge's eyes when he'd told her that she must hang.

"I shall give you a statement," she said to keep O'Brien content.

"You must, you must! You must tell us everything about this man—where you met him, just how he ill-treated you, just what he did. Every single thing! Damn it, woman, this could save your neck!"

Save her? He was so eager that Kate was half persuaded. "I'll do it," she said again. "No, not now. Later, when I've time t'think."

"Was it the same man you made mention of before, the man called Strong?" O'Brien asked. In his hand were the jottings he'd noted down before, Strong's name underscored in red.

Kate shrugged. Who else? And O'Brien realized that she did not want to put this name down on paper. No matter. He knew, and the police would know when he had told them.

Sister Madeline and Father M'Enery came in the afternoon and found Kate trembling with excitement.

"Sister Maddy," the priest introduced a slim, smooth-faced woman. She reminded Kate of a statue of a saint carved in alabaster.

"Your son is as handsome as a rainbow," Sister Madeline said before Kate could ask. Her voice was as gentle as Kate expected. "He is well, he is happy, and he sends you his love."

"He misses his ma?"

"But he misses his ma." Sister Madeline swept over and took Kate's hands. They both sat down but did not disengage their hands. Father M'Enery nodded approvingly from a corner.

II

Much though the serenity of Sister Madeline soothed Kate, the undeniable piety of this new company failed to dampen her pathological need to lie; and since the telling of untruths had been as much a habit throughout Kate's life as the smoking of strong tobacco, it was not surprising that this should be the case. In the event, Kate mulled over what Kevin O'Brien had said, anticipated the kind of statement he was wanting, and prepared the context in her mind. And on the Thursday morning she said to Sister Madeline, "Me solicitor wants me to make a confession setting out the true nature of things. I've thought it over, and I'm ready."

Sister Madeline put down her sewing. She was unaccustomed to prison confessions, so she said nothing.

"Will you witness what I have to say, Sister?" Kate asked her. The signature of a nun upon such a document might carry weight.

But Sister Madeline was not to be drawn into such a thing; her role was simply one of spiritual comfort, not of legal involvement.

"I think it far better you have someone from the prison, Kate," she said and got up to call the wardress. She spoke through the grating in the door, and the other came in, surly and suspicious. "I think Kate would like you to witness something or other," Sister Madeline explained.

The wardress who never spoke continued to chew on her American gum and stared at Kate for so long that it occurred to Kate that perhaps she really had no tongue.

"Couldn't read what you writ even if I wanted," she said finally. "No good at letters, see?" And the chewing began again.

"Then perhaps you could fetch someone who *can* help?" Sister Madeline asked.

"Why not you?"

"I think it would be outside my province, my child."

The wardress looked her up and down with an obvious distaste for the nun's habit. The movement of her jaws became furious as she snapped back, "Don't see what the likes of you's doing here anyway!"

Kate came to her feet, huge and dangerous, and stepped forward.

"Get back you!" shrieked the wardress.

Sister Madeline came swiftly between them. "Now then, none of this!" Her voice was sharp. "You run off and find someone," she told the wardress.

"Daughter of a fornicatin' goat!" Kate growled as the wardress closed the cell door. "If she talks to you like that once more, I'll write me name across her face!"

The wardress returned after some ten minutes, the matron of the prison in tow, and Sister Madeline absented herself lest a further attempt be made to involve her in whatever took place. Outside the cell she tried to make light of the recent unpleasantness with the wardress, but that bovine girl stalked off in a huff, so she went to the Catholic chapel to pray for Kate instead. And while that Sister of Compassion prayed, Kate Webster fabricated a tale as contrary as her powers of imagination allowed, helped with her English by the unsuspecting matron, who didn't know what to believe and cared little about what was being said in any event. When her faculties for extreme distortion dwindled from sheer exhaustion, Kate laid down her pen.

"No more?" the matron asked.

"Later," replied Kate, head in hands.

The matron picked up the seven pages of manuscript. She herself felt weary, for the narrative had taken a full hour to relate. She had offered to lend a hand with the writing herself, but Kate had been adamant—*her* writing only. The matron was there to assist with the usage of words and their spelling and to sign her name as witness—no more.

"Ye'll keep it safe for me?" Kate asked, raising her head and rubbing her aching hands.

The matron nodded. "I'll give it to your solicitor myself. He's certainly got some reading to do!"

" Tis only half of the truth at that," said Kate.

Kevin O'Brien paced up and down, frowning, hands behind his back. The statement lay crumpled on the table, and Kate grew more anxious by the moment.

"Why lie?" Her solicitor suddenly rounded on her.

"Lie, sir?" Kate's stomach turned.

"Yes, lie!" O'Brien reached out, seized her confession, and shook it at her. "I never told you to make any public statement from the dock, did I? No, that was you and you alone, damn it! To say that I was in the *dock* with you . . ." He flung the papers down again.

"Oh that, sir," said Kate, very much relieved. "Well, I'll own that was a little bit of a white lie. But I sees it this way, I does. You being a first-rate and respected man, as it were, and you advisin' me to tell what I know from morn to dusk—ain't it right that you'd have done what I say you did had the circumstances been the way that I say they were?"

O'Brien looked at her and then laughed without humor. "Snakes alive, you're more Irish than me, Mrs. Webster! But what about this black bag?" he continued. "In your statement you say Strong threw a black bag containing the . . . er . . . head of Mrs. Thomas into the river and that you have told me the exact spot where he did so. Another white lie perhaps?"

"It looked better that way," said Kate.

O'Brien frowned. "You must realize that I would be unable to corroborate these matters should I be asked."

"Corroborate, sir?"

"Come, come now! Your knowledge of English is very good, judging by the *flowing* words of your statement; don't play the ninny-hammer with me!"

Kate grinned. Yes, she had even managed to surprise herself *and* the matron with her choice of phrase.

"How's your boy?" O'Brien asked to change the subject.

"Farin' good, bless him! Sister Maddy's seeing him this very aft'noon, and she'll report back to me. God knows, but that's a holy woman!"

O'Brien wondered whether his client's esteem did not have a tendency to be restricted to those who were of use to her.

"Good," he said, retrieving the statement and sliding it into his case. "I'll have this copied. In the meantime you think of what more you have to say and get it down on paper. We need everything we can get, I assure you."

"We?"

O'Brien stopped what he was doing. Should he tell her? He supposed that he should; she, of all people, was entitled to know.

"Quite a petition has been started on your behalf," he said.

"Petition? What petition?"

"There are those who found the evidence of Mrs. Thomas's death unsatisfactory," O'Brien explained. "It does not help that you insist the old lady is dead after all, but some people don't think sentence of death should be carried out." He closed his briefcase.

Kate was up and at him, holding on to the hem of his cloak. "Yer mean they think Katty's innocent?" she demanded.

O'Brien pulled himself free. "Just a few. We can't expect too much, you know."

"And you'll show these folk my statement? I'll make another —another twenty if it helps!"

"No. One will be enough, thank you."

A newspaper had taken up her cause, the *Penny Illustrated*, together with a Kensington councilor. O'Brien could envisage their interest fading at the sight of a hundred pages of foolscap.

"I shall call again soon," he said, ringing the bell to be let out. "I shall keep you informed of developments."

Seven days later Kate sat down solemnly with paper, pen, and ink and wrote far into the night. She did not call for the assistance of the matron on this occasion, for she had decided to make this her confession, a baring of the soul of the kind so much loved by the illustrated papers of the metropolis. She took care over her handwriting, and her choice of what O'Brien had called those "flowing" words demanded concentration and a plowing of her memory for expressions she had heard used by her betters throughout the years. And proud was she to remember "reluctant" and "screen" and "incriminate," as well as "dark-complexioned" and "biased" (although she thought her solicitor had used this word upon one occasion).

When she had done, she blew upon the pages and waggled them about to avoid smudges. Her epistle was complete for whomsoever might be inclined to read it.

Kevin O'Brien was the first to read the confession, on the Friday morning, and he took it away with him without comment, much to Kate's surprise. But O'Brien had read the document twice, so alarmed was he by its content, and he wanted a second opinion before he taxed Kate on what she had written. Knowing that Father M'Enery was within the prison walls, he made for the small annex that served as a chapel, and he found the priest spreading out his chasuble in the vestry.

"I'm glad you're here, Father," O'Brien said at once. "Can you spare me a moment, please?"

Father M'Enery looked at his watch. He had a few moments before the file of Catholic inmates were marched down from their cells.

"Read this," said O'Brien, handing him Kate's statement, and the priest sat down on a nearby chair. O'Brien watched him read and reread various parts of the document. Once or twice the priest shook his head.

"Well?" asked O'Brien when the other had finished.

"Well what, Mr. O'Brien?"

O'Brien drew up another chair and took the document away from the priest. A legal and a spiritual adviser, each distrusting the other by instinct.

"Most of what Mrs. Webster says here is a pack of lies," O'Brien said. He patted the pages in his hand. "First she blamed Church for the murder and involved the man Porter. Then she exonerated both of them and blamed a man called Strong. In her last statement she mentioned another man, and a woman, whom she said she did not know and could not describe. Now she not only describes this other man but tells us of how she had met him with Strong in the past, at Brighton of all places. I don't believe a word, nor will others anxious to save her life."

"I know nothing of this," said Father M'Enery.

"I appreciate that, Father, but I need your help. *I* believe that somebody other than she murdered the old woman and cut her up—Strong or who I cannot say. But this"—he tapped the statement again—"is not the truth and does not look like the truth. Until she stops these absurd lies, my hands are tied."

"What do you want from me?" asked Father M'Enery.

"See her, Father! Speak to her! Make her see the folly of her ways! I must forward an application for her reprieve to the Home Office within the next four days!"

"And what makes you think she will be more honest with me, Mr. O'Brien?"

Kevin O'Brien pointed to the biretta on the priest's head and to the vestments on the table.

"No, no!" The priest laughed. "More lies are told to the likes of us than almost anyone else! No. But seriously, Mr. O'Brien, you were born a Catholic, were you not? Yes, as I thought. You still practice your Faith? No, as I thought. In times of great hardship, would you come to *me?* You hesitate before answering. You see, you do not know! Now, take Kate Webster. She too was born of the Faith, and she too has lost that Faith over the years; and now, when her fellow man is about to break her neck with a rope, does she send for me? Does she call out, 'Help me, Father. I would confess my sins to you!'? No, she does not. Nor will she until there is nothing left for her to do, unless I am much mistaken. *You* are her lawyer, it is in you that she places her trust at the moment, and I am afraid that you will have to cope with her perversities yourself."

"Will you do nothing then?"

Father M'Enery considered the question. "I tell you what I am prepared to do," he said. "I shall go and see your troublesome client and I shall say to her, 'Your solicitor has told me that you are being a very silly woman; if that is so, then stop being silly and tell him what he wants to know.' How is that?"

O'Brien agreed rather graciously. The priest, he thought, did not really want to assist him; the priest was waiting for a summons from Kate for him to attend in his own right, and no doubt Father M'Enery regarded O'Brien as standing in the way of that call.

Armed with a copy of Kate's statement, the prison chaplain saw Kate in the presence of Sister Madeline. Father M'Enery had read the statement over once again. Being only partially acquainted with the facts of the case, he could not apply the lawyer's critical mind to the truth or otherwise of certain parts, but he found much to disconcert him in the latter paragraphs.

"Mr. O'Brien was good enough to lend me this," he said. "He is somewhat unhappy about what you say in it, but that's a matter for the two of you." He smiled at Kate. "Tell me, Katherine, do *you* think this document will be well received?"

Kate looked puzzled. "And why not, Father?"

"Well, let me read you some of what you say. You have been convicted by a jury of what many hold to be a particularly heinous crime; you have lied to incriminate two men, risking their heads; and you now say this: 'For anything I have done, which I now declare before God to be as I have stated, I implore His mercy, and I hereby forgive those who have been ready to

condemn me of actual murder,' and then, 'The public mind
. . . was greatly biased against me, and for all the harsh and
unkind remarks passed upon me in the height of peril and
trouble, I freely from my heart forgive,' and finally, 'I have been
foolishly led away to my ruin by those who should have protected me, and may my miseries, trials, and awful fate serve as
a warning to young girls never to be led away from the path of
virtue and honesty.' Your words, Katherine. How do you think
your harsh and unkind public are going to receive them?"

Kate grew uneasy under his stare, and she was conscious of
Sister Madeline watching her as well.

"What's wrong with 'em, Father?"

"Well, don't you think, Katherine, that your harsh and unkind
public might consider your words somewhat hypocritical and
sanctimonious?"

"Sanctimonious, Father?"

"Holier than thou, smug, self-righteous."

Kate looked at the floor, and Sister Madeline moved over to
her side. Kate turned to her for protection. "I did not mean to
sound that way!" she cried.

The Sister of Compassion gave no sign of her feelings.

"Do you know what is missing from your statement, Katherine?" Father M'Enery said. The smiling priest had disappeared
completely, and Kate was frightened of what she saw. "Remorse. Oh, we have pity for yourself, for your condition, for
your child. But do we have so much as a shred of sorrow for
what happened to old Mrs. Thomas? No, we do not. Within the
next few days this document will be forwarded to Mr. Cross, the
Home Secretary, as part of your petition for him to urge the
Queen to grant you a reprieve—or so Mr. O'Brien tells me. How
much weight do you think the authorities will attach to what

you have to say?" He put the foolscap pages on the table in front of her and turned to Sister Madeline. "I shall leave you now," he said. "I shall be in the building if required."

When he was gone, Kate wiped her nose with her sleeve.

"Sure, he had no right to talk t'me that way!" she complained to Sister Madeline, and she pushed her statement away along the table as if it were infected.

"He's only doing what he thinks is best," said the sister.

"He's thinking he can convert me back, that's what he's thinkin'!"

III

Kate was walking in the smaller exercise yard, Sister Madeline at her side and the surly wardress lurking some way off, when Kevin O'Brien and Captain Colville stepped out of the side entrance and approached.

Captain Colville led the way, lifting his hat to the sister, but Kate was looking at her solicitor. His face was drawn and set, and he seemed more inclined to peer about at the granite walls and brickwork of the prison than to let his eyes rest upon the exercise party. He carried his cane under his arm and fiddled with the silver knob.

"Let us step inside," said the governor as he came up, and Kate knew that whatever news they conveyed must be bad.

In the passageway leading to her cell, O'Brien and the governor formed a semicircle around her, and Sister Madeline was politely sent away. O'Brien looked to the governor, who nodded, and the solicitor opened up his case. A short letter, which he handed to Kate without comment.

"Sir," Kate read to herself. "Mr. Secretary Cross having had before him the memorial forwarded by you on behalf of Katherine Webster, now under sentence of death for murder, I am directed to express to you Mr. Cross's regret that, after full inquiry and careful consideration of all the circumstances of the case, he has failed to discover any sufficient ground to justify him in advising Her Majesty to interfere with the due course of law." The letter was dated July 26—the day before—and was signed by a Godfrey Lushington.

Kevin O'Brien took back the letter. "I'm sorry," was all he could say.

"When?" Kate asked the governor. Neither looked at the other.

"Tuesday morning."

In just two days' time! Was it possible, was it really Katty who was to be hanged after all? She suddenly felt dizzy and leaned against the wall. Hands took hold of her. "Are you all right?"

Kate nodded. Let them take her back to her cell, so she could lie down to think. Two days! Surely there must be some mistake.

O'Brien stayed with her in her cell until it became apparent that she was not prepared to speak to anybody, and when he left, darkness had already fallen. He wondered if he'd call to visit her again, now that his role had come to an abrupt end and he had failed her. Yes, failed her; for O'Brien was the only man Kate Webster had succeeded in convincing of her innocence.

"Get her Father M'Enery," he murmured to Sister Madeline as he took his leave. "And please tell her . . . tell her how very sorry I am . . ." And he walked out of her cell.

They brought Kate a special meal for supper, as there was ordered an improvement in her menu for the remaining period. But Kate did not stir from her bunk, and moaned when

Sister Madeline tried to make her eat. Hugging her bulk, Kate began to slip into a womb of warmth and fantasies.

Then all at once she was sleeping, and her fancies developed into a series of nightmares, so that she tossed and turned on her bed. Finally Kate woke up screaming.

"Easy, easy." It was Sister Madeline.

"Oh, Mother of God!" Kate said, struggling up into a sitting position. She was bathed in perspiration but very cold. Sister Madeline pulled a blanket over her shoulders to stop her shivering.

Kate looked around her cell. A solitary candle burned on the table, low down and almost guttered. A gray light showed through the tiny windows.

"What time is it then?" Kate asked huskily.

"Near dawn, almost daylight." Sister Madeline was taking her pulse. She let go of Kate's wrist and mopped her face with a flannel. "You've been having bad dreams, that's all," she said.

"Is he still here?" Kate asked with a fresh outburst of trembling.

Sister Madeline took away the flannel. "He is. Do you want him now, Kate?"

Kate nodded. The nightmares had been message enough.

Father M'Enery came within minutes. He was fully dressed and wide awake, which surprised Kate, who was not to know that he'd been waiting for her call.

"I wish to shrieve," Kate said, and the priest flicked a stole about his neck. "I would confess to you, Father. And I would confess to all in writing too."

Father M'Enery stood where he was. Was there *no* end to this woman's desire to speak to the world?

353

"Which is it to be first?" he asked quietly. "Your God or your Public?"

His sarcasm was missed by Kate. "My God," she said, getting off the bed. She knelt down at his feet, and he laid his hands on her head.

"Bless me, Father, for I have sinned," she asked, even as he was doing so in Latin. "You see, it was I that murdered Mrs. Thomas. At first I thought her nice enough, and I was comfortable being with her, what with my boy at Mrs. Crease. But then I found her very trying. She used to annoy me—going over the rooms when I had done, pointing out places she said I'd not cleaned, showing a nasty spirit towards me. I formed an ill feeling towards her, you see. But I'd not intended for to kill her. Then one day we had an altercation. It was agreed that I'd be gone—and I think she writ this down in her memorandum book." Kate stopped.

"Go on, Katherine," said the priest. He had sat himself down on a chair and shaded his eyes and forehead with a hand, resting the arm on the cell table.

"Well, on the Sunday evening I was late in. So we had this argument, and she went off to her church very agitated in her mind. She came back and went upstairs. I followed after. We starts this other panny, which ripens into a rare old quarrel. In me anger, I threw her from the top of the stairs to the ground floor. God forgive, but I lost all control o'er myself. I think I ran down and choked her, to stop her calling out, but I can't recall. Maybe I did, maybe I didn't. But I know that I takes her down to the basement. I had to do away with her body as best I could. 'Twas then that the devil himself must have entered into my being."

"No. Fear," said the priest.

"Thank you, Father." Kate's voice sank very low, so that he had to strain to catch the words that followed. "I chopped the head from the body with a razor. And I used the razor and a meat saw and a great big carver to cut up the rest of her. I boiled up the copper, to put the body in. I don't know why now—I think to prevent the identifying of her. There was blood everywhere; the horror was inconceivable; I acted like I was deranged. Many times I was overcome by the scene I saw, and I failed in me determination. But I suppose Satan gave me strength. I burned and boiled the body. You know how I later did away with the pieces."

"Yes, and I think you have told me enough," said Father M'Enery.

"I did not mean to kill her, Father," Kate went on. "I cannot recollect why I did it. I cannot account for the bad feeling I had towards her."

"And are you truly sorry for what you did?"

"God knows I am, Father. Absolve me my sins, I beg of thee!"

So Father M'Enery blessed her again and absolved her. He gave her no penance but urged her to pray for the soul of Mrs. Thomas and her own. Then all was over. He stood up, kissed his stole, and lifted Kate to her feet by her hands.

"And now you want to tell your solicitor the truth?" he asked her.

Kate nodded. She could do herself no harm now, whatever she said. "Will you have the governor send for him this day?" she said.

"I will. But give him time to get here, Katherine. I imagine the poor man is still abed!"

Kate forced a smile. She looked about the cell for Sister Madeline but found her gone.

355

"I shall ask her to return," said Father M'Enery. "And I shall ask your wardress to see about some breakfast for us all."

A runner took the message to Kevin O'Brien, and he laid aside his divorce papers and his pride to catch the nearest hansom at the Aldwych. Clutching the note from Captain Colville, he bid the cabbie make haste to Westminster Bridge, for—to him—this was the last hour of the finest moment of his life. Kate Webster, that cause of worry and wonderment, was to speak at last. During the journey to Wandsworth Prison it did not occur to the solicitor just why the woman had suddenly changed her mind. At the prison O'Brien was escorted to Kate's wing and cell although he knew the way by heart.

"Mrs. Webster!" he cried with relief, as though she might have been plucked away from his meeting. The wardress closed the door on the solicitor's guide.

Kate was scooping porridge onto bread. O'Brien's own stomach was filled with black coffee only, and the sight of slimy food being shoveled away in such a fashion was upsetting it.

"I'm glad you come," said Kate, licking a finger. "I got a mite more to tell you, and I thought it best for you to hear of it yourself." She drank noisily from a mug, her eyes on O'Brien over the brim. "And I daresay you'll not be likin' what I has to say, Mr. O'Brien," she added when she surfaced for air. "I daresay you'll be a-cursin' me for a lying harlot; and I'll no be blamin' you if you do."

"The truth this time?" O'Brien ventured cagily. Another spate of lies on the eve of execution might be too much for even him to bear.

"Aye, 'tis the truth I'll be tellin' now, but I doubts you'll like the hearing of it. Have you pen and paper?"

"Yes." And O'Brien made himself ready at the other end of the table.

Kate sat back in her chair. "I made a statement in the presence of warders to Mr. O'Brien, my solicitor, on the tenth July," she began, "and a second statement in the presence of warders to my said solicitor, Mr. O'Brien, on the seventeenth July, both in reference to the Richmond murder."

O'Brien had stopped writing. "But that's untrue!" he said. "You made neither of those statements to me!"

"Aye, 'tis so. But I've decided that what I've written should be *official* like—with dacent witnesses, such as yourself. History will never know the truth, and even if it learns, it will forgive old Katty this deceitfulness."

"I'll not witness this!" O'Brien replied.

"No, you just do the writing of it, sir," said Kate. It was enough that her last words be in his handwriting.

"Very well. Proceed, Mrs. Webster."

"These statements were untrue in many ways," Kate continued, and she rambled on for a full half hour, pausing only when her solicitor complained of writer's cramp.

"Now let me have it," she said at the end, holding out her hand.

"Don't you want me to read it back to you?"

"No. I'll just sign it and have done." And Kate signed her name with his pen.

O'Brien watched her. "You are an extraordinary woman, Mrs. Webster," he said, "but you are showing great fortitude in the circumstances."

Kate gave him back his pen and her statement. "I'm peaceful in me mind now," she said. "In less than a day I'm to meet my

357

Maker, and there's nought that can be a-changing that." She took out her stub of clay pipe that had been returned to her by Captain Colville, together with some tobacco. She packed the bowl and O'Brien gave her a match. "I've had meself a useless life," she said through the smoke. "I failed meself and I failed me child, and I've come to thinking that the boy's best off without me. So now I'll smoke me a Kemble pipe and sit back tight."

"A Kemble pipe?"

"A dyin' man's last." Strange how she referred to herself as a man; perhaps she should have been born into the other sex.

"Is there any more I can do for you, Mrs. Webster?" O'Brien asked, rising.

"Aye, see me boy, and give him three kisses from his ma."

O'Brien nodded and held out his hand.

IV

And Kate *was* peaceful in her mind. Since both the right and the joy of her life—the right to live and the joy of her child—were beyond her reach, she had become wholly resigned to her fate. Moreover, she had made her peace with her God, whose presence she had never really ceased to fear and therefore never truly disbelieved. Father M'Enery did not trouble her during that last day, reserving himself for what might prove to be unenviable tasks during the night and early morning. Only Sister Madeline remained with Kate in her cell.

As for the wardress, she was banished by noon.

"You can hop it!" Kate informed her. "And if you so much as show yer chawing face in here again, I'll smash it fer yer!" And the girl was happy to be released from the presence of such a wildwoman.

They gave Kate silverside and dumplings for her lunch, which she ate with gusto, sleeping afterward undisturbed by dreams.

They gave Kate boiled fish in a doubtful sauce for her tea, and she ate it up, although she complained the fish was off. And at nine o'clock they brought Kate a glass of brandy and a quid of tobacco for her pipe.

"You don't imbibe?" Kate asked the Sister of Compassion, offering her the glass of brandy.

Sitting on her bed, Kate drank the brandy in one gulp, and the fierce cheap liquid made her flinch. Then she lit her pipe, puffing hard until the clay was almost too hot to hold.

"Some say it's dangerous t'smoke in bed"—she cocked her head at Sister Madeline—"and they may be right. I heard tell once of a nun that used t'smoke in bed—on the sly, mind. Well, one night she falls asleep and fires the bedclothes. The conflagration was a thing to behold, and all they ever found of this nun was her little finger, which they duly buried according to Holy Rites. But 'tis said that if you sleep in that nun's room, you'll be wakened up by a jabbin' in your back through the mattress. 'Tis the nun's little finger, warnin' you not t'smoke in bed."

They laughed, then Sister Madeline asked Kate a question she had wanted answered for some time. "Did you hate Mrs. Thomas, Kate?"

Kate shook her head. "No," she said. "No, I didn't hate her."

Father M'Enery came at ten.

"God's hooks! but I could do with another throat warmer," Kate complained, looking at her empty brandy glass. Father M'Enery explained that a single tot was the ration.

"What d'you think will happen to me boy?" Kate suddenly asked them both.

Father M'Enery coughed. "Well, he'll be educated into a trade of sorts, and let loose upon the land when old enough. He'll be all right, Katherine, I assure you."

"Aha! But will they tell him his mother was a murd'ress?"

"I don't know. Not necessarily."

"He'll learn the truth if they calls him Webster," Kate reasoned. "Now, I've had many names. Can I not invent another for himself?"

Father M'Enery shrugged. Why not?

"I would have them call him . . . call him . . . *Dimas Strong!*" Kate said.

"That's a funny name!" said Sister Madeline.

"The name of the Good Thief," interposed Father M'Enery.

"Aye," said Kate. "You'd forgot, had ye not?" she said to the sister. "So call him Dimas and call him Strong." She turned to the priest. "D'ye think that'll give him a chance, Father?"

Father M'Enery smiled. Why not? The Good Thief was the one known to have found Paradise, and Strong was a good enough name for anyone. "You have much poetry within you, Kate," he said.

"Faith, no! Just a sense of preservation!"

"A long word for you, Kate. 'Preservation,' I mean."

"Ye've read me statements one an' all. I'm not short on words, Father."

The priest nodded, and his face was sad.

"What time tomorrow?" Kate said after a while. All their thoughts were on the same subject.

"Nine o'clock," said the priest. And his reply was overheard by the well-dressed man looking and listening at the grille on the far side of the door.

"Will it be quick?" Kate went on to ask.

"I think so," said the priest, and the well-dressed man nodded.

"I think I shall sleep awhile," said Kate. She put down her pipe and turned her back on the room.

Kate had not expected to be able to sleep, so she was surprised when she awakened. She rolled over. The priest and the sister were still with her, the former slumped drowsing in his chair. Sister Madeline was still knitting.

"What time has it?" Kate asked, rubbing her eyes.

"Past five."

"I'm hungry," Kate said.

Sister Madeline put her knitting aside and left her chair. Kate observed that she now had her own key to the cell door, which she unlocked, letting herself out.

When she returned, she was bearing a tray, which she set down with such a clatter that Father M'Enery stirred and awoke.

"I'm sorry," he said, ashamed that he had shown weakness.

But Kate had fallen upon the contents of the tray. Eggs and bacon, bread and butter, tea with sugar. She was still enjoying her breakfast when Captain Colville appeared.

"Not yet," said the governor when he saw the look of alarm cross his prisoner's face.

"Everything all right?" He addressed his question to Father M'Enery. Then to Kate: "Is there anything you want, any special requests?"

Kate laughed. "Well, you can open up the doors and let me go. I'll be gone like a puff of wind."

The governor smiled nervously. This was his first execution, and he hoped his last. Mr. Marwood had arrived last night, with his bag of ropes, and was at present testing whatever hangmen tested in the makeshift shed.

"Would you care for something strong to drink?" he asked Kate.

"I would. Brandy—double measure—since you're askin'."

The governor was pleased for this excuse to retreat, and he bowed his way out of the cell.

"Sure you'd think it was he who was t'swing!" said Kate when he'd gone. She turned to Father M'Enery. "Do you think it a mortal sin to face Him upstairs smelling a breath fit to carry coal with, Father?"

The priest shook his head. He was about to offer her Communion, and technically her stomach should be empty. But he didn't think it mattered very much this day.

They came for her just before nine—Captain Colville, three male warders, the under-sheriff, and the well-dressed man.

Kate was on her knees, a brass crucifix in her hand, before the cell table, which had been converted into an altar by Father M'Enery. She had received the Eucharist in Holy Viaticum, and she watched the priest blow out the two candles and close the lid of his box of hosts.

Kate got to her feet without turning to look at the assembly by the door. She walked steadily up to Sister Madeline, took her hand, and kissed her on both cheeks; and the nun hung her head with a sob. Then Father M'Enery was at Kate's side, and she leaned on his arm with her free hand, the other still clutching the crucifix. Without taking her eyes from the priest's face, Kate allowed herself to be escorted from the cell, and the procession set off—the governor and the under-sheriff leading the way, Kate and Father M'Enery in the middle, the warders and the well-dressed man taking up the rear.

They followed passages to the south side of the prison and reached a door, which was unlocked by one of the warders. Beyond lay a small courtyard, cobbled and mossy and seldom used, and the prison bell began to toll as they proceeded to walk across.

A shed of new timber was obvious and out of place in one corner of the yard, hugging the high stone wall. But Kate didn't see it at first, her eyes never having left the face of Father M'Enery. The priest, murmuring a mixture of encouragement and prayers for the dying, had literally been her guide since they had left her cell. A short flight of wooden steps led up into the shed, and Kate stopped when she reached them.

"Will it hurt?" she asked the priest in a low voice.

"No," came the answer. And the well-dressed man, who had overheard her question from the back, shook his head in agreement.

Kate mounted the steps and passed into the shed. A thick beam of oak ran across the area above their heads from eave to eave. From the beam there hung a rope, the noose hitched up to form a coil of slack and tied with a thin piece of twine. But Kate was looking at Father M'Enery's stole, marveling at the intricate workmanship.

The well-dressed man now stepped forward and assumed control, and Kate felt rather than saw the broad leather straps he used to pin her arms and legs. He was very quick about his task, and Kate was suddenly plunged into darkness as he slipped the mask over her head. She took a deep breath, and she could still hear the voice of Father M'Enery. What was he saying now?

"May almighty God remit to you all penalties of the present life. . . . May He open to you the Gates of Paradise and lead you to joys everlasting. . . ."

Kate was pleased he spoke in English. Prayers in Latin confused her. Now someone had put something heavier over her head, and she felt she could not hold her breath much longer.

"Benedicat te omnipotens Deus . . . Pater et Filius et Spiritus Sanctus," said Father M'Enery, lapsing into Latin, and Mr. Marwood drew the gallows bolt.

V

John Church caught the nine-fifteen to Richmond, hold-all in hand. Henry Weston had set off earlier in his van, and Church hoped that his grocer friend would reserve him a place at the head of the queue. For today was the day of the auction.

Mrs. Thomas's brother and her solicitor, having terminated the lease on Number Two Mayfield Cottages with the consent of Miss Ives, had decided to dispose of the effects of the deceased as soon as decently possible. Accordingly, an auction was arranged through local agents and, as fate would have it, this sale of personalty took place on the day following Kate's execution.

John Church was very anxious not to miss the sale. Since his release from custody and the trial of Kate for murder, he had made the most of his experiences—holding forth to whomsoever was prepared to listen and offering interviews to the local press. Naturally he concluded that to possess some of the property of the murdered woman would add a tangible proof to his recent adventure.

The train was on time, and Church took a cab to Park Road, where a large crowd had assembled at the front door of the villa. Henry Weston had been true to his word, and waved to him from the step.

"What you going to buy, Jack?" asked a well-wisher as Church went up the garden path.

"The whole bloody lot, friend," said Church, as sunny as the day. He pushed his way to the front, and the remainder of the crowd—either recognizing him as an actor in the recent drama or having just been informed as to his identity—let him pass amid friendly comments.

"We thoughts she'd took every penny-piece of you, Mr. Church!" someone said.

John Church turned. "Not I, friends," he cried. "She cost me a bob or two, I agree, but I'd say she paid for it well yesterday!" A cheer greeted this observation.

Then the front door was opened by the agents, and the mob poured into the hallway. Furniture, bedding, and household utensils were arranged in neat piles; and the auctioneer stood behind the davenport desk, which now served as a dais. When the hall was packed with people, the auctioneer pounded the desk with an ivorine hammer and called for silence.

"I'll pay you twenty pounds for that desk, for that piano, for that sideboard and that there chest o' drawers," Church rattled off before the agent had time to name a single price.

"We'll not outbid Jack Church," shouted a sycophant from the back, and when no one protested otherwise, the auctioneer let his hammer fall.

"Strictly, we're not onto furnishings yet," said the auctioneer, determined not to be browbeaten. "And next I have to offer a parcel of knickknacks. Two copper pots, one chopper, one gold watch and chain, one brooch, one carving knife. How much for the chopper then, one shilling?"

"Two shillings," a voice bid. The small coal ax was probably worth no more than sixpence, but a certain rumor had spread about the ranks of the crowd.

"Gone for two shillings." And the hammer fell.

"I'll take the rest!" Church said. "Ten bob for the pots, two pounds for the clock on the chain, five shillings for the brooch, and you can throw in the knife for free." He passed up a wad of notes and silver.

"Let 'im have 'em!" yelled the same sycophant, and the auctioneer passed the articles down.

"Nice old hunter," Church said to Henry Weston, holding up Mr. Thomas's watch. He examined the carving knife. Strange design, and something written along the blade. "The Celebrated Arkansas Toothpick," he read. Several heads craned to look at it with him.

"Was that what was used for the dis-em-bowel-ment?" a squeaky voice inquired.

Church looked at the owner, a wizened urchin of about twelve years.

"That's it, lad, that's it!" he said and drew it across his throat with a wicked smile. "Still got traces of gore on it!" Rounds of applause greeted the publican's show of wit; he was a popular man indeed that day. He reread the inscription etched along the blade. "Arkansas Toothpick," he mouthed with his little pink lips. What in tarnation did that mean?

And so the sale continued, Church buying at random, cracking jokes, and eventually standing drinks when they all repaired to the Hole in the Wall at lunchtime. It was a good day for one and all, and especially for John Church, and he whistled merrily when Henry Weston took him home with all his acquisitions in the late afternoon.

"What happened to the copper?" Henry asked him as they crossed Kew Bridge.

Church laughed. "Seems it was stuck to the wall and couldn't be budged."

"Pity."

"Aye, a downright shame." Never mind, thought Church. He had the carving knife of peculiar shape. A tale he'd be able to tell his friends about that. And when the telling of it became confused, or stale with time, the blade would still have an edge fine enough for their Sunday roast.

SOME OBSERVATIONS

Q. Who was "Strong"?

A. A man Kate Webster claimed to know, and to be the father of her child. Strong is the "X" in her third and fourth statements. Neither the police nor Kate Webster's lawyers appear to have traced this man. No statement was ever taken from him, nor was he ever questioned with regard to Webster's final allegations. Strong remains very much a mystery figure.

Q. Was Jack Church really a "villain"?

A. Church also remains a sinister figure. His refusal to state his antecedent history, his jocular behavior, did little to endear him to the authorities or Mr. Justice Denman. It may be doubtful that he realized what had been going on at Richmond or knew the man called Strong, but one must assume that either he was aware of his involvement in crooked dealings at Mayfield Cottages or he was far bigger a fool than he chose to represent.

Q. Mary Durden?

A. Kate Webster would probably have been found guilty by her jury and hanged without the need of Mary Durden's evidence, but she was properly called by the Crown to prove premeditation. Unless Kate Webster's instructions to her counsel were vague, the calling of this witness seems to have presented the defense with an insurmountable difficulty. It may be that Webster planned to steal her mistress's property as far back as Shrove Tuesday and blurted out her

368

visions of riches to Mary Durden. But it is almost inconceivable that Kate Webster spoke then with murder in her mind —she was far too cunning. (To suggest that Jack Church rehearsed Mary in her evidence is, of course, gross libel. It's possible that Mary Durden, recalling a *genuine* conversation with Webster about future riches, became "wise after the event" and convinced herself of the worst interpretation.)

Q. Jars of human dripping?

A. A splendid rumor circulated around Richmond—by Mrs. Hayhoe?—which did much to whet (or smother) the appetite of the hearer.

SOME COMMENTS

"I little thought when Kate came in and I chatted with her that she had left her mistress boiling in the copper!"

—Mrs. Hayhoe

"Kate Webster . . . is remembered at the former prison as a defiant, brutal creature, who showed no remorse, but was subject to fits of ungovernable passion, when she broke into language the most appalling."

—*Chronicles of Newgate* by Major Arthur Griffith

"She was remarkably submissive and docile while there [Wandsworth Prison]."

—Captain Colville of Wandsworth Prison

"I have stated that she was primarily a savage. A record of her ancestry, which, unfortunately, it is impossible to obtain, would most likely show that some of them—in the not very remote past—were sheep stealers, cattle raiders, and perhaps cattle maimers too; for there is no reason to suppose that the capacity for cruelty and barbarity is any the less inherent in us than is the faculty for drawing, music or cricket."

—Elliott O'Donnell in his introduction to *The Trial of Kate Webster*

"Two portraits (a sketch and the photograph of her waxwork) illustrate Mr. O'Donnell's essay on the subject. They complete

the dreary little wave of thankfulness with which one reflects that her career was cut short at thirty."
                                        —The author of a "potboiler" of trials, in 1932

Kate Webster caused a fair degree of alarm and despondency among members of the lower middle class able to employ the odd servant in their homes. Letters were written to the press demanding protection from the likes of this Irishwoman, and the press rendered unhelpful replies.

Even before her execution, a wax effigy of Kate Webster was unveiled at Madame Tussaud's Chamber of Horrors, a scowling, brutish figure not unlike Charlie's Aunt. It has been replaced by one less severe and possessing a hint of tragedy.

Sir Hardinge Giffard rose to become Lord Halsbury, Lord High Chancellor and compiler of the monumental *Halsbury's Laws of England,* still used in British courts to this day. Henry Poland became Sir Harry Poland, an eminent barrister who lived on to a ripe old age. Neither ever spoke of Kate Webster in their various writings.

Whatever became of Kate Webster's little boy . . . ?

FIRST STATEMENT OF KATE WEBSTER

made to Inspector John Dowdell
on Sunday, March 30, and on Tuesday, April 1, 1879

I have known John Church for nearly seven years; I first got acquainted when I was living two or three doors from Church's at Porter's. He used to take me out to London and to various public houses. I met him again some months ago, and he came to my mistress's house one night worse for drink. After remaining there for some time, I told him he would have to go as I expected my mistress home from church. My mistress came home and knocked at the door, and I let her in. Church was in the back at this time. My mistress went into the front room, and she said, "Kate, don't you think I am very late?" I said, "No, as I have company." He [Church] had previously told me to say that he was my brother. Mrs Thomas said, "Who have you got there?" and I said, "My brother, who has come to see me." At this time he was getting sober. Mrs Thomas went into the back room and spoke to him, and asked him to come into the front room by the fire, and she asked me if he would wish to remain all night, and he said, "No, I must not stay all night," and, turning round to me, he said, "You know I must not stay out all night," and I said, "No." Shortly after that he left.

A few days after, he came again into the house and, during conversation, I told him the mistress had no money in the house. He said, "Couldn't we put the old woman out of the way?" I said, "What do you mean?" He said, "Oh, poison her." I said, "You

372

must do that yourself; I'll have nothing to do with that." Church said, "We would have her things, and go off to America together and enjoy it, as I am getting tired of my old woman." He left late in the evening.

He came back again on the Monday night, the 3rd of March, and had tea with Mrs Thomas. I waited upon them. After tea, I asked Mrs Thomas to go out to see my little boy. She said, "Yes, Kate, and you need not hurry back." When I returned late in the evening, I noticed the light was turned down. I knocked three times at the door; the third knock, Church opened the front door, when I saw Mrs Thomas lying on the mat in the passage, struggling and groaning, and he said, "Come in." I drew back on to the step, frightened to go in. At this time there was a policeman standing on the opposite side of the road, a tall dark man. Church catched me by the arm, pulled me in, and closed the door. I said, "Whatever have you done?" He said, "Never you mind; I have done for her and, if you say a word about it, I'll put this knife into you—up to the handle." That was a carving knife belonging to Mrs Thomas. I felt very faint and, when he said he would put the knife into me, I said, "No, John, don't; I won't tell." He offered me what I thought was a glass of water. I said "No, I am better now," thinking it was poison, and that he was going to serve me the same as Mrs Thomas. Shortly after we left the house together, leaving Mrs Thomas there, and took a cab. I had told him I would not stay in the house by myself. He drove to near Church's house. Church saw me into Mrs Porter's, and I remained there for the night.

I got up early the next morning and went into Church's house. Mrs Church remarked that I was out early. Church was there, and beckoned me to go up the street. I went up, and he joined me shortly afterwards, and he said, "I can't get over to your house before one o'clock, as I got into a row with my old woman last night for being out so late again, and I must stay at home this morning to make it up with her." I said I should not go back to the house by myself. He had the keys of the front and side door, and said he should be down by two. He asked me what time I would be down; I told him I would not be down there before night. He told me where to meet him, at the Richmond Hotel, over the bridge. I took the boy Porter with me, and as I passed the hotel I saw Church inside. I asked the boy to go on a short distance and wait. I went to the house [hotel], and spoke to Church, and he asked me what I would have to drink. I had some whisky. He then gave me the keys of the house, and said I was to go to the house, take the boy with me, and I should find a box in the back room which he had packed up, tied with cord. The boy was to assist me to bring it away, not to take a cab from the house, but if we passed one on the way to the bridge we were to take it; but we didn't, so we carried it to the bridge. Church told me to let the boy Porter keep back and not see him when I went with the box, but he would be there to see me. I took the box on to the bridge, and placed it up on the bridge; the boy went away and Church appeared. I said, "What are you going to do with the box?" Church said, "That is my business." There was a tall gentleman near, on the opposite side of the bridge. I left him, and he said, "Follow the boy." I left, and heard a splash in the water. I joined the boy Porter at the foot of the bridge, carrying a carpet bag, which we had also brought from the house, containing books and meat. We went to the railway station and found that the last train had gone. The boy asked a cabman what he would take him home for, and he said three shillings. The boy having only two shillings, and I no change, I said, "You shall come home and sleep with me." We both slept in one room. On going downstairs to the kitchen I found the carpeting rolled up, and the table, with a leaf let down, put up against the cupboard, and the boards wet, as if they had been washed, and a large fire in the kitchen, and a large saucepan on the fire, full of water; but I saw no blood.

About two days after, when I was cleaning up the scullery, I saw some blood on the carving knife. There was a meat saw hanging up by the fireside, but on that day I found it on a box in the scullery, quite clean. Since Mrs Thomas disappeared, Church, Porter, and his boy have been frequently at the house,

Church directing me to order meat, as if it was for Mrs Thomas. It has been taken to his house, cooked, and eaten there, likewise to Porter's. He called Porter in to value the goods and furniture in the house, and said to me, "Don't you pay him for the valuation; I'll pay him." I paid several bills; he said, "Never mind paying them, pay Miss Ives, the landlady, to keep her quiet." I went to pay her when they were removing the goods. I went to pay her, and she said, "No." She refused to take the money, and thought there was something wrong. I went back into the house and told Church, and said there was some noise being made. He said, "I'll go out to Porter and say I think there is something wrong about this; don't move the things." He came back and said, "You will have to clear out and go to your friends," and I left soon after. He knew where I was going; he gave me a card with his address, and said I was to write to him, and "I'll ——— stop at home and braze it out." This was on Tuesday, the 19th, and I reached my uncle's house at Greenanne, on the following Friday night. I wrote to Church, to his address in Hammersmith, telling him I had arrived home safely. Before leaving, it was partly arranged, that I should remain at home for about three weeks, that he would send me money to come back with, and then we were to go to America.

I never laid a hand on Mrs Thomas, and had nothing to do with murdering her, but I knew Church had done it. All the money left in the house belonging to Mrs Thomas was a £5 note and thirty shillings. This note I changed at a fishmonger's in Richmond. Church and Porter were with me at the time. I intend to tell the whole truth, as I don't see why I should be blamed for what Church has done. I wouldn't accuse my greatest enemy of anything wrong, let alone a friend, which Church has been to me up till now.

Mr Church wanted to know how to get the furniture away. I told him he could manage that as well as the other business. He then asked my consent to let Porter value the furniture, so as to have a witness; he [Porter] did value the furniture at £50, and Mr

Church drew the receipt himself, but he has not paid the money. On the next evening we were sitting on the sofa in the front room. Porter was there, and another man; I don't know his name. Church told me to look after the furniture till he removed it. He suspected Porter of moving anything. He then gave me £10 in gold, and called Porter's attention to it. I asked him why he wanted Porter to be acquainted with our conversation on the subject. He said, "To keep things on my side square." Porter and the other man went on to Hammersmith. At the same time Church and I remained till the last train; that was on the Saturday night, 15th. On Sunday we went on the water. On Monday, I think about 11 or 12 o'clock, we reached down here [Richmond], and went home about half-past ten on Monday night.

On Tuesday morning we left home about 8 o'clock. He brought a man with him to collect the furniture, and get it ready for the vans. I asked him what he wanted to draw the receipt for, as it was between ourselves. He said, "If I should be stopped by the landlady I shall have the receipt to produce." The vans came at half-past 6. As soon as Miss Ives saw the furniture going out she came in and asked the carman where the furniture was going to be taken, and he declined to answer her. I was in the front room at the time with Mr Church. He asked me who she was, and I told him the landlady; he told me not to show myself, and he would go out and tell the men to stop bringing out the furniture, and then it would not be noticed. He then returned into the house, and came into the front room and asked me to go and see the landlady, and if she wanted the money for the rest he would give it to me to pay her. I asked him what I should say to the landlady. He replied, "If she asks to see Mrs Thomas, say she will be here in a few days." I then saw the landlady, and asked her if she wished to speak to me. She said, "No, I want to see Mrs Thomas." I told her she was not at home. I asked her if she wanted her rent; she said, "No; I want to know where the furniture is going to." I told her it was going to Hammersmith. She then said, "I will see about that." I then went back and told Mr Church what she said, and he said, "I thought she was going to inform the police"; he then said, "I have the agreement to produce, and I am not frightened; you get out of the way." He then told me to write to him, and, in case I should forget his address, he gave me his card and also his own portrait. I then left and went to Rose Gardens, and took my child away. I thought I had not enough money to travel with, and I went on to Mrs Church's, the "Rising Sun", and asked her to lend me a pound. She gave me a half-sovereign and ten shillings in silver, and I left the house. Church took the plate away on the Saturday before the Tuesday the furniture was to be removed. He was accompanied by me and Porter. We had 12 lb of beef and a leg of mutton, 8 lb of cheese, 1 lb butter, 4 lb sugar, 1 lb tea, 1 quartern of flour, 1 lb suet, 1 lb wax candles, and 1 cake; these were taken to Church's and divided, Church taking the beef and candles, and Porter the leg of mutton, cheese, butter, sugar, tea, flour, suet and cake. All I have now told you is quite true.

SECOND STATEMENT OF KATE WEBSTER

made to Inspector John Dowdell
on April 10, 1879

On the 2nd of March, when Church pulled me into the house,
I heard a cough in the back room, and I fell inside the front room
door against a chiffonier, and upon recovering myself I saw
Henry Porter standing on the mat at the front room door. He said
to Church, "What is the matter with her?" Church said, "Oh,
she'll be alright in a minute." Porter said, "Didn't you see me
coming in after you?" I said, "No." He said, "I was coming behind
you for a long way." I suspected he had not followed me, and I
asked him, "What way did I come?" He said, "Straight up the hill
by the church." I said, "No; I came the cemetery way." He then
said, "There was some one very much like you on ahead of me."
Church said, "Don't hesitate; you both got here somehow."
Porter said, "That's quite right, but I never saw any one so much
like her in my life." Church and Porter then went into the back
room. After about twenty minutes Porter came out; he turned
to Church and said, "Jack, I'll go on a little before you." Church
said, "We are all going now in a minute." Porter said, "There'll
be too much notice taken of us all going together." Porter then
took his hat from off the front room table, and said to Church,
"I suppose I'll see you at home tonight, and then we can talk
about matters." Porter left, and afterwards Church and me followed. We went from Richmond to Shaftesbury Road Station,
and when we got to the "Rising Sun", Rose Gardens, Church

said, "They are shut up; but there, come in." I said, "No, I won't; it is too late." Mrs Church then opened the door; she also said, "Isn't Kate coming in?" Church answered, "No, she wants to get home." Church insisted that I should go in, but I would not; he said, "Perhaps Porter wants to see you." I said, "He must see me when he comes home." I then left Church; I did not see Porter that night. I went to Porter's house; the door was opened by me, and I went into the front parlour and went to bed on the sofa. I heard Porter come in about half an hour later; he fastened the door and went into the back room, which is called the kitchen. I have often slept at the same place, and have lodged at Porter's house for six months in 1873. Shortly afterwards I heard the handle of the door of the room where I was sleeping turn, but I had it locked on the inside. I asked who was there, and Mr Porter spoke and said, "It is me, Kate; I want to see you." I told him I was undressed, and he should see me in the morning. He then said, "Good night; I'll be going out at 5, and I'll call you." I saw Porter at 10 minutes past 5 in the morning; he said, "I must go to work today to keep things straight; will you go home to Richmond before I come home tonight? I'll be home at 5." I said, "It all depends, perhaps I won't go then." Porter said, "Church is going down, but he won't go till after dinner." I says, "Where did you see Church so early?" He said, "I was there last night when you came home, didn't you know that?" I said, "Yes, Mrs Church said so." He said, "Church and me has arranged matters," and that "I must see him tonight if I can get off. I'll get off, for I'll not do overtime." He then went away to his work.

I stopped there till 5 o'clock that day, Monday, 3rd March, when Porter came home. I got the tea ready, as Mrs Porter was the worse for drink. After having tea, Porter said, "Are you going down?" I said, "Yes, I think I'll go." He said, "Church is to meet me at Hartley's. Isn't the boy going down with you, Kate?" [meaning his son Robert]. I said, "Yes." The boy went to wash himself, and Porter said, "Don't let that boy know anything, only as little as you can." Porter, me, and the boy then went down to Hammersmith. We went into a public house near the old railway station and had something to drink. This was about 7 o'clock, and I said, "Now, we must get on if we are going to Richmond to-night." We went to the new station, and, finding we had some time to wait, Porter said we might walk to the Shaftesbury Road. We done so, and when we got to the top of the Shaftesbury Road the boy said, "Ain't you going home now, father?" He [Porter] said yes, he would go and have another pint to himself and then he would go. Porter asked me to come into a public house with him, but I said, "No, I'll lose the train if I do." The boy was waiting for me, and he hurried him on, and said, "Kate will catch you in a minute." Porter arranged that he would come on to Richmond by the next train. I said, "Can't you come by this train?" He said, "No, I don't want the boy to know it. I don't suppose I shall see you any more tonight." We then parted, and I went to Richmond with the boy. I saw Church at Hartley's, the Richmond Hotel. I told the boy to go on in front of me. I went in and saw Church there, and spoke to him. I told him Porter was coming by the next train; he asked me to have something to drink, and I had some whisky and water; he then gave me two keys, one of the side door, and one of the glass door at the back of the house, and said, "You'll find a small box in the back room on the ground floor, between the sofa and bookcase; it ain't very heavy. I think the boy and you can manage it; don't take a cab from the house, if you think you can't carry it; if you meet a cab you can bring it with you to Richmond Bridge; I'll be there some time before you; I'll wait here until Porter comes. Does the boy know his father is coming down?" I said, "No, the boy suspects something, for he asked me in the train, 'What is there, Kate, between father, you, and Church?' "

I left Church in the public house and joined the boy up the street, and went to the house with him. We then went in through the side entrance round to the glass door, and into the back room. I lit the lights, and, after stopping in the house a short time, we left by way of the front door, carrying between us the box mentioned by Church, and a large carpet bag. I did not know what was in the box, but the bag contained a large family Bible and seven other books, some meat, and a number of things. We carried the box on all the way; we met no cab. Getting on the middle of the bridge, we put the box down. I said to the boy, "Now, you go on to the station, and I'll catch you"; He said, "Very well, Kate," and went. Then Church came up to me, and I said to him, "How long have you been here?" He said, "Not very long"; I said, "Where is Porter, did you see him?" He said, "Yes, I waited for him; don't let the boy know we are here; go on after him as quick as you can"; I said, "Where is the cab for this box? You can't carry it"; he said, "Never mind that, I'll see about it." I then left Church and, following the boy, I got a short distance away when I heard a splash in the water. Turning round, I saw a tall, dark man standing on the bridge. It was too dark to recognise him. I caught up to the boy and said, "Did you hear anything like falling into the water?" He said, "Yes, Kate, I thought I heard a splash of something." We then went to the station carrying the bag between us. Finding the last train was gone for Hammersmith, the boy insisted on going home; he had two shillings, and I, having no change, I said, "You can't get a cab for two shillings to take you." A cabman said he would take him for three. I said, "You had better come up and stay all night, and we'll go home in the morning early enough. We went, and going in the same way to the house, I told him to go into the front room; I then went upstairs and took my bonnet off, coming downstairs and into the kitchen. I found a large fire there, a large iron saucepan full of water; the table, with one leaf let down, was removed to one side of the kitchen against the cupboard, the carpet pushed back right off the floor; the floor was all wet, as if washed or scrubbed. I missed the meat saw which always hung against the fireplace, but two days afterwards, when I went into the wash house, I found the saw standing on a large box which always stood there, and on that day I also saw a carving knife lying on the scullery floor, partly behind the box. I picked it up and found it rusty, and marks (streaky) of blood on it. I also found at that time brown paper under the sink, with dirty looking marks on it. The boy Porter stopped at the house all night and slept in the same room with me. I made him a bed.

I saw Church and Porter the next evening, Tuesday, 4th March; the two came down together about half past seven; I had been to Hammersmith all day. Church was not at home, and I was home at Richmond some time before them. Church brought a bottle of brandy in his pocket; he asked me for the corkscrew. I told him I couldn't find it. I thought him or Porter had taken it. He said he didn't take it, and Porter commenced laughing. I said to Porter, "You have it, then?" He said, "Yes, of course, I claim some of the things as well as other people." Porter and Church then began talking how they would dispose of the things. I went into the back room, leaving them in the front room, and stopped there some time, then returned into the front room, and found Church and Porter in deep conversation. Porter said, "Do you know how to act, Kate?" I said, "Yes, I know when you tell me." Church said, "It's easy for her to act if she will only listen to what we tell her." I then took a chair and sat down; I said to Church, "Now let me hear what you have got to tell me." Porter then said, "If anyone comes and asks for Mrs Thomas, say she has gone to the country for a few days." He then said to Church, "Ain't that the best thing to say?" Church said, "Yes; and another thing you had better do, when you want anything, order it in Mrs Thomas's name as you have always done since you have been here." Porter then said, "The tradespeople will think by doing that that Mrs Thomas is here." But I said, "When the bills want to be paid, she pays every week, they'll know she is not here." Church said, "Oh, damn the bills; we'll be moved before the bills come in. Let us get all we can while we are about it; it is no good in being too honest in this world, is there, Harry?" Porter said, "No; if we can do it on the quiet; the thing is in not being found out." Church said, "There is only our three selves that know it. I want a piece of the sirloin of beef for Sunday; and what do you want?" Porter said he would like a leg of mutton. Church told me when the butcher came to order it in Mrs Thomas's name. Mrs Thomas had two butchers, one beyond the railway station and one at the top of Richmond Hill, where the beef and mutton was got from. We had supper, and came off to Hammersmith.

The above statement has been read over to me by Inspector Jones, in the presence of Inspector Dowdell, and is correct.

THIRD STATEMENT OF KATE WEBSTER

made in Wandsworth Prison
on Thursday, July 10, 1879

I make this statement in the first place merely thanking my solicitor, Mr O'Brien, who has defended me at the Police Court and upon my trial at Central Criminal Court, and to whom I owe a debt of gratitude for the interest he has taken on my behalf under difficulties most trying to him and myself; and for all he has done for me, I tender my heartfelt thanks and gratitude, as also to my counsel, Mr Sleigh, and Mr Keith, for the attention they have given in my case. In the first place, I am advised that I ought not to be found guilty on the evidence, which was wholly circumstantial, and also upon the plea I have pleaded.

I was born at Killane, in the County of Wexford, and am about 30 years of age. I left home in Ireland about the year 1867, and came to England. I got into trouble upon my arrival, and got 5 years' penal servitude on Feb. 13, 1868. I was discharged on Jan. 28th, 1872.

When I got my discharge I went to Mrs Meredith's Home for Discharged Prisoners at Nine Elms, where I remained for 3 months. I then got a situation through Mrs Meredith at Grove Road, Wandsworth, where I remained for three or four months, and left of my own accord. Upon leaving there, I went to live at Porter's house in 10 Rose Gardens, Hammersmith. I knew the Porters through a fellow-prisoner named Carr, who introduced them to me. I lodged with Carr, about 5 doors from Church's, and afterwards went to live next door to Porter's. I was living in Porter's house for six months, and what he swore respecting this is wholly false. At this time, I was in the habit of going out washing with Mrs Porter. A woman named Lizzie was living at this time at 10 Rose Gardens, and used to do Mrs Smith's washing at No. 10. I became very much attached to Porter's family, and they were very much attached to me. From there I went to Captain Woolbest's, Royal Crescent, Notting Hill, as cook and housemaid. I used to visit Mrs Marsh close to, and made X's [the man called Strong?] acquaintance while there. A charge of felony was made out against Mr Marsh, and X came to bail him out. X at this time was living in at Holloway, and kept an oil shop. I was induced by him to go and live with him at his house, and he seduced me while there, and I became in the family way of my little boy, now about six years of age. At this time, X obtained some goods from America by foul means. The goods consisted of a number of tanks. I assisted him in doing so, and was obliged to leave Holloway and go to live at Kingston. He induced me to live with him at Kingston, and took a room for me at No. 5 Acre Road, where my boy was born on April 19, 1874. I went from there to London Street (Windman's Cottage), for which I was to pay 4s. 6d. a week, and he left me there to do the best I could for myself and child. I became very impoverished, forsaken by him, and committed crimes for the purpose of supporting myself and child. I could not get a place to leave the child, and was open to all kinds of temptations.

I was charged with three offences of stealing at Kingston, and sentenced to eighteen months' hard labour on 14th April, 1875. I was but a short time at my liberty, and on the 18th Jan., 1877, I was sentenced to twelve months' imprisonment at the Surrey Sessions. I was innocent of that charge, although convicted, and upon my discharge from Wandsworth Prison, after suffering that term, I went to live at Mr Mitchell's, at Bridge Cottage, Stanley Road, Teddington. X introduced me in the first instance as a charwoman to that place, where he told me he suspected I would be able to commit a robbery. He desired me to remain there and watch my opportunity to rob the house and give him the proceeds. I found Mr Mitchell and his family very kind to me, and I did not do as X advised me. Mrs Mitchell fell ill, and I attended her and was very kind to her. I left Mr Mitchell's service after twelve months' at X's request, as I told him that the Mitchells were poor and had nothing I could take. X came to Mitchell's and took me away to Mrs Crease's at Richmond, where he took lodging for me, and through Mrs Crease I got acquainted with Miss Loder, who introduced me to Mrs Thomas.

During the whole time since the day I went to X's house at Holloway, I was entirely under his control, and was led and advised by him in every possible manner. It was through him I got into my troubles. His whole aim in keeping me on was to facilitate him in his designs, and it is to him I trace the whole of my misfortune and the awful position I am now placed in. He being the father of my child [?], I did not like to leave him, and I cherished him to the last, even at the sacrifice of my life.

Having been introduced to the vacant situation at Mrs Thomas's at Vine Cottages, Richmond, by Miss Loder, I entered her service about 27th Jan., 1879. I kept up a correspondence with X. He came to see me there. I went out to see my child on 2nd March (the Sunday), and came home about 9.45. When I got to the gate, I met X coming down the gravel walk from the front door. The door was open and he was after coming out. Another man was with him, who returned back and went away through the back door.

X said: "Is that you, Kate?"

I was surprised to see him. He said: "Don't Holloa!"

I said: "Who was with you?"

He said: "Nobody that you know." He said he came on some business, but was not going to tell me. He said: "Come inside and I'll tell you."

Just as I went up on the step of the door, the other man ran down from the back of the house into the street. I did not know him, as there was not light enough for me to see him. I asked who it was that let him in, and how he opened the door. He said his pal got into the house with keys. I asked him: "Did he see the mistress?" He said she would not see him—he said: "No."

I said: "For goodness sake, don't let the mistress see you here!" He said she would not see him.

I asked where the man was gone? He said he was nobody I knew. He went inside. X gave me £5 and 1s. 6d. in silver. He said: "Sit down on the chair."

I asked him what was the matter? And he said he would tell me.

I said: "How long have you been here?"

He said: "About an hour," and that the other man did not wish to see him. He then said while they were in the house, Mrs Thomas came in with her latch key and caught them in the house, and the other man hit her and knocked her down with a chair.

I then fell off the chair, being very frightened. I asked him to let me see where she was. He said it was better for me not to see her and anything to do with it, but that she was in a room downstairs.

When I came to, I went outside and sat on the steps of the hall door. He asked me where the silver was, that they had not found that out. I said I did not know; nor did I remember where it was for the moment. I had not time to clean it on the Saturday, and had placed it under one of the dish covers. He asked me if I would stop in the house or go home with him. I was afraid to stop in the house, and went with him to Kingston. I remained out all night and slept in a shed in the field. X came with me to the shed. I told him I could not go into my house. He left me in the shed.

I returned to Vine Cottage by the first train in the morning before seven o'clock. I found X in the house with a woman I did not know. She left at once when I came. There was a large fire in the kitchen. The copper was lighted. The other man was gone away. X told me he had left. I asked why he went? And X said he was frightened to remain when he heard me come in. This took place in the kitchen. I noticed the boards wet. X would not allow me into the room next to the kitchen. I asked what they had done with Mrs Thomas? And he said I could not see her. X said the other man had done something to her, and that he would not have risked it for £1000. I began to cry, and he told me to keep quiet and that his life remained in my hands. He made me take an oath I would not tell it. I went upstairs and commenced to clean up in the rooms, but I was much too frightened to do much. X remained below. I did not see any portion of the body of Mrs Thomas. I knew from what he said they had done away with her, but I did not see anything. They kept the room next the kitchen locked. X remained until the afternoon and then went away.

I went back to Kingston the next day, by the four o'clock train. We returned by the last train that night to Vine Cottage, and remained all night. He went back early in the morning, and arranged to meet me on Richmond Bridge that night. He asked me if I would get someone to carry the box and did not want a cab. I went to Rose Gardens and brought the boy, Robert Porter, to help me remove the box. He came with me and we removed it, and I met X on the bridge, and gave him the box and returned with the boy. The black bag mentioned at the trial contained the head of Mrs Thomas, and was taken by me to the Porters, and afterwards carried by us to the bridge, where I met X, who disposed of it. I have told my solicitor since the trial where that particular place is. The man on the bridge was the man I have mentioned. I have no doubt that the foot found at Twickenham was part of Mrs Thomas's body, and was removed there by the man I have mentioned. The man who was with X I believe to be a man I once saw with him, and whom he used to call a "house tapper", and used to live and keep a little shop along the Blackfriars Road. X wears an apron during the day, and goes out at times by night in a horse and cart. X asked how they could do away with the furniture, as they did not want to be seen with it. I said: Could he not get a man from London to buy them, like he used to do with other things? He said: No, he would not trust them. He then suggested that I should introduce the matter to Porter, and the statement I have made in respect to the sale to Porter, and Church, as mentioned in my statement respecting same, is true. I said if it were found out it would get them into trouble. He said: No, it would not, unless I told it. I knew Church long before I knew X, and X did not like him for that reason, and it is untrue for Church to say he only knew me from March 9. Church visited me several times at Vine Cottage, and it was at the suggestion of X that I made the statement about Church and Porter incriminating them. And as to my seeing Mrs Thomas lying dead, I never saw her at all, and it was to save X that I was induced to make the false statement against them. In the first instance I did not give my solicitor a true account of the case. I led him to believe it was Church and Porter who did it, and that X was innocent, and it was not until I was about to be sentenced that I declared the truth to Mr O'Brien in the dock. [?] He then at once advised me to confess in public that Church and Porter were innocent, and that their character might be cleared before the public, and but for this I might not have confessed it. And my solicitor, believing in my instructions throughout, defended me well, although I was in great want of pecuniary means, and for which I owe him a great debt of gratitude. Church brought me the earrings and also a pair of new boots, which are in the box at Vine Cottage, and he knew me as well as his own wife. I am now very ill and weak, and unfit to continue my statement at present.

KATHERINE WEBSTER

Statement taken in the presence of J. N. YOUNG HOWISON, Prison Matron

FOURTH STATEMENT OF KATE WEBSTER

made in Wandsworth Prison
on Thursday, July 17, 1879

Upon the last occasion I was not well enough to continue my statement, otherwise I should have done so. I adhere to my statement of 10th July. With respect to the murder of Mrs Thomas, I had no knowledge whatever of such an act myself or any intention to commit, and the first intimation I got of that matter was upon my arrival at Vine Cottage on Ṣunday night, 2nd March, as already stated by me, when I met X at the door of the house.

With regard to the statement I made upon my way from Ireland after being arrested, I declare that before I left London, after the sale of the furniture was stopped, X begged of me not to have his name brought up, and that in case there was any noise over it, I was to say it was Church and Porter that did it. I accordingly yielded to his advice and made accusations against Church and Porter, not knowing at the time the terrible effects it might have against them; and for such a statement, I now humbly beg God's forgiveness. I did not for one moment consider the nature of it, and it was made under a severe trial to me, not only as regarded X, but all the circumstances taken together. With regard to the statement I made that Church said to me: "Do away with the old lady", I declare that my statement in that respect was untrue, as I never had any conversation at all with either Church or Porter upon that subject, and it is but justice to them that I should say so. The only conversation I had with anybody was with X, who planned the whole thing and desired me to act exactly as I did under his guidance and directions. I had no knowledge whatever that X, or the man, were going to the house on the Sunday evening. This I declare now most solemnly, nor did I ever hear it said that anything was to be done to Mrs Thomas, and this I now declare most solemnly. I was in the house at the time the man from the coal company called; X was there at the time, and I was afraid of being seen, and acting under his influence and advice, I answered the door but did not open it wide. Nobody was in the house at the time but myself and X, and I was wholly and entirely subject to his control.

I forgot to say in my last statement that on the Sunday night, the 2nd March, when X brought me from Vine Cottage to Kingston, he left me immediately at Kingston and returned to Richmond with a view to meet the other man, as I understood, and when I returned to Vine Cottage the next morning early, I found him and the other man there in the house. I believe now that the reason X induced me to go away from Vine Cottage on the Sunday night was that I should not be witness or see anything that was going on, and from the relative position I unfortunately had with him I was extremely reluctant to say or do anything that might affect or compromise him, and, therefore, I may say, he exercised almost a right of dominion and, as it were, ownership over the place and myself. I have no doubt whatever in my mind now that the men were in the house on the Sunday night, and that the lights were kept up till their purpose was completed. As we were walking along the road called Richmond Road, X and myself, on the Sunday night, I inquired of him what they had been doing at the house and what became of Mrs Thomas, and he said she came in from church while they were in the house, and they were frightened she would make an alarm, and the man struck her and felled her down at once. When they heard the key in the door, they became alarmed, and X said to the man, when they heard the noise at the door, "Be careful, it is not Kate that is coming." I asked to see her, but he refused, and I have never seen her since.

When Church and Porter came down to Vine Cottage about the sale of the furniture, they knew well I was not Mrs Thomas, and that I was not married, and Church accordingly called me Kate. Church inquired from me who owned the furniture, and I said I would not tell him. He said he suspected they were not mine. He asked me who lived there, and I told him a lady named Mrs Thomas. He says: "I don't mind buying the things if there is no bother and I can get something out of it." But I do not think Church knew what became of Mrs Thomas, however much they might suspect what was going on. X knew well that I was to introduce the sale of the things to Church and Porter and once they got into the matter, if any trouble turned up, I was to make the statement against them, which I afterwards did, and for which I am now sincerely sorry. I never saw Mrs Thomas lying dead on the mat, but I was induced to say so by X, who planned in substance this statement I was to make against Church and Porter in case any trouble turned up, and the substance of this statement was arranged by X in Vine Cottage. As far as I can think now, X suspected some trouble to turn up, and I can see now that he preferred me to give an account which might incriminate Church and Porter and screen him.

With regard to the carpetbag found by the police in Vine Cottage, that belonged to Mrs Thomas, and the chopper was the one that used to be had for breaking coal in the cellar. It used to hang up against the cellar wall. The razor found in the house belonged to Mrs Thomas. It was an old one which she used to cut her nails. She lent it to me to cut a corn, and it was lying in my drawer of the dressing-table, and when I was packing it was wrapped in paper, and within the box in the room on the ground floor. On the Monday morning, 3rd March last, when I got back from Kingston to Vine Cottage, I saw X, the man, and the woman I have mentioned. I never saw the woman before but, as far as

392

I now recollect, she was dark-complexioned, stoutly built, and not as tall as I am. She left the house when I got there, with a bag of something. X introduced her to me at first as a friend of his, but she made no delay in going away. I did not see her again on the Sunday night, but she may have been there for all I know.

I have known the man that was with X at Vine Cottage on the Sunday night. The same man came to me while living at Mr Mitchell's. He brought me a message from X, and wanted me to go to London and live. He was a man about 5 feet 6 inches, and about 35 years old. When he went about, dealing sometimes as a pedlar, he used to wear a white apron, a long overcoat with a velvet collar, and X told me he used to go about during the day with his white apron and a wicker basket, as a sort of cloak to spot the houses that they might attack at night. This same man wrote to me during the time I was at Mitchell's, which letter I was requested to answer to some public-house at Westminster, and the letter asked when I could come to London, and he would meet me. This said letter is now in the hands of the police. I think Inspector Pearman at Richmond has it. This man was a pal of X —as X used to call him—and in his confidence, and the arrangement between X and him was that when X found out a house they would attack, he [X] communicated with this man and made an appointment. I remember about two months before last Christmas, I went to see my little boy on Wednesday, as I used to do. I met X at the railway station. I usually went to visit old Mrs Crease, who was ill. He, X, asked me not to go to Richmond on the following Sunday. I asked why, and he said there was a house going to be tapped, and if I was out they might accuse me, as I had been in prison before. I told him I would go out after warning him, and he said he was not going to do it. He would not be seen in it, but he was going to get it done.

I have no doubt whatever but the man who committed the offence was the same man who was with X at Vine Cottage on Sunday, 2nd March. On the following Monday, I went to see my child, and on getting out of the train at Brighton [?] I saw X and this man sitting on the seats. He said to me, "I am waiting here for you, Kate. I want you to come to London with me." I asked why? He said if I came he would give me some money. He said, "The man has given me £20," and he added that he would give him some more. If I could come up to London, he would give me £5 out of it. I did not go up to London with X and the man. He got out at Vauxhall, and X took us to Westminster Bridge to a public house [?]. The man asked us to remain there while he went home. He came back in about a quarter of an hour and called X out, and X returned and said to me he was going to stop out all night, and wanted me to do so. But I refused, telling him my neighbours did not know I came to London, and I would return home. They came to the station with me, and I took the last train from Waterloo. They went to Kingston to see X the next evening. But X said the chap did not give him any more money. I asked him to give me a pound out of the money he had hidden in the cellar, and if he did not I would tell the police. He then went and got it and gave it to me. . . . The pound was to buy clothes for the child, to take him out of the workhouse, where I was bound to place him by reason of my poverty.

There was a bag I saw at Vine Cottage, containing keys, chisels and tools; a large black bag. Inside it was a small black bag which contained the head of Mrs Thomas, as he told me. On the night of the removal of the black bag from Vine Cottage, I met X down the waterside between Richmond and Hammersmith. He asked me to carry it, as he said nobody would take notice of me carrying it. I think it was close by Kew Bridge. I met him by appointment there. When I took the bag I heard keys and tools rattle inside. One bag was inside the other, and I have explained in my last statement what I knew further about it; and I have also pointed out and explained to my solicitor, Mr O'Brien, the place where the said black bag was disposed of by X.

I have now made an account also with respect to Church and Porter; and from those latter two persons I beg forgiveness. I have acted most foolishly to myself in not at once communicating with the police when I got to Vine Cottage on the Sunday night, and in obeying the dictation of X. I was bewildered at the time between right and wrong, as it were, and the occurrence being so sudden, and having no one to advise or to whom I could go and reveal what had occurred, and being wholly, so to say, under X's influence, and being under his protection, I did not know what to do but yield to his advice. For anything I have done, which I now declare before God to be as I have stated, I implore His mercy, and I hereby forgive those who have been ready to condemn me of actual murder, which I now declare in this, my dying confession, to be as I have stated. The public mind, my solicitor informs me, was greatly biassed against me, and for all the harsh and unkind remarks passed upon me in the height of peril and trouble, I freely from my heart forgive. I have no complaint to make against anybody other than as I have now confessed. I thank the Judge who tried me for the fairness he showed, and for his readiness to have me fairly dealt with; and I now pray Almighty God to have mercy on me in the last moments of my mortal existence.

I have been foolishly led away to my ruin by those who should have protected me, and may my miseries, trials, and awful fate serve as a warning to young girls never to be led away from the path of virtue and honesty.

These are the dying words of the unhappy and unfortunate

KATHERINE WEBSTER

FIFTH AND FINAL STATEMENT OF KATE WEBSTER

made in Wandsworth Prison
on Monday, July 28, 1879

I made a statement in the presence of the warders to Mr O'Brien, my solicitor, on the 10th July, and a second statement in the presence of the warders to my said solicitor, Mr O'Brien, on the 17th July, both in reference to the Richmond murder.

These statements were untrue in many ways, especially that portion of them which referred to the murder of Mrs Thomas and the man, Strong, whom I named in the last one, and I am now informed by Mr O'Brien my solicitor, that the memorial presented on my behalf has not been successful, and I will be executed at 9 o'clock on Tuesday, 29th July. I see therefore that there is no visible hope for a respite of my sentence, and I am advised by him, and feel that I am bound in the sight of Almighty God to clear every one of suspicion, and especially those whose names were mentioned in my said statements, before I die, which I am now happy in doing. In the first place, I heartily beg God's forgiveness and mercy for numerous falsehoods I have told throughout this unfortunate case, especially because they affected the character and reputation of persons whose names are mentioned, and secondly, because of the injury they have done to myself in the sight of Almighty God, whose mercy and forgiveness I have no doubt of having obtained.

Since I was arrested, I was always in dread of the consequences of the crime, and although I had all the assistance of my solicitor, who exercised every possible means, both before and after my trial, to rescue me from my untimely end, yet I had my doubts that I should escape the penalty which I must now pay to the law. I was inwardly unhappy throughout, but bore up under such a terrible trial with the greatest fortitude and courage I possibly could. But when I was approaching the day of my execution, and fearing that nothing could be done to save me, I immediately requested the governor send for Mr O'Brien, my solicitor, that I might open my mind and reveal all things to him immediately, without the slightest hesitation or reserve, which I now proceed to do, knowing that I have no hope of mercy in this world.

With respect to the death of Mrs Thomas, the circumstances surrounding the murder of that lady are as follows: I entered the lady's service in the month of January. At first, I thought her a nice old lady, and imagined I could be comfortable and happy with her—but I found her very trying. She used to do many things to annoy me. When I had finished my work in the rooms, she used to go over it, and point out places where she said I did not clean—thus showing evidence of a nasty spirit towards me. This sort of conduct made me have an ill-feeling towards her, but I had no intention of killing her—at least, not then. One day I had an altercation with her, and we mutually arranged I should leave her service, and she made an entrance [sic] to that effect in her memorandum book.

On the Sunday evening, 2nd March last, Mrs Thomas and I were alone in the house. We had some argument at which she and myself were enraged, and she became very agitated and left the house to go to church in that state, leaving me at home. Upon her return from church, before her usual hour, she came in and went upstairs. I went up after her, and we had an argument which ripened into a quarrel, and in the height of my anger and rage I threw her from the top of the stairs to the ground floor. She had a heavy fall. I felt that she was seriously injured, and I became agitated at what had occurred, lost all control of myself, and, to prevent her screaming or getting me into trouble, I caught her by the throat, and in the struggle she was choked. I threw her on the floor. I then became entirely lost, and without any control over myself, and looking on what had happened, and the fear of being discovered, I determined to do away with the body as best I could. I chopped the head from the body with the assistance of a razor which I used to cut through the flesh afterwards. I also used the meat saw and the carving knife to cut the body up with. I prepared the copper with water, to boil the body to prevent identity; as soon as I had succeeded in cutting it up, I placed it in the copper and boiled it.

I opened the stomach with the carving knife, and burned up as much of the parts as I could.

During the whole of this time, there was nobody in the house but myself. When I looked upon the scene before me, and saw the blood around my feet, the horror and dread I felt was inconceivable. I was bewildered—acted as if I was mad—and did everything I possibly could to conceal the occurrence—keep it quiet, and everything regular—fearing the neighbours might suspect something had happened. I was greatly overcome, both from the horrible sight before me and the smell, and I failed several times in my strength and determination—but was helped on by the devil in this vile purpose. I remained in the house all night, endeavouring to clear up the place and clean away traces of the murder.

I burned one part of the body after chopping it up, and boiled the other. I think I boiled one of the feet. I emptied the copper, throwing the water away after having washed and cleaned the outside. I then put parts of the body into the little wooden box which was produced in court, and tied it up with cord, and determined to deposit it in the Thames—which was afterwards done, in the manner already described, with the help of young Porter.

I remember the coalman, Mr Deane, coming to the house and knocking at the door. I was greatly frightened, but in dread of creating suspicion, I opened the door to answer him, and spoke to him—as he stated in his evidence. When he called, I was engaged in regulating the place, and was in a dreadful state of mind. I also recall the young lady calling at the house about the repairs, and I answered her in the manner she gave in her evidence.

I put the head of Mrs Thomas into the black bag and, being weary and afraid to remain in the house, I carried it to the Porters, and had some tea there. I placed the bag, with the head in it, under the tea table, and afterwards took it away from the house and disposed of it in the way and in the place I have described to my solicitor, Mr O'Brien[?].

The deposition [*sic*] of this black bag gave me great uneasiness, as I feared it might be discovered, and the identity of Mrs Thomas thereby proven, and when I heard a black bag had been found I was greatly troubled. I pretended to Mr O'Brien that the bag contained nothing of the kind. The foot in the dunghill at Kingston was placed there by me, for when I came to realise the true state of things and the great danger I stood in, I resolved to do everything in my power to keep everything secret and prevent being discovered. When I placed the box in the river and disposed of the head and other parts of the body as best I could, and cleared up the place so that a person coming in might not suspect or see anything irregular, it was suggested to my mind to sell all that there was in the house and go away; and with that view I went and saw Porter, and introduced the sale of the things to him.

He accompanied me to Church's, and we bargained for the sale in the manner set forth in the evidence given at the trial respecting that part of the transaction. I gave the chairs to Porter as a gift, and also kept ordering things for the house from tradespeople in order to evade suspicion.

There is no truth in the evidence given by Miss Ives that she heard men talking in the house on Monday night or the voice of a woman called Lizzie. Miss Ives is mistaken in that part of the evidence, as there was nobody in the house but myself; and the statement I made that Strong and a woman were in the house is untrue. I made these statements to save myself, if possible, from my perilous position. At the time of the murder I took possession of Mrs Thomas's gold watch and chain, and also of all the money in the house, which was only seven or eight pounds. I accompanied Church to the watchmaker's and asked for Mrs Thomas's watch. Church only paid me £13, not £18, as stated.

He made me a present of earrings, and the evidence as to my borrowing a sovereign from Mrs Church is correct. I threw the dresses and bonnet of Mrs Thomas into the van which was brought to fetch the furniture, and they were taken to Church's. I thought of getting rid of them in the best manner I could.

When I left Church's house in the evening after the sale of the furniture was stopped, I determined to proceed to Ireland at once, to avoid being discovered, but I was not surprised at being arrested.

I did not murder Mrs Thomas from any premeditation. I was enraged and in a passion, and I cannot now recollect why I did it; something seemed to seize me at the time. I threw her down-stairs in the heat of strong impulse and passion; I acted towards her as I have described. I never had a hatred or what may be termed a bad feeling towards anybody in my lifetime, certainly not such as would have induced me to do them bodily injury; and I cannot account for the awful feelings that came over me from the time Mrs Thomas came home from church until the murder was completed. It is true I went by the name of Mrs Thomas and that I wore her gold watch; and with regard to the false teeth, I took them from Mrs Thomas and gave them to Porter to sell, the proceeds of which he gave me, except one shilling which I gave him. I have now relieved my mind by making a full and sincere confession that myself, without help or assistance of any person whatever, committed the murder. I have accounted for it and described it in this statement to the best of my power and recollection. I heartily exonerate everyone from having any hand or part in it. When I got into trouble in Liverpool it was owing in a great measure to poverty and evil associations, which led me step by step into badness. When I got over that trouble I formed an intimate acquaintance with one who should have protected me, and, being led away by evil associates and bad companions, I became, as it were, forlorn, and forsook everything that might have kept me in the path of rectitude and prevented my unhappy end.

I was afraid to make known the real state of things to my solicitor, lest he might have abandoned my case and taken no interest in it. I therefore concealed the truth from him until I sent for him, when he told me of the reply to the memorial sent up for me. I then fully and candidly confessed to him at the last moment the whole of the facts, in order that everything might be cleared up, and that I alone should be blamed. I am perfectly resigned to my fate, and am full of confidence in a happy eternity. If I had a choice I would almost sooner die than return to a life full of misery, deception and wickedness.

I die with great fortitude and confidence in my faith, and in our Blessed God, whom I beseech to have mercy on my soul.

KATHERINE WEBSTER

GLOSSARY

Some of the terms and expressions that appear in this book are Victorian, or older, and no longer commonplace. For example:

Arkansas Toothpick. One of many names given to bowie-type knives manufactured in England (c. 1845–1900) for export to the U.S. Other names included California Knife, Gold Searcher's Protector, and Nebraska Neckblister.

Beak. A magistrate.

Beef. Tobacco.

Beyond Temple Bar. East End of London.

Brown Bess. A British musket of the eighteenth and the early nineteenth century.

Catchpenny. Gutter ballad or newssheet sold by itinerant vendors for a penny or less.

Character. References carried about by servants from one job to another.

Copper. A large cauldron in which laundry was boiled.

Croppies. Irish rebels of the 1798 revolt against British rule, so called because they cut their hair very short.

The Crowbar Brigade. The Royal Irish Constabulary, who made a habit of breaking down with crowbars the doors of those tenants unable or unwilling to pay their rents and dues.

East of the Griffin. East End of London.

Garrotting. A form of robbery popular at that time, whereby one woman would hold a victim around the neck with a silk handkerchief or rope while her female accomplice would snatch his wallet or purse. A kind of nineteenth-century mugging.

German silver. Silver not hallmarked and of inferior quality, used to adorn cutlery, condiments, and even firearms.

Hump of the devil. Irish folklore had it that the devil's back was humped, but this theory was widespread. Note Punch of the English Punch and Judy shows.

Locker. Davy Jones's Locker, to which sailors went when drowned at sea.

Mutton-shunter. A constable.

Penny-starver. A cheap cigar or cheroot.

Praties. Potatoes (Irish).

Put up the shutters. Close shop, run away.

Ride a white horse. It was said that James II fled on a white horse after his defeat at the Battle of Boyne.

Sflesh, slife, etc. Irish Catholic exclamations. Literally, His flesh, His life, etc.

Six-monthser magistrate. A fierce London magistrate who always imposed the maximum prison sentence if possible (then only six months).

The Slaughter. Sessions House, Surrey Quarter Sessions.

Sunrise London. East End of London.

Tatur-trap. Mouth (Irish).

Ticket of leave. A kind of parole.

Tweeny. A very lowly girl learning to become a servant.

Wearing the broad arrow. Wearing convict garb.